I0715466

DARK WATERS

AN ANTHOLOGY

Collected and Edited by Charles Harrigan

Featuring Stories From

William Hope Hodgson
Edgar Allan Poe
H.G. Wells
Algernon Blackwood
Oscar Wilde
Victor Hugo
and more!

DARLEY
PRESS

Published by
DARLEY PRESS,
Delaware, USA

First Darley Press Edition ©2024
ISBN 978-1-955741-17-0
Cat # DPA003

A NOTE ON THE TEXT:
At the discretion of the editor, the copytext has been brought into
conformity with modern standards of punctuation, capitalization
and spelling.

Book design and formatting by Edgar's Ghost

WWW.DARLEYPRESS.COM

CONTENTS

The Voice in the Night—William Hope Hodgson 7

Descent Into The Maelstrom—Edgar Allan Poe 22

Vanderdecken's Message Home—John Howison 42

The Water Ghost of Harrowby Hall—John Kendrick Bangs 52

The Upper Berth—F. Marion Crawford 63

The Sea Raiders—H.G. Wells 88

The Treasure of Abbot Thomas—M.R. James 100

The Drowned Man—Guy de Maupassant 122

The Captain of the Polestar—Arthur Conan Doyle 132

A Struggle with a Devil Fish—Victor Hugo 160

Sea Curse—Robert E. Howard 171

The Children of the Pool—Arthur Machen 180

The Water Spectre—Francis Lathom 203

The Willows—Algernon Blackwood 221

The Danger From the Deep—Ralph Milne Farley 278

A Bewitched Ship—W. Clark Russel 311

The Terror of the Water Tank—William Hope Hodgson 323

The Striding Place—Gertrude Atherton 341

The Fisherman and His Soul—Oscar Wilde 349

The Ghost Ship—Richard Middleton 388

By Water—Algernon Blackwood 400

THE VOICE IN THE NIGHT

by William Hope Hodgson

IT WAS A DARK, starless night. We were becalmed in the Northern Pacific. Our exact position I do not know, for the sun had been hidden during the course of a weary, breathless week, by a thin haze which had seemed to float above us, about the height of our mastheads, at whiles descending and shrouding the surrounding sea.

With there being no wind, we had steadied the tiller, and I was the only man on deck. The crew, consisting of two men and a boy, were sleeping forward in their den, while Will—my friend, and the master of our little craft—was aft in his bunk on the port side of the little cabin.

Suddenly, from out of the surrounding darkness, there came a hail:

"Schooner, ahoy!"

The cry was so unexpected that I gave no immediate answer, because of my surprise.

It came again—a voice curiously throaty and inhuman, calling from somewhere upon the dark sea away on our port broadside:

"Schooner, ahoy!"

"Hullo!" I sung out, having gathered my wits somewhat. "What are you? What do you want?"

"You need not be afraid," answered the queer voice, having probably noticed some trace of confusion in my tone. "I am only an old... man."

The pause sounded odd, but it was only afterward that it came back to me with any significance.

"Why don't you come alongside, then?" I queried somewhat snappishly, for I liked not his hinting at my having been a trifle shaken.

"I—I—can't. It wouldn't be safe. I—" The voice broke off, and there was silence.

"What do you mean?" I asked, growing more and more astonished. "What's not safe? Where are you?"

I listened for a moment, but there came no answer. And then, a sudden indefinite suspicion, of I knew not what, coming to me, I stepped swiftly to the binnacle and took out the lighted lamp. At the same time, I knocked on the deck with my heel to waken Will. Then I was back at the side, throwing the yellow funnel of light out into the silent immensity beyond our rail. As I did so, I heard a slight muffled cry, and then the sound of a splash, as though someone had dipped oars abruptly. Yet I cannot say with certainty that I saw anything, save, it seemed to me, that with the first flash of the light there had been something upon the waters, where now there was nothing.

"Hullo, there!" I called. "What foolery is this?"

But there came only the indistinct sounds of a boat being pulled away into the night.

Then I heard Will's voice from the direction of the after scuttle:

"What's up, George?"

"Come here, Will!" I said.

"What is it?" he asked, coming across the deck.

I told him the queer thing that had happened. He put several questions, then, after a moment's silence, he raised his hands to his lips and hailed:

"Boat, ahoy!"

From a long distance away there came back to us a faint reply, and my companion repeated his call. Presently, after a short period of silence, there grew on our hearing the muffled sound of oars, at which Will hailed again.

This time there was a reply: "Put away the light."

"I'm damned if I will," I muttered, but Will told me to do as the voice bade, and I shoved it down under the bulwarks.

"Come nearer," he said, and the oar strokes continued. Then, when apparently some half dozen fathoms distant, they again ceased.

"Come alongside!" exclaimed Will. "There's nothing to be frightened of aboard here."

"Promise that you will not show the light?"

"What's to do with you," I burst out, "that you're so infernally afraid of the light?"

"Because—" began the voice, and stopped short.

"Because what?" I asked quickly.

Will put his hand on my shoulder. "Shut up a minute, old man," he said, in a low voice. "Let me tackle him."

He leaned more over the rail.

"See here, mister," he said, "this is a pretty queer business, you coming upon us like this, right out in the middle of the blessed Pacific. How are we to know what sort of a hanky-panky trick you're up to? You say there's only one of you. How are we to know, unless we get a squint at you, eh? What's your objection to the light, anyway?"

As he finished, I heard the noise of the oars again, and then the voice came, but now from a greater distance, and sounding extremely hopeless and pathetic.

"I am sorry—sorry! I would not have troubled you, only I am hungry, and... so is she."

The voice died away, and the sound of the oars, dipping irregularly, was borne to us.

"Stop!" sang out Will. "I don't want to drive you away. Come back! We'll keep the light hidden, if you don't like it."

He turned to me:

"It's a damned queer rig, this, but I think there's nothing to be afraid of?"

There was a question in his tone, and I replied.

"No, I think the poor devil's been wrecked around here, and gone crazy."

The sound of the oars drew nearer.

"Shove that lamp back in the binnacle," said Will, then he leaned over the rail and listened. I replaced the lamp and came back to his side. The dipping of the oars ceased some dozen yards distant.

"Won't you come alongside now?" asked Will in an even voice. "I have had the lamp put back in the binnacle."

"I—I cannot," replied the voice. "I dare not come nearer. I dare not even pay you for the... the provisions."

"That's all right," said Will, and hesitated. "You're welcome to as much grub as you can take..." Again he hesitated.

"You are very good!" exclaimed the voice. "May God, Who understands everything, reward you—" It broke off huskily.

"The—the lady?" said Will abruptly. "Is she—"

"I have left her behind upon the island," came the voice.

"What island?" I cut in.

"I know not its name," returned the voice. "I would to God—" it began, and checked itself as suddenly.

"Could we not send a boat for her?" asked Will at this point.

"No!" said the voice, with extraordinary emphasis. "My God! No!" There was a moment's pause; then it added, in a tone which seemed a merited reproach:

"It was because of our want I ventured, because her agony tortured me."

"I am a forgetful brute!" exclaimed Will. "Just wait a minute, whoever you are, and I will bring you up something at once."

In a couple of minutes he was back again, and his arms were full of various edibles. He paused at the rail.

"Can't you come alongside for them?" he asked.

"No, I *dare not*," replied the voice, and it seemed to me that in its tones I detected a note of stifled craving, as though the owner hushed a mortal desire. It came to me then in a flash that the poor old creature out there in the darkness was *suffering* for actual need for that which Will held in his arms, and yet, because of some unintelligible dread, refraining from dashing to the side of our schooner and receiving it. And with the lightning-like conviction there came the knowledge that the Invisible was not mad, but sanely facing some intolerable horror.

"Damn it, Will!" I said, full of many feelings, over which predominated a vast sympathy. "Get a box. We must float off the stuff to him in it."

This we did, propelling it away from the vessel, out into the darkness, by means of a boat hook. In a minute a slight cry from the Invisible came to us, and we knew that he had secured the box.

A little later he called out a farewell to us, and so heartful a blessing, that I am sure we were the better for it. Then, without more ado, we heard the ply of oars across the darkness.

"Pretty soon off," remarked Will, with perhaps just a little sense of injury.

"Wait," I replied. "I think somehow he'll come back. He must have been badly needing that food."

"And the lady," said Will. For a moment he was silent, then he continued:

"It's the queerest thing ever I've tumbled across since I've been fishing."

"Yes," I said, and fell to pondering.

And so the time slipped away—an hour, another, and still Will stayed with me; for the queer adventure had knocked all desire for sleep out of him.

The third hour was three parts through when we heard again the sound of oars across the silent ocean.

"Listen!" said Will, a low note of excitement in his voice.

"He's coming, just as I thought," I muttered.

The dipping of the oars grew nearer, and I noted that the strokes were firmer and longer. The food had been needed.

They came to a stop a little distance off the broadside, and the queer voice came again to us through the darkness:

"Schooner, ahoy!"

"That you?" asked Will.

"Yes," replied the voice. "I left you suddenly, but—but there was great need."

"The lady?" questioned Will.

"The... lady is grateful now on earth. She will be more grateful soon in—in heaven."

Will began to make some reply, in a puzzled voice, but became confused, and broke off short. I said nothing. I was wondering at the curious pauses, and, apart from my wonder, I was full of a great sympathy.

The voice continued:

"We—she and I, have talked, as we shared the result of God's tenderness and yours—"

Will interposed, but without coherence.

"I beg of you not to—to belittle your deed of Christian charity this night," said the voice. "Be sure that it has not escaped His notice."

It stopped, and there was a full minute's silence. Then it came again:

"We have spoken together upon that which—which has befallen us. We had thought to go out, without telling anyone of the terror which has come into our... lives. She is with me in believing that tonight's happenings are under a special ruling, and that it is God's wish that we should tell to you all that we have suffered since, since—"

"Yes?" said Will softly.

"Since the sinking of the Albatross."

"Ah!" I exclaimed involuntarily. "She left Newcastle for 'Frisco some six months ago, and hasn't been heard of since."

"Yes" answered the voice. "But some few degrees to the North of the line, she was caught in a terrible storm, and dismasted. When the day came, it was found that she was leaking badly, and, presently, it falling to a calm, the sailors took to the boats, leaving—leaving a young lady, my fiancée, and myself upon the wreck.

"We were below, gathering together a few of our belongings, when they left. They were entirely callous, through fear, and when we came up upon the decks, we saw them only as small shapes afar off upon the horizon. Yet we did not despair, but set to work and constructed a small raft. Upon this we put such few matters as it would hold, including a quantity of water and some ship's biscuit. Then, the vessel being very deep in the water, we got ourselves onto the raft and pushed off.

"It was later, when I observed that we seemed to be in the way of some tide or current, which bore us from the ship at an angle, so that in the course of three hours, by my watch, her hull became invisible to our sight, her broken masts remaining in view for a somewhat longer period. Then, towards evening, it grew misty, and so through the night. The next day we were still encompassed by the mist, the weather remaining quiet.

"For four days we drifted through this strange haze, until, on the evening of the fourth day, there grew upon our ears the murmur of breakers at a distance. Gradually it became plainer, and, somewhat after midnight, it appeared to sound upon either hand at no very great space. The raft was raised upon a swell several times, and then we were in smooth water, and the noise of the breakers was behind.

"When the morning came, we found that we were in a sort of great lagoon, but of this we noticed little at the time, for close before us, through the enshrouding mist, loomed the hull of a large sailing vessel. With one accord, we fell upon our knees and thanked God, for we thought that here was an end to our perils. We had much to learn.

"The raft drew near to the ship, and we shouted on them to take us aboard, but none answered. Presently the raft touched against the side of the vessel, and seeing a rope hanging downward, I seized it and began to climb. Yet I had much ado to make my way up, because of a kind of grey, lichenous fungus that had seized upon the rope, and which blotched the side of the ship lividly.

"I reached the rail and clambered over it, onto the deck. Here I saw that the decks were covered, in great patches, with grey masses, some of them rising into nodules several feet in height, but at the time I thought less of this matter than of the possibility of there being people aboard the ship. I shouted, but none answered. Then I went to the door below the poop deck. I opened it, and peered in. There was a great smell of staleness, so that I knew in a moment that nothing living was within, and with the knowledge, I shut the door quickly, for I felt suddenly lonely.

"I went back to the side where I had scrambled up. My—my sweetheart was still sitting quietly upon the raft. Seeing me look down, she called up to know whether there were any aboard of the ship. I replied that the vessel had the appearance of having been long deserted, but that if she would wait a little I would see whether there was anything in the shape of a ladder by which she could ascend to the deck. Then we would make a search through the vessel together. A little later, on the opposite side of the decks, I found a rope side ladder. This I carried across, and a minute afterwards she was beside me.

"Together we explored the cabins and apartments in the after part of the ship; but nowhere was there any sign of life. Here and there, within the cabins themselves, we came across odd patches of that queer fungus, but this, as my sweetheart said, could be cleansed away.

"In the end, having assured ourselves that the after portion of the vessel was empty, we picked our ways to the bows, between the ugly grey nodules of that strange growth, and here we made a further search, which told us that there was indeed none aboard but ourselves.

"This being now beyond any doubt, we returned to the stern of the ship and proceeded to make ourselves as comfortable as possible. Together we cleared out and cleaned two of the cabins, and after that I made examination whether there was anything eatable in the ship. This I soon found was so, and thanked God in my heart for His goodness. In addition to this I discovered the whereabouts of the fresh-water pump, and having fixed it, I found the water drinkable, though somewhat unpleasant to the taste.

"For several days we stayed aboard the ship, without attempting to get to the shore. We were busily engaged in making the place habitable. Yet even thus early we became aware that our lot was even less to be desired than might have been imagined, for though, as a first step, we scraped away the odd patches of growth that studded the floors and walls of the cabins and saloon, yet they returned almost to their original size within the space of twenty-four hours, which not only discouraged us but gave us a feeling of vague unease.

"Still we would nor admit ourselves beaten, so set to work afresh, and not only scraped away the fungus but soaked the places where it had been with carbolic, a can-full of which I had found in the pantry. Yet, by the end of the week the growth had returned in full strength, and, in addition, it had spread to other places, as though our touching it had allowed germs from it to travel elsewhere.

"On the seventh morning, my sweetheart woke to find a small patch of it growing on her pillow, close to her face. At that, she came to me, as soon as she could get her garments upon her. I was in the galley at the time lighting the fire for breakfast.

"'Come here, John,' she said, and led me aft. When I saw the thing upon her pillow I shuddered, and then and there we agreed to go right out of the ship and see whether we could not fare to make ourselves more comfortable ashore.

"Hurriedly we gathered together our few belongings, and even among these I found that the fungus had been at work, for one of her shawls had a little lump of it growing near one edge. I threw the whole thing over the side without saying anything to her.

"The raft was still alongside, but it was too clumsy to guide, and I lowered down a small boat that hung across the stern, and in this we made our way to the shore. Yet, as we drew near to it, I became gradually aware that here the vile fungus, which had driven us from the ship, was growing riot. In places it rose into horrible, fantastic mounds, which seemed almost to quiver, as with a quiet life, when the wind blew across them. Here and there it took on the forms of vast fingers, and in others it just spread out flat and smooth and treacherous. Odd places, it appeared as grotesque stunted trees, seeming extraordinarily kinked and gnarled, the whole quaking vilely at times.

"At first, it seemed to us that there was no single portion of the surrounding shore which was not hidden beneath the masses of the hideous lichen, yet, in this, I found we were mistaken, for somewhat later, coasting along the shore at a little distance, we descried a smooth white patch of what appeared to be fine sand, and there we landed. It was not sand. What it was I do not know. All that I have observed is that upon it the fungus will not grow, while everywhere else, save where the sand-like earth wanders oddly, path-wise, amid the grey desolation of the lichen, there is nothing but that loathsome greyness.

"It is difficult to make you understand how cheered we were to find one place that was absolutely free from the growth, and here we deposited our belongings. Then we went back to the ship for such things as it seemed to us we should need. Among other matters, I managed to bring ashore with me one of the ship's sails, with which I constructed two small tents, which, though exceedingly rough-shaped, served the purposes for which they were intended. In these we lived and stored our various necessities, and thus for a matter of some four weeks all went smoothly and without particular unhappiness. Indeed, I may say with much happiness—for—for we were together.

"It was on the thumb of her right hand that the growth first showed. It was only a small circular spot, much like a little grey mole. My God! how the fear leaped to my heart when she showed me the place. We cleansed it, between us, washing it with carbolic and water. In the morning of the following day she showed her hand to me again. The grey warty thing had returned. For a little while we looked at one another in silence. Then, still wordless, we started again to remove it. In the midst of the operation she spoke suddenly.

"'What's that on the side of your face, dear?' Her voice was sharp with anxiety. I put my hand up to feel.

"'There! Under the hair by your ear. A little to the front a bit.' My finger rested upon the place, and then I knew.

"'Let us get your thumb done first,' I said. And she submitted, only because she was afraid to touch me until it was cleansed. I finished washing and disinfecting her thumb, and then she turned to my face. After it was finished we sat together and talked awhile of many things, for there had come into our lives sudden, very terrible thoughts. We were, all at once, afraid of something worse than death. We spoke of loading the boat with provisions and water and making our way out onto the sea, yet we were helpless, for many causes, and—and the growth had attacked us already. We decided to stay. God would do with us what was His will. We would wait.

"A month, two months, three months passed and the places grew somewhat, and there had come others. Yet we fought so strenuously with the fear that its headway was but slow, comparatively speaking.

"Occasionally we ventured off to the ship for such stores as we needed. There we found that the fungus grew persistently. One of the nodules on the main deck soon became as high as my head.

"We had now given up all thought or hope of leaving the island. We had realized that it would be unallowable to go among healthy humans, with the things from which we were suffering.

"With this determination and knowledge in our minds, we knew that we should have to husband our food and water, for we did not know, at that time, but that we should possibly live for many years.

"This reminds me that I have told you that I am an old man. Judged by years this is not so. But, but—"

He broke off, then continued somewhat abruptly:

"As I was saying, we knew that we should have to use care in the matter of food. But we had no idea then how little food there was left of which to take care. It was a week later that I made the discovery that all the other bread tanks, which I had supposed full, were empty, and that, beyond odd tins of vegetables and meat, and some other matters, we had nothing on which to depend, but the bread in the tank which I had already opened.

"After learning this I bestirred myself to do what I could, and set to work at fishing in the lagoon, but with no success. At this I was somewhat inclined to feel desperate until the thought came to me to try outside the lagoon, in the open sea.

"Here, at times, I caught odd fish, but so infrequently that they proved of but little help in keeping us from the hunger which threatened. It seemed to me that our deaths were likely to come by hunger, and not by the growth of the thing which had seized upon our bodies.

"We were in this state of mind when the fourth month wore out. Then I made a very horrible discovery. One morning, a little before midday, I came off from the ship with a portion of the biscuits which were left. In the mouth of her tent I saw my sweetheart sitting, eating something.

"'What is it, my dear?' I called out as I leaped ashore. Yet, on hearing my voice, she seemed confused, and, turning, slyly threw something toward the edge of the little clearing. It fell short, and a vague suspicion having arisen within me, I walked across and picked it up. It was a piece of the grey fungus.

"As I went to her with it in my hand, she turned deadly pale, then a rose red.

"I felt strangely dazed and frightened.

"'My dear! My dear!' I said, and could say no more. Yet at my words she broke down and cried bitterly. Gradually, as she calmed, I got from her the news that she had tried it the preceding day, and—and liked it. I got her to promise on her knees not to touch it again, however great our hunger. After she had promised, she told me that the desire for it had come suddenly, and that, until the moment of desire, she had experienced nothing toward it but the most extreme repulsion.

"Later in the day, feeling strangely restless and much shaken with the thing which I had discovered, I made my way along one of the twisted paths formed by the white, sand-like substance, which led among the fungoid growth. I had, once before, ventured along there, but not to any great distance. This time, being involved in perplexing thought, I went much farther than hitherto.

"Suddenly I was called to myself by a queer hoarse sound on my left. Turning quickly I saw that there was movement among an extraordinarily shaped mass of fungus, close to my elbow. It was swaying uneasily, as though it possessed life of its own. Abruptly, as I stared, the thought came to me that the thing had a grotesque resemblance to the figure of a distorted human creature. Even as the fancy flashed into my brain, there was a slight, sickening noise of tearing, and I saw that one of the branchlike arms was detaching itself from the surrounding grey masses, and coming toward me. The head of the thing, a shapeless grey ball, inclined in my direction. I stood stupidly, and the vile arm brushed across my face. I gave out a frightened cry, and ran back a few paces. There was a sweetish taste upon my lips where the thing had touched me. I licked them, and was immediately filled with an inhuman desire. I turned and seized a mass of the fungus. Then more, and... more. I was insatiable. In the midst of devouring, the remembrance of the morning's discovery swept into my mazed brain. It was sent by God. I dashed the fragment I held to the ground. Then, utterly wretched and feeling a dreadful guiltiness, I made my way back to the little encampment.

"I think she knew, by some marvelous intuition which love must have given, so soon as she set eyes on me. Her quiet sympathy made it easier for me, and I told her of my sudden weakness, yet omitted to mention the extraordinary thing which had gone before. I desired to spare her all unnecessary terror.

"But, for myself, I had added an intolerable knowledge, to breed an incessant terror in my brain, for I doubted not but that I had seen the end of one of these men who had come to the island in the ship in the lagoon, and in that monstrous ending I had seen our own.

"Thereafter we kept from the abominable food, though the desire for it had entered into our blood. Yet our drear punishment was upon us, for, day by day, with monstrous rapidity, the fungoid growth took hold of our poor bodies. Nothing we could do would check it materially, and so... and so, we who had been human became... Well, it matters less each day. Only... only we had been man and maid!

"And day by day the fight is more dreadful, to withstand the hunger-lust for the terrible lichen.

"A week ago we ate the last of the biscuit, and since that time I have caught three fish. I was out here fishing tonight when your schooner drifted upon me out of the mist. I hailed you. You know the rest, and may God, out of His great heart, bless you for your goodness to a... a couple of poor outcast souls."

There was the dip of an oar, another. Then the voice came again, and for the last time, sounding through the slight surrounding mist, ghostly and mournful.

"God bless you! Good-bye!"

"Good-bye," we shouted together hoarsely, our hearts full of many emotions.

I glanced about me. I became aware that the dawn was upon us.

The sun flung a stray beam across the hidden sea, pierced the mist dully, and lit up the receding boat with a gloomy fire. Indistinctly I saw something nodding between the oars. I thought of a sponge—a great, grey nodding sponge. The oars continued to ply. They were grey, as was the boat, and my eyes searched a moment vainly for the conjunction of hand and oar. My gaze flashed back to the head. It nodded forward as the oars went backward for the stroke. Then the oars were dipped, the boat shot out of the patch of light, and the—the thing went nodding into the mist.

A DESCENT INTO THE MAELSTRÖM

by Edgar Allan Poe

The ways of God in Nature, as in Providence, are not as our ways;
nor are the models that we frame any way commensurate to the
vastness, profundity, and unsearchableness of His works, which
have a depth in them greater than the well of Democritus.
—*Joseph Glanville*

WE HAD NOW REACHED the summit of the loftiest crag. For some minutes the old man seemed too much exhausted to speak.

"Not long ago," said he at length, "and I could have guided you on this route as well as the youngest of my sons; but, about three years past, there happened to me an event such as never happened to mortal man—or at least such as no man ever survived to tell of—and the six hours of deadly terror which I then endured have broken me up body and soul. You suppose me a *very* old man—but I am not. It took less than a single day to change these hairs from a jetty black to white, to weaken my limbs, and to unstring my nerves, so that I tremble at the least exertion, and am frightened at a shadow. Do you know I can scarcely look over this little cliff without getting giddy?"

The "little cliff," upon whose edge he had so carelessly thrown himself down to rest that the weightier portion of his body hung over it, while he was only kept from falling by the tenure of his elbow on its extreme and slippery edge—this "little cliff" arose, a sheer unobstructed precipice of black shining rock, some fifteen or sixteen hundred feet from the world of crags beneath us. Nothing would have tempted me to within half a dozen yards of its brink. In truth so deeply was I excited by the perilous position of my companion, that I fell at full length upon the ground, clung to the shrubs around me, and dared not even glance upward at the sky—while I struggled in vain to divest myself of the idea that the very foundations of the mountain were in danger from the fury of the winds. It was long before I could reason myself into sufficient courage to sit up and look out into the distance.

"You must get over these fancies," said the guide, "for I have brought you here that you might have the best possible view of the scene of that event I mentioned, and to tell you the whole story with the spot just under your eye."

"We are now," he continued, in that particularizing manner which distinguished him, "we are now close upon the Norwegian coast, in the sixty-eighth degree of latitude, in the great province of Nordland, and in the dreary district of Lofoden. The mountain upon whose top we sit is Helseggen, the Cloudy. Now raise yourself up a little higher, hold on to the grass if you feel giddy, so, and look out, beyond the belt of vapor beneath us, into the sea."

I looked dizzily, and beheld a wide expanse of ocean, whose waters wore so inky a hue as to bring at once to my mind the Nubian geographer's account of the *Mare Tenebrarum*. A panorama more deplorably desolate no human imagination can conceive. To the right and left, as far as the eye could reach, there lay outstretched, like ramparts of the world, lines of horridly black and beetling cliff, whose character of gloom was but the more forcibly illustrated by the surf which reared high up against its white and ghastly crest, howling and shrieking forever. Just opposite the promontory upon whose apex we were placed, and at a distance of some five or six miles out at sea, there was visible a small, bleak-looking island; or, more properly, its position was discernible through the wilderness of surge in which it was enveloped. About two miles nearer the land, arose another of smaller size, hideously craggy and barren, and encompassed at various intervals by a cluster of dark rocks.

The appearance of the ocean, in the space between the more distant island and the shore, had something very unusual about it. Although, at the time, so strong a gale was blowing landward that a brig in the remote offing lay to under a double-reefed trysail, and constantly plunged her whole hull out of sight, still there was here nothing like a regular swell, but only a short, quick, angry cross dashing of water in every direction—as well in the teeth of the wind as otherwise. Of foam there was little except in the immediate vicinity of the rocks.

"The island in the distance," resumed the old man, "is called by the Norwegians Vurrgh. The one midway is Moskoe. That a mile to the northward is Ambaaren. Yonder are Islesen, Hotholm, Keildhelm, Suarven, and Buckholm. Farther off— between Moskoe and Vurrgh—are Otterholm, Flimen, Sand-flesen, and Stockholm. These are the true names of the places, but why it has been thought necessary to name them at all, is more than either you or I can understand. Do you hear any-thing? Do you see any change in the water?"

We had now been about ten minutes upon the top of Helseggen, to which we had ascended from the interior of Lofoden, so that we had caught no glimpse of the sea until it had burst upon us from the summit. As the old man spoke, I became aware of a loud and gradually increasing sound, like the moaning of a vast herd of buffaloes upon an American prairie; and at the same moment I perceived that what seamen term the *chopping* character of the ocean beneath us, was rapidly changing into a current which set to the eastward. Even while I gazed, this current acquired a monstrous velocity. Each moment added to its speed—to its headlong impetuosity. In five minutes the whole sea, as far as Vurrgh, was lashed into ungovernable fury; but it was between Moskoe and the coast that the main uproar held its sway. Here the vast bed of the waters, seamed and scarred into a thousand conflicting channels, burst suddenly into phrensied convulsion—heaving, boiling, hissing—gyrating in gigantic and innumerable vortices, and all whirling and plunging on to the eastward with a rapidity which water never elsewhere assumes except in precipitous descents.

In a few minutes more, there came over the scene another radical alteration. The general surface grew somewhat more smooth, and the whirlpools, one by one, disappeared, while prodigious streaks of foam became apparent where none had been seen before. These streaks, at length, spreading out to a great distance, and entering into combination, took unto themselves the gyratory motion of the subsided vortices, and seemed to form the germ of another more vast. Suddenly—very suddenly—this assumed a distinct and definite existence, in a circle of more than a mile in diameter. The edge of the whirl was represented by a broad belt of gleaming spray, but no particle of this slipped into the mouth of the terrific funnel, whose interior, as far as the eye could fathom it, was a smooth, shining, and jet-black wall of water, inclined to the horizon at an angle of some forty-five degrees, speeding dizzily round and round with a swaying and sweltering motion, and sending forth to the winds an appalling voice, half shriek, half roar, such as not even the mighty cataract of Niagara ever lifts up in its agony to Heaven.

The mountain trembled to its very base, and the rock rocked.

I threw myself upon my face, and clung to the scant herbage in an excess of nervous agitation.

"This," said I at length, to the old man, "this *can* be nothing else than the great whirlpool of the Maelström."

"So it is sometimes termed," said he. "We Norwegians call it the Moskoe-ström, from the island of Moskoe in the midway."

The ordinary accounts of this vortex had by no means prepared me for what I saw. That of Jonas Ramus, which is perhaps the most circumstantial of any, cannot impart the faintest conception either of the magnificence, or of the horror of the scene, or of the wild bewildering sense of *the novel* which confounds the beholder. I am not sure from what point of view the writer in question surveyed it, nor at what time, but it could neither have been from the summit of Helseggen, nor during a storm. There are some passages of his description, nevertheless, which may be quoted for their details, although their effect is exceedingly feeble in conveying an impression of the spectacle.

"Between Lofoden and Moskoe," he says, "the depth of the water is between thirty-six and forty fathoms, but on the other side, toward Ver (Vurrgh) this depth decreases so as not to afford a convenient passage for a vessel, without the risk of splitting on the rocks, which happens even in the calmest weather. When it is flood, the stream runs up the country between Lofoden and Moskoe with a boisterous rapidity, but the roar of its impetuous ebb to the sea is scarce equalled by the loudest and most dreadful cataracts; the noise being heard several leagues off, and the vortices or pits are of such an extent and depth, that if a ship comes within its attraction, it is inevitably absorbed and carried down to the bottom, and there beat to pieces against the rocks, and when the water relaxes, the fragments thereof are thrown up again. But these intervals of tranquility are only at the turn of the ebb and flood, and in calm weather, and last but a quarter of an hour, its violence gradually returning. When the stream is most boisterous, and its fury heightened by a storm, it is dangerous to come within a Norway mile of it. Boats, yachts, and ships have been carried away by not guarding against it before they were within its reach. It likewise happens frequently, that whales come too near the stream, and are overpowered by its violence, and then it is impossible to describe their howlings and bellowings in their fruitless struggles to disengage themselves. A bear once, attempting to swim from Lofoden to Moskoe, was caught by the stream and borne down, while he roared terribly, so as to be heard on shore. Large stocks of firs and pine trees, after being absorbed by the current, rise again broken and torn to such a degree as if bristles grew upon them. This plainly shows the bottom to consist of craggy rocks, among which they are whirled to and fro. This stream is regulated by the flux and reflux of the sea—it being constantly high and low water every six hours. In the year 1645, early in the morning of Sexagesima Sunday, it raged with such noise and impetuosity that the very stones of the houses on the coast fell to the ground."

In regard to the depth of the water, I could not see how this could have been ascertained at all in the immediate vicinity of the vortex. The "forty fathoms" must have reference only to portions of the channel close upon the shore either of Moskoe or Lofoden. The depth in the centre of the Moskoe-ström must be immeasurably greater; and no better proof of this fact is necessary than can be obtained from even the sidelong glance into the abyss of the whirl which may be had from the highest crag of Helseggen. Looking down from this pinnacle upon the howling Phlegethon below, I could not help smiling at the simplicity with which the honest Jonas Ramus records, as a matter difficult of belief, the anecdotes of the whales and the bears, for it appeared to me, in fact, a self-evident thing, that the largest ship of the line in existence, coming within the influence of that deadly attraction, could resist it as little as a feather the hurricane, and must disappear bodily and at once.

The attempts to account for the phenomenon—some of which, I remember, seemed to me sufficiently plausible in perusal—now wore a very different and unsatisfactory aspect. The idea generally received is that this, as well as three smaller vortices among the Ferroe islands, "have no other cause than the collision of waves rising and falling, at flux and reflux, against a ridge of rocks and shelves, which confines the water so that it precipitates itself like a cataract, and thus the higher the flood rises, the deeper must the fall be, and the natural result of all is a whirlpool or vortex, the prodigious suction of which is sufficiently known by lesser experiments."—These are the words of the Encyclopædia Britannica. Kircher and others imagine that in the centre of the channel of the Maelström is an abyss penetrating the globe, and issuing in some very remote part, the Gulf of Bothnia being somewhat decidedly named in one instance. This opinion, idle in itself, was the one to which, as I gazed, my imagination most readily assented, and, mentioning it to the guide, I was rather surprised to hear him say that, although it was the view almost universally entertained of the subject by the Norwegians, it nevertheless was not his own. As to the former notion he confessed his inability to comprehend it, and here I agreed with him, for, however conclusive on paper, it becomes altogether unintelligible, and even absurd, amid the thunder of the abyss.

"You have had a good look at the whirl now," said the old man, "and if you will creep round this crag, so as to get in its lee, and deaden the roar of the water, I will tell you a story that will convince you I ought to know something of the Moskoeström."

I placed myself as desired, and he proceeded.

"Myself and my two brothers once owned a schooner, rigged smack of about seventy tons burthen, with which we were in the habit of fishing among the islands beyond Moskoe, nearly to Vurrgh. In all violent eddies at sea there is good fishing, at proper opportunities, if one has only the courage to attempt it, but among the whole of the Lofoden coastmen, we three were the only ones who made a regular business of going out to the islands, as I tell you. The usual grounds are a great way lower down to the southward. There fish can be got at all hours, without much risk, and therefore these places are preferred. The choice spots over here among the rocks, however, not only yield the finest variety, but in far greater abundance, so that we often got in a single day, what the more timid of the craft could not scrape together in a week. In fact, we made it a matter of desperate speculation—the risk of life standing instead of labor, and courage answering for capital.

"We kept the smack in a cove about five miles higher up the coast than this, and it was our practice, in fine weather, to take advantage of the fifteen minutes' slack to push across the main channel of the Moskoe-ström, far above the pool, and then drop down upon anchorage somewhere near Otterholm, or Sandflesen, where the eddies are not so violent as elsewhere. Here we used to remain until nearly time for slack-water again, when we weighed and made for home. We never set out upon this expedition without a steady side wind for going and coming—one that we felt sure would not fail us before our return—and we seldom made a miscalculation upon this point. Twice, during six years, we were forced to stay all night at anchor on account of a dead calm, which is a rare thing indeed just about here, and once we had to remain on the grounds nearly a week, starving to death, owing to a gale which blew up shortly after our arrival, and made the channel too boisterous to be thought of. Upon this occasion we should have been driven out to sea in spite of everything, for the whirlpools threw us round and round so violently, that, at length, we fouled our anchor and dragged it, if it had not been that we drifted into one of the innumerable cross currents—here to-day and gone to-mor-row—which drove us under the lee of Flimen, where, by good luck, we brought up.

"I could not tell you the twentieth part of the difficulties we encountered 'on the grounds'—it is a bad spot to be in, even in good weather—but we made shift always to run the gauntlet of the Moskoe-ström itself without accident, although at times my heart has been in my mouth when we happened to be a minute or so behind or before the slack. The wind sometimes was not as strong as we thought it at starting, and then we made rather less way than we could wish, while the current rendered the smack unmanageable. My eldest brother had a son eighteen years old, and I had two stout boys of my own. These would have been of great assistance at such times, in using the sweeps, as well as afterward in fishing, but, somehow, although we ran the risk ourselves, we had not the heart to let the young ones get into the danger, for, after all is said and done, it *was* a horrible danger, and that is the truth.

"It is now within a few days of three years since what I am going to tell you occurred. It was on the tenth day of July, 18—, a day which the people of this part of the world will never forget, for it was one in which blew the most terrible hurricane that ever came out of the heavens. And yet all the morning, and indeed until late in the afternoon, there was a gentle and steady breeze from the south-west, while the sun shone brightly, so that the oldest seaman among us could not have foreseen what was to follow.

"The three of us—my two brothers and myself—had crossed over to the islands about two o'clock P. M., and had soon nearly loaded the smack with fine fish, which, we all remarked, were more plenty that day than we had ever known them. It was just seven, *by my watch*, when we weighed and started for home, so as to make the worst of the Ström at slack water, which we knew would be at eight.

"We set out with a fresh wind on our starboard quarter, and for some time spanked along at a great rate, never dreaming of danger, for indeed we saw not the slightest reason to apprehend it. All at once we were taken aback by a breeze from over Helseggen. This was most unusual—something that had never happened to us before—and I began to feel a little uneasy, without exactly knowing why. We put the boat on the wind, but could make no headway at all for the eddies, and I was upon the point of proposing to return to the anchorage, when, looking astern, we saw the whole horizon covered with a singular copper-colored cloud that rose with the most amazing velocity.

"In the meantime the breeze that had headed us off fell away, and we were dead becalmed, drifting about in every direction. This state of things, however, did not last long enough to give us time to think about it. In less than a minute the storm was upon us, in less than two the sky was entirely overcast, and what with this and the driving spray, it became suddenly so dark that we could not see each other in the smack.

"Such a hurricane as then blew it is folly to attempt describing. The oldest seaman in Norway never experienced any thing like it. We had let our sails go by the run before it cleverly took us, but, at the first puff, both our masts went by the board as if they had been sawed off—the mainmast taking with it my youngest brother, who had lashed himself to it for safety.

"Our boat was the lightest feather of a thing that ever sat upon water. It had a complete flush deck, with only a small hatch near the bow, and this hatch it had always been our custom to batten down when about to cross the Ström, by way of precaution against the chopping seas. But for this circumstance we should have foundered at once—for we lay entirely buried for some moments. How my elder brother escaped destruction I cannot say, for I never had an opportunity of ascertaining. For my part, as soon as I had let the foresail run, I threw myself flat on deck, with my feet against the narrow gunwale of the bow, and with my hands grasping a ring-bolt near the foot of the fore-mast. It was mere instinct that prompted me to do this, which was undoubtedly the very best thing I could have done, for I was too much flurried to think.

"For some moments we were completely deluged, as I say, and all this time I held my breath, and clung to the bolt. When I could stand it no longer I raised myself upon my knees, still keeping hold with my hands, and thus got my head clear. Presently our little boat gave herself a shake, just as a dog does in coming out of the water, and thus rid herself, in some measure, of the seas. I was now trying to get the better of the stupor that had come over me, and to collect my senses so as to see what was to be done, when I felt somebody grasp my arm. It was my elder brother, and my heart leaped for joy, for I had made sure that he was overboard. But the next moment all this joy was turned into horror, for he put his mouth close to my ear, and screamed out the word *'Moskoe-ström!'*

"No one ever will know what my feelings were at that moment. I shook from head to foot as if I had had the most violent fit of the ague. I knew what he meant by that one word well enough—I knew what he wished to make me understand. With the wind that now drove us on, we were bound for the whirl of the Ström, and nothing could save us!

"You perceive that in crossing the Ström *channel*, we always went a long way up above the whirl, even in the calmest weather, and then had to wait and watch carefully for the slack, but now we were driving right upon the pool itself, and in such a hurricane as this! 'To be sure,' I thought, 'we shall get there just about the slack—there is some little hope in that'—but in the next moment I cursed myself for being so great a fool as to dream of hope at all. I knew very well that we were doomed, had we been ten times a ninety-gun ship.

"By this time the first fury of the tempest had spent itself, or perhaps we did not feel it so much, as we scudded before it, but at all events the seas, which at first had been kept down by the wind, and lay flat and frothing, now got up into absolute mountains. A singular change, too, had come over the heavens. Around in every direction it was still as black as pitch, but nearly overhead there burst out, all at once, a circular rift of clear sky—as clear as I ever saw, and of a deep bright blue—and through it there blazed forth the full moon with a lustre that I never before knew her to wear. She lit up everything about us with the greatest distinctness, but, oh God, what a scene it was to light up!

"I now made one or two attempts to speak to my brother, but, in some manner which I could not understand, the din had so increased that I could not make him hear a single word, although I screamed at the top of my voice in his ear. Presently he shook his head, looking as pale as death, and held up one of his fingers, as if to say *'listen!'*

"At first I could not make out what he meant, but soon a hideous thought flashed upon me. I dragged my watch from its fob. It was not going. I glanced at its face by the moonlight, and then burst into tears as I flung it far away into the ocean. *It had run down at seven o'clock!* We were behind the time of the slack, and the whirl of the Ström was in full fury!

"When a boat is well built, properly trimmed, and not deep laden, the waves in a strong gale, when she is going large, seem always to slip from beneath her—which appears very strange to a landsman—and this is what is called *riding*, in sea phrase.

"Well, so far we had ridden the swells very cleverly, but presently a gigantic sea happened to take us right under the counter, and bore us with it as it rose—up—up—as if into the sky. I would not have believed that any wave could rise so high. And then down we came with a sweep, a slide, and a plunge, that made me feel sick and dizzy, as if I was falling from some lofty mountain-top in a dream. But while we were up I had thrown a quick glance around—and that one glance was all sufficient. I saw our exact position in an instant. The Moskoe-Ström whirlpool was about a quarter of a mile dead ahead—but no more like the every-day Moskoe-Ström than the whirl as you now see it, is like a mill-race. If I had not known where we were, and what we had to expect, I should not have recognised the place at all. As it was, I involuntarily closed my eyes in horror. The lids clenched themselves together as if in a spasm.

"It could not have been more than two minutes afterward until we suddenly felt the waves subside, and were enveloped in foam. The boat made a sharp half turn to larboard, and then shot off in its new direction like a thunderbolt. At the same moment the roaring noise of the water was completely drowned in a kind of shrill shriek—such a sound as you might imagine given out by the waste-pipes of many thousand steam-vessels, letting off their steam all together. We were now in the belt of surf that always surrounds the whirl, and I thought, of course, that another moment would plunge us into the abyss, down which we could only see indistinctly on account of the amazing velocity with which we wore borne along. The boat did not seem to sink into the water at all, but to skim like an air-bubble upon the surface of the surge. Her starboard side was next the whirl, and on the larboard arose the world of ocean we had left. It stood like a huge writhing wall between us and the horizon.

"It may appear strange, but now, when we were in the very jaws of the gulf, I felt more composed than when we were only approaching it. Having made up my mind to hope no more, I got rid of a great deal of that terror which unmanned me at first. I suppose it was despair that strung my nerves.

"It may look like boasting, but what I tell you is truth, I began to reflect how magnificent a thing it was to die in such a manner, and how foolish it was in me to think of so paltry a consideration as my own individual life, in view of so wonderful a manifestation of God's power. I do believe that I blushed with shame when this idea crossed my mind. After a little while I became possessed with the keenest curiosity about the whirl itself. I positively felt a *wish* to explore its depths, even at the sacrifice I was going to make, and my principal grief was that I should never be able to tell my old companions on shore about the mysteries I should see. These, no doubt, were singular fancies to occupy a man's mind in such extremity, and I have often thought since, that the revolutions of the boat around the pool might have rendered me a little light-headed.

"There was another circumstance which tended to restore my self-possession, and this was the cessation of the wind, which could not reach us in our present situation, for, as you saw yourself, the belt of surf is considerably lower than the general bed of the ocean, and this latter now towered above us, a high, black, mountainous ridge. If you have never been at sea in a heavy gale, you can form no idea of the confusion of mind occasioned by the wind and spray together. They blind, deafen, and strangle you, and take away all power of action or reflection. But we were now, in a great measure, rid of these annoyances, just as death-condemned felons in prison are allowed petty indulgences, forbidden them while their doom is yet uncertain.

"How often we made the circuit of the belt it is impossible to say. We careered round and round for perhaps an hour, flying rather than floating, getting gradually more and more into the middle of the surge, and then nearer and nearer to its horrible inner edge. All this time I had never let go of the ring-bolt. My brother was at the stern, holding on to a small empty water-cask which had been securely lashed under the coop of the counter, and was the only thing on deck that had not been swept overboard when the gale first took us. As we approached the brink of the pit he let go his hold upon this, and made for the ring, from which, in the agony of his terror, he endeavored to force my hands, as it was not large enough to afford us both a secure grasp. I never felt deeper grief than when I saw him attempt this act, although I knew he was a madman when he did it, a raving maniac through sheer fright. I did not care, however, to contest the point with him. I knew it could make no difference whether either of us held on at all, so I let him have the bolt, and went astern to the cask. This there was no great difficulty in doing, for the smack flew round steadily enough, and upon an even keel—only swaying to and fro, with the immense sweeps and swelters of the whirl. Scarcely had I secured myself in my new position, when we gave a wild lurch to starboard, and rushed headlong into the abyss. I muttered a hurried prayer to God, and thought all was over.

"As I felt the sickening sweep of the descent, I had instinctively tightened my hold upon the barrel, and closed my eyes. For some seconds I dared not open them, while I expected instant destruction, and wondered that I was not already in my death-struggles with the water. But moment after moment elapsed. I still lived. The sense of falling had ceased, and the motion of the vessel seemed much as it had been before, while in the belt of foam, with the exception that she now lay more along. I took courage, and looked once again upon the scene.

"Never shall I forget the sensations of awe, horror, and admiration with which I gazed about me. The boat appeared to be hanging, as if by magic, midway down, upon the interior surface of a funnel vast in circumference, prodigious in depth, and whose perfectly smooth sides might have been mistaken for ebony, but for the bewildering rapidity with which they spun around, and for the gleaming and ghastly radiance they shot forth, as the rays of the full moon, from that circular rift amid the clouds which I have already described, streamed in a flood of golden glory along the black walls, and far away down into the inmost recesses of the abyss.

"At first I was too much confused to observe anything accurately. The general burst of terrific grandeur was all that I beheld. When I recovered myself a little, however, my gaze fell instinctively downward. In this direction I was able to obtain an unobstructed view, from the manner in which the smack hung on the inclined surface of the pool. She was quite upon an even keel—that is to say, her deck lay in a plane parallel with that of the water—but this latter sloped at an angle of more than forty-five degrees, so that we seemed to be lying upon our beam-ends. I could not help observing, nevertheless, that I had scarcely more difficulty in maintaining my hold and footing in this situation, than if we had been upon a dead level, and this, I suppose, was owing to the speed at which we revolved.

"The rays of the moon seemed to search the very bottom of the profound gulf, but still I could make out nothing distinctly, on account of a thick mist in which everything there was enveloped, and over which there hung a magnificent rainbow, like that narrow and tottering bridge which Mussulmen say is the only pathway between Time and Eternity. This mist, or spray, was no doubt occasioned by the clashing of the great walls of the funnel, as they all met together at the bottom, but the yell that went up to the Heavens from out of that mist, I dare not attempt to describe.

"Our first slide into the abyss itself, from the belt of foam above, had carried us a great distance down the slope, but our farther descent was by no means proportionate. Round and round we swept, not with any uniform movement, but in dizzying swings and jerks, that sent us sometimes only a few hundred yards, sometimes nearly the complete circuit of the whirl. Our progress downward, at each revolution, was slow, but very perceptible.

"Looking about me upon the wide waste of liquid ebony on which we were thus borne, I perceived that our boat was not the only object in the embrace of the whirl. Both above and below us were visible fragments of vessels, large masses of building timber and trunks of trees, with many smaller articles, such as pieces of house furniture, broken boxes, barrels and staves. I have already described the unnatural curiosity which had taken the place of my original terrors. It appeared to grow upon me as I drew nearer and nearer to my dreadful doom. I now began to watch, with a strange interest, the numerous things that floated in our company. I *must* have been delirious, for I even sought *amusement* in speculating upon the relative velocities of their several descents toward the foam below. 'This fir tree,' I found myself at one time saying, 'will certainly be the next thing that takes the awful plunge and disappears,' and then I was disappointed to find that the wreck of a Dutch merchant ship overtook it and went down before. At length, after making several guesses of this nature, and being deceived in all—this fact—the fact of my invariable miscalculation, set me upon a train of reflection that made my limbs again tremble, and my heart beat heavily once more.

"It was not a new terror that thus affected me, but the dawn of a more exciting *hope*. This hope arose partly from memory, and partly from present observation. I called to mind the great variety of buoyant matter that strewed the coast of Lofoden, having been absorbed and then thrown forth by the Moskoeström. By far the greater number of the articles were shattered in the most extraordinary way—so chafed and roughened as to have the appearance of being stuck full of splinters—but then I distinctly recollected that there were *some* of them which were not disfigured at all. Now I could not account for this difference except by supposing that the roughened fragments were the only ones which had been *completely absorbed*, that the others had entered the whirl at so late a period of the tide, or, for some reason, had descended so slowly after entering, that they did not reach the bottom before the turn of the flood came, or of the ebb, as the case might be. I conceived it possible, in either instance, that they might thus be whirled up again to the level of the ocean, without undergoing the fate of those which had been drawn in more early, or absorbed more rapidly. I made, also, three important observations. The first was, that, as a general rule, the larger the bodies were, the more rapid their descent—the second, that, between two masses of equal extent, the one spherical, and the other of any other shape, the superiority in speed of descent was with the sphere—the third, that, between two masses of equal size, the one cylindrical, and the other of *any other shape,* the cylinder was absorbed the more slowly. Since my escape, I have had several conversations on this subject with an old school-master of the district, and it was from him that I learned the use of the words 'cylinder' and 'sphere.' He explained to me—although I have forgotten the explanation—how what I observed was, in fact, the natural consequence of the forms of the floating fragments—and showed me how it happened that a cylinder, swimming in a vortex, offered more resistance to its suction, and was drawn in with greater difficulty than an equally bulky body, of any form whatever.

"There was one startling circumstance which went a great way in enforcing these observations, and rendering me anxious to turn them to account, and this was that, at every revolution, we passed something like a barrel, or else the yard or the mast of a vessel, while many of these things, which had been on our level when I first opened my eyes upon the wonders of the whirlpool, were now high up above us, and seemed to have moved but little from their original station.

"I no longer hesitated what to do. I resolved to lash myself securely to the water cask upon which I now held, to cut it loose from the counter, and to throw myself with it into the water. I attracted my brother's attention by signs, pointed to the floating barrels that came near us, and did everything in my power to make him understand what I was about to do. I thought at length that he comprehended my design, but, whether this was the case or not, he shook his head despairingly, and refused to move from his station by the ring-bolt. It was impossible to reach him; the emergency admitted of no delay; and so, with a bitter struggle, I resigned him to his fate, fastened myself to the cask by means of the lashings which secured it to the counter, and precipitated myself with it into the sea, without another moment's hesitation.

"The result was precisely what I had hoped it might be. As it is myself who now tell you this tale—as you see that I *did* escape—and as you are already in possession of the mode in which this escape was effected, and must therefore anticipate all that I have farther to say, I will bring my story quickly to conclusion. It might have been an hour, or thereabout, after my quitting the smack, when, having descended to a vast distance beneath me, it made three or four wild gyrations in rapid succession, and, bearing my loved brother with it, plunged headlong, at once and forever, into the chaos of foam below. The barrel to which I was attached sunk very little farther than half the distance between the bottom of the gulf and the spot at which I leaped overboard, before a great change took place in the character of the whirlpool. The slope of the sides of the vast funnel became momently less and less steep. The gyrations of the whirl grew, gradually, less and less violent. By degrees, the froth and the rainbow disappeared, and the bottom of the gulf seemed slowly to uprise. The sky was clear, the winds had gone down, and the full moon was setting radiantly in the west, when I found myself on the surface of the ocean, in full view of the shores of Lofoden, and above the spot where the pool of the Moskoe-ström had been. It was the hour of the slack, but the sea still heaved in mountainous waves from the effects of the hurricane. I was borne violently into the channel of the Ström, and in a few minutes was hurried down the coast into the 'grounds' of the fishermen. A boat picked me up, exhausted from fatigue, and, now that the danger was removed, speechless from the memory of its horror. Those who drew me on board were my old mates and daily companions, but they knew me no more than they would have known a traveller from the spirit-land. My hair which had been raven-black the day before, was as white as you see it now. They say too that the whole expression of my countenance had changed. I told them my story—they did not believe it. I now tell it to you, and I can scarcely expect you to put more faith in it than did the merry fishermen of Lofoden."

VANDERDECKEN'S MESSAGE HOME

—~—

by John Howison

Our ship, after touching at the Cape, went out again, and soon losing sight of the Table Mountain, began to be assailed by the impetuous attacks of the sea, which is well known to be more formidable there than in most parts of the known ocean. The day had grown dull and hazy, and the breeze, which had formerly blown fresh, now sometimes subsided almost entirely, and then recovering its strength, for a short time, and changing its direction, blew with temporary violence, and died away again, as if exercising a melancholy caprice. A heavy swell began to come from the southeast. Our sails flapped against the masts, and the ship rolled from side to side, as heavily as if she had been water-logged. There was so little wind that she would not steer.

At two P.M. we had a squall, accompanied by thunder and rain. The seamen, growing restless, looked anxiously ahead. They said we would have a dirty night of it, and that it would not be worth while to turn into their hammocks. As the second mate was describing a gale he had encountered off Cape Race,

Newfoundland, we were suddenly taken all aback, and the blast came upon us furiously. We continued to scud under a double reefed mainsail and foretopsail till dusk, but, as the sea ran high, the captain thought it safest to bring her to. The watch on deck consisted of four men, one of whom was appointed to keep a lookout ahead, for the weather was so hazy, that we could not see two cables' length from the bows. This man, whose name was Tom Willis, went frequently to the bows, as if to observe something, and when the others called to him, inquiring what he was looking at, he would give no definite answer. They therefore went also to the bows, and appeared startled, and at first said nothing.

But presently one of them cried, "William, go call the watch."

The seamen, having been asleep in their hammocks, murmured at this unseasonable summons, and called to know how it looked upon deck. To which Tom Willis replied, "Come up and see. What we are minding is not on deck, but ahead."

On hearing this, they ran up without putting on their jackets, and when they came to the bows there was a whispering.

One of them asked, "Where is she? I do not see her."

To which another replied, "The last flash of lightning showed there was not a reef in one of her sails, but we, who know her history, know that all her canvass will never carry her into port."

By this time, the talking of the seamen had brought some of the passengers on deck. They could see nothing, however, for the ship was surrounded by thick darkness, and by the noise of the dashing waters, and the seamen evaded the questions that were put to them.

At this juncture the chaplain came on deck. He was a man of grave and modest demeanor, and was much liked among the seamen, who called him Gentle George.

He overheard one of the men asking another, if he had

ever seen the Flying Dutchman before, and if he knew the story about her. To which the other replied, "I have heard of her beating about in these seas. What is the reason she never reaches port?"

The first speaker replied, "They give different reasons for it, but my story is this: She was an Amsterdam vessel, and sailed from that port seventy years ago. Her master's name was Vanderdecken. He was a staunch seaman, and would have his own way, in spite of the devil. For all that, never a sailor under him had reason to complain; though how it is on board with them now, nobody knows. The story is this, that in doubling the Cape, they were a long day trying to weather the Table Bay, which we saw this morning. However, the wind headed them, and went against them more and more, and Vanderdecken walked the deck, swearing at the wind. Just after sunset, a vessel spoke him, asking if he did not mean to go into the Bay that night. Vanderdecken replied, 'May I be eternally d__d if I do, though I should beat about here till the day of judgment!' And to be sure, Vanderdecken never did go into that bay; for it is believed that he continues to beat about in these seas still, and will do so long enough. This vessel is never seen but with foul weather along with her."

To which another replied, "We must keep clear of her. They say that her captain mans his jolly boat, when a vessel comes in sight, and tries hard to get alongside, to put letters on board, but no good comes to them who have communication with him."

Tom Willis said, "There is such a sea between us at present, as should keep us safe from such visits."

To which the other answered, "We cannot trust to that, if Vanderdeckcn sends out his men."

Some of this conversation having been overheard by the passengers, there was a commotion among them. In the meantime, the noise of the waves against the vessel, could scarcely be distinguished from the sounds of the distant thunder. The wind had extinguished the light in the binnacle, where the compass was, and no one could tell which way the ship's head lay.

The passengers were afraid to ask questions, lest they should augment the secret sensation of fear which chilled every heart, or learn any more than they already knew. For while they attributed their agitation of mind to the state of the weather, it was sufficiently perceptible that their alarms also arose from a cause which they did not acknowledge.

The lamp at the binnacle being re-lighted, they perceived that the ship lay closer to the wind than she had hitherto done, and the spirits of the passengers were somewhat revived.

Nevertheless, neither the tempestuous state of the atmosphere, nor the thunder had ceased, and soon a vivid flash of lightning showed the waves tumbling around us, and, in the distance, the Flying Dutchman scudding furiously before the wind, under a press of canvass. The sight was but momentary, but it was sufficient to remove doubt from the minds of the passengers.

One of the men cried aloud, "There she goes, top-gallants and all."

The chaplain had brought up his prayer book, in order that he might draw from thence something to fortify and tranquillize the minds of the rest. Therefore, taking his seat near the binnacle, so that the light shone upon the white leaves of the book, he, in a solemn tone, read out the service for those distressed at sea. The sailors stood round with folded arms, and looked as if they thought it would be of little use. But this served to occupy the attention of those on deck for a while.

In the meantime, the flashes of lightning becoming less vivid, showed nothing else, far or near, but the billows weltering round the vessel. The sailors seemed to think that they had not yet seen the worst, but confined their remarks and prognostications to their own circle.

At this time, the captain, who had hitherto remained in his birth, came on deck, and, with a gay and unconcerned air, inquired what was the cause of the general dread. He said he thought they had already seen the worst of the weather, and wondered that his men had raised such a hubbub about a capful of wind. Mention being made of the Flying Dutchman, the captain laughed. He said he would like very much to see any vessel carrying top-gallant-sails in such a night, for it would be a sight worth looking at.

The chaplain, taking him by one of the buttons of his coat, drew him aside, and appeared to enter into serious conversation with him. While they were talking together the captain was heard to say, "Let us look to our own ship, and not mind such things," and accordingly, he sent a man aloft, to see if all was right about the foretop-sail yard, which was chafing the mast with a loud noise.

It was Tom Willis who went up, and when he came down, he said that all was tight, and that he hoped it would soon get clearer, and that they would see no more of what they were most afraid of.

The captain and first mate were heard laughing loudly together, while the chaplain observed, that it would be better to repress such unseasonable gaiety. The second mate, a native of Scotland, whose name was Duncan Saunderson, having attended one of the university classes at Aberdeen, thought himself too wise to believe all that the sailors said, and took part with the captain. He jestingly told Tom Willis, to borrow his grandam's spectacles the next time he was sent to keep a lookout ahead.

Tom walked sulkily away, muttering, that he would nevertheless trust to his own eyes till morning, and accordingly took his station at the bow, and appeared to watch as attentively as before.

The sound of talking soon ceased, for many returned to

their births, and we heard nothing but the clanking of the ropes upon the masts, and the bursting of the billows ahead, as the vessel successively took the seas.

But after a considerable interval of darkness, gleams of lightning began to reappear. Tom Willis suddenly called out, "Vanderdecken, again! Vanderdecken, again! I see, them letting down a boat."

All who were on deck ran to the bows. The next flash of lightning shone far and wide over the raging sea, and showed us not only the Flying Dutchman at a distance, but also a boat coming from her with four men. The boat was within two cables' length of our ship's side. The man who first saw her, ran to the captain, and asked whether they should hail her or not. The captain, walking about in great agitation, made no reply.

The first mate cried, "Who's going to heave a rope to that boat?"

The men looked at each other without offering to do anything. The boat had come very near the chains, when Tom Willis called out, "What do you want, or what devil has blown you here in such weather?"

A piercing voice from the boat replied in English, "We want to speak with your captain."

The captain took no notice of this, and Vanderdecken's boot having come close alongside, one of the men came upon deck, and appeared like a fatigued and weather-beaten seaman, holding some letters in his hand.

Our sailors all drew back. The chaplain, however, looking steadfastly upon him, went forward a few steps, and asked, "What is the purpose of this visit?"

The stranger replied, "We have long been kept here by foul weather, and Vanderdecken wishes to send these letters to his friends in Europe."

Our captain now came forward, and said as firmly as he could, "I wish Vanderdecken would put his letters on board of any other vessel rather than mine."

The stranger replied, "We have tried many a ship, but most of them refuse our letters."

Upon which, Tom Willis muttered, "It will be best for us if we do the same, for they say, there is sometimes a sinking weight in your paper."

The stranger took no notice of this, but asked where we were from. On being told that we were from Portsmouth, he said, as if with strong feeling, "Would that you had rather been from Amsterdam. Oh that we saw it again! We must see our friends again."

When he uttered these words, the men who were in the boat below, wrung their hands, and cried in a piercing tone, in Dutch, "Oh that we saw it again! We have been long here beating about, but we must see our friends again."

The chaplain asked the stranger, "How long have you been at sea?"

He replied, "We have lost our count, for our almanac was blown overboard. Our ship, you see, is there still, so why should you ask how long we have been at sea? For Vanderdecken only wishes to write home and comfort his friends."

To which the chaplain replied, "Your letters, I fear, would be of no use in Amsterdam, even if they were delivered, for the persons to whom they are addressed are probably no longer to be found there, except under very ancient green turf in the churchyard."

The unwelcome stranger then wrung his hands, and appeared to weep, and replied, "It is impossible. We cannot believe you. We have been long driving about here, but country nor relations cannot be so easily forgotten. There is not a raindrop in the air but feels itself kindred to all the rest, and they fall back into the sea to meet with each other again. How then, can kindred blood be made to forget where it came from? Even our bodies are part of the ground of Holland, and Vanderdecken says, if he once were come to Amsterdam, he would rather be changed into a stone post, well fixed into the ground, than leave it again, if that were to die elsewhere. But in the meantime, we only ask you to take these letters."

The chaplain, looking at him with astonishment, said, "This is the insanity of natural affection, which rebels against all measures of time and distance."

The stranger continued, "Here is a letter from our second mate, to his dear and only remaining friend, his uncle, the merchant who lives in the second house on Stuncken Yacht Quay."

He held forth the letter, but no one would approach to take it. Tom Willis raised his voice, and said, "One of our men here says that he was in Amsterdam last summer, and he knows for certain, that the street called Stuncken Yacht Quay, was pulled down sixty years ago, and now there is only a large church at that place."

The man from the Flying Dutchman, said, "It is impossible. We cannot believe you. Here is another letter from myself, in which I have sent a banknote to my dear sister, to buy some gallant lace, to make her a high headdress."

Tom Willis hearing this, said, "It is most likely that her head now lies under a tombstone, which will outlast all the changes of the fashion. But on what house is your banknote?"

The stranger replied, "On the house of Vanderbrucker and Company."

The man, of whom Tom Willis had spoken, said, "I guess there will now be some discount upon it, for that banking house was gone to destruction forty years ago, and Vanderbrucker was afterwards a-missing. But to remember these things is like raking up the bottom of an old canal."

The stranger called out passionately, "It is impossible. We cannot believe it! It is cruel to say such things to people in our condition. There is a letter from our captain himself, to his much-beloved and faithful wife, whom he left at a pleasant summer dwelling, on the border of the Haarlemer Mer. She promised to have the house beautifully painted and gilded before he came back, and to get a new set of looking-glasses for the principal chamber, that she might see as many images of Vanderdecken, as if she had six husbands at once."

The man replied, "There has been time enough for her to have had six husbands since then, but were she alive still, there is no fear that Vanderdecken would ever get home to disturb her."

On hearing this the stranger again shed tears, and said, if they would not take the letters, he would leave them, and looking around he offered the parcel to the captain, chaplain, and to the rest of the crew successively, but each drew back as it was offered, and put his hands behind his back. He then laid the letters upon the deck, and placed upon them a piece of iron, which was lying near, to prevent them from being blown away. Having done this, he swung himself over the gangway, and went into the boat.

We heard the others speak to him, but the rise of a sudden squall prevented us from distinguishing his reply. The boat was seen to quit the ship's side, and, in a few moments, there were no more traces of her than if she had never been there. The sailors rubbed their eyes, as if doubting what they had witnessed, but the parcel still lay upon deck, and proved the reality of all that had passed.

Duncan Saunderson, the Scotch mate, asked the captain if he should take them up, and put them in the letter bag. Receiving no reply, he would have lifted them if it had not been for Tom Willis, who pulled him back, saying that nobody should touch them.

In the meantime the captain went down to the cabin, and the chaplain having followed him, found him at his bottle-case, pouring out a large dram of brandy. The captain, although somewhat disconcerted, immediately offered the glass to him, saying, "Here, Charters, is what is good in a cold night."

The chaplain declined drinking anything, and the captain having swallowed the bumper, they both returned to the deck, where they found the seamen giving their opinions concerning what should be done with the letters. Tom Willis proposed to pick them up on a harpoon and throw it overboard.

Another speaker said, "I have always heard it asserted that it is neither safe to accept them voluntarily, nor when they are left to throw them out of the ship."

"Let no one touch them," said the carpenter. "The way to do with the letters from the Flying Dutchman is to case them upon deck, by nailing boards over them, so that if he sends back for them, they are still there to give him."

The carpenter went to fetch his tools. During his absence, the ship gave so violent a pitch, that the piece of iron slid off the letters, and they were whirled overboard by the wind, like birds of evil omen whirring through the air. There was a cry of joy among the sailors, and they ascribed the favorable change which soon took place in the weather, to our having got quit of Vanderdecken. We soon got underway again. The night watch being set, the rest of the crew retired to their births.

THE WATER GHOST
OF HARROWBY HALL

by John Kendrick Bangs

THE TROUBLE WITH Harrowby Hall was that it was haunted, and, what was worse, the ghost did not content itself with merely appearing at the bedside of the afflicted person who saw it, but persisted in remaining there for one mortal hour before it would disappear.

It never appeared except on Christmas Eve, and then as the clock was striking twelve, in which respect alone was it lacking in that originality which in these days is a sine qua non of success in spectral life. The owners of Harrowby Hall had done their utmost to rid themselves of the damp and dewy lady who rose up out of the best bedroom floor at midnight, but without avail. They had tried stopping the clock, so that the ghost would not know when it was midnight, but she made her appearance just the same, with that fearful miasmatic personality of hers, and there she would stand until everything about her was thoroughly saturated.

Then the owners of Harrowby Hall calked up every crack in the floor with the very best quality of hemp, and over this was placed layers of tar and canvas; the walls were made water-proof, and the doors and windows likewise, the proprietors having conceived the notion that the unexorcised lady would find it difficult to leak into the room after these precautions had been taken, but even this did not suffice. The following Christmas Eve she appeared as promptly as before, and frightened the occupant of the room quite out of his senses by sitting down alongside of him and gazing with her cavernous blue eyes into his, and he noticed, too, that in her long, aqueously bony fingers bits of dripping sea-weed were entwined, the ends hanging down, and these ends she drew across his forehead until he became like one insane. And then he swooned away, and was found unconscious in his bed the next morning by his host, simply saturated with sea-water and fright, from the combined effects of which he never recovered, dying four years later of pneumonia and nervous prostration at the age of seventy-eight.

The next year the master of Harrowby Hall decided not to have the best spare bedroom opened at all, thinking that perhaps the ghost's thirst for making herself disagreeable would be satisfied by haunting the furniture, but the plan was as unavailing as the many that had preceded it.

The ghost appeared as usual in the room—that is, it was supposed she did, for the hangings were dripping wet the next morning, and in the parlor below the haunted room a great damp spot appeared on the ceiling. Finding no one there, she immediately set out to learn the reason why, and she chose none other to haunt than the owner of the Harrowby himself. She found him in his own cozy room drinking whiskey—whiskey undiluted—and felicitating himself upon having foiled her ghostship, when all of a sudden the curl went out of his hair, his whiskey bottle filled and overflowed, and he was himself in a condition similar to that of a man who has fallen into a water-butt. When he recovered from the shock, which was a painful one, he saw before him the lady of the cavernous eyes and sea-weed fingers. The sight was so unexpected and so terri-fying that he fainted, but immediately came to, because of the vast amount of water in his hair, which, trickling down over his face, restored his consciousness.

Now it so happened that the master of Harrowby was a brave man, and while he was not particularly fond of interview-ing ghosts, especially such quenching ghosts as the one before him, he was not to be daunted by an apparition. He had paid the lady the compliment of fainting from the effects of his first surprise, and now that he had come to he intended to find out a few things he felt he had a right to know. He would have liked to put on a dry suit of clothes first, but the apparition declined to leave him for an instant until her hour was up, and he was forced to deny himself that pleasure. Every time he would move she would follow him, with the result that everything she came in contact with got a ducking. In an effort to warm himself up he approached the fire, an unfortunate move as it turned out, because it brought the ghost directly over the fire, which imme-diately was extinguished. The whiskey became utterly valueless as a comforter to his chilled system, because it was by this time diluted to a proportion of ninety per cent of water. The only thing he could do to ward off the evil effects of his encounter he did, and that was to swallow ten two-grain quinine pills, which he managed to put into his mouth before the ghost had time to interfere. Having done this, he turned with some asperity to the ghost, and said:

"Far be it from me to be impolite to a woman, madam, but I'm hanged if it wouldn't please me better if you'd stop these infernal visits of yours to this house. Go sit out on the lake, if you like that sort of thing; soak the water-butt, if you wish; but do not, I implore you, come into a gentleman's house and saturate him and his possessions in this way. It is damned dis-agreeable."

"Henry Hartwick Oglethorpe," said the ghost, in a gurgling

voice, "you don't know what you are talking about."

"Madam," returned the unhappy householder, "I wish that remark were strictly truthful. I was talking about you. It would be shillings and pence—nay, pounds, in my pocket, madam, if I did not know you."

"That is a bit of specious nonsense," returned the ghost, throwing a quart of indignation into the face of the master of Harrowby. "It may rank high as repartee, but as a comment upon my statement that you do not know what you are talking about, it savors of irrelevant impertinence. You do not know that I am compelled to haunt this place year after year by inexorable fate. It is no pleasure to me to enter this house, and ruin and mildew everything I touch. I never aspired to be a shower-bath, but it is my doom. Do you know who I am?"

"No, I don't," returned the master of Harrowby. "I should say you were the Lady of the Lake, or Little Sallie Waters."

"You are a witty man for your years," said the ghost.

"Well, my humor is drier than yours ever will be," returned the master.

"No doubt. I'm never dry. I am the Water Ghost of Harrowby Hall, and dryness is a quality entirely beyond my wildest hope. I have been the incumbent of this highly unpleasant office for two hundred years tonight."

"How the deuce did you ever come to get elected?" asked the master.

"Through a suicide," replied the spectre. "I am the ghost of that fair maiden whose picture hangs over the mantel-piece in the drawing-room. I should have been your great-great-great-great-great-aunt if I had lived, Henry Hartwick Oglethorpe, for I was the own sister of your great-great-great-great-grandfather."

"But what induced you to get this house into such a predicament?"

"I was not to blame, sir," returned the lady. "It was my

father's fault. He it was who built Harrowby Hall, and the haunted chamber was to have been mine. My father had it furnished in pink and yellow, knowing well that blue and gray formed the only combination of color I could tolerate. He did it merely to spite me, and, with what I deem a proper spirit, I declined to live in the room, whereupon my father said I could live there or on the lawn, he didn't care which. That night I ran from the house and jumped over the cliff into the sea."

"That was rash," said the master of Harrowby.

"So I've heard," returned the ghost. "If I had known what the consequences were to be I should not have jumped, but I really never realized what I was doing until after I was drowned. I had been drowned a week when a sea-nymph came to me and informed me that I was to be one of her followers forever afterwards, adding that it should be my doom to haunt Harrowby Hall for one hour every Christmas Eve throughout the rest of eternity. I was to haunt that room on such Christmas Eves as I found it inhabited, and if it should turn out not to be inhabited, I was and am to spend the allotted hour with the head of the house."

"I'll sell the place."

"That you cannot do, for it is also required of me that I shall appear as the deeds are to be delivered to any purchaser, and divulge to him the awful secret of the house."

"Do you mean to tell me that on every Christmas Eve that I don't happen to have somebody in that guest-chamber, you are going to haunt me wherever I may be, ruining my whiskey, taking all the curl out of my hair, extinguishing my fire, and soaking me through to the skin?" demanded the master.

"You have stated the case, Oglethorpe. And what is more," said the water ghost, "it doesn't make the slightest difference where you are, if I find that room empty, wherever you may be I shall douse you with my spectral pres—"

Here the clock struck one, and immediately the apparition

faded away. It was perhaps more of a trickle than a fade, but as a disappearance it was complete.

"By St. George and his Dragon!" ejaculated the master of Harrowby, wringing his hands. "It is guineas to hot-cross buns that next Christmas there's an occupant of the spare room, or I spend the night in a bath-tub."

But the master of Harrowby would have lost his wager had there been any one there to take him up, for when Christmas Eve came again he was in his grave, never having recovered from the cold contracted that awful night. Harrowby Hall was closed, and the heir to the estate was in London, where to him in his chambers came the same experience that his father had gone through, saving only that, being younger and stronger, he survived the shock. Everything in his rooms was ruined—his clocks were rusted in the works, a fine collection of watercolor drawings was entirely obliterated by the onslaught of the water ghost, and what was worse, the apartments below his were drenched with the water soaking through the floors, a damage for which he was compelled to pay, and which resulted in his being requested by his landlady to vacate the premises immediately.

The story of the visitation inflicted upon his family had gone abroad, and no one could be got to invite him out to any function save afternoon teas and receptions. Fathers of daughters declined to permit him to remain in their houses later than eight o'clock at night, not knowing but that some emergency might arise in the supernatural world which would require the unexpected appearance of the water ghost in this on nights other than Christmas Eve, and before the mystic hour when weary churchyards, ignoring the rules which are supposed to govern polite society, begin to yawn. Nor would the maids themselves have aught to do with him, fearing the destruction by the sudden incursion of aqueous femininity of the costumes which they held most dear.

So the heir of Harrowby Hall resolved, as his ancestors for several generations before him had resolved, that something must be done. His first thought was to make one of his servants occupy the haunted room at the crucial moment, but in this he failed, because the servants themselves knew the history of that room and rebelled. None of his friends would consent to sacrifice their personal comfort to his, nor was there to be found in all England a man so poor as to be willing to occupy the doomed chamber on Christmas Eve for pay.

Then the thought came to the heir to have the fireplace in the room enlarged, so that he might evaporate the ghost at its first appearance, and he was felicitating himself upon the ingenuity of his plan, when he remembered what his father had told him—how that no fire could withstand the lady's extremely contagious dampness. And then he bethought him of steam-pipes. These, he remembered, could lie hundreds of feet deep in water, and still retain sufficient heat to drive the water away in vapor, and as a result of this thought the haunted room was heated by steam to a withering degree, and the heir for six months attended daily the Turkish baths, so that when Christmas Eve came he could himself withstand the awful temperature of the room.

The scheme was only partially successful. The water ghost appeared at the specified time, and found the heir of Harrowby prepared, but hot as the room was, it shortened her visit by no more than five minutes in the hour, during which time the nervous system of the young master was wellnigh shattered, and the room itself was cracked and warped to an extent which required the outlay of a large sum of money to remedy. And worse than this, as the last drop of the water ghost was slowly sizzling itself out on the floor, she whispered to her would-be conqueror that his scheme would avail him nothing, because there was still water in great plenty where she came from, and that next year would find her rehabilitated and as exasperatingly saturating as ever.

It was then that the natural action of the mind, in going from one extreme to the other, suggested to the ingenious heir of Harrowby the means by which the water ghost was ultimately conquered, and happiness once more came within the grasp of the house of Oglethorpe.

The heir provided himself with a warm suit of fur under-clothing. Donning this with the furry side in, he placed over it a rubber garment, tightfitting, which he wore just as a woman wears a jersey. On top of this he placed another set of under-clothing, this suit made of wool, and over this was a second rubber garment like the first. Upon his head he placed a light and comfortable diving helmet, and so clad, on the following Christmas Eve he awaited the coming of his tormentor.

It was a bitterly cold night that brought to a close this twenty-fourth day of December. The air outside was still, but the temperature was below zero. Within all was quiet, the servants of Harrowby Hall awaiting with beating hearts the outcome of their master's campaign against his supernatural visitor.

The master himself was lying on the bed in the haunted room, clad as has already been indicated, and then—

The clock clanged out the hour of twelve.

There was a sudden banging of doors, a blast of cold air swept through the halls, the door leading into the haunted chamber flew open, a splash was heard, and the water ghost was seen standing at the side of the heir of Harrowby, from whose outer dress there streamed rivulets of water, but whose own person deep down under the various garments he wore was as dry and as warm as he could have wished.

"Ha!" said the young master of Harrowby. "I'm glad to see you."

"You are the most original man I've met, if that is true," returned the ghost. "May I ask where did you get that hat?"

"Certainly, madam," returned the master, courteously. "It is a little portable observatory I had made for just such emergencies as this. But, tell me, is it true that you are doomed to follow me about for one mortal hour—to stand where I stand, to sit where I sit?"

"That is my delectable fate," returned the lady.

"We'll go out on the lake," said the master, starting up.

"You can't get rid of me that way," returned the ghost. "The water won't swallow me up. In fact, it will just add to my present bulk."

"Nevertheless," said the master, firmly, "we will go out on the lake."

"But, my dear sir," returned the ghost, with a pale reluctance, "it is fearfully cold out there. You will be frozen hard before you've been out ten minutes."

"Oh no, I'll not," replied the master. "I am very warmly dressed. Come!"

This last in a tone of command that made the ghost ripple.

And they started.

They had not gone far before the water ghost showed signs of distress.

"You walk too slowly," she said. "I am nearly frozen. My knees are so stiff now I can hardly move. I beseech you to accelerate your step."

"I should like to oblige a lady," returned the master, courteously, "but my clothes are rather heavy, and a hundred yards an hour is about my speed. Indeed, I think we would better sit down here on this snowdrift, and talk matters over."

"Do not! Do not do so, I beg!" cried the ghost. "Let me move on. I feel myself growing rigid as it is. If we stop here, I shall be frozen stiff."

"That, madam," said the master slowly, and seating himself on an ice-cake, "that is why I have brought you here. We have been on this spot just ten minutes, we have fifty more. Take your time about it, madam, but freeze, that is all I ask of you."

"I cannot move my right leg now," cried the ghost, in despair, "and my overskirt is a solid sheet of ice. Oh, good, kind Mr. Oglethorpe, light a fire, and let me go free from these icy fetters."

"Never, madam. It cannot be. I have you at last."

"Alas!" cried the ghost, a tear trickling down her frozen cheek. "Help me, I beg. I congeal!"

"Congeal, madam, congeal!" returned Oglethorpe, coldly. "You have drenched me and mine for two hundred and three years, madam. Tonight you have had your last drench."

"Ah, but I shall thaw out again, and then you'll see. Instead of the comfortably tepid, genial ghost I have been in my past, sir, I shall be iced-water," cried the lady, threateningly.

"No, you won't, either," returned Oglethorpe; "for when you are frozen quite stiff, I shall send you to a cold-storage warehouse, and there shall you remain an icy work of art forever more."

"But warehouses burn."

"So they do, but this warehouse cannot burn. It is made of asbestos and surrounding it are fire-proof walls, and within those walls the temperature is now and shall forever be 416 degrees below the zero point—low enough to make an icicle of any flame in this world, or the next," the master added, with an ill-suppressed chuckle.

"For the last time let me beseech you. I would go on my knees to you, Oglethorpe, were they not already frozen. I beg of you do not doo—"

Here even the words froze on the water ghost's lips and the clock struck one. There was a momentary tremor throughout the ice-bound form, and the moon, coming out from behind a cloud, shone down on the rigid figure of a beautiful woman sculptured in clear, transparent ice. There stood the ghost of Harrowby Hall, conquered by the cold, a prisoner for all time.

The heir of Harrowby had won at last, and today in a large storage house in London stands the frigid form of one who will never again flood the house of Oglethorpe with woe and sea-water.

As for the heir of Harrowby, his success in coping with a ghost has made him famous, a fame that still lingers about him, although his victory took place some twenty years ago, and so far from being unpopular with the fair sex, as he was when we first knew him, he has not only been married twice, but is to lead a third bride to the altar before the year is out.

THE UPPER BERTH

—◦—

by F. Marion Crawford

SOMEBODY ASKED for the cigars. We had talked long, and the conversation was beginning to languish The tobacco smoke had got into the heavy curtains, the wine had got into those brains which were liable to become heavy, and it was already perfectly evident that, unless somebody did something to rouse our oppressed spirits, the meeting would soon come to its natural conclusion, and we, the guests, would speedily go home to bed, and most certainly to sleep. No one had said anything very remarkable; it may be that no one had anything very remarkable to say. Jones had given us every particular of his last hunting adventure in Yorkshire. Mr. Tompkins, of Boston, had explained at elaborate length those working principles, by the due and careful maintenance of which the Atchison, Topeka, and Santa Fé Railroad not only extended its territory, increased its departmental influence, and transported live stock without starving them to death before the day of actual delivery, but, also, had for years succeeded in deceiving those passengers who bought its tickets into the fallacious belief that the corporation aforesaid was really able to transport human life without destroying it. Signor Tombola had endeavoured to persuade us, by arguments which we took no trouble to oppose, that the unity of his country in no way resembled the average modern torpedo, carefully planned, constructed with all the skill of the greatest European arsenals, but, when constructed, destined to be directed by feeble hands into a region where it must undoubtedly explode, unseen, unfeared, and unheard, into the illimitable wastes of political chaos.

It is unnecessary to go into further details. The conversation had assumed proportions which would have bored Prometheus on his rock, which would have driven Tantalus to distraction, and which would have impelled Ixion to seek relaxation in the simple but instructive dialogues of Herr Ollendorff, rather than submit to the greater evil of listening to our talk. We had sat at table for hours; we were bored, we were tired, and nobody showed signs of moving.

Somebody called for cigars. We all instinctively looked towards the speaker. Brisbane was a man of five-and-thirty years of age, and remarkable for those gifts which chiefly attract the attention of men. He was a strong man. The external proportions of his figure presented nothing extraordinary to the common eye, though his size was above the average. He was a little over six feet in height, and moderately broad in the shoulder; he did not appear to be stout, but, on the other hand, he was certainly not thin His small head was supported by a strong and sinewy neck. His broad muscular hands appeared to possess a peculiar skill in breaking walnuts without the assistance of the ordinary cracker, and, seeing him in profile, one could not help remarking the extraordinary breadth of his sleeves, and the unusual thickness of his chest. He was one of those men who are commonly spoken of among men as deceptive, that is to say, that though he looked exceedingly strong he was in reality very much stronger than he looked. Of his features

I need say little. His head is small, his hair is thin, his eyes are blue, his nose is large, he has a small moustache, and a square jaw. Everybody knows Brisbane, and when he asked for a cigar everybody looked at him.

"It is a very singular thing," said Brisbane.

Everybody stopped talking. Brisbane's voice was not loud, but possessed a peculiar quality of penetrating general conversation, and cutting it like a knife. Everybody listened. Brisbane, perceiving that he had attracted their general attention, lit his cigar with great equanimity.

"It is very singular," he continued, "that thing about ghosts. People are always asking whether anybody has seen a ghost. I have."

"Bosh! What, you? You don't mean to say so, Brisbane? Well, for a man of his intelligence!"

A chorus of exclamations greeted Brisbane's remarkable statement. Everybody called for cigars, and Stubbs the butler suddenly appeared from the depths of nowhere with a fresh bottle of dry champagne. The situation was saved; Brisbane was going to tell a story.

I

I AM AN OLD SAILOR, and as I have to cross the Atlantic pretty often, I have my favourites. Most men have their favourites. I have seen a man wait in a Broadway bar for three-quarters of an hour for a particular car which he liked. I believe the bar-keeper made at least one-third of his living by that man's preference. I have a habit of waiting for certain ships when I am obliged to cross that duck-pond. It may be a prejudice, but I was never cheated out of a good passage but once in my life. I remember it very well. It was a warm morning in June, and the Custom House officials, who were hanging about waiting for a steamer already on her way up from the Quarantine, presented a peculiarly hazy and thoughtful appearance. I had not much luggage—I never have. I mingled with the crowd of passengers, porters, and officious individuals in blue coats and brass buttons, who seemed to spring up like mushrooms from the deck of a moored steamer to obtrude their unnecessary services upon the independent passenger. I have often noticed with a certain interest the spontaneous evolution of these fellows. They are not there when you arrive; five minutes after the pilot has called "Go ahead!" they, or at least their blue coats and brass buttons, have disappeared from deck and gangway as completely as though they had been consigned to that locker which tradition unanimously ascribes to Davy Jones. But, at the moment of starting, they are there, clean-shaved, blue-coated, and ravenous for fees. I hastened on board. The *Kamtschatka* was one of my favourite ships. I say was, because she emphatically no longer is. I cannot conceive of any inducement which could entice me to make another voyage in her. Yes, I know what you are going to say. She is uncommonly clean in the run aft, she has enough bluffing off in the bows to keep her dry, and the lower berths are most of them double. She has a lot of advantages, but I won't cross in her again. Excuse the digression. I got on board. I hailed a steward, whose red nose and redder whiskers were equally familiar to me.

"One hundred and five, lower berth," said I, in the business-like tone peculiar to men who think no more of crossing the Atlantic than taking a whisky cocktail at downtown Delmonico's.

The steward took my portmanteau, great coat, and rug. I shall never forget the expression of his face. Not that he turned pale. It is maintained by the most eminent divines that even miracles cannot change the course of nature. I have no hesitation in saying that he did not turn pale; but, from his expression, I judged that he was either about to shed tears, to sneeze, or to drop my portmanteau. As the latter contained two bottles of particularly fine old sherry presented to me for my voyage by my old friend Snigginson van Pickyns, I felt extremely nervous. But the steward did none of these things.

"Well, I'm d——d!" said he in a low voice, and led the way.

I supposed my Hermes, as he led me to the lower regions, had had a little grog, but I said nothing, and followed him. One hundred and five was on the port side, well aft. There was nothing remarkable about the state-room. The lower berth, like most of those upon the *Kamtschatka*, was double. There was plenty of room. There was the usual washing apparatus, calculated to convey an idea of luxury to the mind of a North-American Indian. There were the usual inefficient racks of brown wood, in which it is more easy to hang a large-sized umbrella than the common tooth-brush of commerce. Upon the uninviting mattresses were carefully folded together those blankets which a great modern humorist has aptly compared to cold buckwheat cakes. The question of towels was left entirely to the imagination. The glass decanters were filled with a transparent liquid faintly tinged with brown, but from which an odor less faint, but not more pleasing, ascended to the nostrils, like a far-off sea-sick reminiscence of oily machinery. Sad-coloured curtains half-closed the upper berth. The hazy June daylight shed a faint illumination upon the desolate little scene. Ugh! how I hate that state-room!

The steward deposited my traps and looked at me, as though he wanted to get away—probably in search of more passengers and more fees. It is always a good plan to start in favour with those functionaries, and I accordingly gave him certain coins there and then.

"I'll try and make yer comfortable all I can," he remarked, as he put the coins in his pocket. Nevertheless, there was a doubtful intonation in his voice which surprised me. Possibly his scale of fees had gone up, and he was not satisfied; but on the whole I was inclined to think that, as he himself would have expressed it, he was "the better for a glass." I was wrong, however, and did the man injustice.

II

NOTHING ESPECIALLY WORTHY of mention occurred during that day. We left the pier punctually, and it was very pleasant to be fairly under way, for the weather was warm and sultry, and the motion of the steamer produced a refreshing breeze. Everybody knows what the first day at sea is like. People pace the decks and stare at each other, and occasionally meet acquaintances whom they did not know to be on board. There is the usual uncertainty as to whether the food will be good, bad, or indifferent, until the first two meals have put the matter beyond a doubt. There is the usual uncertainty about the weather, until the ship is fairly off Fire Island. The tables are crowded at first, and then suddenly thinned. Pale-faced people spring from their seats and precipitate themselves towards the door, and each old sailor breathes more freely as his sea-sick neighbour rushes from his side, leaving him plenty of elbow room and an unlimited command over the mustard.

One passage across the Atlantic is very much like another, and we who cross very often do not make the voyage for the sake of novelty. Whales and icebergs are indeed always objects of interest, but, after all, one whale is very much like another whale, and one rarely sees an iceberg at close quarters. To the majority of us the most delightful moment of the day on board an ocean steamer is when we have taken our last turn on deck, have smoked our last cigar, and having succeeded in tiring ourselves, feel at liberty to turn in with a clear conscience. On that first night of the voyage I felt particularly lazy, and went to bed in one hundred and five rather earlier than I usually do. As I turned in, I was amazed to see that I was to have a companion. A portmanteau, very like my own, lay in the opposite corner, and in the upper berth had been deposited a neatly folded rug with a stick and umbrella. I had hoped to be alone, and I was disappointed, but I wondered who my roommate was to be, and I determined to have a look at him.

Before I had been long in bed he entered. He was, as far as I could see, a very tall man, very thin, very pale, with sandy hair and whiskers and colourless grey eyes. He had about him, I thought, an air of rather dubious fashion, the sort of man you might see in Wall Street, without being able precisely to say what he was doing there—the sort of man who frequents the Café Anglais, who always seems to be alone and who drinks champagne. You might meet him on a race-course, but he would never appear to be doing anything there either. A little over-dressed, a little odd. There are three or four of his kind on every ocean steamer. I made up my mind that I did not care to make his acquaintance, and I went to sleep saying to myself that I would study his habits in order to avoid him. If he rose early, I would rise late; if he went to bed late, I would go to bed early. I did not care to know him. If you once know people of that kind they are always turning up. Poor fellow! I need not have taken the trouble to come to so many decisions about him, for I never saw him again after that first night in one hundred and five.

I was sleeping soundly when I was suddenly waked by a loud noise. To judge from the sound, my roommate must have sprung with a single leap from the upper berth to the floor. I heard him fumbling with the latch and bolt of the door, which opened almost immediately, and then I heard his footsteps as he ran at full speed down the passage, leaving the door open behind him. The ship was rolling a little, and I expected to hear him stumble or fall, but he ran as though he were running for his life. The door swung on its hinges with the motion of the vessel, and the sound annoyed me. I got up and shut it, and groped my way back to my berth in the darkness. I went to sleep again, but I have no idea how long I slept.

When I awoke it was still quite dark, but I felt a disagreeable sensation of cold, and it seemed to me that the air was damp. You know the peculiar smell of a cabin which has been wet with sea water. I covered myself up as well as I could and dozed off again, framing complaints to be made the next day, and selecting the most powerful epithets in the language. I could hear my roommate turn over in the upper berth. He had probably returned while I was asleep. Once I thought I heard him groan, and I argued that he was sea-sick. That is particularly unpleasant when one is below. Nevertheless I dozed off and slept till early daylight.

The ship was rolling heavily, much more than on the previous evening, and the grey light which came in through the porthole changed in tint with every movement according as the angle of the vessel's side turned the glass seawards or skywards. It was very cold—unaccountably so for the month of June. I turned my head and looked at the porthole, and saw to my surprise that it was wide open and hooked back. I believe I swore audibly. Then I got up and shut it. As I turned back I glanced at the upper berth. The curtains were drawn close together; my companion had probably felt cold as well as I. It struck me that I had slept enough. The state-room was uncomfortable, though, strange to say, I could not smell the dampness which had annoyed me in the night. My roommate was still asleep—excellent opportunity for avoiding him, so I dressed at once and went on deck. The day was warm and cloudy, with an oily smell on the water. It was seven o'clock as I came out, much later than I had imagined. I came across the doctor, who was taking his first sniff of the morning air. He was a young man from the West of Ireland, a tremendous fellow, with black hair and blue eyes, already inclined to be stout; he had a happy-go-lucky, healthy look about him which was rather attractive.

"Fine morning," I remarked, by way of introduction.

"Well," said he, eying me with an air of ready interest, "it's a fine morning and it's not a fine morning. I don't think it's much of a morning."

"Well, no, it is not so very fine," said I.

"It's just what I call fuggly weather," replied the doctor.

"It was very cold last night, I thought," I remarked. "However, when I looked about, I found that the porthole was wide open. I had not noticed it when I went to bed. And the state-room was damp, too."

"Damp!" said he. "Whereabouts are you?"

"One hundred and five—"

To my surprise the doctor started visibly, and stared at me.

"What is the matter?" I asked.

"Oh, nothing," he answered, "only everybody has complained of that state-room for the last three trips."

"I shall complain too," I said. "It has certainly not been properly aired. It is a shame!"

"I don't believe it can be helped," answered the doctor. "I believe there is something—well, it is not my business to frighten passengers."

"You need not be afraid of frightening me," I replied. "I can stand any amount of damp. If I should get a bad cold I will come to you."

I offered the doctor a cigar, which he took and examined very critically.

"It is not so much the damp," he remarked. "However, I dare say you will get on very well. Have you a roommate?"

"Yes, a deuce of a fellow, who bolts out in the middle of the night and leaves the door open."

Again the doctor glanced curiously at me. Then he lit the cigar and looked grave.

"Did he come back?" he asked presently.

"Yes. I was asleep, but I waked up and heard him moving. Then I felt cold and went to sleep again. This morning I found the porthole open."

"Look here," said the doctor, quietly, "I don't care much for this ship. I don't care a rap for her reputation. I tell you what I will do. I have a good-sized place up here. I will share it with you, though I don't know you from Adam."

I was very much surprised at the proposition. I could not imagine why he should take such a sudden interest in my welfare. However, his manner as he spoke of the ship was peculiar.

"You are very good, doctor," I said. "But really, I believe even now the cabin could be aired, or cleaned out, or something. Why do you not care for the ship?"

"We are not superstitious in our profession, sir," replied the doctor. "But the sea makes people so. I don't want to prejudice you, and I don't want to frighten you, but if you will take my advice you will move in here. I would as soon see you overboard," he added, "as know that you or any other man was to sleep in one hundred and five."

"Good gracious! Why?" I asked.

"Just because on the last three trips the people who have slept there actually have gone overboard," he answered, gravely.

The intelligence was startling and exceedingly unpleasant, I confess. I looked hard at the doctor to see whether he was making game of me, but he looked perfectly serious. I thanked him warmly for his offer, but told him I intended to be the exception to the rule by which every one who slept in that particular state-room went overboard. He did not say much, but looked as grave as ever, and hinted that before we got across I should probably reconsider his proposal. In the course of time we went to breakfast, at which only an inconsiderable number of passengers assembled. I noticed that one or two of the officers who breakfasted with us looked grave. After breakfast I went into my state-room in order to get a book. The curtains of the upper berth were still closely drawn. Not a word was to be heard. My roommate was probably still asleep.

As I came out I met the steward whose business it was to

look after me. He whispered that the captain wanted to see me, and then scuttled away down the passage as if very anxious to avoid any questions. I went toward the captain's cabin, and found him waiting for me.

"Sir," said he, "I want to ask a favour of you."

I answered that I would do anything to oblige him.

"Your roommate has disappeared," he said. "He is known to have turned in early last night. Did you notice anything extraordinary in his manner?"

The question coming, as it did, in exact confirmation of the fears the doctor had expressed half an hour earlier, staggered me.

"You don't mean to say he has gone overboard?" I asked.

"I fear he has," answered the captain.

"This is the most extraordinary thing—" I began.

"Why?" he asked.

"He is the fourth, then?" I explained. In answer to another question from the captain, I explained, without mentioning the doctor, that I had heard the story concerning one hundred and five. He seemed very much annoyed at hearing that I knew of it. I told him what had occurred in the night.

"What you say," he replied, "coincides almost exactly with what was told me by the roommates of two of the other three. They bolt out of bed and run down the passage. Two of them were seen to go overboard by the watch. We stopped and lowered boats, but they were not found. Nobody, however, saw or heard the man who was lost last night, if he is really lost. The steward, who is a superstitious fellow, perhaps, and expected something to go wrong, went to look for him this morning, and found his berth empty, but his clothes lying about, just as he had left them. The steward was the only man on board who knew him by sight, and he has been searching everywhere for him. He has disappeared! Now, sir, I want to beg you not to mention the circumstance to any of the passengers. I don't want the ship to get a bad name, and nothing hangs about an ocean-goer like stories of suicides. You shall have your choice of any one of the officers' cabins you like, including my own, for the rest of the passage. Is that a fair bargain?"

"Very," said I, "and I am much obliged to you. But since I am alone, and have the state-room to myself, I would rather not move. If the steward will take out that unfortunate man's things, I would as leave stay where I am. I will not say anything about the matter, and I think I can promise you that I will not follow my roommate."

The captain tried to dissuade me from my intention, but I preferred having a state-room alone to being the chum of any officer on board. I do not know whether I acted foolishly, but if I had taken his advice I should have had nothing more to tell. There would have remained the disagreeable coincidence of several suicides occurring among men who had slept in the same cabin, but that would have been all.

That was not the end of the matter, however, by any means. I obstinately made up my mind that I would not be disturbed by such tales, and I even went so far as to argue the question with the captain. There was something wrong about the state-room, I said. It was rather damp. The porthole had been left open last night. My roommate might have been ill when he came on board, and he might have become delirious after he went to bed. He might even now be hiding somewhere on board, and might be found later. The place ought to be aired and the fastening of the port looked to. If the captain would give me leave, I would see that what I thought necessary were done immediately.

"Of course you have a right to stay where you are if you please," he replied, rather petulantly, "but I wish you would turn out and let me lock the place up, and be done with it."

I did not see it in the same light, and left the captain, after promising to be silent concerning the disappearance of my companion. The latter had had no acquaintances on board, and was not missed in the course of the day. Towards evening I met the doctor again, and he asked me whether I had changed my mind. I told him I had not.

"Then you will before long," he said, very gravely.

III

WE PLAYED WHIST in the evening, and I went to bed late. I will confess now that I felt a disagreeable sensation when I entered my state-room. I could not help thinking of the tall man I had seen on the previous night, who was now dead, drowned, tossing about in the long swell, two or three hundred miles astern. His face rose very distinctly before me as I undressed, and I even went so far as to draw back the curtains of the upper berth, as though to persuade myself that he was actually gone. I also bolted the door of the state-room. Suddenly I became aware that the porthole was open, and fastened back. This was more than I could stand. I hastily threw on my dressing-gown and went in search of Robert, the steward of my passage. I was very angry, I remember, and when I found him I dragged him roughly to the door of one hundred and five, and pushed him towards the open porthole.

"What the deuce do you mean, you scoundrel, by leaving that port open every night? Don't you know it is against the regulations? Don't you know that if the ship heeled and the water began to come in, ten men could not shut it? I will report you to the captain, you blackguard, for endangering the ship!"

I was exceedingly wroth. The man trembled and turned pale, and then began to shut the round glass plate with the heavy brass fittings.

"Why don't you answer me?" I said, roughly.

"If you please, sir," faltered Robert, "there's nobody on board as can keep this 'ere port shut at night. You can try it yourself, sir. I ain't a-going to stop hany longer on board o' this vessel, sir, I ain't, indeed. But if I was you, sir, I'd just clear out and go and sleep with the surgeon, or something, I would. Look 'ere, sir, is that fastened what you may call securely, or not, sir? Try it, sir, see if it will move a hinch."

I tried the port, and found it perfectly tight.

"Well, sir," continued Robert, triumphantly, "I wager my reputation as a A1 steward, that in 'arf an hour it will be open again, fastened back, too, sir, that's the horful thing—fastened back!"

I examined the great screw and the looped nut that ran on it.

"If I find it open in the night, Robert, I will give you a sovereign. It is not possible. You may go."

"Soverin' did you say, sir? Very good, sir. Thank ye, sir. Good night, sir. Pleasant reepose, sir, and all manner of hinchantin' dreams, sir."

Robert scuttled away, delighted at being released. Of course, I thought he was trying to account for his negligence by a silly story, intended to frighten me, and I disbelieved him. The consequence was that he got his sovereign, and I spent a very peculiarly unpleasant night.

I went to bed, and five minutes after I had rolled myself up in my blankets the inexorable Robert extinguished the light that burned steadily behind the ground-glass pane near the door. I lay quite still in the dark trying to go to sleep, but I soon found that impossible. It had been some satisfaction to be angry with the steward, and the diversion had banished that unpleasant sensation I had at first experienced when I thought of the drowned man who had been my chum, but I was no longer sleepy, and I lay awake for some time, occasionally glancing at the porthole, which I could just see from where I lay, and which, in the darkness, looked like a faintly-luminous soup-plate suspended in blackness. I believe I must have lain there for an hour, and, as I remember, I was just dozing into sleep when I was roused by a draught of cold air and by distinctly feeling the spray of the sea blown upon my face. I started to my feet, and not having allowed in the dark for the motion of the ship, I was instantly thrown violently across the state-room upon the couch which was placed beneath the porthole. I recovered myself immediately, however, and climbed upon my knees. The porthole was again wide open and fastened back!

Now these things are facts. I was wide awake when I got up, and I should certainly have been waked by the fall had I still been dozing. Moreover, I bruised my elbows and knees badly, and the bruises were there on the following morning to testify to the fact, if I myself had doubted it. The porthole was wide open and fastened back, a thing so unaccountable that I remember very well feeling astonishment rather than fear when I discovered it. I at once closed the plate again and screwed down the loop nut with all my strength. It was very dark in the state-room. I reflected that the port had certainly been opened within an hour after Robert had at first shut it in my presence, and I determined to watch it and see whether it would open again. Those brass fittings are very heavy and by no means easy to move. I could not believe that the clump had been turned by the shaking of the screw. I stood peering out through the thick glass at the alternate white and grey streaks of the sea that foamed beneath the ship's side. I must have remained there a quarter of an hour.

Suddenly, as I stood, I distinctly heard something moving behind me in one of the berths, and a moment afterwards, just as I turned instinctively to look—though I could, of course, see nothing in the darkness—I heard a very faint groan. I sprang across the state-room, and tore the curtains of the upper berth aside, thrusting in my hands to discover if there were any one there. There was someone.

I remember that the sensation as I put my hands forward was as though I were plunging them into the air of a damp cellar, and from behind the curtain came a gust of wind that smelled horribly of stagnant sea-water. I laid hold of something that had the shape of a man's arm, but was smooth, and wet, and icy cold. But suddenly, as I pulled, the creature sprang violently forward against me, a clammy, oozy mass, as it seemed to me, heavy and wet, yet endowed with a sort of supernatural strength. I reeled across the state-room, and in an instant the door opened and the thing rushed out. I had not had time to be frightened, and quickly recovering myself, I sprang through the door and gave chase at the top of my speed, but I was too late. Ten yards before me I could see—I am sure I saw it—a dark shadow moving in the dimly lighted passage, quickly as the shadow of a fast horse thrown before a dog-cart by the lamp on a dark night. But in a moment it had disappeared, and I found myself holding on to the polished rail that ran along the bulkhead where the passage turned towards the companion. My hair stood on end, and the cold perspiration rolled down my face. I am not ashamed of it in the least: I was very badly frightened.

Still I doubted my senses, and pulled myself together. It was absurd, I thought. The Welsh rare-bit I had eaten had disagreed with me. I had been in a nightmare. I made my way back to my state-room, and entered it with an effort. The whole place smelled of stagnant sea-water, as it had when I had waked on the previous evening. It required my utmost strength to go in and grope among my things for a box of wax lights. As I lighted a railway reading lantern which I always carry in case I want to read after the lamps are out, I perceived that the porthole was again open, and a sort of creeping horror began to take possession of me which I never felt before, nor wish to feel again. But I got a light and proceeded to examine the upper berth, expecting to find it drenched with sea-water.

But I was disappointed. The bed had been slept in, and the smell of the sea was strong, but the bedding was as dry as a bone. I fancied that Robert had not had the courage to make the bed after the accident of the previous night—it had all been a hideous dream. I drew the curtains back as far as I could and examined the place very carefully. It was perfectly dry. But the porthole was open again. With a sort of dull bewilderment of horror, I closed it and screwed it down, and thrusting my heavy stick through the brass loop, wrenched it with all my might, till the thick metal began to bend under the pressure. Then I hooked my reading lantern into the red velvet at the head of the couch, and sat down to recover my senses if I could. I sat there all night, unable to think of rest, hardly able to think at all. But the porthole remained closed, and I did not believe it would now open again without the application of a considerable force.

The morning dawned at last, and I dressed myself slowly, thinking over all that had happened in the night. It was a beautiful day and I went on deck, glad to get out in the early, pure sunshine, and to smell the breeze from the blue water, so different from the noisome, stagnant odour from my state-room. Instinctively I turned aft, towards the surgeon's cabin. There he stood, with a pipe in his mouth, taking his morning airing precisely as on the preceding day.

"Good-morning," said he, quietly, but looking at me with evident curiosity.

"Doctor, you were quite right," said I. "There is something wrong about that place."

"I thought you would change your mind," he answered, rather triumphantly. "You have had a bad night, eh? Shall I make you a pick-me-up? I have a capital recipe."

"No, thanks," I cried. "But I would like to tell you what happened."

I then tried to explain as clearly as possible precisely what had occurred, not omitting to state that I had been scared as I had never been scared in my whole life before. I dwelt particularly on the phenomenon of the porthole, which was a fact to which I could testify, even if the rest had been an illusion. I had closed it twice in the night, and the second time I had actually bent the brass in wrenching it with my stick. I believe I insisted a good deal on this point.

"You seem to think I am likely to doubt the story," said the doctor, smiling at the detailed account of the state of the porthole. "I do not doubt it in the least. I renew my invitation to you. Bring your traps here, and take half my cabin."

"Come and take half of mine for one night," I said. "Help me to get at the bottom of this thing."

"You will get to the bottom of something else if you try," answered the doctor.

"What?" I asked.

"The bottom of the sea. I am going to leave the ship. It is not canny."

"Then you will not help me to find out—"

"Not I," said the doctor, quickly. "It is my business to keep my wits about me, not to go fiddling about with ghosts and things."

"Do you really believe it is a ghost?" I inquired, rather contemptuously. But as I spoke I remembered very well the horrible sensation of the supernatural which had got possession of me during the night. The doctor turned sharply on me:

"Have you any reasonable explanation of these things to offer?" he asked. "No, you have not. Well, you say you will find an explanation. I say that you won't, sir, simply because there is not any."

"But, my dear sir," I retorted, "do you, a man of science, mean to tell me that such things cannot be explained?"

"I do," he answered, stoutly. "And, if they could, I would not be concerned in the explanation."

I did not care to spend another night alone in the stateroom, and yet I was obstinately determined to get at the root of the disturbances. I do not believe there are many men who would have slept there alone, after passing two such nights. But I made up my mind to try it, if I could not get any one to share a watch with me. The doctor was evidently not inclined for such an experiment. He said he was a surgeon, and that in case any accident occurred on board he must always be in readiness. He could not afford to have his nerves unsettled. Perhaps he was quite right, but I am inclined to think that his precaution was prompted by his inclination. On inquiry, he informed me that there was no one on board who would be likely to join me in my investigations, and after a little more conversation I left him. A little later I met the captain, and told him my story. I said that if no one would spend the night with me I would ask leave to have the light burning all night, and would try it alone.

"Look here," said he, "I will tell you what I will do. I will share your watch myself, and we will see what happens. It is my belief that we can find out between us. There may be some fellow skulking on board, who steals a passage by frightening the passengers. It is just possible that there may be something queer in the carpentering of that berth."

I suggested taking the ship's carpenter below and examining the place, but I was overjoyed at the captain's offer to spend the night with me. He accordingly sent for the workman and ordered him to do anything I required. We went below at once. I had all the bedding cleared out of the upper berth, and we examined the place thoroughly to see if there was a board loose anywhere, or a panel which could be opened or pushed aside. We tried the planks everywhere, tapped the flooring, unscrewed the fittings of the lower berth and took it to pieces—in short, there was not a square inch of the state-room which was not searched and tested. Everything was in perfect order, and we put everything back in its place. As we were finishing our work, Robert came to the door and looked in.

"Well, sir, find anything, sir?" he asked with a ghastly grin.

"You were right about the porthole, Robert," I said, and I gave him the promised sovereign. The carpenter did his work silently and skilfully, following my directions. When he had done he spoke.

"I'm a plain man, sir," he said. "But it's my belief you had better just turn out your things and let me run half a dozen four inch screws through the door of this cabin. There's no good never came o' this cabin yet, sir, and that's all about it. There's been four lives lost out o' here to my own remembrance, and that in four trips. Better give it up, sir, better give it up!"

"I will try it for one night more," I said.

"Better give it up, sir, better give it up! It's a precious bad job," repeated the workman, putting his tools in his bag and leaving the cabin.

But my spirits had risen considerably at the prospect of having the captain's company, and I made up my mind not to be prevented from going to the end of the strange business. I abstained from Welsh rare-bits and grog that evening, and did not even join in the customary game of whist. I wanted to be quite sure of my nerves, and my vanity made me anxious to make a good figure in the captain's eyes.

IV

THE CAPTAIN WAS ONE of those splendidly tough and cheerful specimens of seafaring humanity whose combined courage, hardihood, and calmness in difficulty leads them naturally into high positions of trust. He was not the man to be led away by an idle tale, and the mere fact that he was willing to join me in the investigation was proof that he thought there was something seriously wrong, which could not be accounted for on ordinary theories, nor laughed down as a common superstition. To some extent, too, his reputation was at stake, as well as the reputation of the ship. It is no light thing to lose passengers overboard, and he knew it.

About ten o'clock that evening, as I was smoking a last cigar, he came up to me and drew me aside from the beat of the other passengers who were patrolling the deck in the warm darkness.

"This is a serious matter, Mr. Brisbane," he said. "We must make up our minds either way—to be disappointed or to have a pretty rough time of it. You see, I cannot afford to laugh at the affair, and I will ask you to sign your name to a statement of whatever occurs. If nothing happens tonight we will try it again tomorrow and next day. Are you ready?"

So we went below, and entered the state-room. As we went in I could see Robert the steward, who stood a little further down the passage, watching us, with his usual grin, as though certain that something dreadful was about to happen. The captain closed the door behind us and bolted it.

"Supposing we put your portmanteau before the door," he suggested. "One of us can sit on it. Nothing can get out then. Is the port screwed down?"

I found it as I had left it in the morning. Indeed, without using a lever, as I had done, no one could have opened it. I drew back the curtains of the upper berth so that I could see well into it. By the captain's advice I lighted my reading-lantern, and placed it so that it shone upon the white sheets above. He insisted upon sitting on the portmanteau, declaring that he wished to be able to swear that he had sat before the door.

Then he requested me to search the state-room thoroughly, an operation very soon accomplished, as it consisted merely in looking beneath the lower berth and under the couch below the porthole. The spaces were quite empty.

"It is impossible for any human being to get in," I said, "or for any human being to open the port."

"Very good," said the captain, calmly. "If we see anything now, it must be either imagination or something supernatural."

I sat down on the edge of the lower berth.

"The first time it happened," said the captain, crossing his legs and leaning back against the door, "was in March. The passenger who slept here, in the upper berth, turned out to have been a lunatic. In any event, he was known to have been a little touched, and he had taken his passage without the knowledge of his friends. He rushed out in the middle of the night, and threw himself overboard, before the officer who had the watch could stop him. We stopped and lowered a boat. It was a quiet night, just before that heavy weather came on, but we could not find him. Of course his suicide was afterwards accounted for on the ground of his insanity."

"I suppose that often happens?" I remarked, rather absently.

"Not often, no," said the captain, "never before in my experience, though I have heard of it happening on board of other ships. Well, as I was saying, that occurred in March. On the very next trip—What are you looking at?" he asked, stopping suddenly in his narration.

I believe I gave no answer. My eyes were riveted upon the porthole. It seemed to me that the brass loop-nut was beginning to turn very slowly upon the screw—so slowly, however, that I was not sure it moved at all. I watched it intently, fixing its position in my mind, and trying to ascertain whether it changed. Seeing where I was looking, the captain looked too.

"It moves!" he exclaimed, in a tone of conviction. "No, it does not," he added, after a minute.

"If it were the jarring of the screw," said I, "it would have opened during the day, but I found it this evening jammed tight as I left it this morning."

I rose and tried the nut. It was certainly loosened, for by an effort I could move it with my hands.

"The queer thing," said the captain, "is that the second man who was lost is supposed to have got through that very port. We had a terrible time over it. It was in the middle of the night, and the weather was very heavy. There was an alarm that one of the ports was open and the sea running in. I came below and found everything flooded, the water pouring in every time she rolled, and the whole port swinging from the top bolts—not the porthole in the middle. Well, we managed to shut it, but the water did some damage. Ever since that the place smells of sea-water from time to time. We supposed the passenger had thrown himself out, though the Lord only knows how he did it. The steward kept telling me that he could not keep anything shut here. Upon my word, I can smell it now, cannot you?" he inquired, sniffing the air suspiciously.

"Yes, distinctly," I said, and I shuddered as that same odour of stagnant sea-water grew stronger in the cabin. "Now, to smell like this, the place must be damp," I continued, "and yet when I examined it with the carpenter this morning everything was perfectly dry. It is most extraordinary—hallo!"

My reading-lantern, which had been placed in the upper berth, was suddenly extinguished. There was still a good deal of light from the pane of ground glass near the door, behind which loomed the regulation lamp. The ship rolled heavily, and the curtain of the upper berth swung far out into the state-room and back again. I rose quickly from my seat on the edge of the bed, and the captain at the same moment started to his feet with a loud cry of surprise. I had turned with the intention of taking down the lantern to examine it, when I heard his exclamation, and immediately afterwards his call for help. I sprang towards him. He was wrestling with all his might, with the brass loop of the port. It seemed to turn against his hands in spite of all his efforts. I caught up my cane, a heavy oak stick I always used to carry, and thrust it through the ring and bore on it with all my strength. But the strong wood snapped suddenly, and I fell upon the couch. When I rose again the port was wide open, and the captain was standing with his back against the door, pale to the lips.

"There is something in that berth!" he cried, in a strange

voice, his eyes almost starting from his head. "Hold the door, while I look—it shall not escape us, whatever it is!"

But instead of taking his place, I sprang upon the lower bed, and seized something which lay in the upper berth.

It was something ghostly, horrible beyond words, and it moved in my grip. It was like the body of a man long drowned, and yet it moved, and had the strength of ten men living, but I gripped it with all my might—the slippery, oozy, horrible thing. The dead white eyes seemed to stare at me out of the dusk. The putrid odour of rank sea-water was about it, and its shiny hair hung in foul wet curls over its dead face. I wrestled with the dead thing. It thrust itself upon me and forced me back and nearly broke my arms. It wound its corpse's arms about my neck, the living death, and overpowered me, so that I, at last, cried aloud and fell, and left my hold.

As I fell the thing sprang across me, and seemed to throw itself upon the captain. When I last saw him on his feet his face was white and his lips set. It seemed to me that he struck a violent blow at the dead being, and then he, too, fell forward upon his face, with an inarticulate cry of horror.

The thing paused an instant, seeming to hover over his prostrate body, and I could have screamed again for very fright, but I had no voice left. The thing vanished suddenly, and it seemed to my disturbed senses that it made its exit through the open port, though how that was possible, considering the smallness of the aperture, is more than anyone can tell. I lay a long time upon the floor, and the captain lay beside me. At last I partially recovered my senses and moved, and I instantly knew that my arm was broken—the small bone of the left forearm near the wrist.

I got upon my feet somehow, and with my remaining hand I tried to raise the captain. He groaned and moved, and at last came to himself. He was not hurt, but he seemed badly stunned.

Well, do you want to hear any more? There is nothing more.

That is the end of my story. The carpenter carried out his scheme of running half a dozen four-inch screws through the door of one hundred and five; and if ever you take a passage in the *Kamtschatka*, you may ask for a berth in that state-room. You will be told that it is engaged, yes, it is engaged by that dead thing.

I finished the trip in the surgeon's cabin. He doctored my broken arm, and advised me not to "fiddle about with ghosts and things" any more. The captain was very silent, and never sailed again in that ship, though it is still running. And I will not sail in her either. It was a very disagreeable experience, and I was very badly frightened, which is a thing I do not like. That is all. That is how I saw a ghost, if it was a ghost. It was dead, anyhow.

THE SEA RAIDERS

by H.G. Wells

I

UNTIL THE EXTRAORDINARY AFFAIR at Sidmouth, the peculiar species *Haploteuthis ferox* was known to science only generically, on the strength of a half-digested tentacle obtained near the Azores, and a decaying body pecked by birds and nibbled by fish, found early in 1896 by Mr. Jennings, near Land's End.

In no department of zoological science, indeed, are we quite so much in the dark as with regard to the deep-sea cephalopods. A mere accident, for instance, it was that led to the Prince of Monaco's discovery of nearly a dozen new forms in the summer of 1895, a discovery in which the before-mentioned tentacle was included. It chanced that a cachalot was killed off Terceira by some sperm whalers, and in its last struggles charged almost to the Prince's yacht, missed it, rolled under, and died within twenty yards of his rudder. And in its agony it threw up a number of large objects, which the Prince, dimly perceiving they were strange and important, was, by a happy expedient, able to secure before they sank. He set his screws in motion, and kept them circling in the vortices thus created until a boat could be lowered. And these specimens were whole cephalopods and fragments of cephalopods, some of gigantic proportions, and almost all of them unknown to science!

It would seem, indeed, that these large and agile creatures, living in the middle depths of the sea, must, to a large extent, forever remain unknown to us, since under water they are too nimble for nets, and it is only by such rare unlooked-for accidents that specimens can be obtained. In the case of *Haploteuthis ferox*, for instance, we are still altogether ignorant of its habitat, as ignorant as we are of the breeding-ground of the herring or the sea-ways of the salmon. And zoologists are altogether at a loss to account for its sudden appearance on our coast. Possibly it was the stress of a hunger migration that drove it hither out of the deep. But it will be, perhaps, better to avoid necessarily inconclusive discussion, and to proceed at once with our narrative.

The first human being to set eyes upon a living *Haploteuthis* —the first human being to survive, that is, for there can be little doubt now that the wave of bathing fatalities and boating accidents that travelled along the coast of Cornwall and Devon in early May was due to this cause—was a retired tea-dealer of the name of Fison, who was stopping at a Sidmouth boarding-house. It was in the afternoon, and he was walking along the cliff path between Sidmouth and Ladram Bay. The cliffs in this direction are very high, but down the red face of them in one place a kind of ladder staircase has been made. He was near this when his attention was attracted by what at first he thought to be a cluster of birds struggling over a fragment of food that caught the sunlight, and glistened pinkish-white. The tide was right out, and this object was not only far below him, but remote across a broad waste of rock reefs covered with dark seaweed and interspersed with silvery shining tidal pools. And he was, moreover, dazzled by the brightness of the further water.

In a minute, regarding this again, he perceived that his judgment was in fault, for over this struggle circled a number of birds, jackdaws and gulls for the most part, the latter gleaming blindingly when the sunlight smote their wings, and they seemed minute in comparison with it. And his curiosity was, perhaps, aroused all the more strongly because of his first insufficient explanations.

As he had nothing better to do than amuse himself, he decided to make this object, whatever it was, the goal of his afternoon walk, instead of Ladram Bay, conceiving it might perhaps be a great fish of some sort, stranded by some chance, and flapping about in its distress. And so he hurried down the long steep ladder, stopping at intervals of thirty feet or so to take breath and scan the mysterious movement.

At the foot of the cliff he was, of course, nearer his object than he had been, but, on the other hand, it now came up against the incandescent sky, beneath the sun, so as to seem dark and indistinct. Whatever was pinkish of it was now hidden by a skerry of weedy boulders. But he perceived that it was made up of seven rounded bodies, distinct or connected, and that the birds kept up a constant croaking and screaming, but seemed afraid to approach it too closely.

Mr. Fison, torn by curiosity, began picking his way across the wave-worn rocks, and, finding the wet seaweed that covered them thickly rendered them extremely slippery, he stopped, removed his shoes and socks, and coiled his trousers above his knees. His object was, of course, merely to avoid stumbling into the rocky pools about him, and perhaps he was rather glad, as all men are, of an excuse to resume, even for a moment, the sensations of his boyhood. At any rate, it is to this, no doubt, that he owes his life.

He approached his mark with all the assurance which the

absolute security of this country against all forms of animal life gives its inhabitants. The round bodies moved to and fro, but it was only when he surmounted the skerry of boulders I have mentioned that he realised the horrible nature of the discovery. It came upon him with some suddenness.

The rounded bodies fell apart as he came into sight over the ridge, and displayed the pinkish object to be the partially devoured body of a human being, but whether of a man or woman he was unable to say. And the rounded bodies were new and ghastly-looking creatures, in shape somewhat resembling an octopus, and with huge and very long and flexible tentacles, coiled copiously on the ground. The skin had a glistening texture, unpleasant to see, like shiny leather. The downward bend of the tentacle-surrounded mouth, the curious excrescence at the bend, the tentacles, and the large intelligent eyes, gave the creatures a grotesque suggestion of a face. They were the size of a fair-sized swine about the body, and the tentacles seemed to him to be many feet in length. There were, he thinks, seven or eight at least of the creatures. Twenty yards beyond them, amid the surf of the now returning tide, two others were emerging from the sea.

Their bodies lay flatly on the rocks, and their eyes regarded him with evil interest, but it does not appear that Mr. Fison was afraid, or that he realised that he was in any danger. Possibly his confidence is to be ascribed to the limpness of their attitudes. But he was horrified, of course, and intensely excited and indignant at such revolting creatures preying upon human flesh. He thought they had chanced upon a drowned body. He shouted to them, with the idea of driving them off, and, finding they did not budge, cast about him, picked up a big rounded lump of rock, and flung it at one.

And then, slowly uncoiling their tentacles, they all began moving towards him—creeping at first deliberately, and making a soft purring sound to each other.

In a moment Mr. Fison realised that he was in danger. He shouted again, threw both his boots, and started off, with a leap, forthwith. Twenty yards off he stopped and faced about, judging them slow, and behold! the tentacles of their leader were already pouring over the rocky ridge on which he had just been standing!

At that he shouted again, but this time not threatening, but a cry of dismay, and began jumping, striding, slipping, wading across the uneven expanse between him and the beach. The tall red cliffs seemed suddenly at a vast distance, and he saw, as though they were creatures in another world, two minute workmen engaged in the repair of the ladder-way, and little suspecting the race for life that was beginning below them. At one time he could hear the creatures splashing in the pools not a dozen feet behind him, and once he slipped and almost fell.

They chased him to the very foot of the cliffs, and desisted only when he had been joined by the workmen at the foot of the ladder-way up the cliff. All three of the men pelted them with stones for a time, and then hurried to the cliff top and along the path towards Sidmouth, to secure assistance and a boat, and to rescue the desecrated body from the clutches of these abominable creatures.

II

A ND, AS IF HE HAD NOT ALREADY been in sufficient peril that day, Mr. Fison went with the boat to point out the exact spot of his adventure.

As the tide was down, it required a considerable detour to reach the spot, and when at last they came off the ladder-way, the mangled body had disappeared. The water was now running in, submerging first one slab of slimy rock and then another, and the four men in the boat—the workmen, that is, the boatman, and Mr. Fison—now turned their attention from the bearings off shore to the water beneath the keel.

At first they could see little below them, save a dark jungle of laminaria, with an occasional darting fish. Their minds were set on adventure, and they expressed their disappointment freely. But presently they saw one of the monsters swimming through the water seaward, with a curious rolling motion that suggested to Mr. Fison the spinning roll of a captive balloon. Almost immediately after, the waving streamers of laminaria were extraordinarily perturbed, parted for a moment, and three of these beasts became darkly visible, struggling for what was probably some fragment of the drowned man. In a moment the copious olive-green ribbons had poured again over this writhing group.

At that all four men, greatly excited, began beating the water with oars and shouting, and immediately they saw a tumultuous movement among the weeds. They desisted to see more clearly, and as soon as the water was smooth, they saw, as it seemed to them, the whole sea bottom among the weeds set with eyes.

"Ugly swine!" cried one of the men. "Why, there's dozens!"

And forthwith the things began to rise through the water about them. Mr. Fison has since described to the writer this startling eruption out of the waving laminaria meadows. To him it seemed to occupy a considerable time, but it is probable that really it was an affair of a few seconds only. For a time nothing but eyes, and then he speaks of tentacles streaming out and parting the weed fronds this way and that. Then these things, growing larger, until at last the bottom was hidden by their intercoiling forms, and the tips of tentacles rose darkly here and there into the air above the swell of the waters.

One came up boldly to the side of the boat, and, clinging to this with three of its sucker-set tentacles, threw four others over the gunwale, as if with an intention either of oversetting the boat or of clambering into it. Mr. Fison at once caught up the boathook, and, jabbing furiously at the soft tentacles, forced it to desist. He was struck in the back and almost pitched overboard by the boatman, who was using his oar to resist a similar attack on the other side of the boat. But the tentacles on either side at once relaxed their hold at this, slid out of sight, and splashed into the water.

"We'd better get out of this," said Mr. Fison, who was trembling violently. He went to the tiller, while the boatman and one of the workmen seated themselves and began rowing. The other workman stood up in the fore part of the boat, with the boathook, ready to strike any more tentacles that might appear. Nothing else seems to have been said. Mr. Fison had expressed the common feeling beyond amendment. In a hushed, scared mood, with faces white and drawn, they set about escaping from the position into which they had so recklessly blundered.

But the oars had scarcely dropped into the water before dark, tapering, serpentine ropes had bound them, and were about the rudder, and creeping up the sides of the boat with a looping motion came the suckers again. The men gripped their oars and pulled, but it was like trying to move a boat in a floating raft of weeds. "Help here!" cried the boatman, and Mr. Fison and the second workman rushed to help lug at the oar.

Then the man with the boathook—his name was Ewan, or Ewen—sprang up with a curse, and began striking downward over the side, as far as he could reach, at the bank of tentacles that now clustered along the boat's bottom. And, at the same time, the two rowers stood up to get a better purchase for the recovery of their oars. The boatman handed his to Mr. Fison, who lugged desperately, and, meanwhile, the boatman opened a big clasp-knife, and, leaning over the side of the boat, began hacking at the spiring arms upon the oar shaft.

Mr. Fison, staggering with the quivering rocking of the boat, his teeth set, his breath coming short, and the veins starting on his hands as he pulled at his oar, suddenly cast his eyes seaward. And there, not fifty yards off, across the long rollers of the incoming tide, was a large boat standing in towards them, with three women and a little child in it. A boatman was rowing, and a little man in a pink-ribboned straw hat and whites stood in the stern, hailing them. For a moment, of course, Mr. Fison thought of help, and then he thought of the child. He abandoned his oar forthwith, threw up his arms in a frantic gesture, and screamed to the party in the boat to keep away "for God's sake!" It says much for the modesty and courage of Mr. Fison that he does not seem to be aware that there was any quality of heroism in his action at this juncture. The oar he had abandoned was at once drawn under, and presently reappeared floating about twenty yards away.

At the same moment Mr. Fison felt the boat under him lurch violently, and a hoarse scream, a prolonged cry of terror from Hill, the boatman, caused him to forget the party of excursionists altogether. He turned, and saw Hill crouching by the forward rowlock, his face convulsed with terror, and his right arm over the side and drawn tightly down. He gave now a succession of short, sharp cries, "Oh! oh! oh!—oh!" Mr. Fison believes that he must have been hacking at the tentacles below the water-line, and have been grasped by them, but, of course, it is quite impossible to say now certainly what had happened. The boat was heeling over, so that the gunwale was within ten inches of the water, and both Ewan and the other labourer were striking down into the water, with oar and boathook, on either side of Hill's arm. Mr. Fison instinctively placed himself to counterpoise them.

Then Hill, who was a burly, powerful man, made a strenuous effort, and rose almost to a standing position. He lifted his arm, indeed, clean out of the water. Hanging to it was a complicated tangle of brown ropes, and the eyes of one of the brutes that had hold of him, glaring straight and resolute, showed momentarily above the surface. The boat heeled more and more, and the green-brown water came pouring in a cascade over the side. Then Hill slipped and fell with his ribs across the side, and his arm and the mass of tentacles about it splashed back into the water. He rolled over. His boot kicked Mr. Fison's knee as that gentleman rushed forward to seize him, and in another moment fresh tentacles had whipped about his waist and neck, and after a brief, convulsive struggle, in which the boat was nearly capsized, Hill was lugged overboard. The boat righted with a violent jerk that all but sent Mr. Fison over the other side, and hid the struggle in the water from his eyes.

He stood staggering to recover his balance for a moment, and as he did so, he became aware that the struggle and the inflowing tide had carried them close upon the weedy rocks again. Not four yards off a table of rock still rose in rhythmic movements above the in-wash of the tide. In a moment Mr. Fison seized the oar from Ewan, gave one vigorous stroke, then, dropping it, ran to the bows and leapt. He felt his feet slide over the rock, and, by a frantic effort, leapt again towards a further mass. He stumbled over this, came to his knees, and rose again.

"Look out!" cried someone, and a large drab body struck him. He was knocked flat into a tidal pool by one of the workmen, and as he went down he heard smothered, choking cries, that he believed at the time came from Hill. Then he found himself marvelling at the shrillness and variety of Hill's voice. Someone jumped over him, and a curving rush of foamy water poured over him, and passed. He scrambled to his feet dripping, and, without looking seaward, ran as fast as his terror would let him shoreward. Before him, over the flat space of scattered rocks, stumbled the two workmen—one a dozen yards in front of the other.

He looked over his shoulder at last, and, seeing that he was not pursued, faced about. He was astonished. From the moment of the rising of the cephalopods out of the water, he had been acting too swiftly to fully comprehend his actions. Now it seemed to him as if he had suddenly jumped out of an evil dream.

For there were the sky, cloudless and blazing with the afternoon sun, the sea weltering under its pitiless brightness, the soft creamy foam of the breaking water, and the low, long, dark ridges of rock. The righted boat floated, rising and falling gently on the swell about a dozen yards from shore. Hill and the monsters, all the stress and tumult of that fierce fight for life, had vanished as though they had never been.

Mr. Fison's heart was beating violently. He was throbbing to the finger-tips, and his breath came deep.

There was something missing. For some seconds he could not think clearly enough what this might be. Sun, sky, sea, rocks—what was it? Then he remembered the boatload of excursionists. It had vanished. He wondered whether he had imagined it. He turned, and saw the two workmen standing side by side under the projecting masses of the tall pink cliffs. He hesitated whether he should make one last attempt to save the man Hill. His physical excitement seemed to desert him suddenly, and leave him aimless and helpless. He turned shoreward, stumbling and wading towards his two companions.

He looked back again, and there were now two boats floating, and the one farthest out at sea pitched clumsily, bottom upward.

III

So it was *Haploteuthis ferox* made its appearance upon the Devonshire coast. So far, this has been its most serious aggression. Mr. Fison's account, taken together with the wave of boating and bathing casualties to which I have already alluded, and the absence of fish from the Cornish coasts that year, points clearly to a shoal of these voracious deep-sea monsters prowling slowly along the sub-tidal coastline. Hunger migration has, I know, been suggested as the force that drove them hither, but, for my own part, I prefer to believe the alternative theory of Hemsley. Hemsley holds that a pack or shoal of these creatures may have become enamoured of human flesh by the accident of a foundered ship sinking among them, and have wandered in search of it out of their accustomed zone, first waylaying and following ships, and so coming to our shores in the wake of the Atlantic traffic. But to discuss Hemsley's cogent and admirably-stated arguments would be out of place here.

It would seem that the appetites of the shoal were satisfied by the catch of eleven people, for so far as can be ascertained, there were ten people in the second boat, and certainly these creatures gave no further signs of their presence off Sidmouth that day. The coast between Seaton and Budleigh Salterton was patrolled all that evening and night by four Preventive Service boats, the men in which were armed with harpoons and cutlasses, and as the evening advanced, a number of more or less similarly equipped expeditions, organised by private individuals, joined them. Mr. Fison took no part in any of these expeditions.

About midnight excited hails were heard from a boat about a couple of miles out at sea to the south-east of Sidmouth, and a lantern was seen waving in a strange manner to and fro and up and down. The nearer boats at once hurried towards the alarm. The venturesome occupants of the boat, a seaman, a curate, and two schoolboys, had actually seen the monsters passing under their boat. The creatures, it seems, like most deep-sea organisms, were phosphorescent, and they had been floating, five fathoms deep or so, like creatures of moonshine through the blackness of the water, their tentacles retracted and as if asleep, rolling over and over, and moving slowly in a wedge-like formation towards the south-east.

These people told their story in gesticulated fragments, as first one boat drew alongside and then another. At last there was a little fleet of eight or nine boats collected together, and from them a tumult, like the chatter of a marketplace, rose into the stillness of the night. There was little or no disposition to pursue the shoal, the people had neither weapons nor experience for such a dubious chase, and presently, even with a certain relief, it may be, the boats turned shoreward.

And now to tell what is perhaps the most astonishing fact in this whole astonishing raid. We have not the slightest knowledge of the subsequent movements of the shoal, although the whole south-west coast was now alert for it. But it may, perhaps, be significant that a cachalot was stranded off Sark on June 3. Two weeks and three days after this Sidmouth affair, a living *Haploteuthis* came ashore on Calais sands. It was alive, because several witnesses saw its tentacles moving in a convulsive way. But it is probable that it was dying. A gentleman named Pouchet obtained a rifle and shot it.

That was the last appearance of a living *Haploteuthis*. No others were seen on the French coast. On the 15th of June a dead body, almost complete, was washed ashore near Torquay, and a few days later a boat from the Marine Biological station, engaged in dredging off Plymouth, picked up a rotting specimen, slashed deeply with a cutlass wound. How the former specimen had come by its death it is impossible to say. And on the last day of June, Mr. Egbert Caine, an artist, bathing near Newlyn, threw up his arms, shrieked, and was drawn under. A friend bathing with him made no attempt to save him, but swam at once for the shore. This is the last fact to tell of this extraordinary raid from the deeper sea. Whether it is really the last of these horrible creatures it is, as yet, premature to say. But it is believed, and certainly it is to be hoped, that they have returned now, and returned for good, to the sunless depths of the middle seas, out of which they have so strangely and so mysteriously arisen.

THE TREASURE OF ABBOT THOMAS

by M.R. James

I

Verum usque in præsentem diem multa garriunt inter se Canonici de abscondito quodam istius Abbatis Thomæ thesauro, quem sæpe, quanquam adhuc incassum, quæsiverunt Steinfeldenses. Ipsum enim Thomam adhuc florida in ætate existentem ingentem auri massam circa monasterium defodisse perhibent; de quo multoties interrogatus ubi esset, cum risu respondere solitus erat: "Job, Johannes, et Zacharias vel vobis vel posteris indicabunt"; idemque aliquando adiicere se inventuris minime invisurum. Inter alia huius Abbatis opera, hoc memoria præcipue dignum iudico quod fenestram magnam in orientali parte alæ australis in ecclesia sua imaginibus optime in vitro depictis impleverit: id quod et ipsius effigies et insignia ibidem posita demonstrant. Domum quoque Abbatialem fere totam restauravit: puteo in atrio ipsius effosso et lapidibus marmoreis pulchre cælatis exornato. Decessit autem, morte aliquantulum subitanea perculsus, ætatis suæ anno lxxiido, incarnationis vero Dominiæ mdxxixo.

I SUPPOSE I SHALL have to translate this," said the antiquary to himself, as he finished copying the above lines from that rather rare and exceedingly diffuse book, the *Sertum Steinfeldense*

Norbertinum.[1] "Well, it may as well be done first as last," and accordingly the following rendering was very quickly produced:

Up to the present day there is much gossip among the Canons about a certain hidden treasure of this Abbot Thomas, for which those of Steinfeld have often made search, though hitherto in vain. The story is that Thomas, while yet in the vigour of life, concealed a very large quantity of gold somewhere in the monastery. He was often asked where it was, and always answered, with a laugh: "Job, John, and Zechariah will tell either you or your successors." He sometimes added that he should feel no grudge against those who might find it. Among other works carried out by this Abbot I may specially mention his filling the great window at the east end of the south aisle of the church with figures admirably painted on glass, as his effigy and arms in the window attest. He also restored almost the whole of the Abbot's lodging, and dug a well in the court of it, which he adorned with beautiful carvings in marble. He died rather suddenly in the seventy-second year of his age, A.D. 1529.

The object which the antiquary had before him at the moment was that of tracing the whereabouts of the painted windows of the Abbey Church of Steinfeld. Shortly after the Revolution, a very large quantity of painted glass made its way from the dissolved abbeys of Germany and Belgium to this country, and may now be seen adorning various of our parish churches, cathedrals, and private chapels. Steinfeld Abbey was among the most considerable of these involuntary contributors to our artistic possessions (I am quoting the somewhat ponderous preamble of the book which the antiquary wrote), and the greater part of the glass from that institution can be identified without much difficulty by the help, either of the

---

1   An account of the Premonstratensian abbey of Steinfeld, in the Eiffel, with lives of the Abbots, published at Cologne in 1712 by Christian Albert Erhard, a resident in the district. The epithet Norbertinum is due to the fact that St Norbert was founder of the Premonstratensian Order.

numerous inscriptions in which the place is mentioned, or of the subjects of the windows, in which several well-defined cycles or narratives were represented.

The passage with which I began my story had set the antiquary on the track of another identification. In a private chapel—no matter where—he had seen three large figures, each occupying a whole light in a window, and evidently the work of one artist. Their style made it plain that that artist had been a German of the sixteenth century, but hitherto the more exact localizing of them had been a puzzle. They represented—will you be surprised to hear it?—Job Patriarcha, Johannes Evangelista, Zacharias Propheta, and each of them held a book or scroll, inscribed with a sentence from his writings. These, as a matter of course, the antiquary had noted, and had been struck by the curious way in which they differed from any text of the Vulgate that he had been able to examine. Thus the scroll in Job's hand was inscribed: *Auro est locus in quo absconditur* (for *conflatur*);[2] on the book of John was: *Habent in vestimentis suis scripturam quam nemo novit*[3] (for in *vestimento scriptum*, the following words being taken from another verse); and Zacharias had: *Super lapidem unum septem oculi sunt*[4] (which alone of the three presents an unaltered text).

A sad perplexity it had been to our investigator to think why these three personages should have been placed together in one window. There was no bond of connection between them, either historic, symbolic, or doctrinal, and he could only suppose that they must have formed part of a very large series of Prophets and Apostles, which might have filled, say, all the clerestory windows of some capacious church. But the passage from the *Sertum* had altered the situation by showing that the

---

2   There is a place for gold where it is hidden.

3   They have on their raiment a writing which no man knoweth.

4   Upon one stone are seven eyes.

names of the actual personages represented in the glass now in Lord D——'s chapel had been constantly on the lips of Abbot Thomas von Eschenhausen of Steinfeld, and that this Abbot had put up a painted window, probably about the year 1520, in the south aisle of his abbey church. It was no very wild conjecture that the three figures might have formed part of Abbot Thomas's offering. It was one which, moreover, could probably be confirmed or set aside by another careful examination of the glass. And, as Mr. Somerton was a man of leisure, he set out on pilgrimage to the private chapel with very little delay. His conjecture was confirmed to the full. Not only did the style and technique of the glass suit perfectly with the date and place required, but in another window of the chapel he found some glass, known to have been bought along with the figures, which contained the arms of Abbot Thomas von Eschenhausen.

At intervals during his researches Mr. Somerton had been haunted by the recollection of the gossip about the hidden treasure, and, as he thought the matter over, it became more and more obvious to him that if the Abbot meant anything by the enigmatical answer which he gave to his questioners, he must have meant that the secret was to be found somewhere in the window he had placed in the abbey church. It was undeniable, furthermore, that the first of the curiously-selected texts on the scrolls in the window might be taken to have a reference to hidden treasure.

Every feature, therefore, or mark which could possibly assist in elucidating the riddle which, he felt sure, the Abbot had set to posterity he noted with scrupulous care, and, returning to his Berkshire manor-house, consumed many a pint of the midnight oil over his tracings and sketches. After two or three weeks, a day came when Mr Somerton announced to his man that he must pack his own and his master's things for a short journey abroad, whither for the moment we will not follow him.

II

M r Gregory, the Rector of Parsbury, had strolled out before breakfast, it being a fine autumn morning, as far as the gate of his carriage-drive, with intent to meet the postman and sniff the cool air. Nor was he disappointed of either purpose. Before he had had time to answer more than ten or eleven of the miscellaneous questions propounded to him in the lightness of their hearts by his young offspring, who had accompanied him, the postman was seen approaching, and among the morning's budget was one letter bearing a foreign postmark and stamp (which became at once the objects of an eager competition among the youthful Gregorys), and was addressed in an uneducated, but plainly an English hand.

When the Rector opened it, and turned to the signature, he realized that it came from the confidential valet of his friend and squire, Mr. Somerton. Thus it ran:

HONOURED SIR,

Has I am in a great anxiety about Master I write at is Wish to beg you Sir if you could be so good as Step over. Master Has add a Nastey Shock and keeps His Bedd. I never Have known Him like this but No wonder and Nothing will serve but you Sir. Master says would I mintion the Short Way Here is Drive to Cobblince and take a Trap. Hopeing I Have maid all Plain, but am much Confused in Myself what with Anxiatey and Weakfulness at Night. If I might be so Bold Sir it will be a Pleasure to see a Honnest Brish Face among all These Forig ones.

I am Sir
Your obedt Servt
William Brown.

P.S.—The Village for Town I will not Turm. It is name Steenfeld.

The reader must be left to picture to himself in detail the surprise, confusion, and hurry of preparation into which the receipt of such a letter would be likely to plunge a quiet Berkshire parsonage in the year of grace 1859. It is enough for me to say that a train to town was caught in the course of the day, and that Mr Gregory was able to secure a cabin in the Antwerp boat and a place in the Coblentz train. Nor was it difficult to manage the transit from that centre to Steinfeld.

I labour under a grave disadvantage as narrator of this story in that I have never visited Steinfeld myself, and that neither of the principal actors in the episode (from whom I derive my information) was able to give me anything but a vague and rather dismal idea of its appearance. I gather that it is a small place, with a large church despoiled of its ancient fittings, a number of rather ruinous great buildings, mostly of the seventeenth century, surround this church, for the abbey, in common with most of those on the Continent, was rebuilt in a luxurious fashion by its inhabitants at that period. It has not seemed to me worthwhile to lavish money on a visit to the place, for though it is probably far more attractive than either Mr Somerton or Mr Gregory thought it, there is evidently little, if anything, of first-rate interest to be seen—except, perhaps, one thing, which I should not care to see.

The inn where the English gentleman and his servant were lodged is, or was, the only "possible" one in the village. Mr Gregory was taken to it at once by his driver, and found Mr Brown waiting at the door. Mr Brown, a model when in his Berkshire home of the impassive whiskered race who are known as confidential valets, was now egregiously out of his element, in a light tweed suit, anxious, almost irritable, and plainly anything but master of the situation. His relief at the sight of the "honest British face" of his Rector was unmeasured, but words to describe it were denied him. He could only say:

"Well, I ham pleased, I'm sure, sir, to see you. And so I'm

sure, sir, will master."

"How *is* your master, Brown?" Mr Gregory eagerly put in.

"I think he's better, sir, thank you, but he's had a dreadful time of it. I 'ope he's gettin' some sleep now, but—"

"What has been the matter—I couldn't make out from your letter? Was it an accident of any kind?"

"Well, sir, I 'ardly know whether I'd better speak about it. Master was very partickler he should be the one to tell you. But there's no bones broke—that's one thing I'm sure we ought to be thankful—"

"What does the doctor say?" asked Mr Gregory.

They were by this time outside Mr Somerton's bedroom door, and speaking in low tones. Mr Gregory, who happened to be in front, was feeling for the handle, and chanced to run his fingers over the panels. Before Brown could answer, there was a terrible cry from within the room.

"In God's name, who is that?" were the first words they heard. "Brown, is it?"

"Yes, sir, me, sir, and Mr Gregory," Brown hastened to answer, and there was an audible groan of relief in reply.

They entered the room, which was darkened against the afternoon sun, and Mr Gregory saw, with a shock of pity, how drawn, how damp with drops of fear, was the usually calm face of his friend, who, sitting up in the curtained bed, stretched out a shaking hand to welcome him.

"Better for seeing you, my dear Gregory," was the reply to the Rector's first question, and it was palpably true.

After five minutes of conversation Mr Somerton was more his own man, Brown afterwards reported, than he had been for days. He was able to eat a more than respectable dinner, and talked confidently of being fit to stand a journey to Coblentz within twenty-four hours.

"But there's one thing," he said, with a return of agitation which Mr Gregory did not like to see, "which I must beg you to do for me, my dear Gregory. Don't," he went on, laying his hand on Gregory's to forestall any interruption, "don't ask me what it is, or why I want it done. I'm not up to explaining it yet. It would throw me back, undo all the good you have done me by coming. The only word I will say about it is that you run no risk whatever by doing it, and that Brown can and will show you tomorrow what it is. It's merely to put back, to keep... something... No, I can't speak of it yet. Do you mind calling Brown?"

"Well, Somerton," said Mr Gregory, as he crossed the room to the door, "I won't ask for any explanations till you see fit to give them. And if this bit of business is as easy as you represent it to be, I will very gladly undertake it for you the first thing in the morning."

"Ah, I was sure you would, my dear Gregory. I was certain I could rely on you. I shall owe you more thanks than I can tell. Now, here is Brown. Brown, one word with you."

"Shall I go?" interjected Mr Gregory.

"Not at all. Dear me, no. Brown, the first thing tomorrow morning—you don't mind early hours, I know, Gregory— you must take the Rector to... *there*, you know" (a nod from Brown, who looked grave and anxious), "and he and you will put that back. You needn't be in the least alarmed. It's *perfectly* safe in the daytime. You know what I mean. It lies on the step, you know, where—where we put it." Brown swallowed dryly once or twice, and, failing to speak, bowed. "And, yes, that's all. Only this one other word, my dear Gregory. If you *can* manage to keep from questioning Brown about this matter, I shall be still more bound to you. Tomorrow evening, at latest, if all goes well, I shall be able, I believe, to tell you the whole story from start to finish. And now I'll wish you good night. Brown will be with me—he sleeps here—and if I were you, I should lock my door. Yes, be particular to do that. They—they like it, the people here, and it's better. Goodnight, goodnight."

They parted upon this, and if Mr Gregory woke once or twice in the small hours and fancied he heard a fumbling about the lower part of his locked door, it was, perhaps, no more than what a quiet man, suddenly plunged into a strange bed and the heart of a mystery, might reasonably expect. Certainly he thought, to the end of his days, that he had heard such a sound twice or three times between midnight and dawn.

He was up with the sun, and out in company with Brown soon after. Perplexing as was the service he had been asked to perform for Mr Somerton, it was not a difficult or an alarming one, and within half an hour from his leaving the inn it was over. What it was I shall not as yet divulge.

Later in the morning Mr Somerton, now almost himself again, was able to make a start from Steinfeld, and that same evening, whether at Coblentz or at some intermediate stage on the journey I am not certain, he settled down to the promised explanation. Brown was present, but how much of the matter was ever really made plain to his comprehension he would never say, and I am unable to conjecture.

III

THIS WAS Mr Somerton's story: "You know roughly, both of you, that this expedition of mine was undertaken with the object of tracing something in connection with some old painted glass in Lord D——'s private chapel. Well, the starting point of the whole matter lies in this passage from an old printed book, to which I will ask your attention."

And at this point Mr Somerton went carefully over some ground with which we are already familiar.

"On my second visit to the chapel," he went on, "my purpose was to take every note I could of figures, lettering, diamond-scratchings on the glass, and even apparently accidental markings. The first point which I tackled was that of the inscribed scrolls. I could not doubt that the first of these, that of Job—'There is a place for the gold where it is hidden'—with its intentional alteration, must refer to the treasure, so I applied myself with some confidence to the next, that of St John—'They have on their vestures a writing which no man knoweth.' The natural question will have occurred to you: Was there an inscription on the robes of the figures? I could see none. Each of the three had a broad black border to his mantle, which made a conspicuous and rather ugly feature in the window. I was nonplussed, I will own, and, but for a curious bit of luck, I think I should have left the search where the Canons of Steinfeld had left it before me. But it so happened that there was a good deal of dust on the surface of the glass, and Lord D——, happening to come in, noticed my blackened hands, and kindly insisted on sending for a Turk's head broom to clean down the window. There must, I suppose, have been a rough piece in the broom. Anyhow, as it passed over the border of one of the mantles, I noticed that it left a long scratch, and that some yellow stain instantly showed up. I asked the man to stop his work for a moment, and ran up the ladder to examine the place. The yellow stain was there, sure enough, and what had come away was a thick black pigment, which had evidently been laid on with the brush after the glass had been burnt, and could therefore be easily scraped off without doing any harm. I scraped, accordingly, and you will hardly believe—no, I do you an injustice; you will have guessed already—that I found under this black pigment two or three clearly-formed capital letters in yellow stain on a clear ground. Of course, I could hardly contain my delight.

"I told Lord D—— that I had detected an inscription which I thought might be very interesting, and begged to be allowed to uncover the whole of it. He made no difficulty about it whatever, told me to do exactly as I pleased, and then, having an engagement, was obliged, rather to my relief I must say, to leave me. I set to work at once, and found the task a fairly easy one. The pigment, disintegrated, of course, by time, came off almost at a touch, and I don't think that it took me a couple of hours, all told, to clean the whole of the black borders in all three lights. Each of the figures had, as the inscription said, 'a writing on their vestures which nobody knew'.

"This discovery, of course, made it absolutely certain to my mind that I was on the right track. And, now, what was the inscription? While I was cleaning the glass I almost took pains not to read the lettering, saving up the treat until I had got the whole thing clear. And when that was done, my dear Gregory, I assure you I could almost have cried from sheer disappointment. What I read was only the most hopeless jumble of letters that was ever shaken up in a hat. Here it is:

Job

DREVICIOPEDMOOMSMVIVLISLCAVIBASBATAOVT

St John

RDIIEAMRLESIPVSPODSEEIRSETTAAESGIAVNNR

Zechariah

DREVICIOPEDMOOMSMVIVLISLCAVIBASBATAOVT

"Blank as I felt and must have looked for the first few minutes, my disappointment didn't last long. I realized almost at once that I was dealing with a cipher or cryptogram, and I reflected that it was likely to be of a pretty simple kind, considering its early date. So I copied the letters with the most anxious care. Another little point, I may tell you, turned up in the process which confirmed my belief in the cipher. After copying the letters on Job's robe I counted them, to make sure that I had them right. There were thirty-eight, and, just as I finished going through them, my eye fell on a scratching made with a sharp point on the edge of the border. It was simply the number xxxviii in Roman numerals. To cut the matter short, there was a similar note, as I may call it, in each of the other lights, and that made it plain to me that the glass-painter had had very strict orders from Abbot Thomas about the inscription, and had taken pains to get it correct.

"Well, after that discovery you may imagine how minutely I went over the whole surface of the glass in search of further light. Of course, I did not neglect the inscription on the scroll of Zechariah, 'Upon one stone are seven eyes,' but I very quickly concluded that this must refer to some mark on a stone which could only be found in situ, where the treasure was concealed. To be short, I made all possible notes and sketches and tracings, and then came back to Parsbury to work out the cipher at leisure. Oh, the agonies I went through! I thought myself very clever at first, for I made sure that the key would be found in some of the old books on secret writing. The *Steganographia* of Joachim Trithemius, who was an earlier contemporary of Abbot Thomas, seemed particularly promising, so I got that and Selenius's *Cryptographia* and Bacon's *de Augmentis Scientiarum* and some more. But I could hit upon nothing. Then I tried the principle of the 'most frequent letter', taking first Latin and then German as a basis. That didn't help, either. Whether it ought to have done so, I am not clear. And then I came back to the window itself, and read over my notes, hoping almost against hope that the Abbot might himself have somewhere supplied the key I wanted. I could make nothing out of the colour or pattern of the robes. There were no landscape backgrounds with subsidiary objects. There was nothing in the canopies. The only resource possible seemed to be in the attitudes of the figures. 'Job,' I read: 'scroll in left hand, forefinger of right hand extended upwards. John: holds inscribed book in left hand, with right hand blesses, with two fingers. Zechariah: scroll in left hand, right hand extended upwards, as Job, but with three fingers pointing up.' In other words, I reflected, Job has *one* finger extended, John has *two*, Zechariah has *three*. May not there be a numeral key concealed in that? My dear Gregory," said Mr Somerton, laying his hand on his friend's knee, "that was the key. I didn't get it to fit at first, but after two or three trials I saw what was meant. After the first letter of the inscription you skip one letter, after the next you skip two, and after that skip three. Now look at the result I got. I've underlined the letters which form words:

[D]R[E]VI[C]IOP[E]D[M]OO[M]SMV[I]V[L]IS[L]
CAV[I]B[A]SB[A]TAO[V]T
[R]DI[I]EAM[R]L[E]SI[P]VSP[O]D[S]EE[I]RSE[T]T[A]
AE[S]GIA[V]N[N]R
F[T]EEA[I]L[N]QD[P]VAI[V]M[T]LE[E]ATT[O]H[I]
OO[N]VMC[A]A[T].H.Q.E.

"Do you see it? *'Decem millia auri reposita sunt in puteo in at...'* 'Ten thousand pieces of gold are laid up in a well in...' followed by an incomplete word beginning *at*. So far so good. I tried the same plan with the remaining letters, but it wouldn't work, and I fancied that perhaps the placing of dots after the three last letters might indicate some difference of procedure. Then I thought to myself, 'Wasn't there some allusion to a well in the account of Abbot Thomas in that book the *"Sertum"*?' Yes, there was: he built a *puteus in atrio* (a well in the court). There, of course, was my word *atrio*. The next step was to copy out the remaining letters of the inscription, omitting those I had already used. That gave what you will see on this slip:

RVIIOPDOOSMVVISCAVBSBTAOTDIEAMLSIVSP-
DEERSETAEGIANRFEEALQDVAIMLEATTHOOVM-
CA.H.Q.E.

"Now, I knew what the three first letters I wanted were—namely, *rio*—to complete the word *atrio*, and, as you will see, these are all to be found in the first five letters. I was a little confused at first by the occurrence of two i's, but very soon I saw that every alternate letter must be taken in the remainder of the inscription. You can work it out for yourself. The result, continuing where the first 'round' left off, is this:

'rio domus abbatialis de Steinfeld a me, Thoma, qui posui custodem super ea. Gare à qui la touche'.

"So the whole secret was out:

'Ten thousand pieces of gold are laid up in the well in the court of the Abbot's house of Steinfeld by me, Thomas, who have set a guardian over them. *Gare à qui la touche.'*

"The last words, I ought to say, are a device which Abbot Thomas had adopted. I found it with his arms in another piece of glass at Lord D——'s, and he drafted it bodily into his cipher, though it doesn't quite fit in point of grammar.

"Well, what would any human being have been tempted to do, my dear Gregory, in my place? Could he have helped setting off, as I did, to Steinfeld, and tracing the secret literally to the fountain-head? I don't believe he could. Anyhow, I couldn't, and, as I needn't tell you, I found myself at Steinfeld as soon as the resources of civilization could put me there, and installed myself in the inn you saw. I must tell you that I was not altogether free from forebodings—on one hand of disappointment, on the other of danger. There was always the possibility that Abbot Thomas's well might have been wholly obliterated, or else that someone, ignorant of cryptograms, and guided only by luck, might have stumbled on the treasure before me. And then"—there was a very perceptible shaking of the voice here—"I was not entirely easy, I need not mind confessing, as to the meaning of the words about the guardian of the treasure. But, if you don't mind, I'll say no more about that until—until it becomes necessary.

"At the first possible opportunity Brown and I began exploring the place. I had naturally represented myself as being interested in the remains of the abbey, and we could not avoid paying a visit to the church, impatient as I was to be elsewhere. Still, it did interest me to see the windows where the glass had been, and especially that at the east end of the south aisle. In the tracery lights of that I was startled to see some fragments and coats-of-arms remaining. Abbot Thomas's shield was there, and a small figure with a scroll inscribed *Oculos habent, et non videbunt* (They have eyes, and shall not see), which, I take it, was a hit of the Abbot at his Canons.

"But, of course, the principal object was to find the Abbot's house. There is no prescribed place for this, so far as I know, in the plan of a monastery. You can't predict of it, as you can of the chapterhouse, that it will be on the eastern side of the cloister, or, as of the dormitory, that it will communicate with a transept of the church. I felt that if I asked many questions I might awaken lingering memories of the treasure, and I thought it best to try first to discover it for myself. It was not a very long or difficult search. That three-sided court south-east of the church, with deserted piles of building round it, and grass-grown pavement, which you saw this morning, was the place. And glad enough I was to see that it was put to no use, and was neither very far from our inn nor overlooked by any inhabited building. There were only orchards and paddocks on the slopes east of the church. I can tell you that fine stone glowed wonderfully in the rather watery yellow sunset that we had on the Tuesday afternoon.

"Next, what about the well? There was not much doubt about that, as you can testify. It is really a very remarkable thing. That curb is, I think, of Italian marble, and the carving I thought must be Italian also. There were reliefs, you will perhaps remember, of Eliezer and Rebekah, and of Jacob opening the well for Rachel, and similar subjects, but, by way of disarming suspicion, I suppose, the Abbot had carefully abstained from any of his cynical and allusive inscriptions.

"I examined the whole structure with the keenest interest, of course. A square well-head with an opening in one side. An arch over it, with a wheel for the rope to pass over, evidently in very good condition still, for it had been used within sixty years, or perhaps even later, though not quite recently. Then there was the question of depth and access to the interior. I suppose the depth was about sixty to seventy feet; and as to the other point, it really seemed as if the Abbot had wished to lead searchers up to the very door of his treasure-house, for, as you tested for yourself, there were big blocks of stone bonded into the masonry, and leading down in a regular staircase round and round the inside of the well.

"It seemed almost too good to be true. I wondered if there was a trap, if the stones were so contrived as to tip over when a weight was placed on them. But I tried a good many with my own weight and with my stick, and all seemed, and actually were, perfectly firm. Of course, I resolved that Brown and I would make an experiment that very night.

"I was well prepared. Knowing the sort of place I should have to explore, I had brought a sufficiency of good rope and bands of webbing to surround my body, and cross-bars to hold to, as well as lanterns and candles and crowbars, all of which would go into a single carpet-bag and excite no suspicion. I satisfied myself that my rope would be long enough, and that the wheel for the bucket was in good working order, and then we went home to dinner.

"I had a little cautious conversation with the landlord, and made out that he would not be overmuch surprised if I went out for a stroll with my man about nine o'clock, to make (Heaven forgive me!) a sketch of the abbey by moonlight. I asked no questions about the well, and am not likely to do so now. I fancy I know as much about it as anyone in Steinfeld: at least"—with a strong shudder—"I don't want to know any more.

"Now we come to the crisis, and, though I hate to think of it, I feel sure, Gregory, that it will be better for me in all ways to recall it just as it happened. We started, Brown and I, at about nine with our bag, and attracted no attention, for we managed to slip out at the hinder end of the inn-yard into an alley which brought us quite to the edge of the village. In five minutes we were at the well, and for some little time we sat on the edge of the well-head to make sure that no one was stirring or spying on us. All we heard was some horses cropping grass out of sight farther down the eastern slope. We were perfectly unobserved, and had plenty of light from the gorgeous full moon to allow us to get the rope properly fitted over the wheel. Then I secured the band round my body beneath the arms. We attached the end of the rope very securely to a ring in the stonework. Brown took the lighted lantern and followed me. I had a crowbar. And so we began to descend cautiously, feeling every step before we set foot on it, and scanning the walls in search of any marked stone.

"Half aloud I counted the steps as we went down, and we got as far as the thirty-eighth before I noted anything at all irregular in the surface of the masonry. Even here there was no mark, and I began to feel very blank, and to wonder if the Abbot's cryptogram could possibly be an elaborate hoax. At the forty-ninth step the staircase ceased. It was with a very sinking heart that I began retracing my steps, and when I was back on the thirty-eighth—Brown, with the lantern, being a step or two above me—I scrutinized the little bit of irregularity in the stonework with all my might. But there was no vestige of a mark.

"Then it struck me that the texture of the surface looked just a little smoother than the rest, or, at least, in some way different. It might possibly be cement and not stone. I gave it a good blow with my iron bar. There was a decidedly hollow sound, though that might be the result of our being in a well. But there was more. A great flake of cement dropped on to my feet, and I saw marks on the stone underneath. I had tracked the Abbot down, my dear Gregory. Even now I think of it with a certain pride. It took but a very few more taps to clear the whole of the cement away, and I saw a slab of stone about two feet square, upon which was engraven a cross. Disappointment again, but only for a moment. It was you, Brown, who reassured me by a casual remark. You said, if I remember right:

"'It's a funny cross: looks like a lot of eyes.'

"I snatched the lantern out of your hand, and saw with inexpressible pleasure that the cross *was* composed of seven eyes, four in a vertical line, three horizontal. The last of the scrolls in the window was explained in the way I had anticipated. Here was my 'stone with the seven eyes'. So far the Abbot's data had been exact, and, as I thought of this, the anxiety about the 'guardian' returned upon me with increased force. Still, I wasn't going to retreat now.

"Without giving myself time to think, I knocked away the cement all round the marked stone, and then gave it a prise on the right side with my crowbar. It moved at once, and I saw that it was but a thin light slab, such as I could easily lift out myself, and that it stopped the entrance to a cavity. I did lift it out unbroken, and set it on the step, for it might be very important to us to be able to replace it. Then I waited for several minutes on the step just above. I don't know why, but I think to see if any dreadful thing would rush out. Nothing happened. Next I lit a candle, and very cautiously I placed it inside the cavity, with some idea of seeing whether there were foul air, and of getting a glimpse of what was inside. There *was* some foulness of air which nearly extinguished the flame, but in no long time it burned quite steadily. The hole went some little way back, and also on the right and left of the entrance, and I could see some rounded light-coloured objects within which might be bags. There was no use in waiting. I faced the cavity, and looked in. There was nothing immediately in the front of the hole. I put my arm in and felt to the right, very gingerly...

"Just give me a glass of cognac, Brown. I'll go on in a moment, Gregory...

"Well, I felt to the right, and my fingers touched something curved, that felt—yes—more or less like leather. Dampish it was, and evidently part of a heavy, full thing. There was nothing, I must say, to alarm one. I grew bolder, and putting both hands in as well as I could, I pulled it to me, and it came. It was heavy, but moved more easily than I had expected. As I pulled it towards the entrance, my left elbow knocked over and extinguished the candle. I got the thing fairly in front of the mouth and began drawing it out. Just then Brown gave a sharp ejaculation and ran quickly up the steps with the lantern. He will tell you why in a moment. Startled as I was, I looked round after him, and saw him stand for a minute at the top and then walk away a few yards. Then I heard him call softly, 'All right, sir,' and went on pulling out the great bag, in complete darkness. It hung for an instant on the edge of the hole, then slipped forward on to my chest, and put its arms round my neck.

"My dear Gregory, I am telling you the exact truth. I believe I am now acquainted with the extremity of terror and repulsion which a man can endure without losing his mind. I can only just manage to tell you now the bare outline of the experience. I was conscious of a most horrible smell of mould, and of a cold kind of face pressed against my own, and moving slowly over it, and of several—I don't know how many—legs or arms or tentacles or something clinging to my body. I screamed out, Brown says, like a beast, and fell away backward from the step on which I stood, and the creature slipped downwards, I suppose, on to that same step. Providentially the band round me held firm. Brown did not lose his head, and was strong enough to pull me up to the top and get me over the edge quite promptly. How he managed it exactly I don't know, and I think he would find it hard to tell you. I believe he contrived to hide our implements in the deserted building near by, and with very great difficulty he got me back to the inn. I was in no state to make explanations, and Brown knows no German, but next morning I told the people some tale of having had a bad fall in the abbey ruins, which, I suppose, they believed. And now, before I go further, I should just like you to hear what Brown's experiences during those few minutes were. Tell the Rector, Brown, what you told me."

"Well, sir," said Brown, speaking low and nervously, "it was just this way. Master was busy down in front of the 'ole, and I was 'olding the lantern and looking on, when I 'eard somethink drop in the water from the top, as I thought. So I looked up, and I see someone's 'ead lookin' over at us. I s'pose I must ha' said somethink, and I 'eld the light up and run up the steps, and my light shone right on the face. That was a bad un, sir, if ever I see one! A holdish man, and the face very much fell in, and larfin', as I thought. And I got up the steps as quick pretty nigh as I'm tellin' you, and when I was out on the ground there warn't a sign of any person. There 'adn't been the time for anyone to get away, let alone a hold chap, and I made sure he warn't crouching down by the well, nor nothink. Next thing I hear master cry out somethink 'orrible, and hall I see was him hanging out by the rope, and, as master says, 'owever I got him up I couldn't tell you."

"You hear that, Gregory?" said Mr Somerton. "Now, does any explanation of that incident strike you?"

"The whole thing is so ghastly and abnormal that I must own it puts me quite off my balance; but the thought did occur to me that possibly the—well, the person who set the trap might have come to see the success of his plan."

"Just so, Gregory, just so. I can think of nothing else so—likely, I should say, if such a word had a place anywhere in my story. I think it must have been the Abbot... Well, I haven't much more to tell you. I spent a miserable night, Brown sitting up with me. Next day I was no better; unable to get up, no doctor to be had, and, if one had been available, I doubt if he could have done much for me. I made Brown write off to you, and spent a second terrible night. And, Gregory, of this I am sure, and I think it affected me more than the first shock, for it lasted longer: there was someone or something on the watch outside my door the whole night. I almost fancy there were two. It wasn't only the faint noises I heard from time to time all through the dark hours, but there was the smell—the hideous smell of mould. Every rag I had had on me on that first evening I had stripped off and made Brown take it away. I believe he stuffed the things into the stove in his room, and yet the smell was there, as intense as it had been in the well. And, what is more, it came from outside the door. But with the first glimmer of dawn it faded out, and the sounds ceased, too, and that convinced me that the thing or things were creatures of darkness, and could not stand the daylight, and so I was sure that if anyone could put back the stone, it or they would be powerless until someone else took it away again. I had to wait until you came to get that done. Of course, I couldn't send Brown to do it by himself, and still less could I tell anyone who belonged to the place.

"Well, there is my story, and, if you don't believe it, I can't help it. But I think you do."

"Indeed," said Mr Gregory, "I can find no alternative. I must believe it! I saw the well and the stone myself, and had a glimpse, I thought, of the bags or something else in the hole. And, to be plain with you, Somerton, I believe my door was watched last night, too."

"I dare say it was, Gregory, but, thank goodness, that is over. Have you, by the way, anything to tell about your visit to that dreadful place?"

"Very little," was the answer. "Brown and I managed easily enough to get the slab into its place, and he fixed it very firmly with the irons and wedges you had desired him to get, and we contrived to smear the surface with mud so that it looks just like the rest of the wall. One thing I did notice in the carving on the well-head, which I think must have escaped you. It was a horrid, grotesque shape—perhaps more like a toad than any-thing else, and there was a label by it inscribed with the two words, 'Depositum custodi'."[5]

---

5   "Keep that which is committed to thee."

THE DROWNED MAN

by Guy de Maupassant

I

Every one in Fécamp was acquainted with the story of Mother Patin. There could be no doubt that Mother Patin had not had a happy life of it with her man, for during his lifetime her man had used to thrash her as they thrash the wheat on the barn-floor.

He was captain of a fishing boat, and had married her, long ago, although she was poor, for her good looks.

Patin, a good sailor, but very much of a brute, was a frequenter of Father Auban's pothouse, where, on ordinary days, he would drink four or five small glasses of tanglefoot, and on days when the luck was good out at sea eight or ten, and even more, according to his gayety of heart, as he used to say. The tanglefoot was served to the customers by Father Auban's daughter, a comely brunette of pleasing aspect, who attracted custom to the house by dint of her good looks alone, for she had never been the subject of scandal.

At the commencement of Patin's visits to the pothouse he would be content to gaze upon her, and his remarks to her would be simply such as were demanded by common politeness, the reasonable remarks of a modest young man. When he had taken his first glass of tanglefoot he began to discover that she was handsomer than before; at the second he would make eyes at her; at the third he would say: "If you were only so minded, Mam'zelle Désirée..." without ever concluding his sentence; at the fourth he would be pulling her by her petticoats and trying to kiss her; and when he reached his tenth, then it was Father Auban who waited on the customers.

The old wineseller, who was up to all the tricks of his trade, used to send Désirée around among the tables to keep the drinking up to a satisfactory pitch, and Désirée, who was Father Auban's own worthy daughter, would whisk her petticoats to and fro among the drinkers and exchange pleasantries with them, a smile on her lips and malice in her eye.

Through drinking many glasses of tanglefoot, Désirée's image became so deeply imprinted on Patin's heart that he was thinking of her constantly, even while he was out at sea, while he was casting his nets into the water, away out on the broad ocean, on the nights when the wind blew and the nights when it was calm, on the nights when the moon shone and the nights when it was dark. He thought of her as he held the tiller in the stern of his boat, while his four shipmates were slumbering with their heads pillowed, on their arms. He always beheld her smiling on him, raising her shoulder to pour out the yellow brandy, and then going away, saying:

"There! Are you satisfied?"

And so, by reason of thus keeping her before his eyes and in his mind, he became possessed of such an inordinate desire of having her to wife that he asked her hand in marriage.

He was well to do, owning his vessel, his nets, and a house on the Retenue down by the end of the beach, while Father

Auban had nothing. He was consequently accepted with avidity, and the wedding was celebrated at the earliest moment possible, both sides, for different reasons of their own, being desirous to have the matter over and ended.

When he had been married three days, however, Patin did not understand at all how he could ever have believed that Désirée was different from other women. True as gospel, he must have been a blockhead to saddle himself with a woman as poor as a church mouse, who had bewitched him with her brandy, that was as plain as a pikestaff, with brandy in which she had put some unclean nostrum to addle his brain. And he swore, and he swore, at all times of the tide, and he smashed his pipe between his teeth, and he blew up his crew. And when he had ripped and stormed, up hill and down, with all the hard words in the dictionary and against everything that he could think of, he would expectorate what bile was left in his stomach upon the fishes and the lobsters as he took them from the nets, one by one, and never consigned them to the hampers without a running accompaniment of insult and unseemly language.

Then when he got home, where his wife, old Auban's daughter, was at the mercy of his tongue and fist, it was not long before he began to treat her as the lowest of the low. Then, as she endured it all with resignation, accustomed as she had been to the outbursts of the paternal abode, her calmness only exasperated him the more, and one night he gave her a thumping. After that life became a terrible affair in his house.

For ten years all the talk on the Retenue was of the kicks and cuffs that Patin gave his wife, and how he never spoke to her without swearing at her, with or without occasion. He had, in truth, a way of swearing that was all his own, a redundancy of idiom and a stentorian lung power such as were possessed by no other man in Fécamp. The moment that his boat was sighted off the entrance of the harbor, returning from the fishing-ground, folks waited to hear the first volley that he would let fly from his deck upon the wharf so soon as he should catch the first glimpse of his helpmate's white cap.

On days when there was a heavy sea on he would be standing at the stern managing his vessel, one eye on the bow and one on the canvas, and notwithstanding the care that was necessitated by the narrow and difficult passage, notwithstanding the great waves that came rolling into the contracted channel, mountain-high, he would manage to keep an eye on the women who stood there, drenched by the spray of the breaking waves, waiting for their sailor lads, so that he might recognize his own wife, old Auban's daughter, the good-for-nothing huzzy!

Then, as soon as he set eyes on her, unmindful of the roaring of the wind and waves, he would salute her with a deafening bellow of abuse, which detonated from his gullet with such explosive violence that every one laughed, though they all felt much compassion for her. When the boat had got up to the wharf, too, he had a way of discharging his ballast of politeness, to make use of his own expression, while at the same time discharging his load of fish, that attracted about his fasts all the blackguards and all the idlers of the harbor.

These things would pour from his mouth, at one time terrific and of short duration, like the report of a cannon, and again reverberating like thunder-claps, which for five minutes at a time would keep up such a rolling fire of bad language that it seemed as if all the tempests of the Everlasting Father must have their home within his breast.

When, after this performance, he had left his vessel and was face to face with her amid the throng of gaping idlers and fishwives, he would summon up from the mysterious recesses of his memory an entirely fresh assortment of outrages and insults, and in this way would conduct her home to their dwelling, she preceding, he following, she weeping, he shouting at the top of his voice.

Then, when the doors were closed and they were alone

together, he would beat her upon the most trifling pretext. Anything sufficed him for an excuse for raising his hand to her, and when he had once begun he never stopped, brutally casting in her face at such times the true reasons of his hatred. At every slap, at every cuff he would roar: "Ah! You beggar, you! You scarecrow, you starveling! A pretty stroke of business I made of it the day when I washed my mouth with the vile stuff of that rascally old father of yours!"

She was living, now, poor woman, in a never-ceasing state of terror, in a continuous tremor of body and of mind, in the despairing expectation of indignities and blows.

And that went on for ten years. She was so entirely cowed that she never spoke to anyone, no matter whom, without changing color. She could think of nothing but the beatings with which she was constantly threatened, and she had become yellower, leaner, and drier than a smoked herring.

II

ONE NIGHT, when her husband was away at sea, she was suddenly awakened by that growling, as of wild beasts, that the wind makes when it rushes upon us like a dog that has broken his chain. She was frightened and sat up in bed, then, hearing it no more, laid down again, but almost instantly there came a roaring in the chimney that seemed to make the whole house tremble, and it extended over all the heavens, as if a drove of maddened animals had passed, snorting and bellowing, through space.

Then she arose and hurried to the harbor. Other women came flocking there from every quarter, bearing lanterns. The men came running up, and they all stood looking out to sea, watching the foam on the crest of the waves as it shone in the darkness of the night.

The storm lasted fifteen hours. There were eleven sailors

who never came back, and Patin was one of them.

What was left of his vessel, the Little Emily, was picked up over Dieppe way. The bodies of his men were recovered in the neighborhood of Saint Valéry, but his was never found. As the boat's hull seemed to have been cut in two, his wife for a long time expected, and feared, to see him come home, for if there had been a collision it might well be that the colliding vessel had taken him aboard, him alone of all the crew, and carried him off to distant parts.

By slow degrees she familiarized herself with the thought that she was a widow, but would never fail to be startled whenever a neighbor or a beggar or a vagrant peddler unexpectedly entered her house.

As she was passing along the Rue aux Juifs one afternoon, about four years after her husband's disappearance, she stopped in front of an old sea-captain's house who had died a short time before, and whose household goods were being auctioned off.

It so chanced that just at that moment they were bidding on a parrot, a green parrot with a blue head, who was considering the assemblage with an air of dejection and anxiety.

"Three francs!" exclaimed the auctioneer. "Three francs, for a bird that can talk like a lawyer!"

A friend of the widow Patin gave her a nudge with her elbow:

"You've got plenty of money," she said. "You ought to buy that bird. It would be company for you. It's worth more than thirty francs, that bird is. You could get twenty or twenty-five for it, any time you wanted to sell it."

"Four francs! Ladies, four francs!" the man continued. "He can sing vespers and preach as good a sermon as M. the curé. He is a wonder, a phenomenon!"

Madame Patin raised the bid fifty centimes and the hook-billed bird was knocked down to her, and she walked off, carrying it with her in a little cage.

When she got home she hung up the cage, and as she was opening the wire door to give the brute a drink he snapped at her finger with his beak and bit it so that the blood came.

"Ah! How cross he is," she said.

Nevertheless she gave him some hemp-seed and corn to eat and then left him to smooth down his rumpled feathers, which he did, casting meanwhile sly, stealthy glances upon his new abode and his new mistress.

The day was just breaking next morning when the widow heard a voice, as distinct as could be, a loud, ringing, resounding voice, old Patin's voice, shouting:

"Will you get up, carrion!"

Her fright was so great that she drew the sheets up over her head, for every morning, in the old days, as soon as he had fairly got his eyes open, her deceased husband had yelled in her ears those five words that were so familiar to her.

Trembling in every limb, curled up like a ball and her back made ready to receive the shower of blows that she already felt in anticipation, she murmured, sinking her face still deeper into the pillow:

"Holy Father, there he is! Holy Father, there he is! He is back again. Holy Father!"

The minutes passed. No further sound disturbed the silence of the chamber. Then, quaking still with her great fear, she protruded her head from the bedclothes in the certainty that she should behold him there, watching her, prepared to beat her.

She saw nothing, nothing but a sunbeam shining through the window-pane, and she thought, "He has hidden himself away somewhere, depend on't."

She waited a long time, then, her fears being somewhat reassured, came to the conclusion, "I must have been dreaming, since he don't come out and show himself."

She was just closing her eyes again, a little emboldened by this reflection, when, close to her ear, as it seemed, exploded the wrathful voice, the drowned man's voice of thunder, vociferating:

"Name of a name, of a name, of a name, will you get up, you—!"

She sprang from her bed, impelled by the instinct of obedience, by the blind obedience of a woman who has known many a beating, who remembers still, after four years have gone by, and who will always remember and always obey that dread voice. And she said:

"Here I am, Patin. What do you want?"

But Patin answered not.

Then she looked about her wildly, distractedly. Then she searched the room through, every part of it, the closets, the fireplace, beneath the bed, and found no one, and at last she sank into a chair, beside herself with terror, certain that Patin's spirit, divested of its earthly garb, was there, at her side, returned again to earth to torment her.

All at once she thought of the garret, which could be reached from outside by means of a ladder. There could be no doubt of it, he had concealed himself up there the better to surprise her. It must have been that the savages had held him prisoner upon some distant coast and he had been unable to escape them until then, and now he was returned, more ruffianly than ever. The mere ring of his voice, was clear enough evidence of that.

Raising her face toward the ceiling, she asked:

"Are you up there, Patin?"

Patin made no answer.

Then she left the house, and, with a horrible fear that seemed to freeze her very heart, climbed the ladder, threw back the shutter of the window, looked into the room, saw nothing, entered, searched, and found nothing.

Seating herself upon a bundle of straw she gave way to tears, but while she sat there sobbing, transpierced by a weird and breathless terror, in her chamber below she heard Patin going over his story. His anger seemed to have subsided, he was calmer, and this was what he was saying:

"Dirty weather! High wind! Dirty weather! I've had no breakfast, name of a name!"

She shouted to him through the ceiling, "Here I am, Patin. I'm going to make the soup for you. Don't be angry, I'm coming." And she hastened down the ladder. There was no one in the room.

She felt her strength failing her, as if Death had touched her with his finger, and was about to take to her heels and ask protection from the neighbors when the voice, right at her ear, shouted:

"I've had no breakfast, name of a name!"

And there was the parrot in his cage, watching her with his round, sly, wicked eye.

She looked at him, too, as if her senses were leaving her, muttering, "Ah! It's you!"

The bird continued, with a movement of its head, "Wait, wait, wait, I'll teach you to dawdle!"

What passed through her mind? She felt, she knew that it was no other than he, the dead man, who had returned, who had disguised himself in the feathers of this brute to begin afresh his old work of torment, that he would swear at her all day long, as he had done before, and bite her, and yell at her with taunting words to raise the neighbors and make them laugh. Then she made a wild rush, opened the cage, seized the bird, which tore her flesh with beak and claws in its struggle to defend itself, but she held him with all her strength, in both her hands, and throwing herself upon the floor she rolled upon him with the frenzy of one possessed, crushed him, reduced him to a rag of flesh, a small, green object, devoid of speech or movement and which dangled from her hand inanimate. Then, taking a dish-clout, she wrapped the shapeless mass in it as in a shroud, went out by the door, barefooted, in her chemise, crossed the wharf, against which the sea was breaking in small waves, and, shaking out the cloth, let fall into the water that small dead object that was like nothing so much as a handful of grass. Then she returned to the house, and throwing herself upon her knees before the empty cage, all wrought up by what she had done, sought forgiveness from God the Comforter, sobbing, the while, as if she had been guilty of some horrible crime.

THE CAPTAIN OF THE POLE-STAR

by Sir Arthur Conan Doyle

[Being an extract from the singular journal of JOHN
M'ALISTER RAY, student of medicine.]

SEPTEMBER 11TH.—Lat. 81 degrees 40' N.; long. 2 degrees
E. Still lying-to amid enormous ice fields. The one which
stretches away to the north of us, and to which our ice-anchor is
attached, cannot be smaller than an English county. To the right
and left unbroken sheets extend to the horizon. This morning
the mate reported that there were signs of pack ice to the southward. Should this form of sufficient thickness to bar our return,
we shall be in a position of danger, as the food, I hear, is already
running somewhat short. It is late in the season, and the nights
are beginning to reappear.

This morning I saw a star twinkling just over the fore-yard,
the first since the beginning of May. There is considerable
discontent among the crew, many of whom are anxious to get
back home to be in time for the herring season, when labour

always commands a high price upon the Scotch coast. As yet their displeasure is only signified by sullen countenances and black looks, but I heard from the second mate this afternoon that they contemplated sending a deputation to the Captain to explain their grievance. I much doubt how he will receive it, as he is a man of fierce temper, and very sensitive about anything approaching to an infringement of his rights. I shall venture after dinner to say a few words to him upon the subject. I have always found that he will tolerate from me what he would resent from any other member of the crew. Amsterdam Island, at the north-west corner of Spitzbergen, is visible upon our starboard quarter—a rugged line of volcanic rocks, intersected by white seams, which represent glaciers. It is curious to think that at the present moment there is probably no human being nearer to us than the Danish settlements in the south of Greenland, a good nine hundred miles as the crow flies. A captain takes a great responsibility upon himself when he risks his vessel under such circumstances. No whaler has ever remained in these latitudes till so advanced a period of the year.

9 P.M.—I have spoken to Captain Craigie, and though the result has been hardly satisfactory, I am bound to say that he listened to what I had to say very quietly and even deferentially. When I had finished he put on that air of iron determination which I have frequently observed upon his face, and paced rapidly backwards and forwards across the narrow cabin for some minutes. At first I feared that I had seriously offended him, but he dispelled the idea by sitting down again, and putting his hand upon my arm with a gesture which almost amounted to a caress. There was a depth of tenderness too in his wild dark eyes which surprised me considerably. "Look here, Doctor," he said, "I'm sorry I ever took you—I am indeed—and I would give fifty pounds this minute to see you standing safe upon the Dundee quay. It's hit or miss with me this time. There are fish to the north of us. How dare you shake your head, sir, when

I tell you I saw them blowing from the masthead?"—this in a sudden burst of fury, though I was not conscious of having shown any signs of doubt. "Two-and-twenty fish in as many minutes as I am a living man, and not one under ten foot.[1] Now, Doctor, do you think I can leave the country when there is only one infernal strip of ice between me and my fortune? If it came on to blow from the north tomorrow we could fill the ship and be away before the frost could catch us. If it came on to blow from the south, well, I suppose the men are paid for risking their lives, and as for myself it matters but little to me, for I have more to bind me to the other world than to this one. I confess that I am sorry for you, though. I wish I had old Angus Tait who was with me last voyage, for he was a man that would never be missed, and you—you said once that you were engaged, did you not?"

"Yes," I answered, snapping the spring of the locket which hung from my watch-chain, and holding up the little vignette of Flora.

"Curse you!" he yelled, springing out of his seat, with his very beard bristling with passion. "What is your happiness to me? What have I to do with her that you must dangle her photograph before my eyes?" I almost thought that he was about to strike me in the frenzy of his rage, but with another imprecation he dashed open the door of the cabin and rushed out upon deck, leaving me considerably astonished at his extraordinary violence. It is the first time that he has ever shown me anything but courtesy and kindness. I can hear him pacing excitedly up and down overhead as I write these lines.

I should like to give a sketch of the character of this man, but it seems presumptuous to attempt such a thing upon paper, when the idea in my own mind is at best a vague and

---

1   A whale is measured among whalers not by the length of its body, but by the length of its whalebone.

uncertain one. Several times I have thought that I grasped the clue which might explain it, but only to be disappointed by his presenting himself in some new light which would upset all my conclusions. It may be that no human eye but my own shall ever rest upon these lines, yet as a psychological study I shall attempt to leave some record of Captain Nicholas Craigie.

A man's outer case generally gives some indication of the soul within. The Captain is tall and well-formed, with dark, handsome face, and a curious way of twitching his limbs, which may arise from nervousness, or be simply an outcome of his excessive energy. His jaw and whole cast of countenance is manly and resolute, but the eyes are the distinctive feature of his face. They are of the very darkest hazel, bright and eager, with a singular mixture of recklessness in their expression, and of something else which I have sometimes thought was more allied with horror than any other emotion. Generally the former predominated, but on occasions, and more particularly when he was thoughtfully inclined, the look of fear would spread and deepen until it imparted a new character to his whole countenance. It is at these times that he is most subject to tempestuous fits of anger, and he seems to be aware of it, for I have known him lock himself up so that no one might approach him until his dark hour was passed. He sleeps badly, and I have heard him shouting during the night, but his cabin is some little distance from mine, and I could never distinguish the words which he said.

This is one phase of his character, and the most disagreeable one. It is only through my close association with him, thrown together as we are day after day, that I have observed it. Otherwise he is an agreeable companion, well-read and entertaining, and as gallant a seaman as ever trod a deck. I shall not easily forget the way in which he handled the ship when we were caught by a gale among the loose ice at the beginning of April. I have never seen him so cheerful, and even hilarious, as he was that night, as he paced backwards and forwards upon the bridge amid the flashing of the lightning and the howling of the wind. He has told me several times that the thought of death was a pleasant one to him, which is a sad thing for a young man to say. He cannot be much more than thirty, though his hair and moustache are already slightly grizzled. Some great sorrow must have overtaken him and blighted his whole life. Perhaps I should be the same if I lost my Flora—God knows! I think if it were not for her that I should care very little whether the wind blew from the north or the south tomorrow.

There, I hear him come down the companion, and he has locked himself up in his room, which shows that he is still in an unamiable mood. And so to bed, as old Pepys would say, for the candle is burning down (we have to use them now since the nights are closing in), and the steward has turned in, so there are no hopes of another one.

September 12th.—Calm, clear day, and still lying in the same position. What wind there is comes from the south-east, but it is very slight. Captain is in a better humour, and apologised to me at breakfast for his rudeness. He still looks somewhat distrait, however, and retains that wild look in his eyes which in a Highlander would mean that he was "fey"—at least so our chief engineer remarked to me, and he has some reputation among the Celtic portion of our crew as a seer and expounder of omens.

It is strange that superstition should have obtained such mastery over this hard-headed and practical race. I could not have believed to what an extent it is carried had I not observed it for myself. We have had a perfect epidemic of it this voyage, until I have felt inclined to serve out rations of sedatives and nerve-tonics with the Saturday allowance of grog. The first symptom of it was that shortly after leaving Shetland the men at the wheel used to complain that they heard plaintive cries and screams in the wake of the ship, as if something were following it and were unable to overtake it. This fiction has been kept up during the whole voyage, and on dark nights at the beginning of the seal-fishing it was only with great difficulty that men could be induced to do their spell. No doubt what they heard was either the creaking of the rudder-chains, or the cry of some passing sea-bird. I have been fetched out of bed several times to listen to it, but I need hardly say that I was never able to distinguish anything unnatural.

The men, however, are so absurdly positive upon the subject that it is hopeless to argue with them. I mentioned the matter to the Captain once, but to my surprise he took it very gravely, and indeed appeared to be considerably disturbed by what I told him. I should have thought that he at least would have been above such vulgar delusions.

All this disquisition upon superstition leads me up to the fact that Mr. Manson, our second mate, saw a ghost last night, or, at least says that he did, which of course is the same thing. It is quite refreshing to have some new topic of conversation after the eternal routine of bears and whales which has served us for so many months. Manson swears the ship is haunted, and that he would not stay in her a day if he had any other place to go to. Indeed the fellow is honestly frightened, and I had to give him some chloral and bromide of potassium this morning to steady him down. He seemed quite indignant when I suggested that he had been having an extra glass the night before, and I was obliged to pacify him by keeping as grave a countenance as possible during his story, which he certainly narrated in a very straight-forward and matter-of-fact way.

"I was on the bridge," he said, "about four bells in the middle watch, just when the night was at its darkest. There was a bit of a moon, but the clouds were blowing across it so that you couldn't see far from the ship. John M'Leod, the harpooner, came aft from the foc'sle-head and reported a strange noise on the starboard bow.

"I went forrard and we both heard it, sometimes like a bairn crying and sometimes like a wench in pain. I've been seventeen years to the country and I never heard seal, old or young, make a sound like that. As we were standing there on the foc's'le-head the moon came out from behind a cloud, and we both saw a sort of white figure moving across the ice field in the same direction that we had heard the cries. We lost sight of it for a while, but it came back on the port bow, and we could just make it out like a shadow on the ice. I sent a hand aft for the rifles, and M'Leod and I went down on to the pack, thinking that maybe it might be a bear. When we got on the ice I lost sight of M'Leod, but I pushed on in the direction where I could still hear the cries. I followed them for a mile or maybe more, and then running round a hummock I came right on to the top of it standing and waiting for me seemingly. I don't know what it was. It wasn't a bear anyway. It was tall and white and straight, and if it wasn't a man nor a woman, I'll stake my davy it was something worse. I made for the ship as hard as I could run, and precious glad I was to find myself aboard. I signed articles to do my duty by the ship, and on the ship I'll stay, but you don't catch me on the ice again after sundown."

That is his story, given as far as I can in his own words. I fancy what he saw must, in spite of his denial, have been a young bear erect upon its hind legs, an attitude which they often assume when alarmed. In the uncertain light this would bear a resemblance to a human figure, especially to a man whose nerves were already somewhat shaken. Whatever it may have been, the occurrence is unfortunate, for it has produced a most unpleasant effect upon the crew. Their looks are more sullen than before, and their discontent more open. The double grievance of being debarred from the herring fishing and of being detained in what they choose to call a haunted vessel, may lead them to do something rash. Even the harpooners, who are the oldest and steadiest among them, are joining in the general agitation.

Apart from this absurd outbreak of superstition, things are looking rather more cheerful. The pack which was forming to the south of us has partly cleared away, and the water is so warm as to lead me to believe that we are lying in one of those branches of the gulf-stream which run up between Greenland and Spitzbergen. There are numerous small Medusae and sealemons about the ship, with abundance of shrimps, so that there is every possibility of "fish" being sighted. Indeed one was seen blowing about dinner-time, but in such a position that it was impossible for the boats to follow it.

September 13th.—Had an interesting conversation with the chief mate, Mr. Milne, upon the bridge. It seems that our Captain is as great an enigma to the seamen, and even to the owners of the vessel, as he has been to me. Mr. Milne tells me that when the ship is paid off, upon returning from a voyage, Captain Craigie disappears, and is not seen again until the approach of another season, when he walks quietly into the office of the company, and asks whether his services will be required. He has no friend in Dundee, nor does any one pretend to be acquainted with his early history. His position depends entirely upon his skill as a seaman, and the name for courage and coolness which he had earned in the capacity of mate, before being entrusted with a separate command. The unanimous opinion seems to be that he is not a Scotchman, and that his name is an assumed one. Mr. Milne thinks that he has devoted himself to whaling simply for the reason that it is the most dangerous occupation which he could select, and that he courts death in every possible manner. He mentioned several instances of this, one of which is rather curious, if true. It seems that on one occasion he did not put in an appearance at the office, and a substitute had to be selected in his place. That was at the time of the last Russian and Turkish war. When he turned up again next spring he had a puckered wound in the side of his neck which he used to endeavour to conceal with his cravat. Whether the mate's inference that he had been engaged in the war is true or not I cannot say. It was certainly a strange coincidence.

The wind is veering round in an easterly direction, but is still very slight. I think the ice is lying closer than it did yesterday. As far as the eye can reach on every side there is one wide expanse of spotless white, only broken by an occasional rift or the dark shadow of a hummock. To the south there is the narrow lane of blue water which is our sole means of escape, and which is closing up every day. The Captain is taking a heavy responsibility upon himself. I hear that the tank of potatoes has been finished, and even the biscuits are running short, but he preserves the same impassible countenance, and spends the greater part of the day at the crow's nest, sweeping the horizon with his glass. His manner is very variable, and he seems to avoid my society, but there has been no repetition of the violence which he showed the other night.

7:30 P.M.—My deliberate opinion is that we are commanded by a madman. Nothing else can account for the extraordinary vagaries of Captain Craigie. It is fortunate that I have kept this journal of our voyage, as it will serve to justify us in case we have to put him under any sort of restraint, a step which I should only consent to as a last resource. Curiously enough it was he himself who suggested lunacy and not mere eccentricity as the secret of his strange conduct. He was standing upon the bridge about an hour ago, peering as usual through his glass, while I was walking up and down the quarterdeck. The majority of the men were below at their tea, for the watches have not been regularly kept of late. Tired of walking, I leaned against the bulwarks, and admired the mellow glow cast by the sinking sun upon the great ice fields which surround us. I was suddenly aroused from the reverie into which I had fallen by a hoarse voice at my elbow, and starting round I found that the Captain had descended and was standing by my side. He was staring out over the ice with an expression in which horror, surprise, and something approaching to joy were contending for the mastery. In spite of the cold, great drops of perspiration were coursing down his forehead, and he was evidently fearfully excited.

His limbs twitched like those of a man upon the verge of an epileptic fit, and the lines about his mouth were drawn and hard.

"Look!" he gasped, seizing me by the wrist, but still keeping his eyes upon the distant ice, and moving his head slowly in a horizontal direction, as if following some object which was moving across the field of vision. "Look! There, man, there! Between the hummocks! Now coming out from behind the far one! You see her, you MUST see her! There still! Flying from me, by God, flying from me—and gone!"

He uttered the last two words in a whisper of concentrated agony which shall never fade from my remembrance. Clinging to the ratlines he endeavoured to climb up upon the top of the bulwarks as if in the hope of obtaining a last glance at the departing object. His strength was not equal to the attempt, however, and he staggered back against the saloon skylights, where he leaned panting and exhausted. His face was so livid that I expected him to become unconscious, so lost no time in leading him down the companion, and stretching him upon one of the sofas in the cabin. I then poured him out some brandy, which I held to his lips, and which had a wonderful effect upon him, bringing the blood back into his white face and steadying his poor shaking limbs. He raised himself up upon his elbow, and looking round to see that we were alone, he beckoned to me to come and sit beside him.

"You saw it, didn't you?" he asked, still in the same subdued awesome tone so foreign to the nature of the man.

"No, I saw nothing."

His head sank back again upon the cushions. "No, he

wouldn't without the glass," he murmured. "He couldn't. It was the glass that showed her to me, and then the eyes of love— the eyes of love.

"I say, Doc, don't let the steward in! He'll think I'm mad. Just bolt the door, will you!"

I rose and did what he had commanded.

He lay quiet for a while, lost in thought apparently, and then raised himself up upon his elbow again, and asked for some more brandy.

"You don't think I am, do you, Doc?" he asked, as I was putting the bottle back into the after-locker. "Tell me now, as man to man, do you think that I am mad?"

"I think you have something on your mind," I answered, "which is exciting you and doing you a good deal of harm."

"Right there, lad!" he cried, his eyes sparkling from the effects of the brandy. "Plenty on my mind, plenty! But I can work out the latitude and the longitude, and I can handle my sextant and manage my logarithms. You couldn't prove me mad in a court of law, could you, now?" It was curious to hear the man lying back and coolly arguing out the question of his own sanity.

"Perhaps not," I said, "but still I think you would be wise to get home as soon as you can, and settle down to a quiet life for a while."

"Get home, eh?" he muttered, with a sneer upon his face. "One word for me and two for yourself, lad. Settle down with Flora, pretty little Flora. Are bad dreams signs of madness?"

"Sometimes," I answered.

"What else? What would be the first symptoms?"

"Pains in the head, noises in the ears, flashes before the eyes, delusions—"

"Ah! What about them?" he interrupted. "What would you call a delusion?"

"Seeing a thing which is not there is a delusion."

"But she WAS there!" he groaned to himself. "She WAS there!" and rising, he unbolted the door and walked with slow and uncertain steps to his own cabin, where I have no doubt that he will remain until tomorrow morning. His system seems to have received a terrible shock, whatever it may have been that he imagined himself to have seen. The man becomes a greater mystery every day, though I fear that the solution which he has himself suggested is the correct one, and that his reason is affected. I do not think that a guilty conscience has anything to do with his behaviour. The idea is a popular one among the officers, and, I believe, the crew, but I have seen nothing to support it. He has not the air of a guilty man, but of one who has had terrible usage at the hands of fortune, and who should be regarded as a martyr rather than a criminal.

The wind is veering round to the south tonight. God help us if it blocks that narrow pass which is our only road to safety! Situated as we are on the edge of the main Arctic pack, or the "barrier" as it is called by the whalers, any wind from the north has the effect of shredding out the ice around us and allowing our escape, while a wind from the south blows up all the loose ice behind us and hems us in between two packs. God help us, I say again!

September 14th.—Sunday, and a day of rest. My fears have been confirmed, and the thin strip of blue water has disappeared from the southward. Nothing but the great motionless ice fields around us, with their weird hummocks and fantastic pinnacles. There is a deathly silence over their wide expanse which is horrible. No lapping of the waves now, no cries of seagulls or straining of sails, but one deep universal silence in which the murmurs of the seamen, and the creak of their boots upon the white shining deck, seem discordant and out of place. Our only visitor was an Arctic fox, a rare animal upon the pack, though common enough upon the land. He did not come near the ship, however, but after surveying us from a distance fled rapidly across the ice. This was curious conduct, as they generally know nothing of man, and being of an inquisitive nature, become so familiar that they are easily captured. Incredible as it may seem, even this little incident produced a bad effect upon the crew. "Yon puir beastie kens mair, ay, an' sees mair nor you nor me!" was the comment of one of the leading harpooners, and the others nodded their acquiescence. It is vain to attempt to argue against such puerile superstition. They have made up their minds that there is a curse upon the ship, and nothing will ever persuade them to the contrary.

The Captain remained in seclusion all day except for about half an hour in the afternoon, when he came out upon the quarterdeck. I observed that he kept his eye fixed upon the spot where the vision of yesterday had appeared, and was quite prepared for another outburst, but none such came. He did not seem to see me although I was standing close beside him. Divine service was read as usual by the chief engineer. It is a curious thing that in whaling vessels the Church of England Prayer-book is always employed, although there is never a member of that Church among either officers or crew. Our men are all Roman Catholics or Presbyterians, the former predominating. Since a ritual is used which is foreign to both, neither can complain that the other is preferred to them, and they listen with all attention and devotion, so that the system has something to recommend it.

A glorious sunset, which made the great fields of ice look like a lake of blood. I have never seen a finer and at the same time more weird effect. Wind is veering round. If it will blow twenty-four hours from the north all will yet be well.

September 15th.—Today is Flora's birthday. Dear lass! It is well that she cannot see her boy, as she used to call me, shut up among the ice fields with a crazy captain and a few weeks' provisions. No doubt she scans the shipping list in the Scotsman every morning to see if we are reported from Shetland. I have to set an example to the men and look cheery and unconcerned, but God knows, my heart is very heavy at times.

The thermometer is at nineteen Fahrenheit today. There is but little wind, and what there is comes from an unfavourable quarter. Captain is in an excellent humour. I think he imagines he has seen some other omen or vision, poor fellow, during the night, for he came into my room early in the morning, and stooping down over my bunk, whispered, "It wasn't a delusion, Doc. It's all right!" After breakfast he asked me to find out how much food was left, which the second mate and I proceeded to do. It is even less than we had expected. Forward they have half a tank full of biscuits, three barrels of salt meat, and a very limited supply of coffee beans and sugar. In the after-hold and lockers there are a good many luxuries, such as tinned salmon, soups, haricot mutton, etc., but they will go a very short way among a crew of fifty men. There are two barrels of flour in the store-room, and an unlimited supply of tobacco. Altogether there is about enough to keep the men on half rations for eighteen or twenty days—certainly not more. When we reported the state of things to the Captain, he ordered all hands to be piped, and addressed them from the quarterdeck. I never saw him to better advantage. With his tall, well-knit figure, and dark animated face, he seemed a man born to command, and he discussed the situation in a cool sailor-like way which showed that while appreciating the danger he had an eye for every loophole of escape.

"My lads," he said, "no doubt you think I brought you into this fix, if it is a fix, and maybe some of you feel bitter against me on account of it. But you must remember that for many a season no ship that comes to the country has brought in as much oil-money as the old Pole-Star, and every one of you has had his share of it. You can leave your wives behind you in comfort while other poor fellows come back to find their lasses on the parish. If you have to thank me for the one you have to thank me for the other, and we may call it quits. We've tried a bold venture before this and succeeded, so now that we've tried one and failed, we've no cause to cry out about it. If the worst comes to the worst, we can make the land across the ice, and lay in a stock of seals which will keep us alive until the spring. It won't come to that, though, for you'll see the Scotch coast again before three weeks are out. At present every man must go on half rations, share and share alike, and no favour to any. Keep up your hearts and you'll pull through this as you've pulled through many a danger before." These few simple words of his had a wonderful effect upon the crew. His former unpopularity was forgotten, and the old harpooner whom I have already mentioned for his superstition, led off three cheers, which were heartily joined in by all hands.

September 16th.—The wind has veered round to the north during the night, and the ice shows some symptoms of opening out. The men are in a good humour in spite of the short allowance upon which they have been placed. Steam is kept up in the engine room, that there may be no delay should an opportunity for escape present itself. The Captain is in exuberant spirits, though he still retains that wild "fey" expression which I have already remarked upon. This burst of cheerfulness puzzles me more than his former gloom. I cannot understand it. I think I mentioned in an early part of this journal that one of his oddities is that he never permits any person to enter his cabin, but insists upon making his own bed, such as it is, and performing every other office for himself. To my surprise he handed me the key today and requested me to go down there and take the time by his chronometer while he measured the altitude of the sun at noon. It is a bare little room, containing a washing-stand and a few books, but little else in the way of luxury, except some pictures upon the walls. The majority of these are small cheap oleographs, but there was one watercolour sketch of the head

146

of a young lady which arrested my attention. It was evidently a portrait, and not one of those fancy types of female beauty which sailors particularly affect. No artist could have evolved from his own mind such a curious mixture of character and weakness. The languid, dreamy eyes, with their drooping lashes, and the broad, low brow, unruffled by thought or care, were in strong contrast with the clean-cut, prominent jaw, and the resolute set of the lower lip. Underneath it in one of the corners was written, "M. B., aet. 19." That any one in the short space of nineteen years of existence could develop such strength of will as was stamped upon her face seemed to me at the time to be well-nigh incredible. She must have been an extraordinary woman. Her features have thrown such a glamour over me that, though I had but a fleeting glance at them, I could, were I a draughtsman, reproduce them line for line upon this page of the journal. I wonder what part she has played in our Captain's life. He has hung her picture at the end of his berth, so that his eyes continually rest upon it. Were he a less reserved man I should make some remark upon the subject. Of the other things in his cabin there was nothing worthy of mention—uniform coats, a camp-stool, small looking-glass, tobacco box, and numerous pipes, including an oriental hookah—which, by-the-bye, gives some colour to Mr. Milne's story about his participation in the war, though the connection may seem rather a distant one.

11:20 P.M.—Captain just gone to bed after a long and interesting conversation on general topics. When he chooses he can be a most fascinating companion, being remarkably well-read, and having the power of expressing his opinion forcibly without appearing to be dogmatic. I hate to have my intellectual toes trod upon. He spoke about the nature of the soul, and sketched out the views of Aristotle and Plato upon the subject in a masterly manner. He seems to have a leaning for metempsychosis and the doctrines of Pythagoras. In discussing them we touched upon modern spiritualism, and I made some joking allusion to the impostures of Slade, upon which, to my surprise, he warned me most impressively against confusing the innocent with the guilty, and argued that it would be as logical to brand Christianity as an error because Judas, who professed that religion, was a villain. He shortly afterwards bade me good-night and retired to his room.

The wind is freshening up, and blows steadily from the north. The nights are as dark now as they are in England. I hope tomorrow may set us free from our frozen fetters.

September 17th.—The Bogie again. Thank Heaven that I have strong nerves! The superstition of these poor fellows, and the circumstantial accounts which they give, with the utmost earnestness and self-conviction, would horrify any man not accustomed to their ways. There are many versions of the matter, but the sum-total of them all is that something uncanny has been flitting round the ship all night, and that Sandie M'Donald of Peterhead and "lang" Peter Williamson of Shetland saw it, as also did Mr. Milne on the bridge—so, having three witnesses, they can make a better case of it than the second mate did. I spoke to Milne after breakfast, and told him that he should be above such nonsense, and that as an officer he ought to set the men a better example. He shook his weather-beaten head ominously, but answered with characteristic caution, "Mebbe aye, mebbe na, Doctor," he said. "I didna ca' it a ghaist. I canna' say I preen my faith in sea-bogles an' the like, though there's a mony as claims to ha' seen a' that and waur. I'm no easy feared, but maybe your ain bluid would run a bit cauld, mun, if instead o' speerin' aboot it in daylicht ye were wi' me last night, an' seed an awfu' like shape, white an' gruesome, whiles here, whiles there, an' it greetin' and ca'ing in the darkness like a bit lambie that hae lost its mither. Ye would na' be sae ready to put it a' doon to auld wives' clavers then, I'm thinkin'." I saw it was hopeless to reason with him, so contented myself with begging him as a personal favour to call me up the next time the spectre appeared, a request to which he acceded with many ejaculations expressive of his hopes that such an opportunity might never arise.

As I had hoped, the white desert behind us has become broken by many thin streaks of water which intersect it in all directions. Our latitude today was 80 degrees 52' N., which shows that there is a strong southerly drift upon the pack. Should the wind continue favourable it will break up as rapidly as it formed. At present we can do nothing but smoke and wait and hope for the best. I am rapidly becoming a fatalist. When dealing with such uncertain factors as wind and ice a man can be nothing else. Perhaps it was the wind and sand of the Arabian deserts which gave the minds of the original followers of Mahomet their tendency to bow to kismet.

These spectral alarms have a very bad effect upon the Captain. I feared that it might excite his sensitive mind, and endeavoured to conceal the absurd story from him, but unfortunately he overheard one of the men making an allusion to it, and insisted upon being informed about it. As I had expected, it brought out all his latent lunacy in an exaggerated form. I can hardly believe that this is the same man who discoursed philosophy last night with the most critical acumen and coolest judgment. He is pacing backwards and forwards upon the quarterdeck like a caged tiger, stopping now and again to throw out his hands with a yearning gesture, and stare impatiently out over the ice. He keeps up a continual mutter to himself, and once he called out, "But a little time, love, but a little time!" Poor fellow, it is sad to see a gallant seaman and accomplished gentleman reduced to such a pass, and to think that imagination and delusion can cow a mind to which real danger was but the salt of life. Was ever a man in such a position as I, between a demented captain and a ghost-seeing mate? I sometimes think I am the only really sane man aboard the vessel, except perhaps the second engineer, who is a kind of ruminant, and would care nothing for all the fiends in the Red Sea so long as they would leave him alone and not disarrange his tools.

The ice is still opening rapidly, and there is every probability of our being able to make a start tomorrow morning. They will think I am inventing when I tell them at home all the strange things that have befallen me.

12 P.M.—I have been a good deal startled, though I feel steadier now, thanks to a stiff glass of brandy. I am hardly myself yet, however, as this handwriting will testify. The fact is, that I have gone through a very strange experience, and am beginning to doubt whether I was justified in branding every one on board as madmen because they professed to have seen things which did not seem reasonable to my understanding. Pshaw! I am a fool to let such a trifle unnerve me, and yet, coming as it does after all these alarms, it has an additional significance, for I cannot doubt either Mr. Manson's story or that of the mate, now that I have experienced that which I used formerly to scoff at.

After all it was nothing very alarming—a mere sound, and that was all. I cannot expect that anyone reading this, if anyone ever should read it, will sympathise with my feelings, or realise the effect which it produced upon me at the time. Supper was over, and I had gone on deck to have a quiet pipe before turning in. The night was very dark—so dark that, standing under the quarter-boat, I was unable to see the officer upon the bridge. I think I have already mentioned the extraordinary silence which prevails in these frozen seas. In other parts of the world, be they ever so barren, there is some slight vibration of the air, some faint hum, be it from the distant haunts of men, or from the leaves of the trees, or the wings of the birds, or even the faint rustle of the grass that covers the ground. One may not actively perceive the sound, and yet if it were withdrawn it would be missed. It is only here in these Arctic seas that stark, unfathomable stillness obtrudes itself upon you in all its gruesome reality. You find your tympanum straining to catch some little murmur, and dwelling eagerly upon every accidental sound within the vessel. In this state I was leaning against the bulwarks when there arose from the ice almost directly underneath me a cry, sharp and shrill, upon the silent air of the night, beginning, as it seemed to me, at a note such as prima donna never reached, and mounting from that ever higher and higher until it culminated in a long wail of agony, which might have been the last cry of a lost soul. The ghastly scream is still ringing in my ears. Grief, unutterable grief, seemed to be expressed in it, and a great longing, and yet through it all there was an occasional wild note of exultation. It shrilled out from close beside me, and yet as I glared into the darkness I could discern nothing. I waited some little time, but without hearing any repetition of the sound, so I came below, more shaken than I have ever been in my life before. As I came down the companion I met Mr. Milne coming up to relieve the watch. "Weel, Doctor," he said, "maybe that's auld wives' clavers tae? Did ye no hear it skirling? Maybe that's a supersteetion? What d'ye think o't noo?" I was obliged to apologise to the honest fellow, and acknowledge that I was as puzzled by it as he was. Perhaps tomorrow things may look different. At present I dare hardly write all that I think. Reading it again in days to come, when I have shaken off all these associations, I should despise myself for having been so weak.

September 18th.—Passed a restless and uneasy night, still haunted by that strange sound. The Captain does not look as if he had had much repose either, for his face is haggard and his eyes bloodshot. I have not told him of my adventure of last night, nor shall I. He is already restless and excited, standing up, sitting down, and apparently utterly unable to keep still.

A fine lead appeared in the pack this morning, as I had expected, and we were able to cast off our ice-anchor, and steam

about twelve miles in a west-sou'-westerly direction. We were
then brought to a halt by a great floe as massive as any which we
have left behind us. It bars our progress completely, so we can
do nothing but anchor again and wait until it breaks up, which
it will probably do within twenty-four hours, if the wind holds.
Several bladder-nosed seals were seen swimming in the water,
and one was shot, an immense creature more than eleven feet
long. They are fierce, pugnacious animals, and are said to be
more than a match for a bear. Fortunately they are slow and
clumsy in their movements, so that there is little danger in attacking them upon the ice.

The Captain evidently does not think we have seen the last
of our troubles, though why he should take a gloomy view of
the situation is more than I can fathom, since every one else on
board considers that we have had a miraculous escape, and are
sure now to reach the open sea.

"I suppose you think it's all right now, Doctor?" he said, as
we sat together after dinner.

"I hope so," I answered.

"We mustn't be too sure, and yet no doubt you are right.
We'll all be in the arms of our own true loves before long, lad,
won't we? But we mustn't be too sure, we mustn't be too sure."

He sat silent a little, swinging his leg thoughtfully backwards
and forwards. "Look here," he continued, "it's a dangerous
place this, even at its best, a treacherous, dangerous place. I
have known men cut off very suddenly in a land like this. A slip
would do it sometimes, a single slip, and down you go through
a crack, and only a bubble on the green water to show where
it was that you sank. It's a queer thing," he continued with
a nervous laugh, "but all the years I've been in this country I
never once thought of making a will—not that I have anything
to leave in particular, but still when a man is exposed to danger
he should have everything arranged and ready, don't you think
so?"

"Certainly," I answered, wondering what on earth he was driving at.

"He feels better for knowing it's all settled," he went on. "Now if anything should ever befall me, I hope that you will look after things for me. There is very little in the cabin, but such as it is I should like it to be sold, and the money divided in the same proportion as the oil-money among the crew. The chronometer I wish you to keep yourself as some slight remembrance of our voyage. Of course all this is a mere precaution, but I thought I would take the opportunity of speaking to you about it. I suppose I might rely upon you if there were any necessity?"

"Most assuredly," I answered, "and since you are taking this step, I may as well—"

"You! You!" he interrupted. "YOU'RE all right. What the devil is the matter with YOU? There, I didn't mean to be peppery, but I don't like to hear a young fellow, that has hardly began life, speculating about death. Go up on deck and get some fresh air into your lungs instead of talking nonsense in the cabin, and encouraging me to do the same."

The more I think of this conversation of ours the less do I like it. Why should the man be settling his affairs at the very time when we seem to be emerging from all danger? There must be some method in his madness. Can it be that he contemplates suicide? I remember that upon one occasion he spoke in a deeply reverent manner of the heinousness of the crime of self-destruction. I shall keep my eye upon him, however, and though I cannot obtrude upon the privacy of his cabin, I shall at least make a point of remaining on deck as long as he stays up.

Mr. Milne pooh-poohs my fears, and says it is only the "skipper's little way." He himself takes a very rosy view of the situation. According to him we shall be out of the ice by the day after tomorrow, pass Jan Meyen two days after that, and sight Shetland in little more than a week. I hope he may not be too sanguine. His opinion may be fairly balanced against the gloomy precautions of the Captain, for he is an old and experienced seaman, and weighs his words well before uttering them.

The long-impending catastrophe has come at last. I hardly know what to write about it. The Captain is gone. He may come back to us again alive, but I fear me—I fear me. It is now seven o'clock of the morning of the 19th of September. I have spent the whole night traversing the great ice-floe in front of us with a party of seamen in the hope of coming upon some trace of him, but in vain. I shall try to give some account of the circumstances which attended upon his disappearance. Should anyone ever chance to read the words which I put down, I trust they will remember that I do not write from conjecture or from hearsay, but that I, a sane and educated man, am describing accurately what actually occurred before my very eyes. My inferences are my own, but I shall be answerable for the facts.

The Captain remained in excellent spirits after the conversation which I have recorded. He appeared to be nervous and impatient, however, frequently changing his position, and moving his limbs in an aimless choreic way which is characteristic of him at times. In a quarter of an hour he went upon deck seven times, only to descend after a few hurried paces. I followed him each time, for there was something about his face which confirmed my resolution of not letting him out of my sight. He seemed to observe the effect which his movements had produced, for he endeavoured by an over-done hilarity, laughing boisterously at the very smallest of jokes, to quiet my apprehensions.

After supper he went on to the poop once more, and I with him. The night was dark and very still, save for the melancholy soughing of the wind among the spars. A thick cloud was coming up from the north-west, and the ragged tentacles which it threw out in front of it were drifting across the face of the moon, which only shone now and again through a rift in the wrack. The Captain paced rapidly backwards and forwards, and then seeing me still dogging him, he came across and hinted that he thought I should be better below, which, I need hardly say, had the effect of strengthening my resolution to remain on deck.

I think he forgot about my presence after this, for he stood silently leaning over the taffrail, and peering out across the great desert of snow, part of which lay in shadow, while part glittered mistily in the moonlight. Several times I could see by his movements that he was referring to his watch, and once he muttered a short sentence, of which I could only catch the one word "ready." I confess to having felt an eerie feeling creeping over me as I watched the loom of his tall figure through the darkness, and noted how completely he fulfilled the idea of a man who is keeping a tryst. A tryst with whom? Some vague perception began to dawn upon me as I pieced one fact with another, but I was utterly unprepared for the sequel.

By the sudden intensity of his attitude I felt that he saw something. I crept up behind him. He was staring with an eager questioning gaze at what seemed to be a wreath of mist, blown swiftly in a line with the ship. It was a dim, nebulous body, devoid of shape, sometimes more, sometimes less apparent, as the light fell on it. The moon was dimmed in its brilliancy at the moment by a canopy of thinnest cloud, like the coating of an anemone.

"Coming, lass, coming," cried the skipper, in a voice of unfathomable tenderness and compassion, like one who soothes a beloved one by some favour long looked for, and as pleasant to bestow as to receive.

What followed happened in an instant. I had no power to interfere.

He gave one spring to the top of the bulwarks, and another which took him on to the ice, almost to the feet of the pale misty figure. He held out his hands as if to clasp it, and so ran into the darkness with outstretched arms and loving words. I still stood rigid and motionless, straining my eyes after his retreating form, until his voice died away in the distance. I never thought to see him again, but at that moment the moon shone out brilliantly through a chink in the cloudy heaven, and illuminated the great field of ice. Then I saw his dark figure already a very long way off, running with prodigious speed across the frozen plain. That was the last glimpse which we caught of him—perhaps the last we ever shall. A party was organised to follow him, and I accompanied them, but the men's hearts were not in the work, and nothing was found. Another will be formed within a few hours. I can hardly believe I have not been dreaming, or suffering from some hideous nightmare, as I write these things down.

7:30 P.M.—Just returned dead beat and utterly tired out from a second unsuccessful search for the Captain. The floe is of enormous extent, for though we have traversed at least twenty miles of its surface, there has been no sign of its coming to an end. The frost has been so severe of late that the overlying snow is frozen as hard as granite, otherwise we might have had the footsteps to guide us. The crew are anxious that we should cast off and steam round the floe and so to the southward, for the ice has opened up during the night, and the sea is visible upon the horizon. They argue that Captain Craigie is certainly dead, and that we are all risking our lives to no purpose by remaining when we have an opportunity of escape. Mr. Milne and I have had the greatest difficulty in persuading them to wait until tomorrow night, and have been compelled to promise that we will not under any circumstances delay our departure longer than that. We propose therefore to take a few hours' sleep, and then to start upon a final search.

September 20th, evening.—I crossed the ice this morning with a party of men exploring the southern part of the floe, while Mr. Milne went off in a northerly direction. We pushed on for ten or twelve miles without seeing a trace of any living thing except a single bird, which fluttered a great way over our heads, and which by its flight I should judge to have been a falcon. The southern extremity of the ice field tapered away into a long narrow spit which projected out into the sea. When we came to the base of this promontory, the men halted, but I begged them to continue to the extreme end of it, that we might have the satisfaction of knowing that no possible chance had been neglected.

We had hardly gone a hundred yards before M'Donald of Peterhead cried out that he saw something in front of us, and began to run. We all got a glimpse of it and ran too. At first it was only a vague darkness against the white ice, but as we raced along together it took the shape of a man, and eventually of the man of whom we were in search. He was lying face downwards upon a frozen bank. Many little crystals of ice and feathers of snow had drifted on to him as he lay, and sparkled upon his dark seaman's jacket. As we came up some wandering puff of wind caught these tiny flakes in its vortex, and they whirled up into the air, partially descended again, and then, caught once more in the current, sped rapidly away in the direction of the sea. To my eyes it seemed but a snow-drift, but many of my companions averred that it started up in the shape of a woman, stooped over the corpse and kissed it, and then hurried away across the floe. I have learned never to ridicule any man's opinion, however strange it may seem. Sure it is that Captain Nicholas Craigie had met with no painful end, for there was a bright smile upon his blue pinched features, and his hands were still outstretched as though grasping at the strange visitor which had summoned him away into the dim world that lies beyond the grave.

We buried him the same afternoon with the ship's ensign around him, and a thirty-two pound shot at his feet. I read the burial service, while the rough sailors wept like children, for there were many who owed much to his kind heart, and who showed now the affection which his strange ways had repelled during his lifetime. He went off the grating with a dull, sullen splash, and as I looked into the green water I saw him go down, down, down until he was but a little flickering patch of white hanging upon the outskirts of eternal darkness. Then even that faded away, and he was gone. There he shall lie, with his secret and his sorrows and his mystery all still buried in his breast, until that great day when the sea shall give up its dead, and Nicholas Craigie come out from among the ice with the smile upon his face, and his stiffened arms outstretched in greeting. I pray that his lot may be a happier one in that life than it has been in this.

I shall not continue my journal. Our road to home lies plain and clear before us, and the great ice field will soon be but a remembrance of the past. It will be some time before I get over the shock produced by recent events. When I began this record of our voyage I little thought of how I should be compelled to finish it. I am writing these final words in the lonely cabin, still starting at times and fancying I hear the quick nervous step of the dead man upon the deck above me. I entered his cabin tonight, as was my duty, to make a list of his effects in order that they might be entered in the official log. All was as it had been upon my previous visit, save that the picture which I have described as having hung at the end of his bed had been cut out of its frame, as with a knife, and was gone. With this last link in a strange chain of evidence I close my diary of the voyage of the Pole-Star.

[NOTE by Dr. John M'Alister Ray, senior.—I have read over the strange events connected with the death of the Captain of the Pole-Star, as narrated in the journal of my son. That everything occurred exactly as he describes it I have the fullest confidence, and, indeed, the most positive certainty, for I know him to be a strong-nerved and unimaginative man, with the strictest regard for veracity. Still, the story is, on the face of it, so vague and so improbable, that I was long opposed to its publication. Within the last few days, however, I have had independent testimony upon the subject which throws a new light upon it. I had run down to Edinburgh to attend a meeting of the British Medical Association, when I chanced to come across Dr. P——, an old college chum of mine, now practising at Saltash, in Devonshire. Upon my telling him of this experience of my son's, he declared to me that he was familiar with the man, and proceeded, to my no small surprise, to give me a description of him, which tallied remarkably well with that given in the journal, except that he depicted him as a younger man. According to his account, he had been engaged to a young lady of singular beauty residing upon the Cornish coast. During his absence at sea his betrothed had died under circumstances of peculiar horror.]

A STRUGGLE WITH A DEVIL FISH

by Victor Hugo

WHEN HE AWAKENED he was hungry.

The sea was growing calmer. But there was still a heavy swell, which made his departure, for the present at least, impossible. The day, too, was far advanced. For the sloop with its burden to get to Guernsey before midnight, it was necessary to start in the morning.

Although pressed by hunger, Gilliatt began by stripping himself, the only means of getting warmth. His clothing was saturated by the storm, but the rain had washed out the sea-water, which rendered it possible to dry them.

He kept nothing on but his trousers, which he turned up nearly to the knees.

His overcoat, jacket, overalls, and sheepskin he spread out and fixed with large round stones here and there.

Then he thought of eating.

He had recourse to his knife, which he was careful to sharpen, and to keep always in good condition, and he detached from the rock a few limpets, similar in kind to the *clonisses* of the Mediterranean. It is well known that these are eaten raw, but after so many labors, so various and so rude, the pittance was meagre. His biscuit was gone, but of water he had now abundance.

He took advantage of the receding tide to wander among the rocks in search of crayfish.

He wandered, not in the gorge of the rocks, but outside among the smaller breakers. It was there that the Durande, ten weeks previously, had struck upon the sunken reef.

For the search that Gilliatt was prosecuting, this part was more favorable than the interior. At low water the crabs are accustomed to crawl out into the air. They seem to like to warm themselves in the sun, where they swarm sometimes to the disgust of the loiterers, who recognize in these creatures, with their awkward sidelong gait, climbing clumsily from crack to crack the lower stages of the rocks like the steps of a staircase, a sort of sea vermin.

For two months Gilliatt had lived upon these vermin of the sea.

On this day, however, the crayfish and crabs were both wanting. The tempest had driven them into their solitary retreats, and they had not yet mustered courage to venture abroad. Gilliatt held his open knife in his hand, and from time to time scraped a cockle from under the bunches of seaweed, which he ate while still walking.

He could not have been far from the very spot where Sieur Clubin had perished.

As Gilliatt was determining to content himself with the sea-urchins and the *chataignes de mer*, a little clattering noise at his feet aroused his attention. A large crab, startled by his approach, had just dropped into a pool. The water was shallow, and he did not lose sight of it.

He chased the crab along the base of the rock. The crab moved fast.

Suddenly it was gone.

It had buried itself in some crevice under the rock.

Gilliatt clutched the protections of the rock, and stretched out to observe where it shelved away under the water.

As he suspected, there was an opening there in which the creature had evidently taken refuge. It was more than a crevice; it was a kind of porch.

The sea entered beneath it, but was not deep. The bottom was visible, covered with large pebbles. The pebbles were green and clothed with *confervæ*, indicating that they were never dry. They were like the tops of a number of heads of infants, covered with a kind of green hair.

Holding his knife between his teeth, Gilliatt descended, by the help of feet and hands, from the upper part of the escarpment, and leaped into the water. It reached almost to his shoulders.

He made his way through the porch, and found himself in a blind passage, with a roof in the form of a rude arch over his head.

The walls were polished and slippery. The crab was nowhere visible. He gained his feet and advanced in daylight growing fainter, so that he began to lose the power to distinguish objects.

At about fifteen paces the vaulted roof ended overhead. He had penetrated beyond the blind passage. There was here more space, and consequently more daylight. The pupils of his eyes, moreover, had dilated; he could see pretty clearly. He was taken by surprise.

He had made his way again into the singular cavern which he had visited in the previous month. The only difference was that he had entered by the way of the sea.

His eyes became more accustomed to the place. His vision became clearer and clearer. He was astonished. He found, above the level of the water, and within reach of his hand, a horizontal fissure. It seemed to him probable that the crab had taken refuge there, and he plunged his hand in as far as he was able, and groped about in that dusky aperture.

Suddenly he felt himself seized by the arm. A strange indescribable horror thrilled through him.

Some living thing, thin, rough, flat, cold, slimy, had twisted itself round his naked arm, in the dark depth below. It crept upward toward his chest. Its pressure was like a tightening cord, its steady persistence like that of a screw. In less than a moment some mysterious spiral form had passed round his wrist and elbow, and had reached his shoulder. A sharp point penetrated beneath the armpit.

Gilliatt recoiled, but he had scarcely power to move! He was, as it were, nailed to the place. With his left hand, which was disengaged, he seized his knife, which he still held between his teeth, and with that hand, holding the knife, he supported himself against the rocks, while he made a desperate effort to withdraw his arm. He succeeded only in disturbing his persecutor, which wound itself still tighter. It was supple as leather, strong as steel, cold as night.

A second form, sharp, elongated, and narrow, issued out of the crevice, like a tongue out of monstrous jaws. It seemed to lick his naked body. Then suddenly stretching out, it became longer and thinner, as it crept over his skin, and wound itself round him. At the same time a terrible sense of pain, comparable to nothing he had ever known, compelled all his muscles to contract. He felt upon his skin a number of flat rounded points. It seemed as if innumerable suckers had fastened to his flesh and were about to drink his blood.

A third long undulating shape issued from the hole in the rock, and seemed to feel its way about his body, lashed round his ribs like a cord, and fixed itself there.

Agony when at its height is mute. Gilliatt uttered no cry. There was sufficient light for him to see the repulsive forms which had entangled themselves about him. A fourth ligature, but this one swift as an arrow, darted toward his stomach, and wound around him there.

It was impossible to sever or tear away the slimy bands which were twisted tightly round his body, and were adhering by a number of points. Each of the points was the focus of frightful and singular pangs. It was as if numberless small mouths were devouring him at the same time.

A fifth long, slimy, riband-shaped strip issued from the hole. It passed over the others, and wound itself tightly around his chest. The compression increased his sufferings. He could scarcely breathe.

These living thongs were pointed at their extremities, but broadened like the blade of a sword toward its hilt. All belonged evidently to the same centre. They crept and glided about him. He felt the strange points of pressure, which seemed to him like mouths, change their places from time to time.

Suddenly a large, round, glutinous mass issued from beneath the crevice. It was the centre. The five thongs were attached to it like spokes to the nave of a wheel. On the opposite side of this disgusting monster appeared the commencement of three other tentacles, the ends of which remained under the rock. In the middle of this slimy mass appeared two eyes.

The eyes were fixed on Gilliatt.

He recognized the devil fish.

It is difficult for those who have not seen it to believe in the existence of the devil fish.

Compared to this creature, the ancient hydras are insignificant.

If terror were the object of its creation, nothing could be imagined more perfect than the devil fish.

The devil fish has no muscular organization, no menacing cry, no breastplate, no horn, no dart, no claw, no tail with which to hold or bruise, no cutting fins, or wings with nails, no prickles, no sword, no electric discharge, no poison, no talons, no beak, no teeth. Yet he is of all creatures the most formidably armed.

What, then, is the devil fish? It is the sea vampire.

This frightful apparition, which is always possible among the rocks in the open sea, is a grayish form, which undulates in the water. It is of the thickness of a man's arm, and in length nearly five feet. Its outline is ragged. Its form resembles an umbrella closed, and without a handle. This irregular mass advances slowly toward you. Suddenly it opens, and eight radii issue abruptly from around a face with two eyes. These radii are alive. Their undulation is like lambent flames. They resemble, when opened, the spokes of a wheel, of four or five feet in diameter. A terrible expansion! It springs upon its prey.

The devil fish harpoons its victim.

It winds around the sufferer, covering and entangling him in its long folds. Underneath it is yellow, above a dull, earthy hue; nothing could render that inexplicable shade dust-colored. Its form is spider-like, but its tints are like those of the chameleon. When irritated, it becomes violet. Its most horrible characteristic is its softness.

Its folds strangle, its contact paralyzes.

It has an aspect like gangrened or scabrous flesh. It is a monstrous embodiment of disease.

It adheres closely to its prey, and cannot be torn away, a fact which is due to its power of exhausting air. The eight antennæ, large at their roots, diminish gradually, and end in needle-like points. Underneath each of these feelers range two rows of pustules, decreasing in size, the largest ones near the head, the smaller at the extremities. Each row contains twenty-five of these. There are, therefore, fifty pustules to each feeler, and the creature possesses in the whole four hundred. These pustules are capable of acting like cupping-glasses. They are cartilaginous substances, cylindrical, horny, and livid. Upon the large species they diminish gradually from the diameter of a five-franc piece to the size of a split pea. These small tubes can be thrust out and withdrawn by the animal at will. They are capable of piercing to a depth of more than an inch.

This sucking apparatus has all the regularity and delicacy of a key-board. It stands forth at one moment and disappears the next. The most perfect sensitiveness cannot equal the contractibility of these suckers, always proportioned to the internal movement of the animal, and its exterior circumstances. The monster is endowed with the qualities of the sensitive plant.

When swimming, the devil fish rests, so to speak, in its sheath. It swims with all its parts drawn close. It may be likened to a sleeve sewn up with a closed fist within. The protuberance, which is the head, pushes the water aside and advances with a vague undulatory movement. Its two eyes, though large, are indistinct, being of the color of the water.

The devil fish not only swims, it walks. It is partly fish, partly reptile. It crawls upon the bed of the sea. At these times, it makes use of its eight feelers, and creeps along in the fashion of a species of swift-moving caterpillar.

It has no blood, no bones, no flesh. It is soft and flabby, a skin with nothing inside. Its eight tentacles may be turned inside out like the fingers of a glove.

It has a single orifice in the centre of its radii, which appears at first to be neither the vent nor the mouth. It is, in fact, both one and the other. The orifice performs a double function. The entire creature is cold.

The jelly-fish of the Mediterranean is repulsive. Contact with that animated gelatinous substance which envelopes the bather, in which the hands sink, and the nails scratch ineffectively, which can be torn without killing it, and which can be plucked off without entirely removing it—that fluid and yet tenacious creature which slips through the fingers, is disgusting. But no horror can equal the sudden apparition of the devil fish, that Medusa with its eight serpents.

It is with the sucking apparatus that it attacks. The victim is oppressed by a vacuum drawing at numberless points; it is not a clawing or a biting, but an indescribable scarification. A tearing of the flesh is terrible, but less terrible than a sucking of the blood. Claws are harmless compared with the horrible action of these natural air-cups. The muscles swell, the fibres of the body are contorted, the skin cracks under the loathsome oppression, the blood spurts out and mingles horribly with the lymph of the monster, which clings to its victim by innumerable hideous mouths. The hydra incorporates itself with the man, the man becomes one with the hydra. The spectre lies upon you. The tiger can only devour you, but the devil fish, horrible, sucks your life-blood away.

He draws you to him, and into himself, while bound down, glued to the ground, powerless, you feel yourself gradually emptied into this horrible pouch, which is the monster itself.

Such was the creature in whose power Gilliatt had fallen for some minutes.

The monster was the inhabitant of the grotto, the terrible genii of the place. A kind of sombre demon of the water.

All the splendors of the cavern existed for it alone.

On the day of the previous month when Gilliatt had first penetrated into the grotto, the dark outline, vaguely perceived by him in the ripples of the secret waters, was this monster. It was here in its home.

When entering for the second time into the cavern in pursuit of the crab, he had observed the crevice in which he supposed that the crab had taken refuge, the *pieuvre* was there lying in wait for prey.

Gilliatt had thrust his arm deep into the opening. The monster had snapped at it. It held him fast, as the spider holds the fly.

He was in the water up to his belt, his naked feet clutching the slippery roundness of the huge stones at the bottom, his right arm bound and rendered powerless by the flat coils of the long tentacles of the creature, and his body almost hidden under the folds and cross folds of this horrible bandage.

Of the eight arms of the devil fish three adhered to the rock, while five encircled Gilliatt. In this way, clinging to the granite on the one hand, and with the other to its human prey, it enchained him to the rock. Two hundred and fifty suckers were upon him, tormenting him with agony and loathing. He was grasped by gigantic hands, the fingers of which were each nearly a yard long, and furnished inside with living blisters eating into the flesh.

It is impossible to tear one's self from the folds of the devil fish. The attempt ends only in a firmer grasp. The monster clings with more determined force. Its effort increases with that of its victim; every struggle produces a tightening of its ligatures.

Gilliatt had but one resource, his knife.

His left hand only was free, but the reader knows with what power he could use it. It might have been said that he had two right hands.

His open knife was in his hand.

The antennæ of the devil fish cannot be cut; it is a leathery substance impossible to divide with the knife, it slips under the edge. Its position in attack also is such that to cut it would be to wound the victim's own flesh.

The creature is formidable, but there is a way of resisting it. The fishermen of Sark know this, as does anyone who has seen them execute certain abrupt movements in the sea. The porpoises know it also; they have a way of biting the cuttle-fish which decapitates it. Hence the frequent sight on the sea of pen-fish, poulps, and cuttle-fish without heads.

The devil fish, in fact, is only vulnerable through the head.

Gilliatt was not ignorant of this fact.

With the devil fish, as with a furious bull, there is a certain moment in the conflict which must be seized. It is the instant when the devil fish advances its head. The movement is rapid. He who loses that moment is destroyed.

The things we have described occupied only a few moments. Gilliatt, however, felt the increasing power of its innumerable suckers.

The monster is cunning. It tries first to stupefy its prey. It seizes and then pauses a while.

Gilliatt grasped his knife. The sucking increased.

He looked at the monster, which seemed to look at him.

Suddenly it loosened from the rock its sixth antenna, and darting it at him, seized him by the left arm.

At the same moment it advanced its head with a violent movement. In one second more its mouth would have fastened on his breast. Bleeding in the sides, and with his two arms entangled, he would have been a dead man.

But Gilliatt was watchful. He avoided the antenna, and at the moment when the monster darted forward to fasten on his breast, he struck it with the knife clenched in his left hand. There were two convulsions in opposite directions, that of the devil fish and that of its prey. The movement was rapid as a double flash of lightning.

He had plunged the blade of his knife into the flat, slimy substance, and by a rapid movement, like the flourish of a whip in the air, describing a circle around the two eyes, he wrenched the head off as a man would draw a tooth.

The struggle was ended. The folds relaxed. The monster dropped away, like the slow detaching of bands. The four hundred suckers, deprived of their sustaining power, dropped at once from the man and the rock. The mass sank to the bottom of the water.

Breathless with the struggle, Gilliatt could perceive upon the stones at his feet two shapeless, slimy heaps, the head on one side, the remainder of the monster on the other.

Fearing, nevertheless, some convulsive return of his agony he recoiled to avoid the reach of the dreaded tentacles.

But the monster was quite dead.

Gilliatt closed his knife.

It was time that he killed the devil fish. He was almost suffocated. His right arm and his chest were purple. Numberless little swellings were distinguishable upon them. The blood flowed from them here and there.

The remedy for these wounds is sea-water. Gilliatt plunged into it, rubbing himself at the same time with the palms of his hands. The swellings disappeared under the friction.

SEA CURSE

by Robert E. Howard

Tᴀᴇʏ ᴡᴇʀᴇ ᴛʜᴇ brawlers and braggarts, the loud boasters and hard drinkers, of Faring town, John Kulrek and his crony Lie-lip Canool. Many a time have I, a tousle-haired lad, stolen to the tavern door to listen to their curses, their profane arguments and wild sea songs, half fearful and half in admiration of these wild rovers. Aye, all the people of Faring town gazed on them with fear and admiration, for they were not like the rest of the Faring men; they were not content to ply their trade along the coasts and among the shark-teeth shoals. No yawls, no skiffs for them! They fared far, farther than any other man in the village, for they shipped on the great sailing-ships that went out on the white tides to brave the restless grey ocean and make ports in strange lands.

Ah, I mind it was swift times in the little sea-coast village of Faring when John Kulrek came home, with the furtive Lie-lip at his side, swaggering down the gang-plank, in his tarry sea-clothes, and the broad leather belt that held his ever-ready dagger, shouting condescending greeting to some favored acquaintance, kissing some maiden who ventured too near, then up the street, roaring some scarcely decent song of the sea. How the cringers and the idlers, the hangers-on, would swarm about the two desperate heroes, flattering and smirking, guffawing hilariously at each nasty jest. For to the tavern loafers and to some of the weaker among the straightforward villagers, these men with their wild talk and their brutal deeds, their tales of the Seven Seas and the far countries, these men, I say, were valiant knights, nature's noblemen who dared to be men of blood and brawn.

And all feared them, so that when a man was beaten or a woman insulted, the villagers muttered, and did nothing. And so when Moll Farrell's niece was put to shame by John Kulrek, none dared even to put into words what all thought. Moll had never married, and she and the girl lived alone in a little hut down close to the beach, so close that in high tide the waves came almost to the door.

The people of the village accounted old Moll something of a witch, and she was a grim, gaunt old dame who had little to say to anyone. But she minded her own business, and eked out a slim living by gathering clams, and picking up bits of driftwood.

The girl was a pretty, foolish little thing, vain and easily befooled, else she had never yielded to the shark-like blandishments of John Kulrek.

I mind the day was a cold winter day with a sharp breeze out of the east when the old dame came into the village street shrieking that the girl had vanished. All scattered over the beach and back among the bleak inland hills to search for her, all save John Kulrek and his cronies who sat in the tavern dicing and toping. All the while beyond the shoals, we heard the never-ceasing droning of the heaving, restless grey monster, and in the dim light of the ghostly dawn Moll Farrell's girl came home.

The tides bore her gently across the wet sands and laid her

almost at her own door. Virgin-white she was, and her arms were folded across her still bosom. Calm was her face, and the grey tides sighed about her slender limbs. Moll Farrell's eyes were stones, yet she stood above her dead girl and spoke no word till John Kulrek and his crony came reeling down from the tavern, their drinking-jacks still in their hands. Drunk was John Kulrek, and the people gave back for him, murder in their souls, so he came and laughed at Moll Farrell across the body of her girl.

"Zounds!" swore John Kulrek, "the wench has drowned herself, Lie-lip!"

Lie-lip laughed, with the twist of his thin mouth. He always hated Moll Farrell, for it was she that had given him the name of Lie-lip.

Then John Kulrek lifted his drinking-jack, swaying on his uncertain legs. "A health to the wench's ghost!" he bellowed, while all stood aghast.

Then Moll Farrell spoke, and the words broke from her in a scream which sent ripples of cold up and down the spines of the throng.

"The curse of the Foul Fiend upon you, John Kulrek!" she screamed. "The curse of God rest upon your vile soul through-out eternity! May you gaze on sights that shall sear the eyes of you and scorch the soul of you! May you die a bloody death and writhe in hell's flames for a million and a million and yet a million years! I curse you by sea and by land, by earth and by air, by the demons of the swamplands, the fiends of the forest and the goblins of the hills! And you"—her lean finger stabbed at Lie-lip Canool and he started backward, his face paling—"you shall be the death of John Kulrek and he shall be the death of you! You shall bring John Kulrek to the doors of hell and John Kulrek shall bring you to the gallows-tree! I set the seal of death upon your brow, John Kulrek! You shall live in terror and die in horror far out upon the cold grey sea! But the sea that took the soul of innocence to her bosom shall not take you, but shall fling forth your vile carcass to the sands! Aye, John Kulrek"—and she spoke with such a terrible intensity that the drunken mockery on the man's face changed to one of swinish stupidity—"the sea roars for the victim it will not keep! There is snow upon the hills, John Kulrek, and ere it melts your corpse will lie at my feet. And I shall spit upon it and be content."

Kulrek and his crony sailed at dawn for a long voyage, and Moll went back to her hut and her clam-gathering. She seemed to grow leaner and more grim than ever and her eyes smoldered with a light not sane. The days glided by and people whispered among themselves that Moll's days were numbered, for she faded to a ghost of a woman, but she went her way, refusing all aid.

That was a short, cold summer and the snow on the barren inland hills never melted, a thing very unusual, which caused much comment among the villagers. At dusk and at dawn Moll would come up on the beach, gaze up at the snow which glittered on the hills, then out to sea with a fierce intensity in her gaze.

Then the days grew shorter, the nights longer and darker, and the cold grey tides came sweeping along the bleak strands, bearing the rain and sleet of the sharp east breezes.

And upon a bleak day a trading-vessel sailed into the bay and anchored. And all the idlers and the wastrels flocked to the wharfs, for that was the ship upon which John Kulrek and Lie-lip Canool had sailed. Down the gang-plank came Lie-lip, more furtive than ever, but John Kulrek was not there.

To shouted queries, Canool shook his head. "Kulrek deserted ship at a port of Sumatra," said he. "He had a row with the skipper, lads. Wanted me to desert, too, but no! I had to see you fine lads again, eh boys?"

Almost cringing was Lie-lip Canool, and suddenly he

recoiled as Moll Farrell came through the throng. A moment they stood eyeing each other, then Moll's grim lips bent in a terrible smile.

"There's blood on your hand, Canool!" she lashed out suddenly, so suddenly that Lie-lip started and rubbed his right hand across his left sleeve.

"Stand aside, witch!" he snarled in sudden anger, striding through the crowd which gave back for him. His admirers followed him to the tavern.

Now, I mind that the next day was even colder. Grey fogs came drifting out of the east and veiled the sea and the beaches. There would be no sailing that day, and so all the villagers were in their snug houses or matching tales at the tavern. So it came that Joe, my friend, a lad of my own age, and I, were the ones who saw the first of the strange things that happened.

Being harum-scarum lads of no wisdom, we were sitting in a small rowboat, floating at the end of the wharfs, each shivering and wishing the other would suggest leaving, there being no reason whatever for our being there, save that it was a good place to build air-castles undisturbed.

Suddenly Joe raised his hand. "Say," he said, "d'ye hear? Who can be out on the bay upon a day like this?"

"Nobody. What d'ye hear?"

"Oars. Or I'm a lubber. Listen."

There was no seeing anything in that fog, and I heard nothing. Yet Joe swore he did, and suddenly his face assumed a strange look.

"Somebody rowing out there, I tell you! The bay is alive with oars from the sound! A score of boats at the least! Ye dolt, can ye not hear?"

Then, as I shook my head, he leaped and began to undo the painter.

"I'm off to see. Name me liar if the bay is not full of boats, all together like a close fleet. Are you with me?"

Yes, I was with him, though I heard nothing. Then out in the greyness we went, and the fog closed behind and before so that we drifted in a vague world of smoke, seeing naught and hearing naught. We were lost in no time, and I cursed Joe for leading us upon a wild goose chase that was like to end with our being swept out to sea. I thought of Moll Farrell's girl and shuddered.

How long we drifted I know not. Minutes faded into hours, hours into centuries. Still Joe swore he heard the oars, now close at hand, now far away, and for hours we followed them, steering our course toward the sound, as the noise grew or receded. This I later thought of, and could not understand.

Then, when my hands were so numb that I could no longer hold the oar, and the forerunning drowsiness of cold and exhaustion was stealing over me, bleak white stars broke through the fog which glided suddenly away, fading like a ghost of smoke, and we found ourselves afloat just outside the mouth of the bay. The waters lay smooth as a pond, all dark green and silver in the starlight, and the cold came crisper than ever. I was swinging the boat about, to put back into the bay, when Joe gave a shout, and for the first time I heard the clack of oar-locks. I glanced over my shoulder and my blood went cold.

A great beaked prow loomed above us, a weird, unfamiliar shape against the stars, and as I caught my breath, sheered sharply and swept by us, with a curious swishing I never heard any other craft make. Joe screamed and backed oars frantically, and the boat walled out of the way just in time, for though the prow missed us, still otherwise we had died. For from the sides of the ship stood long oars, bank upon bank which swept her along. Though I had never seen such a craft, I knew her for a galley. But what was she doing upon our coasts? They said, the far-farers, that such ships were still in use among the heathens of Barbary. But it was many a long, heaving mile to Barbary, and even so she did not resemble the ships described by those who had sailed far.

We started in pursuit, and this was strange, for though the waters broke about her prow, and she seemed fairly to fly through the waves, yet she was making little speed, and it was no time before we caught up with her. Making our painter fast to a chain far back beyond the reach of the swishing oars, we hailed those on deck. But there came no answer, and at last, conquering our fears, we clambered up the chain and found ourselves upon the strangest deck man has trod for many a long, roaring century.

"This is no Barbary rover!" Joe muttered fearsomely. "Look, how old it seems! Almost ready to fall to pieces. Why, 'tis fairly rotten!"

There was no one on deck, no one at the long sweep with which the craft was steered. We stole to the hold and looked down the stair. Then and there, if ever men were on the verge of insanity, it was we. For there were rowers there, it is true; they sat upon the rowers' benches and drove the creaking oars through the grey waters. And they that rowed were skeletons!

Shrieking, we plunged across the deck, to fling ourselves into the sea. But at the rail I tripped upon something and fell headlong, and as I lay, I saw a thing which vanquished my fear of the horrors below for an instant. The thing upon which I had tripped was a human body, and in the dim grey light that was beginning to steal across the eastern waves I saw a dagger hilt standing up between his shoulders. Joe was at the rail, urging me to haste, and together we slid down the chain and cut the painter.

Then we stood off into the bay. Straight on kept the grim galley, and we followed, slowly, wondering. She seemed to be heading straight for the beach beside the wharfs, and as we approached, we saw the wharfs thronged with people. They had missed us, no doubt, and now they stood, there in the early dawn light, struck dumb by the apparition which had come up out of the night and the grim ocean.

Straight on swept the galley, her oars a-swish, then ere she reached the shallow water—crash!—a terrific reverberation shook the bay. Before our eyes the grim craft seemed to melt away, then she vanished, and the green waters seethed where she had ridden, but there floated no driftwood there, nor did there ever float any ashore. Aye, something floated ashore, but it was grim driftwood!

We made the landing amid a hum of excited conversation that stopped suddenly. Moll Farrell stood before her hut, limned gauntly against the ghostly dawn, her lean hand pointing sea-ward. And across the sighing wet sands, borne by the grey tide, something came floating, something that the waves dropped at Moll Farrell's feet. And there looked up at us, as we crowded about, a pair of unseeing eyes set in a still, white face. John Kulrek had come home.

Still and grim he lay, rocked by the tide, and as he lurched sideways, all saw the dagger hilt that stood from his back—the dagger all of us had seen a thousand times at the belt of Lie-lip Canool.

"Aye, I killed him!" came Canool's shriek, as he writhed and groveled before our gaze. "At sea on a still night in a drunken brawl I slew him and hurled him overboard! And from the far seas he has followed me," his voice sank to a hideous whisper, "because of the curse, the sea would not keep his body!"

And the wretch sank down, trembling, the shadow of the gallows already in his eyes.

"Aye!" Strong, deep and exultant was Moll Farrell's voice. "From the hell of lost craft Satan sent a ship of bygone ages! A ship red with gore and stained with the memory of horrid crimes! None other would bear such a vile carcass! The sea has taken vengeance and has given me mine. See now, how I spit upon the face of John Kulrek."

And with a ghastly laugh, she pitched forward, the blood starting to her lips. And the sun came up across the restless sea.

THE CHILDREN OF THE POOL

by Arthur Machen

A COUPLE OF SUMMERS AGO I was staying with old friends in my native county, on the Welsh border. It was in the heat and drought of a hot and dry year, and I came into those green, well-watered valleys with a sense of a great refreshment. Here was relief from the burning of London streets, from the close and airless nights, when all the myriad walls of brick and stone and concrete and the pavements that are endless give out into the heavy darkness the fires that all day long have been drawn from the sun. And from those roadways that have become like railways, with their changing lamps, and their yellow globes, and their bars and studs of steel, from the menace of instant death if your feet stray from the track—from all this what a rest to walk under the green leaf in quiet, and hear the stream trickling from the heart of the hill.

My friends were old friends, and they were urgent that I should go my own way. There was breakfast at nine, but it was equally serviceable and excellent at ten, and I could be in for something cold for lunch, if I liked. And if I didn't like, I could stay away till dinner at half past seven, and then there was all the evening for talks about old times and about the changes, with comfortable drinks, and bed soothed by memories and tobacco, and by the brook that twisted under dark alders through the meadow below. And not a red bungalow to be seen for many a mile around! Sometimes, when the heat even in that green land was more than burning, and the wind from the mountains in the west ceased, I would stay all day under shade on the lawn, but more often I went afield and trod remembered ways, and tried to find new ones, in that happy and bewildered country. There, paths go wandering into undiscovered valleys, there from deep and narrow lanes with overshadowing hedges, still smaller tracks that I suppose are old bridlepaths, creep obscurely, obviously leading nowhere in particular.

It was on a day of cooler air that I went adventuring abroad on such an expedition. It was a "day of the veil." There were no clouds in the sky, but a high mist, grey and luminous, had been drawn all over it. At one moment, it would seem that the sun must shine through, and the blue appear, and then the trees in the wood would seem to blossom, and the meadows lightened, and then again the veil would be drawn. I struck off by the stony lane that led from the back of the house up over the hill. I had last gone that way a-many years ago, of a winter afternoon, when the ruts were frozen into hard ridges, and dark pines on high places rose above snow, and the sun was red and still above the mountain. I remembered that the way had given good sport, with twists to right and left, and unexpected descents, and then risings to places of thorn and bracken, till it darkened to the hushed stillness of a winter's night, and I turned homeward reluctant. Now I took another chance with all the summer day before me, and resolved to come to some end and conclusion of the matter.

I think I had gone beyond the point at which I had stopped and turned back as the frozen darkness and the bright stars came on me. I remembered the dip in the hedge, from which I saw the round tumulus on high at the end of the mountain wall, and there was the white farm on the hill-side, and the farmer was still calling to his dog, as he—or his father—had called before, his voice high and thin in the distance. After this point, I seemed to be in undiscovered country. The ash trees grew densely on either side of the way and met above it. I went on and on into the unknown in the manner of the only good guide-books, which are the tales of old knights. The road went down, and climbed, and again descended, all through the deep of the wood. Then, on both sides, the trees ceased, though the hedges were so high that I could see nothing of the way of the land about me. And just at the wood's ending, there was one of those tracks or little paths of which I have spoken, going off from my lane on the right, and winding out of sight quickly under all its leafage of hazel and wild rose, maple and hornbeam, with a holly here and there, and honeysuckle golden, and dark briony shining and twining everywhere. I could not resist the invitation of a path so obscure and uncertain, and set out on its track of green and profuse grass, with the ground beneath still soft to the feet, even in the drought of that fiery summer. The way wound, as far as I could make out, on the slope of a hill, neither ascending nor descending, and after a mile or more of this rich walking, it suddenly ceased, and I found myself on a bare hill-side, on a rough track that went down to a grey house. It was now a farm by its looks and surroundings, but there were signs of old state about it: good sixteenth-century mullioned windows and a Jacobean porch projecting from the centre, with dim armorial bearings mouldering above the door.

It struck me that bread and cheese and cider would be grateful, and I beat upon the door with my stick, and brought a pleasant woman to open it.

"Do you think," I began, "you could be so good as..."

And then came a shout from somewhere at the end of the

stone passage, and a great voice called, "Come in, then, come in, you old scoundrel, if your name is Meyrick, as I'm sure it is."

I was amazed. The pleasant woman grinned and said, "It seems you are well known here, sir, already. But perhaps you had heard that Mr. Roberts was staying here."

My old acquaintance, James Roberts, came tumbling out from his den at the back. He was a man whom I had known a long time, but not very well. Our affairs in London moved on different lines, and so we did not often meet. But I was glad to see him in that unexpected place. He was a round man, always florid and growing redder in the face with his years. He was a countryman of mine, but I had hardly known him before we both went to town, since his home had been at the northern end of the county.

He shook me cordially by the hand, and looked as if he would like to smack me on the back—he was, a little, that kind of man—and repeated his "Come in, come in!" adding to the pleasant woman, "And bring you another plate, Mrs. Morgan, and all the rest of it. I hope you've not forgotten how to eat Caerphilly cheese, Meyrick. I can tell you, there is none better than Mrs. Morgan's making. And, Mrs. Morgan, another jug of cider, and *seidr dda*, mind you."

I never knew whether he had been brought up as a boy to speak Welsh. In London he had lost all but the faintest trace of accent, but down here in Gwent the tones of the country had quickly returned to him, and he smacked as strongly of the land in his speech as the cheerful farmer's wife herself. I judged his accent was a part of his holiday.

He drew me into the little parlour with its old furniture and its pleasant old-fashioned ornaments and faintly flowering wallpaper, and set me in an elbow-chair at the round table, and gave me, as I told him, exactly what I had meant to ask for— bread and cheese and cider. All very good. Mrs. Morgan, it was clear, had the art of making a Caerphilly cheese that was succulent, a sort of white bel paese—far different from those dry and stony cheeses that often bring dishonour on the Caerphilly name. And afterwards there was gooseberry jam and cream. And the tobacco that the country uses: Shag-on-the-Back, from the Welsh Back, Bristol. And then there was gin.

This last we partook of out of doors, in an old stone summer house, in the garden at the side. A white rose had grown all over the summer-house, and shaded and glorified it. The water in the big jug had just been drawn from the well in the limestone rock, and I told Roberts gratefully that I felt a great deal better than when I had knocked at the farmhouse door. I told him where I was staying—he knew my host by name—and he, in turn, informed me that it was his first visit to Lanypwll, as the farm was called. A neighbour of his at Lee had recommended Mrs. Morgan's cooking very highly, and, as he said, you could not speak too well of her in that way or any other.

We sipped and smoked through the afternoon in that pleasant retreat under the white roses, I meditated gratefully on the fact that I should not dare to enjoy Shag-on-the-Back so freely in London—a potent tobacco, of full and ripe savour, but not for the hard streets.

"You say the farm is called Lanypwll," I interjected, "that means 'by the pool,' doesn't it? Where is the pool? I don't see it."

"Come you," said Roberts, "and I will show you."

He took me by a little gate through the garden hedge of laurels, thick and high, and round to the left of the house, the opposite side to that by which I had made my approach. And there we climbed a green rounded bastion of the old ages, and he pointed down to a narrow valley, shut in by steep wooded hills. There at the bottom was a level, half marshland and half black water lying in still pools, with green islands of iris and of all manner of rank and strange growths that love to have their roots in slime.

"There is your pool for you," said Roberts.

It was the most strange place. I thought, hidden away under the hills as if it were a secret. The steeps that went down to it were a tangle of undergrowth, of all manner of boughs mingled with taller trees rising above the mass, and down at the edge of the marsh some of these had perished in the swampy water, and stood white and bare and ghastly, with leprous limbs.

"An ugly looking place," I said to Roberts.

"I quite agree with you. It is an ugly place enough. They tell me at the farm it's not safe to go near it, or you may get fever and I don't know what else. And, indeed, if you didn't go down carefully and watch your steps, you might easily find yourself up to the neck in that black muck there."

We turned back into the garden and to our summer-house, and soon after, it was time for me to make my way home.

"How long are you staying with Nichol?" Roberts asked me as we parted. I told him, and he insisted on my dining with him at the end of the week.

"I will 'send' you," he said. "I will take you by a short cut across the fields and see that you don't lose your way. Roast duck and green peas," he added alluringly, "and something good for the digestion afterwards."

It was a fine evening when I next journeyed to the farm, but indeed we got tired of saying "fine weathers" throughout that wonderful summer. I found Roberts cheery and welcoming, but, I thought, hardly in such rosy spirits as on my former visit. We were having a cocktail of his composition in the summer-house, as the famous duck gained the last glow of brown perfection, and I noticed that his speech was not bubbling so freely from him as before. He fell silent once or twice and looked thoughtful. He told me he'd ventured down to the pool, the swampy place at the bottom. "And it looks no better when you see it close at hand. Black, oily stuff that isn't like water, with a scum upon it, and weeds like a lot of monsters. I never saw such queer, ugly plants. There's one rank-looking thing down there covered with dull crimson blossoms, all bloated out and speckled like a toad."

"You're no botanist," I remarked.

"No, not I. I know buttercups and daisies and not much more. Mrs. Morgan here was quite frightened when I told her where I'd been. She said she hoped I mightn't be sorry for it. But I feel as well as ever. I don't think there are many places left in the country now where you can get malaria."

We proceeded to the duck and the green peas and rejoiced in their perfection. There was some very old ale that Mr. Morgan had bought when an ancient tavern in the neighbourhood had been pulled down Its age and original excellence had combined to make a drink like a rare wine. The "something good for the digestion" turned out to be a mellow brandy that Roberts had brought with him from town. I told him that I had never known a better hour. He warmed up with the good meat and drink and was cheery enough, and yet I thought there was a reserve, something obscure at the back of his mind that was by no means cheerful.

We had a second glass of the mellow brandy, and Roberts, after a moment's indecision, spoke out. He dropped his holiday game of Welsh countryman completely.

"You wouldn't think, would you," he began, "that a man would come down to a place like this to be blackmailed at the end of the journey?"

"Good Lord!" I gasped in amazement, "I should think not indeed. What's happened?"

He looked very grave. I thought even that he looked frightened.

"Well, I'll tell you. A couple of nights ago, I went for a stroll after my dinner—a beautiful night, with the moon shining, and a nice, clean breeze. So I walked up over the hill, and then took the path that leads down through the wood to the brook. I'd got into the wood, fifty yards or so, when I heard my name called out: 'Roberts! James Roberts!' in a shrill, piercing voice, a young girl's voice, and I jumped pretty well out of my skin, I can tell you. I stopped dead and stared all about me. Of course I could see nothing at all—bright moonlight and black shadow and all those trees—anybody could hide. Then it came to me that it was some girl of the place having a game with her sweetheart. James Roberts is a common enough name, especially in this part of the country. So I was just going on, not bothering my head about the local love-affairs, when that scream came right in my ear: 'Roberts! Roberts! James Roberts!'—and then half a dozen words that I won't trouble you with. Not yet, at any rate."

I have said that Roberts was by no means an intimate friend of mine. But I had always known him as a genial, cordial fellow, a thoroughly good-natured man, and I was sorry and shocked, too, to see him sitting there wretched and dismayed. He looked as if he had seen a ghost. He looked much worse than that—he looked as if he had seen terror.

But it was too early to press him closely. I said, "What did you do then?"

"I turned about, and ran back through the wood, and tumbled over the stile. I got home here as quick as ever I could, and shut myself up in this room, dripping with fright and gasping for breath. I was almost crazy, I believe. I walked up and down. I sat down in the chair and got up again. I wondered whether I should wake up in my bed and find I'd been having a nightmare. I cried at last. I'll tell you the truth, I put my head in my hands, and the tears ran down my cheeks. I was quite broken."

"But, look here," I said, "isn't this making a great to-do about very little? I can quite see it must have been a nasty shock. But, how long did you say you had been staying here?

Ten days, was it?"

"A fortnight, tomorrow."

"Well, you know country ways as well as I do. You may be sure that everybody within three or four miles of Lanypwll knows about a gentleman from London, a Mr. James Roberts, staying at the farm. And there are always unpleasant young people to be found, wherever you go. I gather that this girl used very abusive language when she hailed you. She probably thought it was a good joke. You had taken that walk through the wood in the evening a couple of times before? No doubt, you had been noticed going that way, and the girl and her friend or friends planned to give you a shock. I wouldn't think any more of it, if I were you."

He almost cried out.

"Think any more of it! What will the world think of it?" There was an anguish of terror in his voice. I thought it was time to come to cues. I spoke up pretty briskly.

"Now, look here, Roberts, it's no good beating about the bush. Before we can do anything, we've got to have the whole tale, fair and square. What I've gathered is this: you go for a walk in a wood near here one evening, and a girl, you say it was a girl's voice, hails you by your name, and then screams out a lot of filthy language. Is there anything more in it than that?"

"There's a lot more than that. I was going to ask you not to let it go any further, but as far as I can see, there won't be any secret in it much longer. There's another end to the story, and it goes back a good many years, to the time when I first came to London as a young man. That's twenty-five years ago."

He stopped speaking. When he began again, I could feel that he spoke with unutterable repugnance. Every word was a horror to him.

"You know as well as I do, that there are all sorts of turnings in London that a young fellow can take—good, bad, and indifferent. There was a good deal of bad luck about it. I do believe, and I was too young to know or care much where I was going, but I got into a turning with the black pit at the end of it."

He beckoned me to lean forward across the table, and whispered for a minute or two in my ear. In my turn, I heard not without horror. I said nothing.

"That was what I heard shrieked out in the wood. What do you say?"

"You've done with all that long ago?"

"It was done with very soon after it was begun. It was no more than a bad dream. And then it all flashed back on me like deadly lightning. What do you say? What can I do?"

I told him that I had to admit that it was no good to try to put the business in the wood down to accident, the casual filthy language of a depraved village girl. As I said, it couldn't be a case of a bow drawn at a venture.

"There must be somebody behind it. Can you think of anybody?"

"There may be one or two left. I can't say. I haven't heard of any of them for years. I thought they had all gone. Dead, or at the other side of the world."

"Yes, but people can get back from the other side of the world pretty quickly in these days. Yokohama is not much farther off than Yarmouth. But you haven't heard of any of these people lately?"

"As I said, not for years. But the secret's out."

"But, let's consider. Who is this girl? Where does she live? We must get at her, and try if we can't frighten the life out of her. And, in the first place, we'll find out the source of her information. Then we shall know where we are. I suppose you have discovered who she is?"

"I've not a notion of who she is or where she lives."

"I daresay you wouldn't care to ask the Morgans any questions. But to go back to the beginning, you spoke of blackmail.

Did this damned girl ask you for money to shut her mouth?"

"No, I shouldn't have called it blackmail. She didn't say anything about money."

"Well, that sounds more helpful. Let's see... Tonight is Saturday. You took this unfortunate walk of yours a couple of nights ago, on Thursday night. And you haven't heard anything more since. I should keep away from that wood, and try to find out who the young lady is. That's the first thing to be done, clearly."

I was trying to cheer him up a little, but he only stared at me with his horror-stricken eyes.

"It didn't finish with the wood," he groaned. "My bedroom is next door to this room where we are. When I had pulled myself together a bit that night, I had a stiff glass, about double my allowance, and went off to bed and to sleep. I woke up with a noise of tapping at the window, just by the head of the bed. Tap, tap, tap, it went. I thought it might be a bough beating on the glass. And then I heard that voice calling me: 'James Roberts, open, open!'

"I tell you, my flesh crawled on my bones. I would have cried out, but I couldn't make a sound. The moon had gone down, and there's a great old pear tree close to the window, and it was quite dark. I sat up in my bed, shaking for fear. It was dead still, and I began to think that the fright I had got in the wood had given me a nightmare. Then the voice called again, and louder.

"'James Roberts! Open. Quick.'

"And I had to open. I leaned half out of bed, and got at the latch, and opened the window a little. I didn't dare to look out. But it was too dark to see anything in the shadow of the tree. And then she began to talk to me. She told me all about it from the beginning. She knew all the names. She knew where my business was in London, and where I lived, and who my friends were. She said that they should all know. And she said, 'And you yourself shall tell them, and you shall not be able to keep back a single word!'"

The wretched man fell back in his chair, shuddering and gasping for breath. He beat his hands up and down, with a gesture of hopeless fear and misery, and his lips grinned with dread.

I won't say that I began to see light. But I saw a hint of certain possibilities of light or, let us say, of a lessening of the darkness. I said a soothing word or two, and let him get a little more quiet. The telling of this extraordinary and very dreadful experience had set his nerves all dancing, and yet, having made a clean breast of it all, I could see that he felt some relief. His hands lay quiet on the table, and his lips ceased their horrible grimacing. He looked at me with a faint expectancy, I thought, as if he had begun to cherish a dim hope that I might have some sort of help for him. He could not see himself the possibility of rescue. Still, one never knew what resources and freedoms the other man might bring.

That, at least, was what his poor, miserable face seemed to me to express, and I hoped I was right, and let him simmer a little, and gather to himself such twigs and straws of hope as he could. Then, I began again.

"This was on the Thursday night. And last night? Another visit?"

"The same as before. Almost word for word."

"And it was all true, what she said? The girl was not lying?"

"Every word of it was true. There were some things that I had forgotten myself, but when she spoke of them, I remembered at once. There was the number of a house in a certain street, for example. If you had asked me for that number a week ago I should have told you, quite honestly, that I knew nothing about it. But when I heard it, I knew it in the instant. I could see that number in the light of a street lamp. The sky was dark and cloudy, and a bitter wind was blowing, and driving the leaves on the pavement—that November night."

"When the fire was lit?"

"That night. When they appeared."

"And you haven't seen this girl? You couldn't describe her?"

"I was afraid to look, I told you. I waited when she stopped speaking. I sat there for half an hour or an hour. Then I lit my candle and shut the window-latch. It was three o'clock and growing light."

I was thinking it over. I noted, that Roberts confessed that every word spoken by his visitant was true. She had sprung no surprises on him. There had been no suggestion of fresh details, names, or circumstances. That struck me as having a certain possible significance, and the knowledge of Roberts's present circumstances, his City address, and his home address, and the names of his friends—that was interesting, too.

There was a glimpse of a possible hypothesis. I could not be sure, but I told Roberts that I thought something might be done. To begin with, I said, I was going to keep him company for the night. Nichol would guess that I had shirked the walk home after nightfall, that would be quite all right. And in the morning he was to pay Mrs. Morgan for the two extra weeks he had arranged to stay, with something by way of compensation. "And it should be something handsome," I added with emotion, thinking of the duck and the old ale. "And then," I finished, "I shall pack you off to the other side of the island."

Of that old ale I made him drink a liberal dose by way of sleeping-draught. He hardly needed a hypnotic. The terror that he had endured and the stress of telling it had worn him out. I saw him fall into bed and fall asleep in a moment, and I curled up, comfortably enough, in a roomy armchair. There was no trouble in the night, and when I writhed myself awake, I saw Roberts sleeping peacefully. I let him alone, and wandered about the house and the shining morning garden, till I came upon Mrs. Morgan, busy in the kitchen.

I broke the trouble to her. I told her that I was afraid that the place was not agreeing at all with Mr. Roberts. "Indeed," I said, "he was taken so ill last night that I was afraid to leave him. His nerves seem to be in a very bad way."

"Indeed, then, I don't wonder at all," replied Mrs. Morgan, with a very grave face. But I wondered a good deal at this remark of hers, not having a notion as to what she meant.

I went on to explain what I had arranged for our patient, as I called him: east-coast breezes, and crowds of people, the noisier the better, and, indeed, that was the cure that I had in mind. I said that I was sure Mr. Roberts would do the proper thing.

"That will be all right, sir, I am sure. Don't you trouble yourself about that. But the sooner you get him away after I have given you both your breakfasts, the better I shall be pleased. I am frightened to death for him, I can tell you."

And she went off to her work, murmuring something that sounded like "Plant y pwll, plant y pwll."

I gave Roberts no time for reflection. I woke him up, bustled him out of bed, hurried him through his breakfast, saw him pack his suitcase, make his farewells to the Morgans, and had him sitting in the shade on Nichol's lawn well before the family were back from church. I gave Nichol a vague outline of the circumstances, nervous breakdown and so forth, introduced them to one another, and left them talking about the Black Mountains, Roberts's land of origin. The next day I saw him off at the station, on his way to Great Yarmouth, via London. I told him with an air of authority that he would have no more trouble, "from any quarter," I emphasized. And he was to write to me at my town address in a week's time.

"And, by the way," I said, Just before the train slid along the platform, "here's a bit of Welsh for you. What does 'plant y pwll' mean? Something of the pool?"

"'Plant y pwll,'" he explained, "means 'children of the pool.'"

When my holiday was ended, and I had got back to town,

I began my investigations into the case of James Roberts and his nocturnal visitant. When he began his story I was extremely distressed. I made no doubt as to the bare truth of it, and was shocked to think of a very kindly man threatened with overwhelming disgrace and disaster. There seemed nothing impossible in the tale stated at large, and in the first outline. It is not altogether unheard of for very decent men to have had a black patch in their lives, which they have done their best to live down and atone for and forget. Often enough, the explanation of such misadventure is not hard to seek. You have a young fellow, very decently but very simply brought up among simple country people, suddenly pitched into the labyrinth of London, into a maze in which there are many turnings, as the unfortunate Roberts put it, which lead to disaster, or to something blacker than disaster. The more experienced man, the man of keen instincts and perceptions, knows the aspect of these tempting passages and avoids them. Some have the wit to turn back in time, a few are caught in the trap at the end. And in some cases, though there may be apparent escape, and peace and security for many years, the teeth of the snare are about the man's leg all the while, and close at last on highly reputable chairmen and churchwardens and pillars of all sorts of seemly institutions. And then gaol, or at best, hissing and extinction.

So, on the first face of it, I was by no means prepared to pooh-pooh Robert's tale. But when he came to detail, and I had time to think it over, that entirely illogical faculty, which sometimes takes charge of our thoughts and judgments, told me that there was some huge flaw in all this, that somehow or other, things had not happened so. This mental process, I may say, is strictly indefinable and unjustifiable by any laws of thought that I have ever heard of. It won't do to take our stand with Bishop Butler, and declare with him that probability is the guide of life, deducing from this premise the conclusion that the improbable doesn't happen. Any man who cares to glance over his experience of the world and of things in general is aware that the most wildly improbable events are constantly happening. For example, I take up today's paper, sure that I shall find something to my purpose, and in a minute I come across the headline: "Damaging a Model Elephant." A father, evidently a man of substance, accuses his son of this strange offence. Last summer, the father told the court, his son constructed in their front garden a large model of an elephant, the material being bought by witness. The skeleton of the elephant was made of tubing, and it was covered with soil and fibre, and held together with wire netting. Flowers were planted on it, and it cost £3 5s.

A photograph of the elephant was produced in court, and the clerk remarked, "It is a fearsome-looking thing."

And then the catastrophe. The son got to know a married woman much older than himself, and his parents frowned, and there were quarrels. And so, one night, the young man came to his father's house, jumped over the garden wall and tried to push the elephant over. Failing, he proceeded to disembowel the elephant with a pair of wire clippers.

There! Nothing can be much more improbable than that tale, but it all happened so, as the Daily Telegraph assures me, and I believe every word of it. And I have no doubt that if I care to look I shall find something as improbable, or even more improbable, in the newspaper columns three or perhaps four times a week. What about the old man, unknown, unidentified, found in the Thames: in one pocket, a stone Buddha, in the other, a leather wallet, with the inscription: "The hen that sits on the china egg is best off?"

The improbable happens and is constantly happening, but, using that faculty which I am unable to define, I rejected Roberts's girl of the wood and the window. I did not suspect him for a moment of leg-pulling of an offensive and vicious kind. His misery and terror were too clearly manifest for that, and I was certain that he was suffering from a very serious and dreadful shock, and yet I didn't believe in the truth of the story he had told me. I felt convinced that there was no girl in the case, neither in the wood nor at the window. And when Roberts told me, with increased horror, that every word she spoke was true, that she had even reminded him of matters that he had himself forgotten, I was greatly encouraged in my growing surmise. For, it seemed to me at least probable that if the case had been such as he supposed it, there would have been new and damning circumstances in the story, utterly unknown to him and unsuspected by him. But, as it was, everything that he was told he accepted, as a man in a dream accepts without hesitation the wildest fantasies as matters and incidents of his daily experience. Decidedly, there was no girl there.

On the Sunday that he spent with me at the Wern, Nichol's place, I took advantage of his calmer condition (the night's rest had done him good) to get some facts and dates out of him, and when I returned to town, I put these to the test. It was not altogether an easy investigation since, on the surface, at least, the matters to be investigated were eminently trivial—the early days of a young man from the country up in London in a business house, and twenty-five years ago. Even really exciting murder trials and changes of ministries become blurred and uncertain in outline, if not forgotten, in twenty-five years, or in twelve years for that matter, and compared with such events, the affair of James Roberts seemed perilously like nothing at all.

However, I had made the best use I could of the information that Roberts had given me, and I was fortified for the task by a letter I received from him. He told me that there had been no recurrence of the trouble (as he expressed it), that he felt quite well, and was enjoying himself immensely at Yarmouth. He said that the shows and entertainments on the sands were doing him "no end of good. There's a retired executioner who does his old business in a tent, with the drop and everything. And there's a bloke who calls himself Archbishop of London, who fasts in a glass case, with his mitre and all his togs on." Certainly, my patient was either recovered, or in a very fair way to recovery. I could set about my researches in a calm spirit of scientific curiosity, without the nervous tension of the surgeon called upon at short notice to perform a life-or-death operation.

As a matter of fact it was all more simple than I thought it would be. True, the results were nothing, or almost nothing, but that was exactly what I had expected and hoped. With the slight sketch of his early career in London, furnished me by Roberts, the horrors omitted by my request, with a name or two and a date or two, I got along very well. And what did it come to? Simply this: here was a lad, he was just seventeen, who had been brought up amongst lonely hills and educated at a small grammar school, furnished through a London uncle with a very small stool in a City office. By arrangement, settled after a long and elaborate correspondence, he was to board with some distant cousins, who lived in the Cricklewood-Kilburn-Brondesbury region, and with them he settled down, comfortably enough, as it seemed, though Cousin Ellen objected to his learning to smoke in his bedroom, and begged him to desist. The household consisted of Cousin Ellen, her husband, Henry Watts, and the two daughters, Helen and Justine. Justine was about Robert's own age, Helen three or four years older. Mr. Watts had married rather late in life, and had retired from his office a year or so before. He interested himself chiefly in tuberous-rooted begonias, and in the season went out a few miles to his cricket club Pool watched the game on Saturday afternoons. Every morning there was breakfast at eight, every evening there was high tea at seven, and in the meantime young Roberts did his best in the City, and liked his job well enough. He was shy with the two girls at first, but Justine was lively, and couldn't help having a voice like a peacock, and Helen was adorable. And so things went on very pleasantly for a year or perhaps eighteen months, on this basis, that Justine was a great joke, and that Helen was adorable. The trouble was that Justine didn't think she was a great joke.

For, it must be said that Roberts's stay with his cousins ended in disaster. I rather gather that the young man and the quiet Helen were guilty of, shall we say, amiable indiscretions, though without serious consequences. But it appeared that Cousin Justine, a girl with black eyes and black hair, made discoveries which she resented savagely, denouncing the offenders at the top of that piercing voice of hers, in the waste hours of the Brondesbury night, to the immense rage, horror, and consternation of the whole house. In fact, there was the devil to pay, and Mr. Watts then and there turned young Roberts out of the house. And there is no doubt that he should have been thoroughly ashamed of himself. But young men…

Nothing very much happened. Old Watts had cried in his rage that he would let Roberts's chief in the City hear the whole story, but, on reflection, he held his tongue. Roberts roamed about London for the rest of the night, refreshing himself occasionally at coffee-stalls. When the shops opened, he had a wash and brush-up, and was prompt and bright at his office. At midday, in the underground smoking-room of the tea-shop, he conferred with a fellow clerk over their dominoes, and arranged to share rooms with him out Norwood way. From that point onwards, the career of James Roberts had been eminently quiet, uneventful, successful.

Now, everybody, I suppose, is aware that in recent years the silly business of divination by dreams has ceased to be a joke and has become a very serious science. It is called "Psychoanalysis," and is compounded, I would say, by mingling one grain of sense with a hundred of pure nonsense. From the simplest and most obvious dreams, the psychoanalyst deduces the most incongruous and extravagant results. A black savage tells him that he has dreamed of being chased by lions, or, maybe, by crocodiles, and the psycho man knows at once that the black is suffering from the Œdipus complex. That is, he is madly in love with his own mother, and is, therefore, afraid of the vengeance of his father. Everybody knows, of course, that "lion" and "crocodile" are symbols of "father." And I understand that there are educated people who believe this stuff.

It is all nonsense, to be sure, and so much the greater nonsense inasmuch as the true interpretation of many dreams—not by any means of all dreams—moves, it may be said, in the opposite direction to the method of psychoanalysis. The psychoanalyst infers the monstrous and abnormal from a trifle. It is often safe to reverse the process. If a man dreams that he has committed a sin before which the sun hid his face, it is often safe to conjecture that, in sheer forgetfulness, he wore a red tie, or brown boots with evening dress. A slight dispute with the vicar may deliver him in sleep into the clutches of the Spanish Inquisition, and the torment of a fiery death. Failure to catch the post with a rather important letter will sometimes bring a great realm to ruin in the world of dreams. And here, I have no doubt, we have the explanation of part of the explanation of the Roberts affair. Without question, he had been a bad boy. There was something more than a trifle at the heart of his trouble. But his original offence, grave as we may think it, had in his hidden consciousness, swollen and exaggerated itself into a monstrous mythology of evil. Some time ago, a learned and curious investigator demonstrated how Coleridge had taken a bald sentence from an old chronicler, and had made it the nucleus of *The Ancient Mariner*. With a vast gesture of the spirit, he had unconsciously gathered from all the four seas of his vast reading all manner of creatures into his net, till the bare hint of the old book glowed into one of the great masterpieces of the world's poetry. Roberts had nothing in him of the poetic faculty, nothing of the shaping power of the imagination, no trace of the gift of expression, by which the artist delivers his soul of its burden. In him, as in many men, there was a great gulf fixed between the hidden and the open consciousness, so that which could not come out into the light grew and swelled secretly, hugely, horribly in the darkness. If Roberts had been a poet or a painter or a musician, we might have had a masterpiece. As he was neither, we had a monster. And I do not at all believe that his years had consciously been vexed by a deep sense of guilt. I gathered in the course of my researches that not long after the flight from Brondesbury, Roberts was made aware of unfortunate incidents in the Watts saga, if we may use this honoured term, which convinced him that there were extenuating circumstances in his offence, and excuses for his wrongdoing. The actual fact had, no doubt, been forgotten or remembered very slightly, rarely, casually, without any sense of grave moment or culpability attached to it, while, all the while, a pageantry of horror was being secretly formed in the hidden places of the man's soul. And at last, after the years of growth and swelling in the darkness, the monster leapt into the light, and with such violence that to the victim it seemed an actual and objective entity.

And, in a sense, it had risen from the black waters of the pool. I was reading a few days ago, in a review of a grave book on psychology, the following very striking sentences:

> The things which we distinguish as qualities or values are inherent in the real environment to make the configuration that they do make with our sensory response to them. There is such a thing as a "sad" landscape, even when we who look at it are feeling jovial, and if we think it is "sad" only because we attribute to it something derived from our own past associations with sadness, Professor Koffka gives us good reason to regard the view as superficial. That is not imputing human attributes to what are described as "demand characters" in the environment, but giving proper recognition to the other end of a nexus, of which only one

end is organised in our own mind.

Psychology is, I am sure, a difficult and subtle science, which, perhaps naturally, must be expressed in subtle and difficult language. But so far as I can gather the sense of the passage which I have quoted, it comes to this: that a landscape, a certain configuration of wood, water, height and depth, light and dark, flower and rock, is, in fact, an objective reality, a thing, just as opium and wine are things, not clotted fancies, mere creatures of our make-believe, to which we give a kind of spurious reality and efficacy. The dreams of De Quincey were a synthesis of De Quincey, plus opium. The riotous gaiety of Charles Surface and his friends was the product and result of the wine they had drunk, plus their personalities. So, the profound Professor Koffka (his book is called *Principles of Gestalt Psychology*) insists that the "sadness" which we attribute to a particular landscape is really and efficiently in the landscape and not merely in ourselves, and consequently that the landscape can affect us and produce results in us, in precisely the same manner as drugs and meat and drink affect us in their several ways. Poe, who knew many secrets, knew this, and taught that landscape gardening was as truly a fine art as poetry or painting, since it availed to communicate the mysteries to the human spirit.

And perhaps, Mrs. Morgan of Lanypwll Farm put all this much better in the speech of symbolism, when she murmured about the children of the pool. For if there is a landscape of sadness, there is certainly also a landscape of a horror of darkness and evil, and that black and oily depth, overshadowed with twisted woods, with its growth of foul weeds and, its dead trees and leprous boughs was assuredly potent in terror. To Roberts it was a strong drug, a drag of evocation, the black deep without calling to the black deep within, and summoning the inhabitant thereof to come forth. I made no attempt to extract the legend of that dark place from Mrs. Morgan, and I do not suppose that she would have been communicative if I had questioned her. But it has struck me as possible, and even probable that Roberts was by no means the first to experience the power of the pool. Old stories often turn out to be true.

THE WATER SPECTRE

by Francis Lathom

Muchardus, the usurping Thane of Dungivan, had murdered Roderic the late owner of that title, whom he had treacherously invited to an entertainment in a castle that he possessed on the banks of the Clyde. As soon as the banquet was nearly concluded, Roderic arose, courteously took leave of his entertainer and his guests, and descended the stairs. But he was not allowed to quit Boswell Castle. His faithful followers had been previously dispatched, and buried in one of the vaults beneath the edifice. To one of these, which was formed into a kind of dungeon, the hapless Roderic was forcibly dragged, and fastened to the stone wall by an iron chain.

Three days and nights did the unfortunate Roderic remain in this wretched lodging, his bed the cold ground, with oaten cake and water for food, and this vile treatment he received from one on whom he had heaped innumerable favours, and honoured with his confidence.

On the fourth night of Roderic's dreadful confinement, Muchardus entered his dungeon. In one hand he carried a written paper, in the other a dagger. The man who had always brought Roderic's food, carried a torch before the recreant lord. Roderic surveyed his foe with silent indignation.

After a pause of a few minutes, Muchardus presented to the Thane the paper which he had brought, and desired him to peruse it with attention. He did so, and found it to be drawn up as a will, by which he bequeathed to his treacherous friend all his vast possessions, and the Thaneship of Dungivan.

"For what vile purpose have you brought me this infamous scroll?" demanded the Thane.

"By signing that paper," replied Muchardus, "you will preserve your existence. Liberty, 'tis true, I cannot grant you, consistent with my own designs and safety, yet you shall be secreted in the best apartment my castle affords, and every wish you can form, that will not tend to a discovery of your still being an inhabitant of this world, shall be attended to with the most scrupulous exactness."

The Thane's eyes darted fire at this disclosure of the premeditated villainy of Muchardus, and he tore the paper to atoms.

The enraged Muchardus flew towards his victim, and repeatedly plunged his dagger in his breast, till, with a heavy groan, he fell, and expired at the feet of his murderer.

Muchardus then left the dungeon, and returned to his own apartment, where he employed one of his emissaries, whom he had sworn to secrecy, to draw up another paper of the same purport as that which the Thane had destroyed. Muchardus had several papers in his possession, which had been written by Roderic, and to most of them his signature was affixed. This they copied with great exactness, and then prepared to reap the fruits of their wicked design.

The corpse of the murdered Thane was taken ere the dawn of day, and flung into a briery dell, where it was left, having been previously stripped of every article of value.

The absence of the Thane and his attendants from the Castle

of Dungivan, had caused a very serious alarm to his vassals and adherents, who had made many unsuccessful researches in the mountains, and inquired at every habitation, if they could give any tidings of their lord, but no one had seen the Thane since the day he went to Boswell Castle.

Some days after the murder had been committed, the body of the Thane was found in the dell, by some huntsmen, who were led to the spot by the sagacity of their hounds. The marks of violence on his person, and his being despoiled of the property about it, which was known to have been of great value on that fatal day, as he had arrayed himself most sumptuously, and put on a variety of ornaments to honour the banquet of Muchardus, led the persons interested in the discovery, to conjecture that his attendants had murdered him, and made off with the booty. And as their bodies could no where be found, the report strengthened every day. Nor was Muchardus in the least suspected of the murder.

That chief having proceeded so far with a success equal to his most sanguine wishes, hastened to put the finishing blow to his manoeuvres. He carried the forged will to be placed in a drawer in one of the chambers where he was sure it would not be overlooked. It was accordingly found by persons empowered to search for the papers of the deceased. Muchardus was accordingly declared sole heir of the late Thane of Dungivan: not much to the surprise of any person, as the great intimacy between him and Roderic had been so apparent, yet they greatly regretted the change, as the tyrannical disposition of Muchardus was too well known, and often experienced by those whom fortune had placed under him.

Muchardus (now Thane of Dungivan) had attained the height of his ambition, yet his pillow was strewed with mental thorns. Ah! How unlike the prosperity of the good man! Conscience, from whose reproaches we cannot flee, perpetually reminded him of his crimes, and made him shudder with apprehension, lest retributive vengeance should overtake his guilty head.

The late Thane married, in early youth, a most beauteous lady, the heiress of a neighbouring chieftain. With her he fondly hoped for many years of happiness, but his hopes were vain; the peerless Matilda expired in giving birth to her first born, the lovely Donald, the traitor Muchardus being one of the sponsors that answered for his faith at the font.

Two years passed on, and the widowed Thane still indulged his grief, undiminished by the lapse of time. Muchardus artfully endeavoured to learn the sentiments of his friend, as far as regarded his re-engaging in matrimonial ties. To his great, though concealed satisfaction, he heard from Dungivan, that he had solemnly vowed never to take a second bride, but to cherish a tender remembrance of his Matilda, and pray for a reunion with her in those realms of bliss where the pangs of separation should be unknown.

Muchardus had for some time past viewed the possessions of Dungivan with a coveting eye, and he thought it feasible to obtain the Thaneship by the murder of the father and son, as they had no near relatives to make a claim. After much deliberation, he concluded that it would be most prudent to remove the child first from this world, as, in case of the death of the Thane preceding that of Donald, the latter might be placed out of his reach.

Annie, the young woman who nursed the little Lord, was walking on the banks of the Clyde, when she was seized by four men masked and armed, who tore Donald from her arms. Two of them ran off with the child, and the other two bound Annie to a tree, and then followed their companions. The length of time that his son was absent alarmed the Thane, and he sent some of the domestics to search for Annie and her charge, and require their immediate return.

They soon discovered the nurse, and heard her dismal

story. They led her back to the castle in an agony of grief, and acquainted the Thane with the tidings. He tore his hair, and rent his garments. Nor would he listen to the consolations that Muchardus seemed so eager to administer.

Various conjectures were formed who could be the perpetrator of such a deed, but no one, upon mature reflection, appeared feasible.

The Thane had not, to his knowledge, an enemy existing, for his demeanour had been goodwill to all. Nor did he conceive how any person, as he had no immediate heir, could be benefitted by the death or removal of his son. Alas! He clasped to his bosom as a chosen friend, his deadly foe, the cause of all his sorrow: for it was Muchardus that had employed ruffians to seize young Donald.

Allan, the man who was trusted with the management of this vile plot, was ordered by his employer, to take the child and precipitate him into the Clyde as soon as he had got rid of the men who were joined with him in the enterprise.

Allan took the young Lord to his cottage, where he intended to secrete him till the surrounding objects were enveloped in the gloom of night, and then execute the horrid design which he had pledged his faith to commit. When he entered his humble habitation, he found Jannette, his wife, bitterly lamenting over the corpse of her son, their only child. When Allan departed in the morning, he had left the young Ambrose playing before the door of the cottage, with the rose of health glowing on his cheeks. A few hours after, death had seized his victim, and on the father's return, he found himself bereft of his only hope. Nor did he fail to attribute this calamity as the vengeance of an offended God. He felt what it was to lose a child, and he pitied the sufferings that the Thane must endure.

"They are more than my own," ejaculated the now penitent Allan, "I know the end of mine, but the poor Lord is uncertain what is the fate of his at this moment.

"But tomorrow," continued Allan, after a pause, in which he recollected the injunctions of his employer, "tomorrow thy corpse will, perhaps, be discovered floating in the Clyde, and his apprehensions will be confirmed by a horrid reality."

"You will not, surely, murder this sweet babe," exclaimed Jannette in agony, and clasped the young Donald to her breast.

"I must," said Allan, "I have sworn. Behold the price of my villainy," emptying the contents of a well-filled purse on the table, "and I am to have as much more when Lord Muchardus is convinced that the deed is executed."

"I will not part with him," said Jannette, "he shall supply the place of my child. You have been very wicked, Allan, but you are not yet a murderer. The children are nearly of a size, nor are their features much different, only the heir of Dungivan is so beautifully fair, and our Ambrose is nearly olive. Yet that will not be when the poor babe has lain in the water."

"What mean you?" said Allan, who instantly comprehended and applauded the plan which she had in part expressed.

Jannette gave the young Donald some food, and exchanging his apparel for some belonging to her own deceased baby, she lulled him asleep, and placing him in the cradle of his predecessor, she began to prepare her design.

She dressed her lifeless infant in the costly robes which had been worn by the heir of Dungivan, placing also the ornaments of that nobleman about the little corpse, only reserving a gold chain with a small miniature of the Thane attached to it, and which hanging loosely round the neck, might well be supposed to have dropt off in the water. As soon as it was dark, Allan went and flung the child into the river Clyde, accompanying the act with many heartfelt tears and sorrowful lamentations.

Jannette, most fortunately for their plan, had not mentioned to any of the neighbouring cottagers the death of her Ambrose. Under the pretence of the child's being afflicted with a contagious disease, she contrived to keep him in the upper chamber of her cottage, from which she so completely excluded the light, that, if anyone entered by chance, it was impossible to discover the deceit that had been practised.

The body of the infant was not discovered till the third day, when it was brought on shore by some young men who had been out in a boat fishing. It was soon recognized by the dress to be the young Lord Donald, (for the features were not now discernible), and was conveyed to the Castle of Dungivan. The Thane was overwhelmed with despair. He ordered a sumptuous funeral, and then immured himself in a solitary apartment of the north tower.

Allan waited on Muchardus to claim his promised reward, which he gave him, with much praise for his adroitness in performing his commands. Allan then repaired to Jannette, and gathering together what they wished to convey with them, left the cottage at the dead of night, and procured a conveyance to Perth, from whence they meant to travel to some remote part of Scotland, where they might dwell in safety, for they were not without fear of Muchardus, as they supposed that he would devise schemes to annihilate all those who were acquainted with his atrocities. Nor were their conjectures ill-founded. Muchardus rested not till he had removed those whose aid he had purchased with his gold, and he felt great disappointment on discovering that Allan had escaped with safety. To murder the Thane was the next purpose of Muchardus, but while he was deliberating on the best means to facilitate his design with safety to his own person, Dungivan was suddenly ordered to attend his monarch to England, where he was going to ratify some agreement he had entered into with the monarch of that kingdom, and the schemes of his treacherous friend were at that time defeated.

After passing some time in England, the Thane of Dungivan joined the Crusaders, and repaired to the Holy Land, where he performed wonders with his single arm against infidels. He passed sixteen years in foreign countries ere he revisited his native place, which he did with a determination to domesticate there in peace for the remainder of his days.

He was yet in the prime of his age, and his valour had made him an object of esteem and admiration. All the neighbouring nobility gave splendid entertainments in honour of his return. Among the rest, Muchardus, with whom he had instantly renewed the friendship of their youth, was not slow in preparing the banquet, and planning the death of his unsuspecting guest.

The manner in which Muchardus obtained his ill-acquired grandeur has already been described, but he was not happy. To divert his thoughts from dwelling on the past events of his life, which were not of a nature to bear retrospection, he resolved to marry. There was an heiress of great property, who had been consigned to his guardianship by her deceased father. The beauty of Lady Catharine fascinated his senses, while her accumulating wealth held out a lure to his avarice, and fondness for ostentatious parade. Muchardus was still handsome; few men were more indebted to nature for the gifts she had so lavishly bestowed on him. His countenance was formed to command, but the tyrannical passions and habits he had for many years imbibed, sometimes spread over his features a fierceness almost terrific. Lady Catharine beheld him with a fixed aversion. Two years she had resided at Dungivan, and had witnessed enough of his disposition to make her shrink with terror, and daily deplore the infatuation by which her parent was blinded, when he chose the Thane daring her minority.

At this period, Caledonia was much governed by the influence of the Weird Sisters. From the birth of young Donald, they had resolved to protect him, and work his weal, and the woe of his father's murderer.

Allan had long since lost his Jannette. He beheld Donald with the most fervent affection. The noble and heroic mind of the youth often called forth his wonder and admiration.

A native dignity, that adorned his soul, was not subdued by present poverty, or the small expectations he had of acquiring any worldly wealth. Allan could not subdue the regret that constantly arose when Donald met his view. He wished to see him fill the place in society which was his right, but his fears, and the improbability of his tale being believed, made him bury the secret in his bosom.

He had been very successful in the tilling of a small farm, which he had purchased with part of the money which Muchardus had given him as a reward for the supposed murder of the child. All the savings which arose from this source were hoarded for Donald, for he had always retained that appellation from the time of his protectors leaving the precincts of Dungivan. The youth was now in his twentieth year, and the above-mentioned savings Allan was debating with himself how he could best lay out for the benefit of Donald, when he received an intimation from one of the Weird Sisters, that he was to return with his young charge to the banks of the Clyde. Allan disposed of his farm, and obeyed the commands he had received, and he was once more settled in a cottage among the mountains of Dungivan, and heard with horror of the murder of the late Thane, which, from the proofs he had already had of the villainy of the present one, he was not slow in attributing to him.

Time had silvered over the head of Allan, and so altered his person, that no one recognized him as Allan, under the name he thought it now expedient with his own safety to assume. According to the instructions he had received from the Weird Sisters, he repaired to all the neighbouring Thanes, and made an avowal of the transaction in which he had been engaged with respect to the heir of Dungivan, and the way he was preserved by Jannette's interposition.

A particular mark, which Allan asserted to be on the back of Donald's neck, was well known to several of the nobles, who had heard it remarked while the heir was yet in his infancy. This, and several other convincing circumstances, placed his identity beyond a doubt, but none of them were willing to make an enemy of the fierce Muchardus, whose power and undaunted exploits had effectually awed the neighbouring chieftains from interfering in his concerns. Nor could all the endeavours of the aged Allan raise the hapless youth one friend to assert his rights, and the poor old man soon expired under the pressure of the regret that he experienced.

Donald was ignorant of these applications, and the purport of them, for Allan had never disclosed to him the nobleness of his birth. He knew his lofty spirit would not suffer him to sink into silent obscurity while an usurper enjoyed his domains. And what could his single arm effect against his deadliest foe, who would inevitably hurl him to destruction?

Though none of the chieftains would engage in the cause of the orphan, yet their converse on the subject was not carried on so secretly, but that it reached the ears of Muchardus, and gave him the most dire apprehensions, though he openly derided the report as a most absurd imposture.

Anxious to know if he should possess his guilty honours un-molested, and win the love of the beauteous Lady Catharine, he resolved to seek the Weird Sisters. For this purpose he left Dungivan Castle, attended by Sandy, the only domestic he took with him, and repaired to a forest near the cave of Fingal, where the mysterious Sisters were said to resort, and perform their midnight orgies.

When he approached the spot, he directed Sandy to wait his return at the foot of a large tree, which he pointed out to his notice. He then proceeded fearfully on. The soul of the Thane was appalled. The wind rose to a tremendous height, the thunder rolled over his head, and the blue lightning flashed in his face. Terror-struck, he resolved to give up his design of visiting the Sisters, but he had lost the path which led back to the castle, and he wandered he knew not whither. Now and then he beheld a faint light, which he hoped proceeded from the cave of some anchorite, where he could obtain shelter.

He soon came to a rock, in the hollow of which was a door partly open, whence issued a pale gleam of light. The door flew back at his touch, and he entered a misty cavern. The light increased to a supernatural brightness, and in a few moments the Weird Sisters appeared, and saluted him with a discordant voice.

"Hail! We know what brought thee here.
Wicked chieftain, shake with fear,
The assassin shuns his downy head
Can he shun the restless dead?
No, while in the forest drear,
Roderic, rise, and meet him here!
And the wounds he gave display.
Remorse be his by night and day."

The mysterious Sisters then severally requested what he sought to know. "Ask! Require! Demand!" exclaimed the Weird Beings.

Muchardus inquired if he should perish by an avenging sword.

The first Sister replied, "That no human power should harm Muchardus."

He then demanded who was next to enjoy the domains of Dungivan.

The second Sister answered, "That the lawful heir of the murdered Roderic, and his bride, Lady Catharine, the peerless rose of the Clyde, would succeed him."

Muchardus's heart appeared to die within him at these words, and it was not till the third Sister again repeated the question, of what he sought to know, that he recovered sufficiently to ask how many years of his existence still remained.

The bearded sister would not give an explicit answer to this important question, but remarked to him, that he had once seen the apparition of the murdered Roderic.

Muchardus, while his frame trembled with horror at the recollection of the appalling scene he had witnessed in one of the galleries of the castle, faintly replied in the affirmative.

"Mark me then," said the witch, "you will not survive the third appearance of the dreadful spectre."

The sisters then vanished from his view and Muchardus, affrighted at the gloom (for the witches had left him in total darkness), was going to quit the cave with precipitation, when the murdered Roderic stood before him, and intercepted his progress.

Muchardus gazed on the hairy form with the greatest agony, till a chilling sweat bedewed his forehead. His limbs failed him, and he fell senseless on the floor of the cave.

In this situation he was found by Sandy, who alarmed by the Thane's long absence, ventured from his leafy shelter, as soon as the storm had abated, to seek him in which charitable design he succeeded with some difficulty, and was much terrified with meeting the Weird Sisters in his path, who maliciously diverted themselves with exciting his fears, and then suffered him to proceed.

He found his master just recovering from a death-like swoon. He assisted him to rise, and Muchardus, having glanced his eye around, and, to his great relief, perceiving no spectre, exerted himself to leave the horrid cave, and was led by Sandy to the Castle, where he retired to his splendid couch the most miserable of human beings.

Donald, since the death of Allan, his supposed parent, had remained in his cottage, as he had not yet met with the opportunity he coveted of embracing a military life.

In his solitary walks about the mountains, he frequently met Lady Catharine, and her attendant, Moggy Cameron. A fervent passion for the noble fair one took possession of his bosom, and he reasoned with himself in vain against its increasing influence, for Love, that leveller of rank, was constantly inspiring him with hope.

Lady Catharine was not insensible to the attentions of Donald, and she often breathed forth a secret prayer that he had been of equal birth with herself.

Near five weeks had elapsed since their first casual meeting, when one morning the Lady Catharine being with some of her attendants on the Clyde, in a small sailing-boat, a sudden gust of wind upset it, and the fair lady was precipitated into the water, Donald, who had been walking on the banks for some time, and surveying the lovely Catharine with delight, as the vessel slowly glided along, immediately saw her danger, and plunged into the stream to snatch her from impending death. He happily succeeded in bearing his lovely burthen safe to the shore, and led her till they arrived at the castle gates, where he abruptly left her, ere she could express her thanks for the service he had rendered so opportunely.

From this auspicious day, gratitude, united to love, created for Donald a strong interest in her heart, yet prudence bade her avoid him. There was no prospect that the prejudices which her friends would entertain against such a suitor, could be overcome, and she resolved to spare him and herself, if possible from the pangs of a hopeless passion.

Donald no longer met her in his walks. He felt the change in her behaviour most severely, and became a votary of sorrow and despair, courting the influence of these passions in the still hours of the night, wandering among precipices and dreary forests. Chance led him to the cave where Muchardus had obtained an audience with the Weird Sisters, about an hour after that Thane had quitted it. The Sisters again appeared. Instead of cringing to them with the abject servility of Dungivan's usurping lord, he demanded with some sternness, what they wanted with him. But his asperity was soon transformed into profound respect, when they expressed their solicitude for his weal, and claimed his attention to what they had to impart.

The eldest of the Weird Sisters then gave a concise account of the crimes of the present Thane, and informed Donald that he was at that time plotting his destruction, being in dread of his revenge, and his gaining the affections of Lady Catharine.

The Weird Sisters then joined in admonishing him as to his future conduct, and one of them delivered to Donald a white silk flag, on which were woven some mysterious characters. This, she told him, would once, and once only, be of singular service to him in extreme danger, and that being the case, she exhorted him not to try its efficacy till all other resources had failed, and his own exertions proved abortive.

Donald took a courteous leave of the bounteous Sisters, and repaired to his cottage in a far different frame of mind from that he had ever experienced before. His birth was noble worthy of Lady Catharine, and he felt that it was possible for time and perseverance to bestow on him a happiness which the preceding day he had regarded as unattainable.

The next day he was informed by a person who had a sincere regard for his safety that the Thane had discovered him to be the lawful heir of the domain, and had privately suborned persons to assassinate him, not assigning the true reason for that horrid design, but charging him with the attempt to seduce Lady Catharine from her duty, by persuading her to leave the castle of her guardian, and share a beggar's fate. That lady, the informant added, was now strictly confined within the circle of her own apartments, and forced to listen to the hateful addresses of the Thane.

Donald, on receiving this intimation, thought it most prudent to leave his present habitation, and repair to the court of King Malcolm, and submit the case to him. In searching the papers of the deceased Allan, he discovered a written attestation of the deceit he had practised to save the infant's life, describing some particular marks of fruit he had on his body, together with the chain he wore round his neck, which was now fastened to the paper.

These proofs were very consoling to Donald, and made him commence his journey with more alacrity, and by the noon of the day on which he set out, he had travelled many miles. The heat of the midday sun greatly incommoded him, and he grew faint and weary.

A neat cottage presented itself to view, and he knocked at the door to request admittance, that he might rest till the cool of the evening. This the loquacious hostess denied him, and during his expostulations with her on the subject, she unguardedly betrayed to his knowledge, that her inhospitable refusal was owing to her having sheltered Lady Catharine, who had escaped from the Castle to her humble roof, she having been led hither by her attendant, Moggy Cameron, who was daughter to the cottager.

Donald had betrayed so much emotion during the recital, that the good dame, alarmed at the consequences that might ensue from her communicating so much to a stranger, entered the dwelling, and closed the door.

Donald, hurt at her manner, and disappointed at not obtaining an interview with Lady Catharine, to whom he wished to impart the intelligence he had received from the Weird Sisters, and worn out by fatigue, fainted at the door of the cottage. The noise he made in falling, brought its inmates to his relief, and Lady Catharine instantly recognized her faithful Donald. He soon revived, and the fair one had just listened with pleasing surprise to his narrative, when a party of Muchardus's soldiers, who had been sent in pursuit of the fugitives, arrived, and conveyed the lovers to the Castle, where Donald was confined in a dungeon, and Sandy, having interfered in the behalf of the young lord, was also made a prisoner, and guards were set over them. But, by a successful stratagem of Moggy, who intoxicated their keepers, and procured the keys, they were liberated, and quitted the Castle walls.

By the direction of Moggy, they repaired to an isolated building about two miles from Dungivan, and in less than an hour they were joined by Lady Catharine and her attendants, they having escaped from the spies which Muchardus had set round them, by means of a subterraneous winding, which led from the stairs of the north tower to a grotto that terminated one of the avenues of the Castle grounds.

They proceeded in their flight for two days unmolested when, alas! they were again taken in the toils, and the Thane in person headed the pursuers.

As soon as they arrived at the Castle, Muchardus ordered some of his followers to take young Donald to the cave of Fingal (a long subterraneous passage cut through a rock, and filled with a branch of the river), in a boat, and destroy him. In vain Catharine knelt, and besought him to avert the sentence. He was inexorable, and the fair one, frantic with despair, rushed out of the Castle ere the Thane had time to intercept her progress. Sandy, who had attentively watched her, followed, and by her directions procured a boat, and repaired with her to the cave of Fingal. They arrived there first, and securing the boat in one of the inlets, Lady Catharine hid herself behind a projection of the rock, to watch the actions of the Thane, who soon arrived in a boat only, attended by the man who handled the oars. Contrary to the expectations of Catharine, Muchardus suspected her being in the cave, and soon discovered her hiding place, from which he dragged her into his boat, just at the instant that the one in which Donald and his intended assassins were sitting, entered the place pitched on for the scene of his destruction.

Catharine, in her struggles to get from the Thane fell into the water, and would have perished, but for the activity of Sandy, who succeeded in replacing her in the boat which had conveyed her hither, while Donald, who was a confined spectator of the accident, was almost senseless with despair.

The Thane now offered to grant Donald his life, if he would renounce his presumptuous claim, and the hand of Lady Catharine. But the youth rejected the proposal with the scorn it merited. A secret impulse made Muchardus wish to save the youth's life, if he could consistent with his own terms, and he vowed to release him, and provide for his future weal, if Lady Catharine would instantly become his bride, and resign all thought of Donald. She gave an heroic refusal, and the enraged Thane ordered the assassins to strangle their victim. Struggles were of no avail. The youth remembered the injunctions of the Weird Sisters, and waved the flag three times in the air. The Spectre of his Sire arose in the midst of the water, and pronounced the doom of his vile murderer, who sank with the boat and perished.

Donald was instantly conveyed with Lady Catharine back to the Castle, where the most lively transports of joy took place among the domestics at receiving the son of Roderic for their lord, for they had groaned under the tyranny of Muchardus.

Donald found no difficulty in getting his title acknowledged by his sovereign, and his union with the fair Catharine was productive of the utmost felicity to themselves and their off-spring.

THE WILLOWS

by Algernon Blackwood

I

After leaving Vienna, and long before you come to Buda-Pesth, the Danube enters a region of singular loneliness and desolation, where its waters spread away on all sides regardless of a main channel, and the country becomes a swamp for miles upon miles, covered by a vast sea of low willow bushes. On the big maps this deserted area is painted in a fluffy blue, growing fainter in color as it leaves the banks, and across it may be seen in large straggling letters the word *Sümpfe*, meaning marshes.

In high flood this great acreage of sand, shingle-beds, and willow-grown islands is almost topped by the water, but in normal seasons the bushes bend and rustle in the free winds, showing their silver leaves to the sunshine in an ever-moving plain of bewildering beauty. These willows never attain to the dignity of trees; they have no rigid trunks; they remain humble bushes, with rounded tops and soft outline, swaying on slender stems that answer to the least pressure of the wind; supple as grasses, and so continually shifting that they somehow give the impression that the entire plain is moving and alive. For the wind sends waves rising and falling over the whole surface, waves of leaves instead of waves of water, green swells like the sea, too, until the branches turn and lift, and then silvery white as their under-side turns to the sun.

Happy to slip beyond the control of stern banks, the Danube here wanders about at will among the intricate network of channels intersecting the islands everywhere with broad avenues down which the waters pour with a shouting sound, making whirlpools, eddies, and foaming rapids, tearing at the sandy banks, carrying away masses of shore and willow-clumps, and forming new islands innumerable which shift daily in size and shape and possess at best an impermanent life, since the flood-time obliterates their very existence.

Properly speaking, this fascinating part of the river's life begins soon after leaving Pressburg, and we, in our Canadian canoe, with gipsy tent and frying-pan on board, reached it on the crest of a rising flood about mid-July. That very same morning, when the sky was reddening before sunrise, we had slipped swiftly through still-sleeping Vienna, leaving it a couple of hours later a mere patch of smoke against the blue hills of the Wienerwald on the horizon. We had breakfasted below Fischeramend under a grove of birch trees roaring in the wind, and had then swept on the tearing current past Orth, Hainburg, Petronell (the old Roman Carnuntum of Marcus Aurelius), and so under the frowning heights of Theben on a spur of the Carpathians, where the March steals in quietly from the left and the frontier is crossed between Austria and Hungary.

Racing along at twelve kilometers an hour soon took us well into Hungary, and the muddy waters—sure sign of flood— sent us aground on many a shingle-bed, and twisted us like a cork in many a sudden belching whirlpool before the towers of Pressburg (Hungarian, Poszóny) showed against the sky, and then the canoe, leaping like a spirited horse, flew at top speed under the gray walls, negotiated safely the sunken chain of the Fliegende Brücke ferry, turned the corner sharply to the left, and plunged on yellow foam into the wilderness of islands, sand-banks, and swamp-land beyond—the land of the willows.

The change came suddenly, as when a series of bioscope pictures snaps down on the streets of a town and shifts without warning into the scenery of lake and forest. We entered the land of desolation on wings, and in less than half an hour there was neither boat nor fishing-hut nor red roof, nor any single sign of human habitation and civilization within sight. The sense of remoteness from the world of human kind, the utter isolation, the fascination of this singular world of willows, winds, and waters, instantly laid its spell upon us both, so that we allowed laughingly to one another that we ought by rights to have held some special kind of passport to admit us, and that we had, somewhat audaciously, come without asking leave into a separate little kingdom of wonder and magic—a kingdom that was reserved for the use of others who had a right to it, with everywhere unwritten warnings to trespassers for those who had the imagination to discover them.

Though still early in the afternoon, the ceaseless buffetings of a most tempestuous wind made us feel weary, and we at once began casting about for a suitable camping ground for the night. But the bewildering character of the islands made landing difficult; the swirling flood carried us in-shore and then swept us out again. The willow branches tore our hands as we seized them to stop the canoe, and we pulled many a yard of sandy bank into the water before at length we shot with a great sideways blow from the wind into a backwater and managed to beach the bows in a cloud of spray. Then we lay panting and laughing after our exertions on hot yellow sand, sheltered from the wind, and in the full blaze of a scorching sun, a cloudless blue sky above, and an immense army of dancing, shouting willow bushes, closing in from all sides, shining with spray and clapping their thousand little hands as though to applaud the success of our efforts.

"What a river!" I said to my companion, thinking of all the way we had traveled from the source in the Black Forest, and how we had often been obliged to wade and push in the upper shallows at the beginning of June.

"Won't stand much nonsense now, will it?" he said, pulling the canoe a little farther into safety up the sand, and then composing himself for a nap.

I lay by his side, happy and peaceful in the bath of the elements—water, wind, sand, and the great fire of the sun—thinking of the long journey that lay behind us, and of the great stretch before us to the Black Sea, and how lucky I was to have such a delightful and charming traveling companion as my friend, the Swede.

We had made many similar journeys together, but the Danube, more than any other river I knew, impressed us from the very beginning with its aliveness. From its tiny bubbling entry into the world among the pinewood gardens of Donaueschingen, until this moment when it began to play the great river-game of losing itself among the deserted swamps, unobserved, unrestrained, it had seemed to us like following the growth of some living creature. Sleepy at first, but later developing violent desires as it became conscious of its deep soul, it rolled, like some huge fluid being, through all the countries we had passed, holding our little craft on its mighty shoulders, playing roughly with us sometimes, yet always friendly and well-meaning, till at length we had come inevitably to regard it as a Great Personage.

How, indeed, could it be otherwise, since it told us so much of its secret life? At night we heard it singing to the moon as we lay in our tent, uttering that odd sibilant note peculiar to itself and said to be caused by the rapid tearing of the pebbles along its bed, so great is its hurrying speed. We knew, too, the voice of its gurgling whirlpools, suddenly bubbling up on a surface previously quite calm, the roar of its shallows and swift rapids, its constant steady thundering below all mere surface sounds, and that ceaseless tearing of its icy waters at the banks. How it stood up and shouted when the rains fell flat upon its face! And how its laughter roared out when the wind blew upstream and tried to stop its growing speed! We knew all its sounds and voices, its tumblings and foamings, its unnecessary splashing against the bridges, that self-conscious chatter when there were hills to look on, the affected dignity of its speech when it passed through the little towns, far too important to laugh, and all these faint, sweet whisperings when the sun caught it fairly in some slow curve and poured down upon it till the steam rose.

It was full of tricks, too, in its early life before the great world knew it. There were places in the upper reaches among the Swabian forests, when yet the first whispers of its destiny had not reached it, where it elected to disappear through holes in the ground, to appear again on the other side of the porous limestone hills and start a new river with another name, leaving, too, so little water in its own bed that we had to climb out and wade and push the canoe through miles of shallows!

And a chief pleasure, in those early days of its irresponsible youth, was to lie low, like Brer Fox, just before the little turbulent tributaries came to join it from the Alps, and to refuse to acknowledge them when in, but to run for miles side by side, the dividing line well marked, the very levels different, the Danube utterly declining to recognize the new-comer. Below Passau, however, it gave up this particular trick, for there the Inn comes in with a thundering power impossible to ignore, and so pushes and incommodes the parent river that there is hardly room for them in the long twisting gorge that follows, and the Danube is shoved this way and that against the cliffs, and forced to hurry itself with great waves and much dashing to and fro in order to get through in time. And during the fight our canoe slipped down from its shoulder to its breast, and had the time of its life among the struggling waves. But the Inn taught the old river a lesson, and after Passau it no longer pretended to ignore new arrivals.

This was many days back, of course, and since then we had come to know other aspects of the great creature, and across the Bavarian wheat plain of Straubing she wandered so slowly under the blazing June sun that we could well imagine only the surface inches were water, while below there moved, concealed as by a silken mantle, a whole army of Undines, passing silently and unseen down to the sea, and very leisurely too, lest they be discovered.

Much, too, we forgave her because of her friendliness to the birds and animals that haunted the shores. Cormorants lined the banks in lonely places in rows like short black palings; gray crows crowded the shingle-beds; storks stood fishing in the vistas of shallower water that opened up between the islands, and hawks, swans, and marsh birds of all sorts filled the air with glinting wings and singing, petulant cries. It was impossible to feel annoyed with the river's vagaries after seeing a deer leap with a splash into the water at sunrise and swim past the bows of the canoe, and often we saw fawns peering at us from the underbrush, or looked straight into the brown eyes of a stag as we charged full tilt round a corner and entered another reach of the river. Foxes, too, everywhere haunted the banks, tripping daintily among the driftwood and disappearing so suddenly that it was impossible to see how they managed it.

But now, after leaving Pressburg, everything changed a little, and the Danube became more serious. It ceased trifling. It was halfway to the Black Sea, within scenting distance almost of other, stranger countries where no tricks would be permitted or understood. It became suddenly grown-up, and claimed our respect and even our awe. It broke out into three arms, for one thing, that only met again a hundred kilometers farther down, and for a canoe there were no indications which one was intended to be followed.

"If you take a side channel," said the Hungarian officer we met in the Pressburg shop while buying provisions, "you may find yourselves, when the flood subsides, forty miles from anywhere, high and dry, and you may easily starve. There are no people, no farms, no fishermen. I warn you not to continue. The river, too, is still rising, and this wind will increase."

The rising river did not alarm us in the least, but the matter of being left high and dry by a sudden subsidence of the waters might be serious, and we had consequently laid in an extra stock of provisions. For the rest, the officer's prophecy held true, and the wind, blowing down a perfectly clear sky, increased steadily till it reached the dignity of a westerly gale.

It was earlier than usual when we camped, for the sun was a good hour or two from the horizon, and leaving my friend still asleep on the hot sand, I wandered about in desultory examination of our hotel. The island, I found, was less than an acre in extent, a mere sandy bank standing some two or three feet above the level of the river. The far end, pointing into the sunset, was covered with flying spray which the tremendous wind drove off the crests of the broken waves. It was triangular in shape, with the apex upstream.

I stood there for several minutes, watching the impetuous crimson flood bearing down with a shouting roar, dashing in waves against the bank as though to sweep it bodily away, and then swirling by in two foaming streams on either side. The ground seemed to shake with the shock and rush while the furious movement of the willow bushes as the wind poured over them increased the curious illusion that the island itself actually moved. Above, for a mile or two, I could see the great river descending upon me: it was like looking up the slope of a sliding hill, white with foam, and leaping up everywhere to show itself to the sun.

The rest of the island was too thickly grown with willows to make walking pleasant, but I made the tour, nevertheless. From the lower end the light, of course, changed, and the river looked dark and angry. Only the backs of the flying waves were visible, streaked with foam, and pushed forcibly by the great puffs of wind that fell upon them from behind. For a short mile it was visible, pouring in and out among the islands, and then disappearing with a huge sweep into the willows, which closed about it like a herd of monstrous antediluvian creatures crowding down to drink. They made me think of gigantic sponge-like growths that sucked the river up into themselves. They caused it to vanish from sight. They herded there together in such overpowering numbers.

Altogether it was an impressive scene, with its utter loneliness, its bizarre suggestion, and as I gazed, long and curiously, a singular emotion began stir somewhere in the depths of me. Midway in my delight of the wild beauty, there crept unbidden and unexplained, a curious feeling of disquietude, almost of alarm.

A rising river, perhaps, always suggests something of the ominous: many of the little islands I saw before me would probably have been swept away by the morning; this resistless, thundering flood of water touched the sense of awe. Yet I was aware that my uneasiness lay deeper far than the emotions of awe and wonder. It was not that I felt. Nor had it directly to do with the power of the driving wind—this shouting hurricane that might almost carry up a few acres of willows into the air and scatter them like so much chaff over the landscape. The wind was simply enjoying itself, for nothing rose out of the flat landscape to stop it, and I was conscious of sharing its great game with a kind of pleasurable excitement. Yet this novel emotion had nothing to do with the wind. Indeed, so vague was the sense of distress I experienced, that it was impossible to trace it to its source and deal with it accordingly, though I was aware somehow that it had to do with my realization of our utter insignificance before this unrestrained power of the elements about me. The huge-grown river had something to do with it too—a vague, unpleasant idea that we had somehow trifled with these great elemental forces in whose power we lay helpless every hour of the day and night. For here, indeed, they were gigantically at play together, and the sight appealed to the imagination.

But my emotion, so far as I could understand it, seemed to attach itself more particularly to the willow bushes, to these acres and acres of willows, crowding, so thickly growing there, swarming everywhere the eye could reach, pressing upon the river as though to suffocate it, standing in dense array mile after mile beneath the sky, watching, waiting, listening. And, apart quite from the elements, the willows connected themselves subtly with my malaise, attacking the mind insidiously somehow by reason of their vast numbers, and contriving in some way or other to represent to the imagination a new and mighty power, a power, moreover, not altogether friendly to us.

Great revelations of nature, of course, never fail to impress in one way or another, and I was no stranger to moods of the kind. Mountains overawe and oceans terrify, while the mystery of great forests exercises a spell peculiarly its own. But all these, at one point or another, somewhere link on intimately with human life and human experience. They stir comprehensible, even if alarming, emotions. They tend on the whole to exalt.

With this multitude of willows, however, it was something far different, I felt. Some essence emanated from them that besieged the heart. A sense of awe awakened, true, but of awe touched somewhere by a vague terror. Their serried ranks growing everywhere darker about me as the shadows deepened, moving furiously yet softly in the wind, woke in me the curious and unwelcome suggestion that we had trespassed here upon the borders of an alien world, a world where we were intruders, a world where we were not wanted or invited to remain—where we ran grave risks perhaps!

The feeling, however, though it refused to yield its meaning entirely to analysis, did not at the time trouble me by passing into menace. Yet it never left me quite, even during the very practical business of putting up the tent in a hurricane of wind and building a fire for the stew-pot. It remained, just enough to bother and perplex, and to rob a most delightful camping ground of a good portion of its charm. To my companion, however, I said nothing, for he was a man I considered devoid of imagination. In the first place, I could never have explained to him what I meant, and in the second, he would have laughed stupidly at me if I had.

There was a slight depression in the center of the island, and here we pitched the tent. The surrounding willows broke the wind a bit.

"A poor camp," observed the imperturbable Swede when at last the tent stood upright. "No stones and precious little firewood. I'm for moving on early tomorrow—eh? This sand won't hold anything."

But the experience of a collapsing tent at midnight had taught us many devices, and we made the cosy gipsy house as safe as possible, and then set about collecting a store of wood to last till bedtime. Willow bushes drop no branches, and driftwood was our only source of supply. We hunted the shores pretty thoroughly. Everywhere the banks were crumbling as the rising flood tore at them and carried away great portions with a splash and a gurgle.

"The island's much smaller than when we landed," said the accurate Swede. "It won't last long at this rate. We'd better drag the canoe close to the tent, and be ready to start at a moment's notice. I shall sleep in my clothes."

He was a little distance off, climbing along the bank, and I heard his rather jolly laugh as he spoke.

"By Jove!" I heard him call, a moment later, and turned to see what had caused his exclamation, but for the moment he was hidden by the willows, and I could not find him.

"What in the world's this?" I heard him cry again, and this time his voice had become serious.

I ran up quickly and joined him on the bank. He was looking over the river, pointing at something in the water.

"Good Heavens, it's a man's body!" he cried excitedly. "Look!"

A black thing, turning over and over in the foaming waves, swept rapidly past. It kept disappearing and coming up to the surface again. It was about twenty feet from the shore, and just as it was opposite to where we stood it lurched round and looked straight at us. We saw its eyes reflecting the sunset, and gleaming an odd yellow as the body turned over. Then it gave a swift, gulping plunge, and dived out of sight in a flash.

"An otter, by gad!" we exclaimed in the same breath, laughing.

It was an otter, alive, and out on the hunt, yet it had looked exactly like the body of a drowned man turning helplessly in the current. Far below it came to the surface once again, and we saw its black skin, wet and shining in the sunlight.

Then, too, just as we turned back, our arms full of driftwood, another thing happened to recall us to the river bank. This time it really was a man, and what was more, a man in a boat. Now a small boat on the Danube was an unusual sight at any time, but here in this deserted region, and at flood time, it was so unexpected as to constitute a real event. We stood and stared.

Whether it was due to the slanting sunlight, or the refraction from the wonderfully illumined water, I cannot say, but, whatever the cause, I found it difficult to focus my sight properly upon the flying apparition. It seemed, however, to be a man standing upright in a sort of flat-bottomed boat, steering with a long oar, and being carried down the opposite shore at a tremendous pace. He apparently was looking across in our direction, but the distance was too great and the light too uncertain for us to make out very plainly what he was about. It seemed to me that he was gesticulating and making signs at us. His voice came across the water to us shouting something furiously but the wind drowned it so that no single word was audible. There was something curious about the whole appearance—man, boat, signs, voice—that made an impression on me out of all proportion to its cause.

"He's crossing himself!" I cried. "Look, he's making the sign of the cross!"

"I believe you're right," the Swede said, shading his eyes with his hand and watching the man out of sight. He seemed to be gone in a moment, melting away down there into the sea of willows where the sun caught them in the bend of the river and turned them into a great crimson wall of beauty. Mist, too, had begun to rise, so that the air was hazy.

"But what in the world is he doing at nightfall on this flooded river?" I said, half to myself. "Where is he going at such a time, and what did he mean by his signs and shouting? D'you think he wished to warn us about something?"

"He saw our smoke, and thought we were spirits probably," laughed my companion. "These Hungarians believe in all sorts of rubbish: you remember the shopwoman at Pressburg warning us that no one ever landed here because it belonged to some sort of beings outside man's world! I suppose they believe in fairies and elementals, possibly demons too. That peasant in the boat saw people on the islands for the first time in his life," he added, after a slight pause, "and it scared him, that's all." The Swede's tone of voice was not convincing, and his manner lacked something that was usually there. I noted the change instantly while he talked, though without being able to label it precisely.

"If they had enough imagination," I laughed loudly—I remember trying to make as much noise as I could—"they might well people a place like this with the old gods of antiquity. The Romans must have haunted all this region more or less with their shrines and sacred groves and elemental deities."

The subject dropped and we returned to our stew-pot, for my friend was not given to imaginative conversation as a rule. Moreover, just then I remember feeling distinctly glad that he was not imaginative. His stolid, practical nature suddenly seemed to me welcome and comforting. It was an admirable temperament, I felt. He could steer down rapids like a red Indian, shoot dangerous bridges and whirlpools better than any white man I ever saw in a canoe. He was a grand fellow for an adventurous trip, a tower of strength when untoward things happened. I looked at his strong face and light curly hair as he staggered along under his pile of driftwood (twice the size of mine!), and I experienced a feeling of relief. Yes, I was distinctly glad just then that the Swede was—what he was, and that he never made remarks that suggested more than they said.

"The river's still rising, though," he added, as if following out some thoughts of his own, and dropping his load with a gasp. "This island will be under water in two days if it goes on."

"I wish the wind would go down," I said. "I don't care a fig for the river."

The flood, indeed, had no terrors for us. We could get off at ten minutes' notice, and the more water the better we liked it. It meant an increasing current and the obliteration of the treacherous shingle-beds that so often threatened to tear the bottom out of our canoe.

Contrary to our expectations, the wind did not go down with the sun. It seemed to increase with the darkness, howling overhead and shaking the willows round us like straws. Curious sounds accompanied it sometimes, like the explosion of heavy guns, and it fell upon the water and the island in great flat blows of immense power. It made me think of the sounds a planet must make, could we only hear it, driving along through space.

But the sky kept wholly clear of clouds, and soon after supper the full moon rose up in the east and covered the river and the plain of shouting willows with a light like the day.

We lay on the sandy patch beside the fire, smoking, listening to the noises of the night round us, and talking happily of the journey we had already made, and of our plans ahead. The map lay spread in the door of the tent, but the high wind made it hard to study, and presently we lowered the curtain and extinguished the lantern. The firelight was enough to smoke and see each other's faces by, and the sparks flew about overhead like fireworks. A few yards beyond, the river gurgled and hissed, and from time to time a heavy splash announced the falling away of further portions of the bank.

Our talk, I noticed, had to do with the far-away scenes and incidents of our first camps in the Black Forest, or of other subjects altogether remote from the present setting, for neither of us spoke of the actual moment more than was necessary—almost as though we had agreed tacitly to avoid discussion of the camp and its incidents. Neither the otter nor the boatman, for instance, received the honor of a single mention, though ordinarily these would have furnished discussion for the greater part of the evening. They were, of course, distinct events in such a place.

The scarcity of wood made it a business to keep the fire going, for the wind, that drove the smoke in our faces wherever we sat, helped at the same time to make a forced draught. We took it in turn to make foraging expeditions into the darkness, and the quantity the Swede brought back always made me feel that he took an absurdly long time finding it, for the fact was I did not care much about being left alone, and yet it always seemed to be my turn to grub about among the bushes or scramble along the slippery banks in the moonlight. The long day's battle with wind and water—such wind and such water!—had tired us both, and an early bed was the obvious program. Yet neither of us made the move for the tent. We lay there, tending the fire, talking in desultory fashion, peering about us into the dense willow bushes, and listening to the thunder of wind and river. The loneliness of the place had entered our very bones, and silence seemed natural, for after a bit the sound of our voices became a trifle unreal and forced. Whispering would have been the fitting mode of communication, I felt, and the human voice, always rather absurd amid the roar of the elements, now carried with it something almost illegitimate. It was like talking out loud in church, or in some place where it was not lawful, perhaps not quite safe, to be overheard.

The eeriness of this lonely island, set among a million willows, swept by a hurricane, and surrounded by hurrying deep waters, touched us both, I fancy. Untrodden by man, almost unknown to man, it lay there beneath the moon, remote from human influence, on the frontier of another world, an alien world, a world tenanted by willows only and the souls of willows. And we, in our rashness, had dared to invade it, even to make use of it! Something more than the power of its mystery stirred in me as I lay on the sand, feet to fire, and peered up through the leaves at the stars. For the last time I rose to get firewood.

"When this has burnt up," I said firmly, "I shall turn in," and my companion watched me lazily as I moved off into the surrounding shadows.

For an unimaginative man I thought he seemed unusually receptive that night, unusually open to suggestion of things other than sensory. He too was touched by the beauty and loneliness of the place. I was not altogether pleased, I remember, to recognize this slight change in him, and instead of immediately collecting sticks, I made my way to the far point of the island where the moonlight on plain and river could be seen to better advantage. The desire to be alone had come suddenly upon me. My former dread returned in force; there was a vague feeling in me I wished to face and probe to the bottom.

When I reached the point of sand jutting out among the waves, the spell of the place descended upon me with a positive shock. No mere "scenery" could have produced such an effect. There was something more here, something to alarm.

I gazed across the waste of wild waters. I watched the whispering willows. I heard the ceaseless beating of the tireless wind, and, one and all, each in its own way, stirred in me this sensation of a strange distress. But the willows especially: forever they went on chattering and talking among themselves, laughing a little, shrilly crying out, sometimes sighing—but what it was they made so much to-do about belonged to the secret life of the great plain they inhabited. And it was utterly alien to the world I knew, or to that of the wild yet kindly elements. They made me think of a host of beings from another plane of life, another evolution altogether, perhaps, all discussing a mystery known only to themselves. I watched them moving busily together, oddly shaking their big bushy heads, twirling their myriad leaves even when there was no wind. They moved of their own will as though alive, and they touched, by some incalculable method, my own keen sense of the horrible.

There they stood in the moonlight, like a vast army surrounding our camp, shaking their innumerable silver spears defiantly, formed all ready for an attack.

The psychology of places, for some imaginations at least, is very vivid; for the wanderer, especially, camps have their "note" either of welcome or rejection. At first it may not always be apparent, because the busy preparations of tent and cooking prevent, but with the first pause—after supper usually—it comes and announces itself. And the note of this willow-camp now became unmistakably plain to me: we were interlopers, trespassers, we were not welcomed. The sense of unfamiliarity grew upon me as I stood there watching. We touched the frontier of a region where our presence was resented. For a night's lodging we might perhaps be tolerated, but for a prolonged and inquisitive stay—No! by all the gods of the trees and the wilderness, no! We were the first human influences upon this island, and we were not wanted. The willows were against us.

Strange thoughts like these, bizarre fancies, borne I know not whence, found lodgment in my mind as I stood listening. What, I thought, if, after all, these crouching willows proved to be alive; if suddenly they should rise up, like a swarm of living creatures, marshaled by the gods whose territory we had invaded, sweep towards us off the vast swamps, booming overhead in the night—and then settle down! As I looked it was so easy to imagine they actually moved, crept nearer, retreated a little, huddled together in masses, hostile, waiting for the great wind that should finally start them a-running. I could have sworn their aspect changed a little, and their ranks deepened and pressed more closely together.

The melancholy shrill cry of a night bird sounded overhead, and suddenly I nearly lost my balance as the piece of bank I stood upon fell with a great splash into the river, undermined by the flood. I stepped back just in time, and went on hunting for firewood again, half laughing at the odd fancies that crowded so thickly into my mind and cast their spell upon me. I recall the Swede's remark about moving on next day, and I was just thinking that I fully agreed with him, when I turned with a start and saw the subject of my thoughts standing immediately in front of me. He was quite close. The roar of the elements had covered his approach.

"You've been gone so long," he shouted above the wind, "I thought something must have happened to you."

But there was that in his tone, and a certain look in his face as well, that conveyed to me more than his actual words, and in a flash I understood the real reason for his coming. It was because the spell of the place had entered his soul too, and he did not like being alone.

"River still rising," he cried, pointing to the flood in the moonlight, "and the wind's simply awful."

He always said the same things, but it was the cry for companionship that gave the real importance to his words.

"Lucky," I cried back, "our tent's in the hollow. I think it'll hold all right." I added something about the difficulty of finding wood, in order to explain my absence, but the wind caught my words and flung them across the river, so that he did not hear, but just looked at me through the branches, nodding his head.

"Lucky if we get away without disaster!" he shouted, or words to that effect, and I remember feeling half angry with him for putting the thought into words, for it was exactly what I felt myself. There was disaster impending somewhere, and the sense of presentiment lay unpleasantly upon me.

We went back to the fire and made a final blaze, poking it up with our feet. We took a last look round. But for the wind the heat would have been unpleasant. I put this thought into words, and I remember my friend's reply struck me oddly: that he would rather have the heat, the ordinary July weather, than this "diabolical wind."

Everything was snug for the night; the canoe lying turned over beside the tent, with both yellow paddles beneath her; the provision sack hanging from a willow stem, and the washed-up dishes removed to a safe distance from the fire, all ready for the morning meal.

We smothered the embers of the fire with sand, and then turned in. The flap of the tent door was up, and I saw the branches and the stars and the white moonlight. The shaking willows and the heavy buffetings of the wind against our taut little house were the last things I remembered as sleep came down and covered all with its soft and delicious forgetfulness.

II

SUDDENLY I FOUND MYSELF lying awake, peering from my sandy mattress through the door of the tent. I looked at my watch pinned against the canvas, and saw by the bright moonlight that it was past twelve o'clock—the threshold of a new day—and I had therefore slept a couple of hours. The Swede was asleep still beside me; the wind howled as before something plucked at my heart and made me feel afraid. There was a sense of disturbance in my immediate neighborhood.

I sat up quickly and looked out. The trees were swaying violently to and fro as the gusts smote them, but our little bit of green canvas lay snugly safe in the hollow, for the wind passed over it without meeting enough resistance to make it vicious. The feeling of disquietude did not pass however, and I crawled quietly out of the tent to see if our belongings were safe. I moved carefully so as not to waken my companion. A curious excitement was on me.

I was halfway out, kneeling on all fours, when my eye first took in that the tops of the bushes opposite, with their moving tracery of leaves, made shapes against the sky. I sat back on my haunches and stared. It was incredible, surely, but there, opposite and slightly above me, were shapes of some indeterminate sort among the willows, and as the branches swayed in the wind they seemed to group themselves about these shapes, forming a series of monstrous outlines that shifted rapidly beneath the moon. Close, about fifty feet in front of me, I saw these things.

My first instinct was to waken my companion that he too might see them, but something made me hesitate—the sudden realization, probably, that I should not welcome corroboration, and meanwhile I crouched there staring in amazement with smarting eyes. I was wide awake. I remember saying to myself that I was not dreaming.

They first became properly visible, these huge figures, just within the tops of the bushes—immense bronze-colored, moving, and wholly independent of the swaying of the branches. I saw them plainly and noted, now I came to examine them more calmly, that they were very much larger than human, and indeed that something in their appearance proclaimed them to be not human at all. Certainly they were not merely the moving tracery of the branches against the moonlight. They shifted independently. They rose upwards in a continuous stream from earth to sky, vanishing utterly as soon as they reached the dark of the sky. They were interlaced one with another, making a great column, and I saw their limbs and huge bodies melting in and out of each other, forming this serpentine line that bent and swayed and twisted spirally with the contortions of the wind-tossed trees. They were nude, fluid shapes, passing up the bushes, within the leaves almost—rising up in a living column into the heavens. Their faces I never could see. Unceasingly they poured upwards, swaying in great bending curves, with a hue of dull bronze upon their skins.

I stared, trying to force every atom of vision from my eyes. For a long time I thought they must every moment disappear and resolve themselves into the movements of the branches and prove to be an optical illusion. I searched everywhere for a proof of reality, when all the while I understood quite well that the standard of reality had changed. For the longer I looked the more certain I became that these figures were real and living, though perhaps not according to the standards that the camera and the biologist would insist upon.

Far from feeling fear, I was possessed with a sense of awe and wonder such as I have never known. I seemed to be gazing at the personified elemental forces of this haunted and primeval region. Our intrusion had stirred the powers of the place into activity. It was we who were the cause of the disturbance, and my brain filled to bursting with stories and legends of the spirits and deities of places that have been acknowledged and worshiped by men in all ages of the world's history. But, before I could arrive at any possible explanation, something impelled me to go farther out, and I crept forward on to the sand and stood upright. I felt the ground still warm under my bare feet; the wind tore at my hair and face, and the sound of the river burst upon my ears with a sudden roar. These things, I knew, were real, and proved that my senses were acting normally. Yet the figures still rose from earth to heaven, silent, majestically, in a great spiral of grace and strength that overwhelmed me at length with a genuine deep emotion of worship. I felt that I must fall down and worship—absolutely worship.

Perhaps in another minute I might have done so, when a gust of wind swept against me with such force that it blew me sideways, and I nearly stumbled and fell. It seemed to shake the dream violently out of me. At least it gave me another point of view somehow. The figures still remained, still ascended into heaven from the heart of the night, but my reason at last began to assert itself. It must be a subjective experience, I argued— none the less real for that, but still subjective. The moonlight and the branches combined to work out these pictures upon the mirror of my imagination, and for some reason I projected them outwards and made them appear objective. I knew this must be the case, of course. I was the subject of a vivid and interesting hallucination. I took courage, and began to move forward across the open patches of sand. By Jove, though, was it all hallucination? Was it merely subjective? Did not my reason argue in the old futile way from the little standard of the known?

I only know that great column of figures ascended darkly into the sky for what seemed a very long period of time, and with a very complete measure of reality as most men are accustomed to gauge reality. Then suddenly they were gone!

And, once they were gone and the immediate wonder of their great presence had passed, fear came down upon me with a cold rush. The esoteric meaning of this lonely and haunted region suddenly flamed up within me and I began to tremble dreadfully. I took a quick look round—a look of horror that came near to panic—calculating vainly ways of escape, and then, realizing how helpless I was to achieve anything really effective, I crept back silently into the tent and lay down again upon my sandy mattress, first lowering the door-curtain to shut out the sight of the willows in the moonlight, and then burying my head as deeply as possible beneath the blankets to deaden the sound of the terrifying wind.

III

A S THOUGH FURTHER to convince me that I had not been dreaming, I remember that it was a long time before I fell again into a troubled and restless sleep, and even then only the upper crust of me slept, and underneath there was something that never quite lost consciousness, but lay alert and on the watch.

But this second time I jumped up with a genuine start of terror. It was neither the wind nor the river that woke me, but the slow approach of something that caused the sleeping portion of me to grow smaller and smaller till at last it vanished altogether, and I found myself sitting bolt upright—listening.

Outside there was a sound of multitudinous little patterings. They had been coming, I was aware, for a long time, and in my sleep they had first become audible. I sat there nervously wide awake as though I had not slept at all. It seemed to me that my breathing came with difficulty, and that there was a great weight upon the surface of my body. In spite of the hot night, I felt clammy with cold and shivered. Something surely was pressing steadily against the sides of the tent and weighing down upon it from above. Was it the body of the wind? Was this the pattering rain, the dripping of the leaves? The spray blown from the river by the wind and gathering in big drops? I thought quickly of a dozen things.

Then suddenly the explanation leaped into my mind: a bough from the poplar, the only large tree on the island, had fallen with the wind. Still half caught by the other branches, it would fall with the next gust and crush us, and meanwhile its leaves brushed and tapped upon the tight canvas surface of the tent. I raised the loose flap and rushed out, calling to the Swede to follow.

But when I got out and stood upright I saw that the tent was free. There was no hanging bough, there was no rain or spray, nothing approached.

A cold, gray light filtered down through the bushes and lay on the faintly gleaming sand. Stars still crowded the sky directly overhead, and the wind howled magnificently, but the fire no longer gave out any glow, and I saw the east reddening in streaks through the trees. Several hours must have passed since I stood there before, watching the ascending figures, and the memory of it now came back to me horribly, like an evil dream. Oh, how tired it made me feel, that ceaseless raging wind! Yet, though the deep lassitude of a sleepless night was on me, my nerves were tingling with the activity of an equally tireless apprehension, and all idea of repose was out of the question. The river I saw had risen further. Its thunder filled the air, and a fine spray made itself felt through my thin sleeping shirt.

Yet nowhere did I discover the slightest evidences of anything to cause alarm. This deep, prolonged disturbance in my heart remained wholly unaccounted for.

My companion had not stirred when I called him, and there was no need to waken him now. I looked about me carefully, noting everything: the turned-over canoe, the yellow paddles—two of them, I'm certain—the provision sack and the extra lantern hanging together from the tree, and, crowding everywhere about me, enveloping all, the willows, those endless, shaking willows. A bird uttered its morning cry, and a string of duck passed with whirring flight overhead in the twilight. The sand whirled, dry and stinging, about my bare feet in the wind.

I walked round the tent and then went out a little way into the bush, so that I could see across the river to the farther landscape, and the same profound yet indefinable emotion of distress seized upon me again as I saw the interminable sea of bushes stretching to the horizon, looking ghostly and unreal in the wan light of dawn. I walked softly here and there, still puzzling over that odd sound of infinite pattering, and of that pressure upon the tent that had wakened me. It must have been the wind, I reflected—the wind beating upon the loose, hot sand, driving the dry particles smartly against the taut canvas—the wind dropping heavily upon our fragile roof.

Yet all the time my nervousness and malaise increased appreciably.

I crossed over to the farther shore and noted how the coast line had altered in the night, and what masses of sand the river had torn away. I dipped my hands and feet into the cool current, and bathed my forehead. Already there was a glow of sunrise in the sky and the exquisite freshness of coming day. On my way back I passed purposely beneath the very bushes where I had seen the column of figures rising into the air, and midway among the clumps I suddenly found myself overtaken by a sense of vast terror. From the shadows a large figure went swiftly by. Some one passed me, as sure as ever man did...

It was a great staggering blow from the wind that helped me forward again, and once out in the more open space, the sense of terror diminished strangely. The winds were about and walking, I remember saying to myself, for the winds often move like great presences under the trees. And altogether the fear that hovered about me was such an unknown and immense kind of fear, so unlike anything I had ever felt before, that it woke a sense of awe and wonder in me that did much to counteract its worst effects, and when I reached a high point in the middle of the island from which I could see the wide stretch of river, crimson in the sunrise, the whole magical beauty of it all was so overpowering that a sort of wild yearning woke in me and almost brought a cry up into the throat.

But this cry found no expression, for as my eyes wandered from the plain beyond to the island round me and noted our little tent half hidden among the willows, a dreadful discovery leaped out at me, compared to which my terror of the walking winds seemed as nothing at all.

For a change, I thought, had somehow come about in the arrangement of the landscape. It was not that my point of vantage gave me a different view, but that an alteration had apparently been effected in the relation of the tent to the willows, and of the willows to the tent. Surely the bushes now crowded much closer—unnecessarily, unpleasantly close. They had moved nearer.

Creeping with silent feet over the shifting sands, drawing imperceptibly nearer by soft, unhurried movements, the willows had come closer during the night. But had the wind moved them, or had they moved of themselves? I recalled the sound of infinite small patterings and the pressure upon the tent and upon my own heart that caused me to wake in terror. I swayed for a moment in the wind like a tree, finding it hard to keep my upright position on the sandy hillock. There was a suggestion here of personal agency, of deliberate intention, of aggressive hostility, and it terrified me into a sort of rigidity.

Then the reaction followed quickly. The idea was so bizarre, so absurd, that I felt inclined to laugh. But the laughter came no more readily than the cry, for the knowledge that my mind was so receptive to such dangerous imaginings brought the additional terror that it was through our minds and not through our physical bodies that the attack would come, and was coming.

The wind buffeted me about, and, very quickly it seemed, the sun came up over the horizon, for it was after four o'clock, and I must have stood on that little pinnacle of sand longer than I knew, afraid to come down at close quarters with the willows. I returned quietly, creepily, to the tent, first taking another exhaustive look round and—yes, I confess it—making a few measurements. I paced out on the warm sand the distances between the willows and the tent, making a note of the shortest distance particularly.

I crawled stealthily into my blankets. My companion, to all appearances, still slept soundly, and I was glad that this was so. Provided my experiences were not corroborated, I could find strength somehow to deny them, perhaps. With the daylight I could persuade myself that it was all a subjective hallucination, a fantasy of the night, a projection of the excited imagination.

Nothing further came to disturb me, and I fell asleep almost at once, utterly exhausted, yet still in dread of hearing again that weird sound of multitudinous pattering, or of feeling the pressure upon my heart that had made it difficult to breathe.

IV

THE SUN WAS HIGH in the heavens when my companion woke me from a heavy sleep and announced that the porridge was cooked and there was just time to bathe. The grateful smell of frizzling bacon entered the tent door.

"River still rising," he said, "and several islands out in midstream have disappeared altogether. Our own island's much smaller."

"Any wood left?" I asked sleepily.

"The wood and the island will finish tomorrow in a dead heat," he laughed, "but there's enough to last us till then."

I plunged in from the point of the island, which had indeed altered a lot in size and shape during the night, and was swept down in a moment to the landing place opposite the tent. The water was icy, and the banks flew by like the country from an express train. Bathing under such conditions was an exhilarating operation, and the terror of the night seemed cleansed out of me by a process of evaporation in the brain. The sun was blazing hot; not a cloud showed itself anywhere. The wind, however, had not abated one little jot.

Quite suddenly then the implied meaning of the Swede's words flashed across me, showing that he no longer wished to leave posthaste, and had changed his mind. "Enough to last till tomorrow"—he assumed we should stay on the island another night. It struck me as odd. The night before he was so positive the other way. How had the change come about?

Great crumblings of the banks occurred at breakfast, with heavy splashings and clouds of spray which the wind brought into our frying-pan, and my fellow-traveler talked incessantly about the difficulty the Vienna-Pesth steamers must have to find the channel in flood. But the state of his mind interested and impressed me far more than the state of the river or the difficulties of the steamers. He had changed somehow since the evening before. His manner was different—a trifle excited, a trifle shy, with a sort of suspicion about his voice and gestures. I hardly know how to describe it now in cold blood, but at the time I remember being quite certain of one thing, viz., that he had become frightened!

He ate very little breakfast, and for once omitted to smoke his pipe. He had the map spread open beside him, and kept studying its markings.

"We'd better get off sharp in an hour," I said presently, feeling for an opening that must bring him indirectly to a partial confession at any rate. And his answer puzzled me uncomfortably: "Rather! If they'll let us."

"Who'll let us? The elements?" I asked quickly, with affected indifference.

"The powers of this awful place, whoever they are," he replied, keeping his eyes on the map. "The gods are here, if they are anywhere at all in the world."

"The elements are always the true immortals," I replied, laughing as naturally as I could manage, yet knowing quite well that my face reflected my true feelings when he looked up gravely at me and spoke across the smoke:

"We shall be fortunate if we get away without further disaster."

This was exactly what I had dreaded, and I screwed myself up to the point of the direct question. It was like agreeing to allow the dentist to extract the tooth; it had to come anyhow in the long run, and the rest was all pretense.

"Further disaster! Why, what's happened?"

"For one thing—the steering paddle's gone," he said quietly.

"The steering paddle gone!" I repeated, greatly excited, for this was our rudder, and the Danube in flood without a rudder was suicide. "But what—"

"And there's a tear in the bottom of the canoe," he added, with a genuine little tremor in his voice.

I continued staring at him, able only to repeat the words in his face somewhat foolishly. There, in the heat of the sun, and on this burning sand, I was aware of a freezing atmosphere descending round us. I got up to follow him, for he merely nodded his head gravely and led the way towards the tent a few yards on the other side of the fireplace. The canoe still lay there as I had last seen her in the night, ribs uppermost, the paddles, or rather, the paddle, on the sand beside her.

"There's only one," he said, stooping to pick it up. "And here's the rent in the base-board."

It was on the tip of my tongue to tell him that I had clearly noticed two paddles a few hours before, but a second impulse made me think better of it, and I said nothing. I approached to see.

There was a long, finely made tear in the bottom of the canoe where a little slither of wood had been neatly taken clean out. It looked as if the tooth of a sharp rock or snag had eaten down her length, and investigation showed that the hole went through. Had we launched out in her without observing it we must inevitably have foundered. At first the water would have made the wood swell so as to close the hole, but once out in midstream the water must have poured in, and the canoe, never more than two inches above the surface, would have filled and sunk very rapidly.

"There, you see, an attempt to prepare a victim for the sacrifice," I heard him saying, more to himself than to me, "two victims rather," he added as he bent over and ran his fingers along the slit.

I began to whistle—a thing I always do unconsciously when utterly nonplused—and purposely paid no attention to his words. I was determined to consider them foolish.

"It wasn't there last night," he said presently, straightening up from his examination and looking anywhere but at me.

"We must have scratched her in landing, of course," I stopped whistling to say, "The stones are very sharp—"

I stopped abruptly, for at that moment he turned round and met my eye squarely. I knew just as well as he did how impossible my explanation was. There were no stones, to begin with.

"And then there's this to explain too," he added quietly, handing me the paddle and pointing to the blade.

A new and curious emotion spread freezingly over me as I took and examined it. The blade was scraped down all over, beautifully scraped, as though someone had sand-papered it with care, making it so thin that the first vigorous stroke must have snapped it off at the elbow.

"One of us walked in his sleep and did this thing," I said feebly, "or—or it has been filed by the constant stream of sand particles blown against it by the wind, perhaps."

"Ah," said the Swede, turning away, laughing a little, "you can explain everything!"

"The same wind that caught the steering paddle and flung it so near the bank that it fell in with the next lump that crumbled," I called out after him, absolutely determined to find an explanation for everything he showed me.

"I see," he shouted back, turning his head to look at me before disappearing among the willow bushes.

Once alone with these perplexing evidences of personal agency, I think my first thought took the form of "One of us must have done this thing, and it certainly was not I." But my second thought decided how impossible it was to suppose, under all the circumstances, that either of us had done it. That my companion, the trusted friend of a dozen similar expeditions, could have knowingly had a hand in it, was a suggestion not to be entertained for a moment. Equally absurd seemed the explanation that this imperturbable and densely practical nature had suddenly become insane and was busied with insane purposes.

Yet the fact remained that what disturbed me most, and kept my fear actively alive even in this blaze of sunshine and wild beauty, was the clear certainty that some curious alteration had come about in his mind—that he was nervous, timid, suspicious, aware of goings on he did not speak about, watching a series of secret and hitherto unmentionable events—waiting, in a word, for a climax that he expected, and, I thought, expected very soon. This grew up in my mind intuitively—I hardly knew how.

I made a hurried examination of the tent and its surroundings, but the measurements of the night remained the same. There were deep hollows formed in the sand, I now noticed for the first time, basin-shaped and of various depths and sizes, varying from that of a teacup to a large bowl. The wind, no doubt, was responsible for these miniature craters, just as it was for lifting the paddle and tossing it towards the water. The rent in the canoe was the only thing that seemed quite inexplicable, and, after all, it was conceivable that a sharp point had caught it when we landed. The examination I made of the shore did not assist this theory, but all the same I clung to it with that diminishing portion of my intelligence which I called my "reason." An explanation of some kind was an absolute necessity, just as some working explanation of the universe is necessary—however absurd—to the happiness of every individual who seeks to do his duty in the world and face the problems of life. The simile seemed to me at the time an exact parallel.

I at once set the pitch melting, and presently the Swede joined me at the work, though under the best conditions in the world the canoe could not be safe for traveling till the following day. I drew his attention casually to the hollows in the sand.

"Yes," he said, "I know. They're all over the island. But you can explain them, no doubt!"

"Wind, of course," I answered without hesitation. "Have you never watched those little whirlwinds in the street that twist and twirl everything into a circle? This sand's loose enough to yield, that's all."

He made no reply, and we worked on in silence for a bit. I watched him surreptitiously all the time, and I had an idea he was watching me. He seemed, too, to be always listening attentively to something I could not hear, or perhaps for something that he expected to hear, for he kept turning about and staring into the bushes, and up into the sky, and out across the water where it was visible through the openings among the willows. Sometimes he even put his hand to his ear and held it there for several minutes. He said nothing to me, however, about it, and I asked no questions. And meanwhile, as he mended that torn canoe with the skill and address of a red Indian, I was glad to notice his absorption in the work, for there was a vague dread in my heart that he would speak of the changed aspect of the willows. And, if he had noticed that, my imagination could no longer be held a sufficient explanation of it.

At length, after a long pause, he began to talk.

"Queer thing," he added in a hurried sort of voice, as though he wanted to say something and get it over. "Queer thing, I mean, about that otter last night."

I had expected something so totally different that he caught me with surprise, and I looked up sharply.

"Shows how lonely this place is. Otters are awfully shy things—"

"I don't mean that, of course," he interrupted. "I mean—do you think—did you think it really was an otter?"

"What else, in the name of Heaven, what else?"

"You know, I saw it before you did, and at first it seemed—so much bigger than an otter."

"The sunset as you looked upstream magnified it, or something," I replied.

He looked at me absently a moment, as though his mind were busy with other thoughts.

"It had such extraordinary yellow eyes," he went on half to himself.

"That was the sun too," I laughed, a trifle boisterously. "I suppose you'll wonder next if that fellow in the boat—"

I suddenly decided not to finish the sentence. He was in the act again of listening, turning his head to the wind, and something in the expression of his face made me halt. The subject dropped, and we went on with our caulking. Apparently he had not noticed my unfinished sentence. Five minutes later, however, he looked at me across the canoe, the smoking pitch in his hand, his face exceedingly grave.

"I did rather wonder, if you want to know," he said slowly,

"what that thing in the boat was. I remember thinking at the time it was not a man. The whole business seemed to rise quite suddenly out of the water."

I laughed again boisterously in his face, but this time there was impatience and a strain of anger too, in my feeling.

"Look here now," I cried, "this place is quite queer enough without going out of our way to imagine things! That boat was an ordinary boat, and the man in it was an ordinary man, and they were both going downstream as fast as they could lick. And that otter was an otter, so don't let's play the fool about it!"

He looked steadily at me with the same grave expression. He was not in the least annoyed. I took courage from his silence.

"And for heaven's sake," I went on, "don't keep pretending you hear things, because it only gives me the jumps, and there's nothing to hear but the river and this cursed old thundering wind."

"You fool!" he answered in a low, shocked voice, "you utter fool. That's just the way all victims talk. As if you didn't understand just as well as I do!" he sneered with scorn in his voice, and a sort of resignation. "The best thing you can do is to keep quiet and try to hold your mind as firm as possible. This feeble attempt at self-deception only makes the truth harder when you're forced to meet it."

My little effort was over, and I found nothing more to say, for I knew quite well his words were true, and that I was the fool, not he. Up to a certain stage in the adventure he kept ahead of me easily, and I think I felt annoyed to be out of it, to be thus proved less psychic, less sensitive than himself to these extraordinary happenings, and half ignorant all the time of what was going on under my very nose. He knew from the very beginning, apparently. But at the moment I wholly missed the point of his words about the necessity of there being a victim, and that we ourselves were destined to satisfy the want. I dropped all pretense thenceforward, but thenceforward likewise my fear increased steadily to the climax.

"But you're quite right about one thing," he added, before the subject passed, "and that is that we're wiser not to talk about it, or even to think about it, because what one thinks finds expression in words, and what one says, happens."

That afternoon, while the canoe dried and hardened, we spent trying to fish, testing the leak, collecting wood, and watching the enormous flood of rising water. Masses of driftwood swept near our shores sometimes, and we fished for them with long willow branches. The island grew perceptibly smaller as the banks were torn away with great gulps and splashes. The weather kept brilliantly fine till about four o'clock, and then for the first time for three days the wind showed signs of abating. Clouds began to gather in the southwest, spreading thence slowly over the sky.

This lessening of the wind came as a great relief, for the incessant roaring, banging, and thundering had irritated our nerves. Yet the silence that came about five o'clock with its sudden cessation was in a manner quite as oppressive. The booming of the river had everything its own way then: it filled the air with deep murmurs, more musical than the wind noises, but infinitely more monotonous. The wind held many notes, rising, falling, always beating out some sort of great elemental tune; whereas the river's song lay between three notes at most—dull pedal notes, that held a lugubrious quality foreign to the wind, and somehow seemed to me, in my then nervous state, to sound wonderfully well the music of doom.

It was extraordinary, too, how the withdrawal suddenly of bright sunlight took everything out of the landscape that made for cheerfulness, and since this particular landscape had already managed to convey the suggestion of something sinister, the change of course was all the more unwelcome and noticeable. For me, I know, the darkening outlook became distinctly more alarming, and I found myself more than once calculating how soon after sunset the full moon would get up in the east, and whether the gathering clouds would greatly interfere with her lighting of the little island.

With this general hush of the wind—though it still indulged in occasional brief gusts—the river seemed to me to grow blacker, the willows to stand more densely together. The latter, too, kept up a sort of independent movement of their own, rustling among themselves when no wind stirred, and shaking oddly from the roots upwards. When common objects in this way become charged with the suggestion of horror, they stimulate the imagination far more than things of unusual appearance, and these bushes, crowding huddled about us, assumed for me in the darkness a bizarre grotesquerie of appearance that lent to them somehow the aspect of purposeful and living creatures. Their very ordinariness, I felt, masked what was malignant and hostile to us. The forces of the region drew nearer with the coming of night. They were focusing upon our island, and more particularly upon ourselves. For thus, somehow, in the terms of the imagination, did my really indescribable sensations in this extraordinary place present themselves.

I had slept a good deal in the early afternoon, and had thus recovered somewhat from the exhaustion of a disturbed night, but this only served apparently to render me more susceptible than before to the obsessing spell of the haunting. I fought against it, laughing at my feelings as absurd and childish, with very obvious physiological explanations, yet, in spite of every effort, they gained in strength upon me so that I dreaded the night as a child lost in a forest must dread the approach of darkness.

The canoe we had carefully covered with a waterproof sheet during the day, and the one remaining paddle had been securely tied by the Swede to the base of a tree, lest the wind should rob us of that too. From five o'clock onwards I busied myself with the stew-pot and preparations for dinner, it being my turn to cook that night. We had potatoes, onions, bits of bacon fat to add flavour, and a general thick residue from former stews at the bottom of the pot. With black bread broken up into it the result was most excellent, and it was followed by a stew of plums with sugar and a brew of strong tea with dried milk. A good pile of wood lay close at hand, and the absence of wind made my duties easy. My companion sat lazily watching me, dividing his attentions between cleaning his pipe and giving useless advice—an admitted privilege of the off-duty man. He had been very quiet all the afternoon, engaged in re-caulking the canoe, strengthening the tent ropes, and fishing for drift-wood while I slept. No more talk about undesirable things had passed between us, and I think his only remarks had to do with the gradual destruction of the island, which he declared was now fully a third smaller than when we first landed.

The pot had just begun to bubble when I heard his voice calling to me from the bank, where he had wandered away without my noticing. I ran up.

"Come and listen," he said, "and see what you make of it." He held his hand cupwise to his ear, as so often before.

"Now do you hear anything?" he asked, watching me curiously.

We stood there, listening attentively together. At first I heard only the deep note of the water and the hissings rising from its turbulent surface. The willows, for once, were motionless and silent. Then a sound began to reach my ears faintly, a peculiar sound—something like the humming of a distant gong. It seemed to come across to us in the darkness from the waste of swamps and willows opposite. It was repeated at regular intervals, but it was certainly neither the sound of a bell nor the hooting of a distant steamer. I can liken it to nothing so much as to the sound of an immense gong, suspended far up in the sky, repeating incessantly its muffled metallic note, soft and musical, as it was repeatedly struck. My heart quickened as I listened.

"I've heard it all day," said my companion. "While you slept this afternoon it came all round the island. I hunted it down, but could never get near enough to see—to localize it correctly. Sometimes it was overhead, and sometimes it seemed under the water. Once or twice, too, I could have sworn it was not outside at all, but within myself—you know—the way a sound in the fourth dimension is supposed to come."

I was too much puzzled to pay much attention to his words. I listened carefully, striving to associate it with any known familiar sound I could think of, but without success. It changed in direction, too, coming nearer, and then sinking utterly away into remote distance. I cannot say that it was ominous in quality, because to me it seemed distinctly musical, yet I must admit it set going a distressing feeling that made me wish I had never heard it.

"The wind blowing in those sand-funnels," I said, determined to find an explanation, "or the bushes rubbing together after the storm perhaps."

"It comes off the whole swamp," my friend answered. "It comes from everywhere at once." He ignored my explanations. "It comes from the willow bushes somehow—"

"But now the wind has dropped," I objected "The willows can hardly make a noise by themselves, can they?"

His answer frightened me, first because I had dreaded it, and secondly, because I knew intuitively it was true.

"It is because the wind has dropped we now hear it. It was drowned before. It is the cry, I believe of the—"

I dashed back to my fire, warned by a sound of bubbling that the stew was in danger, but determined at the same time to escape from further conversation. I was resolute, if possible, to avoid the exchanging of views. I dreaded, too, that he would begin again about the gods, or the elemental forces, or something else disquieting, and I wanted to keep myself well in hand for what might happen later. There was another night to be faced before we escaped from this distressing place, and there was no knowing yet what it might bring forth.

"Come and cut up bread for the pot," I called to him, vigorously stirring the appetizing mixture. That stew-pot held sanity for us both, and the thought made me laugh.

He came over slowly and took the provision sack from the tree, fumbling in its mysterious depths, and then emptying the entire contents upon the ground-sheet at his feet.

"Hurry up!" I cried. "It's boiling."

The Swede burst out into a roar of laughter that startled me. It was forced laughter, not artificial exactly, but mirthless.

"There's nothing here!" he shouted, holding his sides.

"Bread, I mean."

"It's gone. There is no bread. They've taken it!"

I dropped the long spoon and ran up. Everything the sack had contained lay upon the ground-sheet, but there was no loaf.

The whole dead weight of my growing fear fell upon me and shook me. Then I burst out laughing too. It was the only thing to do, and the sound of my own laughter also made me understand his. The strain of psychical pressure caused it—this explosion of unnatural laughter in both of us. It was an effort of repressed forces to seek relief; it was a temporary safety valve. And with both of us it ceased quite suddenly.

"How criminally stupid of me!" I cried, still determined to be consistent and find an explanation. "I clean forgot to buy a loaf at Pressburg. That chattering woman put everything out of my head, and I must have left it lying on the counter or—"

"The oatmeal, too, is much less than it was this morning," the Swede interrupted.

Why in the world need he draw attention to it? I thought angrily.

"There's enough for tomorrow," I said, stirring vigorously, "and we can get lots more at Komorn or Gran. In twenty-four hours we shall be miles from here."

"I hope so—to God," he muttered, putting the things back into the sack. "Unless we're claimed first as victims for the sacrifice," he added with a foolish laugh. He dragged the sack into the tent, for safety's sake, I suppose, and I heard him mumbling on to himself, but so indistinctly that it seemed quite natural for me to ignore his words.

Our meal was beyond question a gloomy one, and we ate it almost in silence, avoiding one another's eyes, and keeping the fire bright. Then we washed up and prepared for the night, and, once smoking, our minds unoccupied with any definite duties, the apprehension I had felt all day long became more and more acute. It was not then active fear, I think, but the very vagueness of its origin distressed me far more than if I had been able to ticket and face it squarely. The curious sound I have likened to the note of a gong became now almost incessant, and filled the stillness of the night with a faint, continuous ringing rather than a series of distinct notes. At one time it was behind and at another time in front of us. Sometimes I fancied it came from the bushes on our left, and then again from the clumps on our right. More often it hovered directly overhead like the whirring of wings. It was really everywhere at once, behind, in front, at our sides and over our heads, completely surrounding us. The sound really defies description. But nothing within my knowledge is like that ceaseless muffled humming rising off the deserted world of swamps and willows.

We sat smoking in comparative silence, the strain growing every minute greater. The worst feature of the situation seemed to me that we did not know what to expect, and could therefore make no sort of preparation by way of defense. We could anticipate nothing. My explanations made in the sunshine, moreover, now came to haunt me with their foolish and wholly unsatisfactory nature, and it was more and more clear to me that some kind of plain talk with my companion was inevitable, whether I liked it or not. After all, we had to spend the night together, and to sleep in the same tent side by side. I saw that I could not get along much longer without the support of his mind, and for that, of course, plain talk was imperative. As long as possible, however, I postponed this little climax, and tried to ignore or laugh at the occasional sentences he flung into the emptiness.

Some of these sentences, moreover, were confoundedly disquieting to me, coming as they did to corroborate much that I felt myself: corroboration, too—which made it so much more convincing—from a totally different point of view. He composed such curious sentences, and hurled them at me in such an inconsequential sort of way, as though his main line of thought was secret to himself, and these fragments were the bits he found it impossible to digest. He got rid of them by uttering them. Speech relieved him. It was like being sick.

"There are things about us, I'm sure, that make for disorder, disintegration, destruction, our destruction," he said once, while the fire blazed between us. "We've strayed out of a safe line somewhere."

And another time, when the gong sounds had come nearer, ringing much louder than before, and directly over our heads, he said, as though talking to himself:

"I don't think a phonograph would show any record of that. The sound doesn't come to me by the ears at all. The vibrations reach me in another manner altogether, and seem to be within me, which is precisely how a fourth dimension sound might be supposed to make itself heard."

I purposely made no reply to this, but I sat up a little closer to the fire and peered about me into the darkness. The clouds were massed all over the sky and no trace of moonlight came through. Very still, too, everything was, so that the river and the frogs had things all their own way.

"It has that about it," he went on, "which is utterly out of common experience. It is unknown. Only one thing describes it really: it is a non-human sound—I mean a sound outside humanity."

Having rid himself of this indigestible morsel, he lay quiet for a time, but he had so admirably expressed my own feeling that it was a relief to have the thought out, and to have confined it by the limitation of words from dangerous wandering to and fro in the mind.

The solitude of that Danube camping-place, can I ever forget it? The feeling of being utterly alone on an empty planet! My thoughts ran incessantly upon cities and the haunts of men. I would have given my soul, as the saying is, for the "feel" of those Bavarian villages we had passed through by the score; for the normal, human commonplaces, peasants drinking beer, tables beneath the trees, hot sunshine, and a ruined castle on the rocks behind the red-roofed church. Even the tourists would have been welcome.

Yet what I felt of dread was no ordinary ghostly fear. It was infinitely greater, stranger, and seemed to arise from some dim ancestral sense of terror more profoundly disturbing than anything I had known or dreamed of. We had "strayed," as the Swede put it, into some region or some set of conditions where the risks were great, yet unintelligible to us, where the frontiers of some unknown world lay close about us. It was a spot held by the dwellers in some outer space, a sort of peephole whence they could spy upon the earth, themselves unseen, a point where the veil between had worn a little thin. As the final result of too long a sojourn here, we should be carried over the border and deprived of what we called "our lives," yet by mental, not physical, processes. In that sense, as he said, we should be the victims of our adventure—a sacrifice.

It took us in different fashion, each according to the measure of his sensitiveness and powers of resistance. I translated it vaguely into a personification of the mightily disturbed elements, investing them with the horror of a deliberate and malefic purpose, resentful of our audacious intrusion into their breeding-place; whereas my friend threw it into the unoriginal form at first of a trespass on some ancient shrine, some place where the old gods still held sway, where the emotional forces of former worshipers still clung, and the ancestral portion of him yielded to the old pagan spell.

At any rate, here was a place unpolluted by men, kept clean by the winds from coarsening human influences, a place where spiritual agencies were within reach and aggressive. Never, before or since, have I been so attacked by indescribable suggestions of a "beyond region," of another scheme of life, another evolution not parallel to the human. And in the end our minds would succumb under the weight of the awful spell, and we should be drawn across the frontier into their world.

Small things testified to this amazing influence of the place, and now in the silence round the fire they allowed themselves to be noted by the mind. The very atmosphere had proved itself a magnifying medium to distort every indication: the otter rolling in the current, the hurrying boatman making signs, the shifting willows, one and all had been robbed of its natural character, and revealed in something of its other aspect—as it existed across the border in that other region. And this changed aspect I felt was new not merely to me, but to the race. The whole experience whose verge we touched was unknown to humanity at all. It was a new order of experience, and in the true sense of the word unearthly.

"It's the deliberate, calculating purpose that reduces one's courage to zero," the Swede said suddenly, as if he had been actually following my thoughts. "Otherwise imagination might count for much. But the paddle, the canoe, the lessening food—"

"Haven't I explained all that once?" I interrupted viciously.

"You have," he answered dryly, "you have indeed."

He made other remarks too, as usual, about what he called the "plain determination to provide a victim," but, having now arranged my thoughts better, I recognized that this was simply the cry of his frightened soul against the knowledge that he was being attacked in a vital part, and that he would be somehow taken or destroyed. The situation called for a courage and calmness of reasoning that neither of us could compass, and I have never before been so clearly conscious of two persons in me—the one that explained everything, and the other that laughed at such foolish explanations, yet was horribly afraid.

Meanwhile, in the pitchy night the fire died down and the woodpile grew small. Neither of us moved to replenish the stock, and the darkness consequently came up very close to our faces. A few feet beyond the circle of firelight it was inky black. Occasionally a stray puff of wind set the billows shivering about us, but apart from this not very welcome sound a deep and depressing silence reigned, broken only by the gurgling of the river and the humming in the air overhead.

We both missed, I think, the shouting company of the winds.

At length, at a moment when a stray puff prolonged itself as though the wind were about to rise again, I reached the point for me of saturation, the point where it was absolutely necessary to find relief in plain speech, or else to betray myself by some hysterical extravagance that must have been far worse in its effect upon both of us. I kicked the fire into a blaze, and turned to my companion abruptly. He looked up with a start.

"I can't disguise it any longer," I said. "I don't like this place, and the darkness, and the noises, and the awful feelings I get. There's something here that beats me utterly. I'm in a blue funk, and that's the plain truth. If the other shore was—different, I swear I'd be inclined to swim for it!"

The Swede's face turned very white beneath the deep tan of

sun and wind. He stared straight at me and answered quietly, but his voice betrayed his huge excitement by its unnatural calmness. For the moment, at any rate, he was the strong man of the two. He was more phlegmatic, for one thing.

"It's not a physical condition we can escape from by running away," he replied, in the tone of a doctor diagnosing some grave disease. "We must sit tight and wait. There are forces close here that could kill a herd of elephants in a second as easily as you or I could squash a fly. Our only chance is to keep perfectly still. Our insignificance perhaps may save us."

I put a dozen questions into my expression of face, but found no words. It was precisely like listening to an accurate description of a disease whose symptoms had puzzled me.

"I mean that so far, although aware of our disturbing presence, they have not found us—not 'located' us, as the Americans say," he went on. "They're blundering about like men hunting for a leak of gas. The paddle and canoe and provisions prove that. I think they feel us, but cannot actually see us. We must keep our minds quiet—it's our minds they feel. We must control our thoughts, or it's all up with us."

"Death you mean?" I stammered, icy with the horror of his suggestion.

"Worse—by far," he said. "Death, according to one's belief, means either annihilation or release from the limitations of the senses, but it involves no change of character. You don't suddenly alter just because the body's gone. But this means a radical alteration, a complete change, a horrible loss of oneself by substitution—far worse than death, and not even annihilation. We happen to have camped in a spot where their region touches ours where the veil between has worn thin"—horrors! he was using my very own phrase, my actual words—"so that they are aware of our being in their neighborhood."

"But who are aware?" I asked.

I forgot the shaking of the willows in the windless calm, the humming overhead, everything except that I was waiting for an answer that I dreaded more than I can possibly explain.

He lowered his voice at once to reply, leaning forward a little over the fire, an indefinable change in his face that made me avoid his eyes and look down upon the ground.

"All my life," he said, "I have been strangely, vividly conscious of another region—not far removed from our own world in one sense, yet wholly different in kind—where great things go on unceasingly, where immense and terrible personalities hurry by, intent on vast purposes compared to which earthly affairs, the rise and fall of nations, the destinies of empires, the fate of armies and continents, are all as dust in the balance; vast purposes, I mean, that deal directly with the soul, and not indirectly with mere expressions of the soul—"

"I suggest just now—" I began, seeking to stop him, feeling as though I was face to face with a madman. But he instantly overbore me with his torrent that had to come.

"You think," he said, "it is the spirits of the elements, and I thought perhaps it was the old gods. But I tell you now it is—neither. These would be comprehensible entities, for they have relations with men, depending upon them for worship or sacrifice, whereas these beings who are now about us have absolutely nothing to do with mankind, and it is mere chance that their space happens just at this spot to touch our own."

The mere conception, which his words somehow made so convincing, as I listened to them there in the dark stillness of that lonely island, set me shaking a little all over. I found it impossible to control my movements.

"And what do you propose?" I began again.

"A sacrifice, a victim, might save us by distracting them until we could get away," he went on, "just as the wolves stop to devour the dogs and give the sleigh another start. But, I see no chance of any other victim now."

I stared blankly at him. The gleam in his eyes was dreadful.

Presently he continued.

"It's the willows, of course. The willows mask the others, but the others are feeling about for us. If we let our minds betray our fear, we're lost, lost utterly." He looked at me with an expression so calm, so determined, so sincere, that I no longer had any doubts as to his sanity. He was as sane as any man ever was. "If we can hold out through the night," he added, "we may get off in the daylight unnoticed, or rather, undiscovered."

"But you really think a sacrifice would—"

That gong-like humming came down very close over our heads as I spoke, but it was my friend's scared face that really stopped my mouth.

"Hush!" he whispered, holding up his hand. "Do not mention them more than you can help. Do not refer to them by name. To name is to reveal: it is the inevitable clue, and our only hope lies in ignoring them, in order that they may ignore us."

"Even in thought?" He was extraordinarily agitated.

"Especially in thought. Our thoughts make spirals in their world. We must keep them out of our minds at all costs if possible."

I raked the fire together to prevent the darkness having everything its own way. I never longed for the sun as I longed for it then in the awful blackness of that summer night.

"Were you awake all last night?" he went on suddenly.

"I slept badly a little after dawn," I replied evasively, trying to follow his instructions, which I knew instinctively were true, "but the wind, of course—"

"I know. But the wind won't account for all the noises."

"Then you heard it too?"

"The multiplying countless little footsteps I heard," he said, adding, after a moment's hesitation, "and that other sound—"

"You mean above the tent, and the pressing down upon us of something tremendous, gigantic?"

He nodded significantly.

"It was like the beginning of a sort of inner suffocation?" I said.

"Partly, yes. It seemed to me that the weight of the atmosphere had been altered—had increased enormously, so that we should be crushed."

"And that," I went on, determined to have it all out, pointing upwards where the gong-like note hummed ceaselessly, rising and falling like wind. "What do you make of that?"

"It's their sound," he whispered gravely. "It's the sound of their world, the humming in their region. The division here is so thin that it leaks through somehow. But, if you listen carefully, you'll find it's not above so much as around us. It's in the willows. It's the willows themselves humming, because here the willows have been made symbols of the forces that are against us."

I could not follow exactly what he meant by this, yet the thought and idea in my mind were beyond question the thought and idea in his. I realized what he realized, only with less power of analysis than his. It was on the tip of my tongue to tell him at last about my hallucination of the ascending figures and the moving bushes, when he suddenly thrust his face again close into mine across the firelight and began to speak in a very earnest whisper. He amazed me by his calmness and pluck, his apparent control of the situation. This man I had for years deemed unimaginative, stolid!

"Now listen," he said. "The only thing for us to do is to go on as though nothing had happened, follow our usual habits, go to bed, and so forth; pretend we feel nothing and notice nothing. It is a question wholly of the mind, and the less we think about them the better our chance of escape. Above all, don't think, for what you think happens!"

"All right," I managed to reply, simply breathless with his words and the strangeness of it all, "all right, I'll try, but tell me one thing more first. Tell me what you make of those hollows in the ground all about us, those sand-funnels?"

"No!" he cried, forgetting to whisper in his excitement. "I dare not, simply dare not, put the thought into words. If you have not guessed I am glad. Don't try to. They have put it into my mind. Try your hardest to prevent their putting it into yours."

He sank his voice again to a whisper before he finished, and I did not press him to explain. There was already just about as much horror in me as I could hold. The conversation came to an end, and we smoked our pipes busily in silence.

Then something happened, something unimportant apparently, as the way is when the nerves are in a very great state of tension, and this small thing for a brief space gave me an entirely different point of view. I chanced to look down at my sand-shoe—the sort we used for the canoe—and something to do with the hole at the toe suddenly recalled to me the London shop where I had bought them, the difficulty the man had in fitting me, and other details of the uninteresting but practical operation. At once, in its train, followed a wholesome view of the modern skeptical world I was accustomed to move in at home. I thought of roast beef and ale, motor-cars, policemen, brass bands, and a dozen other things that proclaimed the soul of ordinariness or utility. The effect was immediate and astonishing even to myself. Psychologically, I suppose, it was simply a sudden and violent reaction after the strain of living in an atmosphere of things that to the normal consciousness must seem impossible and incredible. But, whatever the cause, it momentarily lifted the spell from my heart, and left me for the short space of a minute feeling free and utterly unafraid. I looked up at my friend opposite.

"You damned old pagan!" I cried, laughing aloud in his face. "You imaginative idiot! You superstitious idolator! You—"

I stopped in the middle, seized anew by the old horror. I

tried to smother the sound of my voice as something sacrilegious. The Swede, of course, heard it too—that strange cry overhead in the darkness—and that sudden drop in the air as though something had come nearer.

He had turned ashen white under the tan. He stood bolt upright in front of the fire, stiff as a rod, staring at me.

"After that," he said in a sort of helpless, frantic way, "we must go! We can't stay now. We must strike camp this very instant and go on—down the river."

He was talking, I saw, quite wildly, his words dictated by abject terror—the terror he had resisted so long, but which had caught him at last.

"In the dark?" I exclaimed, shaking with fear after my hysterical outburst, but still realizing our position better than he did. "Sheer madness! The river's in flood, and we've only got a single paddle. Besides, we only go deeper into their country! There's nothing ahead for fifty miles but willows, willows, willows!"

He sat down again in a state of semi-collapse. The positions, by one of those kaleidoscopic changes nature loves, were suddenly reversed, and the control of our forces passed over into my hands. His mind at last had reached the point where it was beginning to weaken.

"What on earth possessed you to do such a thing?" he whispered, with the awe of genuine terror in his voice and face.

I crossed round to his side of the fire. I took both his hands in mine, kneeling down beside him and looking straight into his frightened eyes.

"We'll make one more blaze," I said firmly, "and then turn in for the night. At sunrise we'll be off full speed for Komorn. Now, pull yourself together a bit, and remember your own advice about not thinking fear!"

He said no more, and I saw that he would agree and obey. In some measure, too, it was a sort of relief to get up and make an excursion into the darkness for more wood. We kept close together, almost touching, groping among the bushes and along the bank. The humming overhead never ceased, but seemed to me to grow louder as we increased our distance from the fire. It was shivery work!

We were grubbing away in the middle of a thickish clump of willows where some driftwood from a former flood had caught high among the branches, when my body was seized in a grip that made me half drop upon the sand. It was the Swede. He had fallen against me, and was clutching me for support. I heard his breath coming and going in short gasps.

"Look! By my soul!" he whispered, and for the first time in my experience I knew what it was to hear tears of terror in a human voice. He was pointing to the fire, some fifty feet away. I followed the direction of his finger, and I swear my heart missed a beat.

There, in front of the dim glow, something was moving.

I saw it through a veil that hung before my eyes like the gauze drop-curtain used at the back of a theater—hazily a little. It was neither a human figure nor an animal. To me it gave the strange impression of being as large as several animals grouped together, like horses, two or three, moving slowly. The Swede, too, got a similar result, though expressing it differently, for he thought it was shaped and sized like a clump of willow bushes, rounded at the top, and moving all over upon its surface, "coiling upon itself like smoke," he said afterwards.

"I watched it settle downwards through the bushes," he sobbed at me. "Look, by God! It's coming this way! Oh, oh!" He gave a kind of whistling cry. "They've found us."

I gave one terrified glance, which just enabled me to see that the shadowy form was swinging towards us through the bushes, and then I collapsed backwards with a crash into the branches. These failed, of course, to support my weight, so that with the Swede on the top of me we fell in a struggling heap upon the sand. I really hardly knew what was happening. I was conscious only of a sort of enveloping sensation of icy fear that plucked the nerves out of their fleshly covering, twisted them this way and that, and replaced them quivering. My eyes were tightly shut. Something in my throat choked me. A feeling that my consciousness was expanding, extending out into space, swiftly gave way to another feeling that I was losing it altogether, and about to die.

An acute spasm of pain passed through me, and I was aware that the Swede had hold of me in such a way that he hurt me abominably. It was the way he caught at me in falling.

But it was this pain, he declared afterwards, that saved me: it caused me to forget them and think of something else at the very instant when they were about to find me. It concealed my mind from them at the moment of discovery, yet just in time to evade their terrible seizing of me. He himself, he says, actually swooned at the same moment, and that was what saved him.

I only know that at a later time, how long or short is impossible to say, I found myself scrambling up out of the slippery network of willow branches, and saw my companion standing in front of me holding out a hand to assist me. I stared at him in a dazed way, rubbing the arm he had twisted for me. Nothing came to me to say, somehow.

"I lost consciousness for a moment or two," I heard him say. "That's what saved me. It made me stop thinking about them."

"You nearly broke my arm in two," I said, uttering my only connected thought at the moment. A numbness came over me.

"That's what saved you!" he replied. "Between us, we've managed to set them off on a false tack somewhere. The humming has ceased. It's gone—for the moment at any rate!"

A wave of hysterical laughter seized me again, and this time spread to my friend too—great healing gusts of shaking laughter that brought a tremendous sense of relief in their train. We made our way back to the fire and put the wood on so that it blazed at once. Then we saw that the tent had fallen over and lay in a tangled heap upon the ground.

We picked it up, and during the process tripped more than once and caught our feet in sand.

"It's those sand-funnels," exclaimed the Swede, when the tent was up again and the firelight lit up the ground for several yards about us. "And look at the size of them!"

All round the tent and about the fireplace where we had seen the moving shadows there were deep funnel-shaped hollows in the sand, exactly similar to the ones we had already found over the island, only far bigger and deeper, beautifully formed, and wide enough in some instances to admit the whole of my foot and leg.

Neither of us said a word. We both knew that sleep was the safest thing we could do, and to bed we went accordingly without further delay, having first thrown sand on the fire and taken the provision sack and the paddle inside the tent with us. The canoe, too, we propped in such a way at the end of the tent that our feet touched it, and the least motion would disturb and wake us.

In case of emergency, too, we again went to bed in our clothes, ready for a sudden start.

V

I T WAS MY FIRM INTENTION to lie awake all night and watch, but the exhaustion of nerves and body decreed otherwise, and sleep after a while came over me with a welcome blanket of oblivion. The fact that my companion also slept quickened its approach. At first he fidgeted and constantly sat up, asking me if I "heard this" or "heard that." He tossed about on his cork mattress, and said the tent was moving and the river had risen over the point of the island, but each time I went out to look I returned with the report that all was well, and finally he grew calmer and lay still. Then at length his breathing became regular and I heard unmistakable sounds of snoring—the first and only time in my life when snoring has been a welcome and calming influence.

This, I remember, was the last thought in my mind before dozing off.

A difficulty in breathing woke me, and I found the blanket over my face. But something else besides the blanket was pressing upon me, and my first thought was that my companion had rolled off his mattress on to my own in his sleep. I called to him and sat up, and at the same moment it came to me that the tent was surrounded. That sound of multitudinous soft pattering was again audible outside, filling the night with horror.

I called again to him, louder than before. He did not answer, but I missed the sound of his snoring, and also noticed that the flap of the tent door was down. This was the unpardonable sin. I crawled out in the darkness to hook it back securely, and it was then for the first time I realized positively that the Swede was not there. He had gone.

I dashed out in a mad run, seized by a dreadful agitation, and the moment I was out I plunged into a sort of torrent of humming that surrounded me completely and came out of every quarter of the heavens at once. It was that same familiar humming—gone mad! A swarm of great invisible bees might have been about me in the air. The sound seemed to thicken the very atmosphere, and I felt that my lungs worked with difficulty.

But my friend was in danger, and I could not hesitate.

The dawn was just about to break, and a faint whitish light spread upwards over the clouds from a thin strip of clear horizon. No wind stirred. I could just make out the bushes and river beyond, and the pale sandy patches. In my excitement I ran frantically to and fro about the island, calling him by name, shouting at the top of my voice the first words that came into my head. But the willows smothered my voice, and the humming muffled it, so that the sound only traveled a few feet round me. I plunged among the bushes, tripping headlong, tumbling over roots, and scraping my face as I tore this way and that among the preventing branches.

Then, quite unexpectedly, I came out upon the island's point and saw a dark figure outlined between the water and the sky. It was the Swede. And already he had one foot in the river! A moment more and he would have taken the plunge.

I threw myself upon him, flinging my arms about his waist and dragging him shorewards with all my strength. Of course he struggled furiously, making a noise all the time just like that cursed humming, and using the most outlandish phrases in his anger about "going inside to Them," and "taking the way of the water and the wind," and God only knows what more besides, that I tried in vain to recall afterwards, but which turned me sick with horror and amazement as I listened. But in the end I managed to get him into the comparative safety of the tent, and flung him breathless and cursing upon the mattress, where I held him until the fit had passed.

I think the suddenness with which it all went and he grew calm, coinciding as it did with the equally abrupt cessation of the humming and pattering outside—I think this was almost the strangest part of the whole business perhaps. For he just opened his eyes and turned his tired face up to me so that the dawn threw a pale light upon it through the doorway, and said, for all the world just like a frightened child:

"My life, old man—it's my life I owe you. But it's all over now anyhow. They've found a victim in our place!"

Then he dropped back upon his blankets and went to sleep literally under my eyes. He simply collapsed, and began to snore again as healthily as though nothing had happened and he had never tried to offer his own life as a sacrifice by drowning. And when the sunlight woke him three hours later—hours of ceaseless vigil for me—it became so clear to me that he remembered absolutely nothing of what he had attempted to do, that I deemed it wise to hold my peace and ask no dangerous questions.

He woke naturally and easily, as I have said, when the sun was already high in a windless hot sky, and he at once got up and set about the preparation of the fire for breakfast. I followed him anxiously at bathing, but he did not attempt to plunge in, merely dipping his head and making some remark about the extra coldness of the water.

"River's falling at last," he said, "and I'm glad of it."

"The humming has stopped too," I said.

He looked up at me quietly with his normal expression. Evidently he remembered everything except his own attempt at suicide.

"Everything has stopped," he said, "because..."

He hesitated. But I knew some reference to that remark he had made just before he fainted was in his mind, and I was determined to know it.

"Because 'They've found another victim'?" I said, forcing a little laugh.

"Exactly," he answered, "exactly! I feel as positive of it as though, as though—I feel quite safe again, I mean," he finished.

He began to look curiously about him. The sunlight lay in hot patches on the sand. There was no wind. The willows were motionless. He slowly rose to feet.

"Come," he said. "I think if we look, we shall find it."

He started off on a run, and I followed him. He kept to the banks, poking with a stick among the sandy bays and caves and little back-waters, myself always close on his heels.

"Ah!" he exclaimed presently, "ah!"

The tone of his voice somehow brought back to me a vivid sense of the horror of the last twenty-four hours, and I hurried up to join him. He was pointing with his stick at a large black object that lay half in the water and half on the sand. It appeared to be caught by some twisted willow roots so that the river could not sweep it away. A few hours before the spot must have been under water.

"See," he said quietly, "the victim that made our escape possible!"

And when I peered across his shoulder I saw that his stick rested on the body of a man. He turned it over. It was the corpse of a peasant, and the face was hidden in the sand. Clearly the man had been drowned but a few hours before, and his body must have been swept down upon our island somewhere about the hour of the dawn—at the very time the fit had passed.

"We must give it a decent burial, you know."

"I suppose so," I replied. I shuddered a little in spite of myself, for there was something about the appearance of that poor drowned man that turned me cold.

The Swede glanced up sharply at me, and began clambering down the bank. I followed him more leisurely. The current, I noticed, had torn away much of the clothing from the body, so that the neck and part of the chest lay bare.

Halfway down the bank my companion suddenly stopped and held up his hand in warning, but either my foot slipped, or I had gained too much momentum to bring myself quickly to a halt, for I bumped into him and sent him forward with a sort of leap to save himself. We tumbled together on to the hard sand so that our feet splashed into the water. And, before anything could be done, we had collided a little heavily against the corpse.

The Swede uttered a sharp cry. And I sprang back as if I had been shot.

At the moment we touched the body there arose from its surface the loud sound of humming—the sound of several hummings—which passed with a vast commotion as of winged things in the air about us and disappeared upwards into the sky, growing fainter and fainter till they finally ceased in the distance. It was exactly as though we had disturbed some living yet invisible creatures at work.

My companion clutched me, and I think I clutched him, but before either of us had time properly to recover from the unexpected shock, we saw that a movement of the current was turning the corpse round so that it became released from the grip of the willow roots. A moment later it had turned completely over, the dead face uppermost, staring at the sky. It lay on the edge of the main stream. In another moment it would be swept away.

The Swede started to save it, shouting again something I did not catch about a "proper burial" and then abruptly dropped upon his knees on the sand and covered his eyes with his hands. I was beside him in an instant.

I saw what he had seen.

For just as the body swung round to the current the face and the exposed chest turned full towards us, and showed plainly how the skin and flesh were indented with small hollows, beautifully formed, and exactly similar in shape and kind to the sand-funnels that we had found all over the island.

"Their mark!" I heard my companion mutter under his breath. "Their awful mark!"

And when I turned my eyes again from his ghastly face to the river, the current had done its work, and the body had been swept away into midstream and was already beyond our reach and almost out of sight, turning over and over on the waves like an otter.

THE DANGER FROM THE DEEP

by Ralph Milne Farley

WITHIN A THICK-WALLED SPHERE of steel eight feet in diameter, with crystal-clear fused-quartz windows, there crouched an alert young scientist, George Abbot. The sphere rested on the primeval muck and slime at the bottom of the Pacific Ocean, one mile beneath the surface.

Marooned on the sea-floor, his hoisting cable cut, young Abbot is left at the mercy of the man-sharks.

The beam from his 200-watt searchlight, which shot out through one of his three windows into the dark blue depths beyond, seemed faint indeed, yet it served to illuminate anything which crossed it, or on which it fell.

For a considerable length of time since his descent to the ocean floor, young Abbot had clung to one of the thick windows of his bathysphere, absorbed by the marine life outside. Slender small fish with stereoscopic eyes, darted in and out of the beam of light. Swimming snails floated by, carrying their own phosphorescent lanterns. Paper-thin transparent crustaceans swam into view, followed by a few white shrimps, pale as ghosts. Then a mist of tiny fish swept across his field of vision. Abbot cupped his face in his hands, and stared out.

The incongruous thought flashed across his mind that thus he had often sat by the window of his club in New York, and gazed out at the passing motor traffic.

His searchlight cut a sharp swath through the blue muck. More than once he thought he saw large moving fish-like forms far away.

"Speed up the generator," he called into his phone.

Immediately the shaft of light brightened. He set about trying to focus upon one of those dim elusive shapes which had so intrigued him.

But suddenly the searchlight went out! Intent on repairing the apparatus as rapidly as possible, Abbot snapped the button-switch, which ought to have illuminated the interior of his diving-sphere, but the lights did not go on. Then he noticed that the electric fan, on which he depended to keep his air-supply properly mixed, had stopped.

He spoke into the telephone transmitter, which hung in front of his mouth: "Hi, there, up on the boat! My electric power is cut off. I'm down here with my fan stopped and my heat cut off. Hoist me up, and be quick about it!"

"O.K., sir."

As the young man waited for the winch to get under way on the boat a mile above him, he pulled out his electric pocket flashlight and sent its feeble ray out through his quartz-glass window into the dim royal-purple depths beyond, in one last attempt to get a look at those mysterious fish-shapes which had so intrigued him.

And then he saw one of them distinctly.

Evidently they had swum closer when the glow of his searchlight had stopped, and so the sudden flash of his pocket-light had taken them by surprise.

For, as he snapped it on, he caught an instant's glimpse of a grinning fish-face pressed close against the outside of his thick window-pane, as though trying to peer in at him. The fish-face somewhat resembled the head of a shark, except that the mouth was a bit smaller and not quite so leeringly brutal, and the forehead was rather high and domed.

But what most attracted Abbot's attention, in the brief instant before the startled fish whisked away in a swirl of phosphorescent foam, was the fact that, from beneath each of the two pectoral fins, there protruded what appeared to be a skinny human arm, terminating in three fingers and a thumb!

Then the fish was gone. Abbot snapped off his little light.

The diving-sphere quivered, as the hoisting-cable tautened. But suddenly the sphere settled back to the bottom of the sea with a jarring thud. "Cable's parted, sir!" spoke a frantic voice in his ear-phones.

For a moment George Abbot sat stunned with horror. Then his mind began to race, like a squirrel in a cage, seeking some way of escape.

Perhaps he could manage to unscrew the 400-pound trap door at the top of the sphere, and shoot to the surface, with the bubbling-out of the confined air. But his scientifically trained mind made some rapid calculations which showed him this was absurd.

At the depth of a mile, the pressure is roughly 156 atmospheres, that is to say, 156 times the air-pressure at the surface of the earth, and the moment that his sphere was opened to this pressure, he would be blown back inwardly away from the man-hole, and the air inside his sphere would suddenly be compressed to only 1/156 of its former volume.

Not only would this pressure be sufficient to squash him into a mangled pulp, but also the sudden compression of the air inside the sphere would generate enough heat to fry that mangled pulp to a crisp cinder almost instantly.

As George Abbot came to a full realization of the horror of

these facts, he recoiled from the trap-door as though it were charged with death.

"For Heaven's sakes, do something!" he shrieked in agony into the transmitter.

"Courage, sir," came back the reply. "We are rigging up a grapple just as fast as we can. Long before your oxygen gives out, we shall slide it down to you along the telephone line, which is the only remaining connection between us. When it settles about your sphere, and you can see its hooks outside your window by the light of your pocket-flash, let us know, and we'll trip the grapple and haul you up."

"Thank you," replied the young man.

He was calm now, but it was an enforced and numb kind of calmness. Mechanically he throttled down his oxygen supply, so as to make it last longer. Mechanically he took out his notebook and pencil and started to write down, in the dark, his experiences, for he was determined to leave a full account for posterity, even though he himself should perish.

After setting down a categorical description of the successive partings of the electric light cable and the hoist cable, and his thoughts and feelings in that connection, he described in detail the shark with hands, which he had seen through the window of his sphere. He tried to be very explicit about this, for he realized that his account would probably be laid, by everyone, to the disordered imagination of his last dying moments. Being a true scientist, George Abbot wanted the world to believe him, so that another sphere would be built and sent down to the ocean depths, to find out more about these peculiar denizens of the deep.

Of course, no one would believe him. This thought kept drumming in his ears. No one—except Professor Osborne. Old Osborne would believe!

George Abbot's mind flashed back to a conversation he had had with the old professor, just before the oil interests had sent him on this exploring trip to discover the source of the large quantities of petroleum which had begun to bubble up from the bottom of a certain section of the Pacific very near where Abbot now was.

Osborne had said, "This petroleum suggests a gusher to me. And what causes gushers? Human beings, boring for oil, to satisfy human needs."

"But, Professor," Abbot had objected, "there can't be any human beings at the bottom of the sea!"

"Why not?" Professor Osborne had countered. "Life is supposed to have originated spontaneously in the slime of the ocean depths, therefore that part of the earth has had a head-start on us in the game of evolution. May not this head-start have been maintained right down to date, thus producing at the bottom of the sea a race superior to anything upon the dry land?"

"But," Abbot had objected further, "if so, why haven't they come up to visit or conquer us? And why haven't we ever found any trace of them?"

"Quite simple to explain," the old professor had replied. "Any creature who can live at the frightful pressures of the ocean depths could never survive a journey even halfway to the surface. It would be like our trying to live in an almost perfect vacuum. We should explode, and so would these denizens of the deep, if they tried to come up here. Even one of their dead bodies could not be brought to the surface in recognizable form. No contact with them will ever be possible, nor will they ever constitute a menace to any one—for which we may thank the Lord!"

George Abbot now reviewed this conversation as he crouched in his diving-sphere in the purple darkness of the marine depths. Yes, old Osborne would believe him. The diary must be written for Osborne's eyes.

Abbot sent another beam from his pocket light suddenly

out into the water, and this time he surprised several of the peculiar fish. These, like the first, had arms and hands and high intelligent foreheads.

Then suddenly Abbot laughed a harsh laugh. Old Osborne had been wrong in one thing, namely in saying that the super-race of the deep would never be a menace to anyone. They were being a menace to George Abbot, right now, for it was undoubtedly they who had cut his cables. Probably they were possessed of much the same scientific curiosity with regard to him as he was with regard to them, and so they had determined to secure him as a museum specimen.

The idea was a weird one. He laughed again, mirthlessly.

"What is the matter, sir?" came an anxious voice in his earphones.

"Hurry that grapple!" was his reply. "I have found out what cut my cables. There are some very intelligent-looking fish down here, and I think they want me for—"

An ominous click sounded in his ears. Then silence.

"Hello! Hello there!" he shouted. "Can you hear me up on the boat?"

But no answer came back. The line remained dead. The strange fish had cut George Abbot's last contact with the upper world. The grapple-hooks could never find him now, for there was now not even a telephone cable to guide them down to his sphere.

The realization that he was hopelessly lost, and that he had not much longer to live, came as a real relief to him, after the last few moments of frantic uncertainty.

Hoping that his sphere would eventually be found, even though too late to do him any good, he set assiduously to work jotting down all the details which he could remember of those strange denizens of the deep, the man-handed sharks, which he was now firmly convinced were the cause of his present predicament.

He stared out through one of his windows into the brilliant blue darkness, but did not turn on his flashlight. How near were these enemies of his, he wondered?

The presence of those menacing man-sharks, just outside the four-inch-thick steel shell, which withstood a ton of pressure for each square inch of its surface, began to obsess young Abbot. What were they doing out there in the watery-blue midnight? Perhaps, having secured his sphere as a scientific specimen, they were already preparing to cut into it so as to see what was inside. That these fish could cut through four inches of steel was not so improbable as it sounded, for had they not already succeeded in severing a rubber cable an inch and a half thick, containing two heavy copper wires, and also two inches of the finest, non-kinking steel rope!

The young scientist flashed his pocket torch out through the thick quartz pane, but his enemies were nowhere in sight. Then he fell to calculating his oxygen supply. His normal consumption was about half a quart per minute, at which rate his two tanks would be good for thirty-six hours. His chemical racks contained enough soda-lime to absorb the excess carbon dioxide, enough calcium chloride to keep down the humidity and enough charcoal to sweeten the body odors for much more than that period.

For a moment, the thought of these facts encouraged him. He had been down less than two hours. Perhaps the boat above him could affect his rescue in the more than thirty-four hours which remained!

But then he realized that he had failed to take into consideration the near-freezing temperature of the ocean depths. This temperature he knew to be in the neighborhood of 39 degrees Fahrenheit—even though no thermometer hung outside his window, as none could withstand the frightful pressures at the bottom of the sea. For it is one of the remarkable facts of inductive science that man has been able to figure out a priori that the temperature at all deep points of the ocean, tropic as well as arctic, must always be stable at approximately 39 degrees.

Abbot was clad only in a light cotton sailor suit, and now that his source of heat had been cut off by the severing of his power lines, his prison was rapidly becoming unbearably chilly. His thick steel sphere constituted such a perfect transmitter of heat that he might almost as well have been actually swimming in water of 39 degrees temperature, so far as comfort was concerned.

Abbot's emotions ran all the gamut from stupefaction, through dull calmness, clear-headed thought, intense but aimless mental activity, nervousness, frenzy, and insane delirium, back to stupefaction again.

During one of his periods of calmness, he figured out what an almost total impossibility there was of the chance that his ship, one mile above him on the surface, could ever find his sphere with grappling hooks. Yet he prayed for that chance. A single chance in a million sometimes does happen.

Several hours had by now elapsed since the parting of the young scientist's cables. It was bitterly cold inside the sphere. In order to keep warm, he had to exercise during his calm moments as systematically as his cramped quarters would permit. During his frantic moments he got plenty of exercise automatically. And of course all this movement used up more than the normal amount of oxygen, so that he was forced to open the valves on his tanks to two or three times their normal flow. His span of further life was thereby cut to ten or twelve hours, if indeed he could keep himself warm for that long.

Why didn't the people on the boat do something!

He was just about to indulge in one of his frantic fits of despair, when he heard or felt—the two senses being strangely commingled in his present situation—a clank or thump upon the top of his bathysphere. Instantly hope flooded him. Could it be that the one chance in a million had actually happened, and that a grapple from the boat above had actually found him?

With feverish expectation, he pressed the button of his little electric pocket flashlight, and sent its feeble beam out through one of the quartz-glass windows into the blue-black depths beyond.

No hooks in front of this window. He tried the others. No hooks there, either. But he did see plenty of the superhuman fish. Eighteen of them, he counted, in sight at one time. And also two huge snake-like creatures with crested backs and maned heads, veritable sea-serpents.

As there was nothing the young man could do to assist in the grappling of his sphere by his friends in the boat above, he devoted his time to jotting down a detailed description of these two new beasts and of their behavior.

One of the sharks appeared to be leading or driving them up to the bathysphere, and when they got close enough, Abbot was surprised to see that they wore what appeared to be a harness!

The clanking upon the bathysphere continued, and now the young man learned its cause. It was not the grapple hooks from his ship, but chains—chains which the man-armed sharks were wrapping around the bathysphere.

Two more of the harnessed sea-serpents swam into view, and these two were hitched to a flat cart: an actual cart with wheels. The chains were attached to the harness of the original two beasts. They swam upward and disappeared from view, and the sphere slowly rose from the mucky bottom of the sea, to be lowered again squarely on top of the cart. The cart jerked forward, and a journey over the ocean floor began.

Then the little pocket torch dimmed to a dull red glow, and the scene outside faded gradually from view. Abbot switched off the now useless light and set to work with scientific precision to record all these unbelievable events.

In his interest and excitement, he had forgotten the ever-increasing cold, but gradually, as he wrote, the frigidity of his surroundings was forced on his consciousness. He turned on more oxygen, and exercised frantically. Meanwhile the cart, carrying his bathysphere, bumped along over an uneven road.

From time to time, he tried his almost exhausted little light, but its dim red beam was completely absorbed by the blue of the ocean depths, and he could make out nothing except two bulking indistinct shapes, writhing on ahead of him. Finally even this degree of visibility failed, and he could see absolutely nothing outside.

He was now so chilled and numb that he could no longer write. With a last effort, he noted down that fact, and then put the book away in its rack.

He began to feel drowsy. Rousing himself, he turned on more oxygen. The effect was exhilaration and a feeling of silly joy. He began to babble drunkenly to himself. His head swam. His mind was in a daze.

It seemed hours later when he awoke. Ahead of him in the distance there was a dim pale-blue light, against which there could be seen, in silhouette, the forms of the two serpentine steeds and their fish-like drivers. Abbot's hands and feet were completely numb, but his head was clear.

As they drew nearer to the light, it gradually took form, until it turned out to be the mouth of a cave. The cart entered it.

Down a long tunnel they progressed, the light getting brighter and brighter as they advanced. The color of the light became a golden green. The rough stone walls of the tunnel could now be seen, and finally there appeared, ahead, two semi-circular doors, swung back against the sides of the passage.

Beyond these doors, the tunnel walls were smooth and exactly cylindrical, and on the ceiling there were many luminous tubes, which lit up the place as brightly as daylight. The cart came to a stop.

The young scientist could now see with surprising distinctness his captors and their serpentine steeds, and even the details of the chains and the harness. He tried to pick up his diary, so as to jot down some points which he had theretofore missed; but his hands were too numb. But at least he could keep on observing; so he glued his eyes to the thick quartz window-pane once more.

A short distance ahead in the passage there was another pair of doors. Presently these swung open and the cavalcade moved forward. Five or six successive pairs of doors were passed in this manner, and then the sea-serpents began to thrash about and become almost unmanageable. It was evident that some change not to their liking had taken place in their surroundings.

At last, as one of the portals swung open, young Abbot saw what appeared to be four deep-sea diving-suits. Could these suits contain human beings? And if so, who? It seemed incredible, for no diving-suit had ever been devised in which a man could descend to the depth of one mile, and live.

These four figures, whatever they were, came stolidly forward and took charge of the cart. One of the sharks swam up to them and appeared to talk to them with its hands. Then the sharks unhitched the two sea-serpents and led them to the rear, and Abbot saw them no more.

The four divers picked up the chains, and slowly towed the cart forward, their clumsy, ponderous movements contrasting markedly with the swift and sure swishings which had characterized the man-sharks and their snake-like steeds.

Several more pairs of doors were passed, and then there met them four figures in less cumbersome diving-suits, like those ordinarily used by men just below the surface of the sea. One of the deep-sea divers then pressed his face close to the outside of one of the windows of the bathysphere, as though to take a look inside, but the four newcomers waved him away, and hurriedly picked up the chains. Nevertheless, in that brief instant, Abbot had seen within the head-piece of the diver what appeared to be a bearded human face.

Several more pairs of doors were passed. The four deep-sea divers floundered along beside the cart, quite evidently having more and more difficulty of locomotion as each successive doorway was passed, until finally they lay down and were left behind.

At last the procession entered a section of tunnel which was square, instead of circular, and in which there was a wide shelf along one side about three feet above the floor. The four divers then dropped the chains, and one by one took a look at Abbot through his window.

And he at the same time took a most interested look at them.

They had unmistakable human faces!

He must be dreaming! For even if Osborne was right about his supposed super-race at the bottom of the sea, this race could not be human, for the pressures here would be entirely too great. No human being could possibly stand two thousand pounds per square inch!

Having satisfied their curiosity, the four divers pulled themselves up onto the shelf, and sat there in a row with their legs hanging over.

Abbot glanced upward at the ceiling lights, but these had become strangely blurred. There seemed to be an opaque barrier above him, and this barrier seemed to be slowly descending. The lights blurred out completely, and were replaced by a diffused illumination over the entire ripply barrier. And then it dawned on the young man that this descending sheet of silver was the surface of the water. He was in a lock, and the water was being pumped out.

The surface settled about the helmets of the divers, and their helmets disappeared, then their shoulders and the rest of them. At last it reached the level of Abbot's window. The divers could again be seen, and among then on the shelf there stood a half dozen naked bearded men, clad only in loin-cloths. They had evidently entered the lock while the water was subsiding.

These men unbuckled the helmets of the divers and helped them out, and then splashed down into the water and peered in through the windows of the bathysphere. Presently some of them left through a door at the end of the platform, but soon reappeared with staging, which they set up around the sphere. Then, climbing on top, they got to work on the man-hole cover.

As George Abbot realized their purpose, he became frantic. Although these men appeared to be human, just like himself, yet his scientifically-trained mind told him that they must be of some very special anatomical structure, in order to be able to withstand the immense pressures at the bottom of the Pacific. It was all right for them to be out there, but it would be fatal to him!

And then the heavy circular door above him began slowly to revolve.

This was terrible! In a moment the crushing pressures of the depths would come seeping in. Rising unsteadily upon his knees, the young man tried with his fingers to resist the rotation of the door, but it continued to turn.

Yet no pressure could be felt. The door became completely unscrewed. It was pried up, and slid off the top of the bathysphere, to crash upon the floor outside. Inquisitive bearded faces peered down through the hole.

Young Abbot slumped to the cold bottom of the sphere and stared back at them. He was saved—incredibly saved! These were real people, the air was real air and he must therefore be on the surface of the earth, instead of at the bottom of the Pacific as he had imagined! With a sigh of relief, he fainted...

When he came to his senses again, he was lying in a bed in a small room. Bending over him was the sweetest feminine face that he had ever seen.

The girl seemed to be about twenty years of age. She was clad in a clinging robe of some filmy green substance. Her hair was honey-brown, short and curly, and her forehead high and intelligent. Her eyes, an indescribable shade of deep violet, were matchlessly set off by her ivory skin.

The young man smiled up at her, and she smiled back. Thus far it had not occurred to him to wonder where he was, or why. No recollection of his recent strange adventures came to him. To him this was an exotic dream, from which he did not care to awake.

She spoke. Her words were unintelligible, and unlike any language which George Abbot knew or had even heard, and he was an accomplished linguist in addition to his other attainments.

And her words were not all that was strange about her speech, for the very tones of her voice sounded completely unhuman, although not displeasing. Her talk had a metallic ring to it, like the brassy blare of temple gongs, and yet was so smooth and subdued as to be sweeter than any sound that the young scientist had ever heard before.

"Beautiful dream fairy," replied the enraptured young man, "I haven't the slightest idea what you are saying, but keep right on. I like it."

His own voice sounded crass and crude compared to hers. At his first words she gave a start of surprise, but thereafter the sound did not appear to grate on her ears.

Then one of the bearded men in loin-cloths entered, and he and the girl talked together, quite evidently about their patient. The man's voice had the same strange metallic quality to it as that of the girl, but was deeper, so that it boomed with the rich notes of a bell.

At the sight of the man, young Abbot's memory swept back, and he remembered the adventure of his diving-sphere, and its capture, one mile down, by the strange shark-fish with human hands and arms. But how he had reached the surface of the earth again, he couldn't figure out. Nor did he particularly care.

The strange man withdrew, and the girl sat down beside the bed and smiled at Abbot. He smiled back at her.

Presently another girl entered and called, "Milli!"

The girl beside the bed started, and looking up asked some question, to which the other replied.

The newcomer brought in some strange warm food in a covered dish and then withdrew. The first girl proceeded to feed her patient.

After the meal, which tasted unlike anything which the young man had ever eaten before, the beautiful nurse again essayed conversation with him. She seemed perplexed and a bit frightened that he could not understand her words. Somehow, the young man sensed that this girl had never heard any other language than her own, and that she did not even know that other languages existed.

Strengthened by his food, he determined to set about learning her language as soon as possible. So he pointed at her and asked, "Milli?"

She nodded, and spoke some word which he took for "yes."

Then he pointed to himself and said, "George."

She understood, but the word was a difficult one for her to duplicate in the metallic tongue of her people. She made several attempts, until he laughingly spoke her word for "yes."

Then he pointed to other objects about the room. She gave him the names of these, but he could easily see that she felt that, if he did not know the names for all these common things, there must be something the matter with him.

He wondered how he could make her understand that there were other languages in the world than her own, and then he remembered the sharks with their hands and what he had taken to be their sign language. Perhaps Milli at least knew of the existence of the sign language. This would afford a parallel, for if she realized that there were two languages in the world, might there not be three?

So Abbot made some meaningless signs with his fingers. Milli quite evidently was accustomed to this kind of talk, but she was further perplexed to find that George talked gibberish with his hands as well as with his mouth.

She made some signs with her hands, and then said something orally. Young Abbot instantly pointed to her mouth, and held up one finger, then to her hands, and held up two, then to his own mouth, and held up three, at the same time speaking a sentence of English. Instantly she caught on: there were three languages in the world. And thereafter she no longer regarded him as crazy.

For several hours she taught him. Then another meal was brought, after which she left him, and the lights went out.

He awakened feeling thoroughly rested and well. The lights were on and Milli was beside him.

He asked for his clothes. They were brought. Milli withdrew and he put them on.

After breakfast, which they ate together, one of the bearded men came and led him out through a number of winding corridors into a larger room, in which there was a closed spherical glass tank, about ten feet in diameter, containing one of the human sharks. Around the tank stood five of the bearded men.

One of them proceeded to address Abbot, but of course the young American could not make out what he was saying. This apparent lack of intelligence seemed to exasperate the man, and finally he turned toward the tank, and engaged in a sign language conference with the fish, then turned back to Abbot again and spoke to him very sternly.

But Abbot shook his head and replied, "Milli. Bring Milli."

One of the other men flashed a look of triumph at their leader, and laughed.

"Yes," he added, "bring Milli."

The leader scowled at him, and some words were interchanged, but it ended in Milli being sent for. She apparently explained the situation to the satisfaction of the fish, to the intense glee of the man who had sent for her, and to the rather complete discomfiture of the leader of the five.

Abbot later learned that the leader's name was Thig, and that the name of the gleeful man was Dolf.

The reception over, Milli led Abbot back to his room.

There ensued many days—very pleasant days—of language instruction from Milli. Dolf and Thig and others of the five came frequently, to note his progress and to talk with him and ask him questions.

A sitting room was provided for him, adjoining his sleeping quarters. Milli occupied quarters nearby.

Within a week he had mastered enough of the language of these people, for their strange history began to be intelligible to him.

In spite of the fact that the air here was at merely atmospheric pressure, nevertheless this place was one mile beneath the surface of the Pacific. Milli and her people lived in a city hollowed out of a reef of rocks, reinforced against the terrific weight of the water and filled with laboratory-made air. They had never been to the surface of the sea.

The fish with the human arms were their creators and their masters.

Professor Osborne had been right. The fish of the deep, having a head start on the rest of the world, had evolved to a perfectly unbelievable degree of intelligence. Centuries ago they had built for themselves the exact analog of George Abbot's bathysphere, and in it they had made much the same sort of exploring trips to the surface that he had made down into the deeps. But their spheres had been constructed to keep in, rather than to keep out, great pressure.

Their scientists had gathered a wealth of data as to conditions on the surface, and had even seen and studied human beings. But their insatiable scientific curiosity had led them to want to know more about the strange country above them and the strange persons who inhabited it. And so they set about breeding, in their own laboratories, creatures which should be as like as possible to those whom they had observed on the surface.

Of course, this experiment necessitated their first setting up an air-filled partial vacuum similar to that which surrounds the earth. But they had persisted. They had brought down samples of air from the surface of the sea, and had analyzed and duplicated it on a large scale.

Finally, through long years, they had so directed—and controlled the course of evolution, in their breederies, as first to be able to produce creatures which could live in air at low pressures, and then to evolve the descendants of those creatures into intelligent human beings.

Some of the lower types of this evolutionary process, both in the direct line of descent of man, and among the collateral offshoots, had been retained for food and other purposes. Abbot, with intense scientific interest, studied these specimens in the zoo of the underwater city where he was staying.

Plans had been in progress for some time, among the fish-folk and their human subjects, to send an expedition to the surface. And now the shark masters had fortunately been able to secure alive an actual specimen of the surface folk—namely, George Abbot. The expedition was accordingly postponed until they could pump out of the young scientist all the information possible.

Abbot was naturally overjoyed at the prospect. This would not only get him out of here—but think what it would mean to science!

The plans of the sharks were entirely peaceful. Furthermore there were only about two hundred of their laboratory-bred synthetic human beings, and so these could constitute no menace to mankind. Accordingly he enthusiastically assured them that they could depend upon the hearty cooperation of the scientists of the outer earth.

During all his stay so far in this cave city, Abbot had been permitted to come in contact only with Milli, the members of the Committee of Five, and an occasional guard or laboratory assistant. Yet, in spite of the absence of personal contacts with other members of this strange race, Abbot was constantly aware of a background of many people and tense activity, which kept the wheels of industry and domestic economy turning in this undersea city.

Although the young man readily accustomed himself to the speech and food and customs of this strange race, his personal modesty and neatness revolted at the loin-cloths and beards of the men, and so, by special dispensation, he was permitted to wear his sailor suit and to shave.

The Committee of Five, who constituted a sort of ruling body for the city, interviewed him at length, cross-examined him most skilfully and took copious notes. But there seemed to be a strange lack of common meeting ground between their minds and his, so that very often they were forced to call on Milli to act as an intermediary. The beautiful young girl seemed able to understand both George Abbot and the leaders of her own people with equal facility.

A number of specially constructed submarines had already been built to carry the expedition to the surface. Before it came time to use them, Abbot tried to paint as glowing a picture as possible of life on earth, but he found it necessary to gloss over a great many things. How could he explain and justify war, liquor, crime, poverty, graft, and the other evils to which constant acquaintance has rendered the human race so calloused?

He was unable to deceive the men of the deep. With their super-intelligence, they relentlessly unearthed from him all the salient facts. And, as a result of their discoveries, their initial friendly feeling for the world of men rapidly developed into supreme contempt.

But Abbot on the other hand developed a deep respect for them. Their chemistry and their electrical and mechanical devices amazed and astounded him. They even were able to keep sun-time and tell the seasons, by means of gyroscopes!

Age was measured much as it is on the surface. This fact was brought to Abbot's attention by the approach of Milli's twentieth birthday.

Strange to relate, she seemed to dread the approach of that anniversary, and finally told Abbot the reason.

"It is the custom," said she, "when a girl or a boy reaches twenty, to give a very rigorous intelligence test. In fact, such a test is given on every birthday, but the one on the twentieth is the hardest. So far, I have just barely passed each test, which fact marks me as of very low mentality indeed. And, if I fail this time, they will kill me, so as to make room for others who have a better right to live."

"Impossible!" exclaimed the young man indignantly. "Why, you have a better mind than those of many of the leading scientists of the outer world!"

"All the same," she gloomily replied, "it is way below standard for down here."

On the day of the test, he did his best to cheer her up. Dolf also came—she seemed to be an especial protege of his—and gave her his encouragement. He had been coaching her heavily for the examinations for some time previous.

But later in the day she returned in tears to report to Abbot that she had failed, and had only twenty-four hours to live. Before he realized what he was doing, Abbot had seized her in his arms, and was pouring out to her a love which up to that moment he had not realized existed.

Finally her sobbing ceased, and she smiled through her tears.

"George, dear," said she, "it is worth dying, to know that

you care for me like this."

"I won't let them kill you!" asserted the young man belligerently. "They owe me something for the assistance which I am to give them on their expedition. I shall demand your life as the price of my cooperation. Besides, you are the only one of all your people who has brains enough to understand what I tell them about the outer earth. It is they who are weak-minded, not you!"

But she sadly shook her head.

"It would never do for you to sponsor me," said she, "for it would alienate my one friend in power, Dolf. He loves me—no, don't scowl, for I do not love him. But, for the safety of both of us, we must not let him know of our love—yet."

"Yet?" exclaimed Abbot, "when you have less than a day to live?"

"You have given me hope," the girl replied, "and also an idea. Dolf promised to appeal to the other members of the Five. I have just thought of a good ground for his appeal—namely, my ability to translate your clumsy description into a form suited to the high intelligence of our superiors."

"Clumsy?" exclaimed the young man, a bit nettled.

"Oh, pardon me, dear. I'm so sorry," said she contritely. "I didn't mean to let it slip. And now I must rush to Dolf and tell him my idea."

"Don't let him make love to you, though!" admonished Abbot gloomily.

She kissed him lightly, and fled.

A half hour later she was back, all smiles. The idea had gone across big. Dolf, as the leader of the projected expedition, had demanded that Milli be brought along as liaison officer between them and their guide, and the other four committeemen had reluctantly acceded. The execution was accordingly indefinitely postponed.

The young couple spent the evening making happy plans for

their life together on the outer earth, for as soon as they should arrive in America, Dolf would have no further hold over them.

The next day, the Committee of Five announced that, for a change, they were going to give George Abbot an intelligence test. He had represented himself as being one of the scientists of the outer earth; accordingly, they could gauge the caliber of his fellow countrymen by determining his I.Q.

Milli was quite agitated when this program was announced, but the ordeal held no terrors for George Abbot. Had he not taken many such tests on earth and passed them easily?

So he appeared before the Committee of Five with a rather cocky air. He had yet to see an intelligence test too tricky for him to eat alive.

"Start him with something easy," suggested Dolf. "Perhaps they don't have tests on the outer earth. You know, one gains a certain facility by practice."

"Milli didn't, in spite of all the practicing which you gave her," maliciously remarked Thig.

Dolf glowered at him.

What is the cube root of 378?" suddenly asked one of the other members of the committee.

"Oh, a little over seven," hazarded Abbot.

"Come, come," boomed Thig, "give it to us exactly."

"Well, seven-point-two, I guess."

"Don't guess. Give it exact, to four decimal places."

"In my head?" asked Abbot incredulously.

"Certainly!" replied Thig. "Even a child could do that. We're giving you easy questions to start with."

"Start him on square root," suggested Dolf kindly. "Remember he isn't used to these tests like our people are."

So they tried him with square root, in which he turned out to be equally dumb.

Abstract questions of physics and chemistry he did better on, but the actual quantitative problems, which they expected him to solve in his head, stumped him completely.

Then they asked him about education on earth, and the qualifications for becoming a scientist, and who were the leaders in his field, and what degrees they held, and what one had to do to get those degrees, etc. Finally they dismissed him. Dolf then sent for Milli.

She was gone about an hour, and returned to Abbot wide-eyed and incredulous.

"Oh, George," said she, lowering her voice. "Dolf tells me that your intelligence is below that of a five-year-old child! Perhaps that is why you and I get along so well together: we are both morons."

He started to protest, but she silenced him with a gesture and hurried on. "I am not supposed to tell you this, but I want you to know that your examination today has resulted in a complete change in their plans for the expedition to the surface. They have consulted with the leaders of our masters, and they agree with them."

She was plainly agitated.

"What is it, dear?" asked Abbot, with ominous foreboding.

Milli continued. "Early during your test, when you demonstrated that you couldn't do the very simplest mathematical problems in your head, they began to doubt your boastings that you are a scientist. But you were so ingenuous in your answers about conditions on the surface, that finally their faith in your honesty returned. If you are a scientist among men, as they now believe, then the average run of your people must be mere animals. This explains what has puzzled them before; namely, how the people of the earth tolerate poverty and unemployment and crime, and disease and war."

"Well?"

"And so a mere handful of our people, by purely peaceful means, could easily make themselves the rulers of the earth. Probably this would be all for the best, but somehow, my feelings tell me that it is not. I know only too well what it is to be an inferior among intelligent beings, so will not your people be happier, left alone to their stupidity, just as I would be?"

George Abbot was crushed. This frank acceptance by Milli of the alleged fact that he was a mere moron, was most humiliating. And swiftly he realized what a real menace to the earth, was this contemplated invasion from the deeps.

All that was worst in the world above would taint these intellectual giants of the undersea. They would rise to supremacy, and then would become rapacious tyrants over those whom they would regard as being no more than animals.

He had witnessed jealousies among them down below. Might not these jealousies flame into huge wars when translated to the world above? Giants striving for mastery, using the human cattle as cannon fodder! He painted to the girl a word-picture of the horrible vision which he foresaw.

The invasion must be stopped at all costs! He and Milli must pit their puny wits against these supermen!

But what could they do? As they were pondering this problem, a girl entered their sitting room—the same who had brought Abbot's breakfast on his first day in the caves. Milli introduced George to the newcomer, whose name was Romehl.

Romehl appeared so woebegone that the young American ventured to inquire if she too had been having difficulty with one of her tests. But that was not the trouble; hers was rather of the heart.

About the same age as Milli, Romehl had recently passed her twentieth birthday test and hence was eligible to marry, so she and a young man named Hakin had requested the fish-masters to give them the requisite permission. But their overlords for some reason had peremptorily denied the request. Romehl and Hakin were desolate.

Young Abbot's sympathies were at once aroused.

"Can't something be done?" he started to ask.

But Milli silenced him with a warning glance. "Of course not!" she said. "Who are we to question the judgment of our all-knowing masters?"

Romehl had really come to Milli just to pour her troubles into a friendly ear, rather than because she hoped to get any helpful ideas. So she had a good cry, and finally left, somewhat comforted.

George and Milli then took up again the problem of saving the outer earth from the threatened invasion. Milli suggested that they go peaceably with the expedition, and then warn the authorities of America at the first opportunity after their arrival, but Abbot pointed out that this would merely result in their both being shut up in some insane asylum, as no one would believe such a crazy story as theirs.

The time for lights to be put out arrived without their thinking of any better idea.

Next day Milli spent considerable time with Dolf, and on her return excitedly informed Abbot that he had evolved a most diabolical plot. There were sufficient quantities of explosives in storage to blast a hole through the wall of the caves, letting in the sea and killing everyone in the city. Dolf planned to set this off with a time fuse, upon the departure of the expedition. Thus Thig and the people who were left behind—about two-thirds of the total population of the city—would be destroyed, and the fish would have no one to send after Dolf and his followers to dictate to them on the upper earth.

Relieved of the thraldom of the fish, Dolf could make himself Emperor of the World, and rule over the human cattle, with Milli at his side as Empress. An alluring program—from Dolf's point of view.

I didn't expect such treason even from Dolf!" exclaimed the young American. "We must tell Thig!"

"What good would that do?" remonstrated the girl. "If you failed to convince Thig, Dolf would make an end of us both.

And if you convinced Thig, it would mean the end of Dolf, whose influence is all that keeps me alive. We must think of something else."

"Right, as always," replied Abbot.

A growl came from the doorway. It was Dolf, his bearded face black with wrath.

"So?" he sputtered. "Treachery, eh?"

He whistled twice and two guards appeared.

"Take them to the prison!" he raged, indicating Abbot and Milli. "Our expedition will have to do without a guide. I have learned enough of the American language to make a good start, and I guess I can pick up another guide when we reach the surface." Then, bending close to the frightened girl, he whispered, "And another Empress."

The guards hustled them away and locked them up. As an added precaution, a sentinel was posted in front of each cell door.

Abbot immediately got busy.

"Can you get word for me at once to Thig?" he whispered to the man on guard.

"Perhaps," replied that individual non-committally.

"Then tell him," said Abbot, "that I have proof that Dolf is planning to destroy this city behind him, and never return from the surface."

The sentry became immediately agitated.

"So you know this?" he exclaimed. "How did it leak out? But—through Milli, of course. And the guard on her cell is not a member of the expedition! Curses! I must get word to Dolf, and have that guard changed at once."

And he darted swiftly away.

The young prisoner was plunged into gloom. Now he'd gone and done it! Why hadn't he first made appropriate inquiries of his guard?

A new guard appeared in front of the door.

"Are you going on the expedition?" asked Abbot.

"Yes, worse luck," replied the guard.

The prisoner forgot his own gloom, in his surprise at the gloominess of the other.

"Don't you want to go?" he exclaimed incredulously.

"No."

"Why not?"

"Do you know Romehl?" asked the guard.

"Yes," Abbot replied.

"Well, that's why."

"Then you must be Hakin!" exclaimed Abbot, with sudden understanding.

"Yes," replied the other dully.

"You are going on the expedition, and Romehl is not?"

"Quite correct."

"Say, look here!" exclaimed Abbot, and then he launched into the description of a plan, which just that moment had occurred to him, for him, Milli, Romehl and Hakin to make their getaway ahead of the expedition—in fact, that very night—and to set off the time-fuse before leaving.

It turned out that Hakin knew where the explosives were planted, and where the submarines were kept, and even how to operate them. He eagerly accepted the plan, and when next relieved as sentinel, he hurried away to inform Romehl.

Three hours later he was back on post. Quickly he explained to his prisoner all about the workings of the submarines of the expedition. The lights-out bell rang, and all the city became dark, except for dim lights in the passageways. Hakin at once unlocked the door of Abbot's cell, and together the two young men sneaked down the corridor to the cell where Milli was confined.

Silently Hakin and Abbot sprang upon the guard and throttled him, then released Milli. There was no time for more than a few hurried words of explanation before the three of them left the prison and made for the locks of the subterranean canal, picking up Romehl at a preappointed spot on the way.

The canal locks were unguarded, as well as the storerooms of the submarines. Each of the rooms held two subs, and could open onto the second lock and be separately flooded.

The submarines were of steel as thick as Abbot's bathysphere. Their shape was that of an elongated rain drop, with fins. In the pointed tip of their tails were motors which could operate at any pressure. At the front end were quartz windows. In the top fin was an expanding device which could be filled with buoyant gas, produced by chemicals, when the craft neared the surface. Each submarine also contained a radio set, so tuned as to be capable of opening and closing the radio-controlled gates of the locks. Each would carry comfortably two or three persons.

Having picked out two submarines and found them to be in order, Hakin sneaked back into the corridor to set off the time-fuse, leaving his three companions in the dark in the storeroom. Abbot put a protecting arm around Milli, while Romehl snuggled close to her other side.

Their hearts were all racing madly with excitement, and this was intensified when they heard Hakin talking with someone just outside their door.

Then Hakin returned unexpectedly.

"Something terrible has happened!" he breathed. "The explosives have been discovered and are gone. One of the expedition men has just informed me. Someone must have gotten word to Thig—"

"Why, I did," interrupted Milli. "I told my guard, just before they came and changed him."

Abbot groaned.

Hakin continued hurriedly, "So Dolf plans to leave at once. He is already rounding up his followers. Come on! We must get out ahead of him!"

An uproar could be heard drawing near in the corridor outside. Abbot opened the door and peered out; then shut it again and whispered, "The two factions are fighting already."

"Then come on!" exclaimed Hakin.

As he spoke he turned on the lights, wedged the door tight against its gaskets and threw the switch which started the water seeping into the storeroom, then he led Romehl hurriedly to one of the two submarines, while George and Milli rushed to the other. Heavy blows sounded against the storeroom door.

The water rapidly rose about them, and the four friends crawled inside the two machines and clamped the lids tight. Then they waited for sufficient depth, so that they could get under way.

The water rose above their bow windows, but suddenly and inexplicably it began to subside again. A man waded by around the bow of Abbot's machine.

"They've crashed in the door, and are pumping out the water again!" exclaimed Abbot. "We're trapped!"

"Not yet!" grimly replied the girl at his side. "Can you work the radio door controls?"

"Yes."

"Then quick! Open the doors into the lock!"

He pressed a button. Ahead of them two gates swung inward, followed by a deluge of water.

"Come on!" spoke the girl. "Full speed ahead, before the water gets too low."

Abbot did so. Out into the lock they sped, in the face of the surging current. Then Abbot pushed another button to close the gates behind them. But the water continued to fall, and they grounded before they reached the end of the lock. Quite evidently the rush of the current had kept the doors from closing behind them. The city was being flooded through the broken door of the storeroom.

But Abbot opened the next gate, and again they breasted

the incoming torrent. This time, although the level continued to fall, their craft did not quite ground.

"They must have got the gates shut behind us at last," said he, as he opened the next set and pressed on.

And then he had an idea. Why not omit to close any further gates behind him? As a result, the sea pressure would eventually break down the inmost barriers, and destroy the city as effectively as Dolf's bomb would have done. But he said nothing to Milli of this plan: she might wish to save her people.

Gate after gate they passed. This was too simple. A few more locks and they would be out in open water. The submarine of Hakin and Romehl swept by—evidently to let George and Milli know their presence—and then dropped behind again. But was it their two friends after all? It might have been some enemy! They could not be sure.

This uncertainty cast a chill of apprehension over them, which was immediately heightened by the sudden extinguishing of the overhead lights of the tunnel. Abbot pressed the radio button for the next set of locks, but they did not budge.

"What can be the matter?" he asked frantically.

"My people must have turned off the electric current," Milli replied. "The gates won't open without electricity to feed the motors. We're trapped again."

For a moment they lay stunned by a realization that their escape was blocked.

"Kiss me goodbye, dear," breathed Milli. "This is the end."

As the young man reached over to take her in his arms, the submarine was suddenly lifted up and spun backward, end over end, then tumbled and bumped along, as though it were a chip on an angry mountain torrent.

Stunned and bruised and bleeding, the young American finally lost consciousness....

When he came to his senses again, his first words were, "Milli, where are you?"

"My darling!" breathed a voice at his side. "Are you all right?"

"Yes," he replied. "Where are we? What has happened?"

"The entire system of locks must have crashed in and flooded the city," said she.

Instantly Abbott's mind grasped the explanation of this occurrence: their leaving open so many gates behind them had made it impossible for the few remaining gates ahead to withstand the terrific pressures of the ocean depths, and they had crumpled. But he did not tell Milli his part in this.

She continued, "I was pretty badly shaken up myself, but I've got this boat going again, and we're on our way out of the tunnel. See—I've found out how to work our searchlight."

He looked. A broad beam of light from their bow, illuminated the tunnel ahead of them.

Presently another beam appeared, shooting by them from behind.

"Hakin and Romehl!" exclaimed the girl. "Then they're safe, too!"

The tunnel walls grew rough, then disappeared. They were out in the open sea at last, although still one mile beneath the surface.

But in front of them was an angry seething school of the man-sharks, clearly illumined by the two rays of light. Behind the sharks were a score or more of serpentine steeds.

The sharks saw the two submarines and charged down upon them, but Milli, with great presence of mind, shut off her searchlight and swung sharply to the left.

"Up! Up!" urged the young man, so she turned the craft upward.

On and on they went, with no interference. Presently they turned the light on again, so as to see what progress they were making. But they were making absolutely none! They were merely standing on their tail. They had reached a height of such relatively low pressure that it took all the churning of their propeller just merely to counteract the great weight of their submarine.

Abbot switched on their chemical gas supply, and as their top fin expanded into a balloon they again began to rise.

One thing, however, perplexed the young man: the water about him seemed jet black rather than blue. They must by now be close to the surface of the sea, where at least a twilight blue should be visible. Even at the one mile depth in his bathysphere, the water had been brilliant, yet here, almost at the surface, he could see absolutely nothing.

He switched on the searchlight again to make sure that their window wasn't clouded over, but it wasn't.

Then suddenly a rippling veil of pale silver appeared ahead, then a blue-black sky and twinkling stars. They had reached the surface, and it was night.

He pointed out the stars to the girl at his side, then swung the nose of the submarine around and showed her the moon.

Where next? George Abbot picked out his position by the stars and headed east. East across the Pacific, toward America.

But soon he noticed that their little craft was dropping beneath the surface. He kept heading up more and more; he threw the lever for more and more chemical gas, yet still they continued to sink.

"Milli!" he exclaimed, "we've got to get out of here!"

She clutched him in fear, for to her the pressure of the open sea meant death, certain death. But he pushed her firmly away, and unclamped the lid of the submarine. In another instant he had hauled her out and was battling his way to the surface, while their little boat sunk slowly beneath them.

Milli was an experienced swimmer, for the undersea folk enjoyed the privilege of a large indoor pool. As soon as she found that the open sea did not kill her, she became calm.

Side by side they floated in the moonlight. The sky began to pink in the east. Dawn came, the first dawn that Milli had ever seen.

Suddenly she called George's attention to two bobbing heads some distance away in the path of light the rising sun made on the ocean.

"Hakin and Romehl!" he exclaimed. Long since they had given them up for dead, but evidently fate had treated them in much the same way as themselves.

And a moment later his own salt-stung eyes noticed a long gray shape to one side.

As the day brightened, Abbot suddenly noticed a large bulking shape nearby.

It was his own boat!—the one which had lowered him into the depths in his bathysphere so many weeks and weeks ago! Evidently it was still sticking around, grappling for his long dead body.

"Come on, dear," said he, and side by side they swam over to it.

He helped her up the ship's ladder. The ship's cook sleepily stuck his head out of the galley door.

"Hullo, Mike," sang out George Abbot merrily to the astonished man. "I've brought company for breakfast. And there'll be two more when we can lower a boat."

A BEWITCHED SHIP

by W. Clark Russell

ABOUT TEN YEARS AGO," began my friend, Captain Green, "I went as second mate of a ship named the 'Ocean King.' She'd been an old Indiaman in her time, and had a poop and topgallant forecastle, though alterations had knocked some of the dignity out of her. Her channels had been changed into plates with dead-eyes above the rail, and the eye missed the spread of the lower rigging that it naturally sought in looking at a craft with a square stern and windows in it, and checkered sides rounding out into curves, that made a complete tub of the old hooker. Yet, spite of changes, the old-fashioned grace would break through. She looked like a lady who has seen better days, who has got to do work which servants did for her in the times when she was well off, but who, let her set her hand to what she will, makes you see that the breeding and the instincts are still there, and that she's as little to be vulgarized by poverty and its coarse struggles as she could be made a truer lady than she is by money. Ships, like human beings, have their careers, and the close of some of them is strange, and sometimes hard, I think.

"The 'Ocean King' had been turned into a collier, and I went second mate of her when she was full up with coal for a South African port. Yet, this ship, that was now carrying one of the dirtiest cargoes you could name, barring phosphate manure, had been reckoned in her day a fine passenger vessel, a noble Indiaman indeed—her tonnage was something over eleven hundred—with a cuddy fitted up royally. Many a freight of soldiers had she carried round the Cape, many an old nabob had she conveyed—ay, and Indian potentates, who smoked out of jeweled hookahs, and who were waited upon by crowds of black servants in turbans and slippers. I used to moralize over her just as I would over a tomb, when I had the watch and was alone and could let my thoughts run loose.

"The sumptuous cabin trappings were all gone, and I seemed to smell coal in the wind, even when my head was over the weather side, and when the breeze that blew along came fresh across a thousand miles of sea, but there was a good deal of the fittings left—fittings which, I don't doubt, made the newspapers give a long account of this 'fine, great ship' when she was launched—quite enough of them to enable a man to reconstruct a picture of the cuddy of the 'Ocean King' as it was in the days of her glory, when the soft oil-lamps shone bright on the draped tables and sparkled on silver and glass, when the old skipper, sitting with the mizzenmast behind him, would look, with his red face and white hair, down the rows of ladies and gentlemen eating and drinking, stewards running about, trays hanging from the deck above, and globes full of gold-fish swinging to the roll of the vessel as she swung stately, with her stunsails hanging out, over the long blue swell, wrinkled by the wind. The ship is still afloat. Where are the people she carried? The crews who have worked her? The captains who have commanded her? There is nothing that should be fuller of ghosts than an old ship, and I very well remember that when I first visited the 'Victory,' at Portsmouth, and descended into

312

her cockpit, what I saw was not a well-preserved and cleanly length of massive deck, but groups of wounded and bleeding and dying men littering the dark floor, and the hatchway shadowed by groaning figures handed below, while the smell of English, French, and Spanish gunpowder, even down there, was so strong—phew! I could have spat the flavor out!

"Well, the old 'Ocean King' had once upon a time been said to be haunted. She had certainly been long enough afloat to own a hundred stories, and she was so stanch and true that if ever a superstition got into her there was no chance of its getting out again. I only remember one of these yarns. It was told to me by the dockmaster, who had been at sea for many years, was an old man, and knew the history of all such craft as the 'Ocean King.' He said that, in '51, I think it was, there had been a row among the crew: an Italian sailor stabbed an Englishman, who bled to death. To avenge the Englishman's death the rest of the crew, who were chiefly English, thrust the Italian into the forepeak and let him lie there in darkness. When he was asked for they reported that he had fallen overboard, and this seems to have been believed. Whether the crew meant to starve him or not is not certain, but, after he had been in the forepeak three or four days, a fellow going behind the galley out of the way of the wind to light his pipe—it being then four bells in the first watch—came running into the forecastle, with his hair on end, and the sweat pouring off his face, swearing he had seen the Italian's ghost. This frightened the men prettily. Some of them went down into the forepeak, and found the Italian lying there dead, with a score of rats upon him, which scampered off when the men dropped below. During all the rest of the voyage his ghost was constantly seen, sometimes at the lee wheel, sometimes astride of the flying-jibboom. What was the end of it—I mean, whether the men confessed the murder, and, if so, what became of them—the dockmaster said he didn't know. But, be this as it may, I discovered shortly after we had begun our voyage that the crew had got to hear of this story, and the chief mate said it had been brought aboard by the carpenter, who had picked it up from some of the dockyard laborers.

"I well recollect two uncomfortable circumstances. We sailed on a Friday, and the able and ordinary seamen were thirteen in number, the idlers and ourselves aft bringing up the ship's company to nineteen souls when, I suppose, in her prime the 'Ocean King' never left port short of seventy or eighty seamen, not to mention stewards, cooks, cooks' mates, butcher, butcher's mate, baker, and the rest of them. But double topsail yards were now in. Besides, I understood that the vessel's masts had been reduced and her yards shortened, and we carried stump fore and mizzen-topgallant masts.

"All being ready, a tug got hold of our tow-rope, and away we went down the river and out to sea.

"I don't believe myself that any stories which had been told the men about the ship impressed them much. Sailors are very superstitious, but they are not to be scared till something has happened to frighten them. Your merely telling them that there's a ghost aboard the ship they're in won't alarm them till they've caught sight of the ghost. But once let a man say to the others: 'There's a bloomin' sperrit in this ship. Lay your head agin the forehatch, and you'll hear him gnashing his teeth and rattlin' his chains,' and then let another man go and listen, and swear, and perhaps very honestly, that he 'heerd the noises plain,' and you'll have all hands in a funk, talking in whispers, and going aloft in the dark nervously.

"In our ship nothing happened for some days. We were deep and slow, and rolled along solemnly, the sea falling away from the vessel's powerful round bows as from a rock. Pile what we could upon her, with tacks aboard, staysails drawing, and the wind hitting her best sailing point, we could seldom manage to get more than seven knots out of her. One night I had the first watch. It was about two bells. There was a nice wind, sea smooth, and a red moon crawling up over our starboard beam. We were under all plain sail, leaning away from the wind a trifle, and the water washed along under the bends in lines through which the starlight ran glimmering.

"I was thinking over the five or six months' voyages which old wagons after the pattern of this ship took in getting to India, when, seeing a squall coming along, I sung out for hands to stand by the main-royal and mizzen-topgallant halliards. It drove down dark, and not knowing what was behind I ordered the main-royal to be clewed up and furled. Two youngsters went aloft. By the time they were on the yard the squall thinned, but I fancied there was another bearing down, and thought it best to let the ordinary seamen roll the sail up. On a sudden down they both trotted, hand over hand, leaving the sail flapping in the clutch of the clew-lines.

"I roared out: 'What d'ye mean by coming down before you've furled that sail?'

"They stood together in the main rigging, and one of them answered: 'Please, sir, there's a ghost somewhere up aloft on the foretopsail-yard.'

"'A ghost, you fool!' I cried.

"'Yes, sir,' he answered. 'He says: "Jim, your mother wants yer." I says: "What?" and he says: "Your mother wants yer," in the hollowest o' voices. Dick here heard it. There's no one aloft forrard, sir.'

"I sung out to them to jump aloft again, and finding that they didn't move I made a spring, on which they dropped like lightning on deck, and began to beg and pray of me in the eagerest manner not to send them aloft, as they were too frightened to hold on. Indeed, the fellow named Jim actually began to shiver and cry when I threatened him. So as the royal had to be furled I sent an able seaman aloft, who, after rolling up the sail, came down and said that no voice had called to him, and that he rather reckoned it was a bit of skylarking on the part of the boys to get out of stowing the sail. However, I noticed that the man was wonderfully quick over the job, and that afterward the watch on deck stood talking in low voices in the waist.

"Jim was a fool of a youth, but Dick was a smart lad, aged about nineteen, and good-looking, with a lively tongue, and I heard afterward that he could spin a yarn to perfection all out of his imagination. I called him to me, and asked him if he had really heard a voice, and he swore he had.

"'Did it say,' said I, 'Jim, your mother wants you?'

"'Ay, sir,' he answered, with a bit of a shudder, 'as plain as you yourself say it. It seemed to come off the foretop-gallant yard, where I fancied I see something dark a-moving, but I was too frightened to take particular notice.'

"Well, it was not long after this, about eleven o'clock in the morning, that, the captain being on deck, the cook steps out of the galley, comes walking along the poop, and going up to the skipper touches his cap, and stands looking at him.

"'What d'ye want?' said the captain, eying him as if he took him to be mad.

"'Didn't you call, sir?' says the cook.

"'Call!' cries the skipper. 'Certainly not.'

"The man looked stupid with surprise, and, muttering something to himself, went forward. Ten minutes after he came up again to the skipper, and says: 'Yes, sir!' as a man might who answers to a call. The skipper began to swear at him, and called him a lunatic, and so on, but the man, finding he was wrong again, grew white, and swore that if he was on his death-bed he'd maintain that the captain had called him twice.

"The skipper, who was a rather nervous man, turned to me, and said: 'What do you make of this, Mr. Green? I can't doubt the cook's word. Who's calling him in my voice?'

"'Oh, it's some illusion, sir,' said I, feeling puzzled for all that.

"But the cook, with the tears actually standing in his eyes, declared it was no illusion; he'd know the captain's voice if it was nine miles off. And he then walked in a dazed way toward the forecastle, singing out that whether the voice he had heard belonged to a ghost or a Christian man, it might go on calling 'Cook!' for the next twenty years without his taking further notice of it. This thing, coming so soon after the call to Jim that had so greatly alarmed the two ordinary seamen, made a great impression on the crew, and I never regret anything more than that my position should have prevented me from getting into their confidence, and learning their thoughts, for there is no doubt I should have stowed away memories enough to serve me for many a hearty laugh in after years.

"A few days rolled by without anything particular happening. One night it came to my turn to have the first watch. It was a quiet night, with wind enough to keep the sails still while the old ship went drowsily rolling along her course to the African port. Suddenly I heard a commotion forward, and fearing that some accident had happened, I called out to know what the matter was. A voice answered: 'Ghost or no ghost, there's somebody a-talking in the forehold; come and listen, sir.' The silence that followed suggested a good deal of alarm. I sang out as I approached the men, 'Perhaps there's a stowaway below.'

"'It's no living voice,' was the reply, 'it sounds as if it comes from a skelington.'

"I found a crowd of men standing in awed postures near the hatch, and the most frightened of all looked to me to be the ordinary seaman Dick, who had backed away on the other side of the hatch, and stood looking on, leaning with his hands on his knees, and staring as if he were fascinated. I waited a couple or three minutes, which, in a business of this kind, seems a long time, and, hearing nothing, I was going to ridicule the men for their nervousness, when a hollow voice under the hatch said distinctly, 'It's a terrible thing to be a ghost and not be able to get out.'

"I was greatly startled, and ran aft to tell the captain, who agreed with me that there must be a stowaway in the hold, and that he had gone mad. We both went forward, and the hatch was lifted, and we looked on top of the coal, and I was then about to ask some of the men to join me in a search in the forepeak, for upon my word I had no taste single-handed for a job of that kind at such a moment, when the voice said, 'There's no use looking, you'll never find me. I'm not to be seen.'

"'Confound me!' cried the skipper, polishing his forehead with a pocket-handkerchief, 'if ever I heard of such a thing. I'll tell you what it is,' he shouted, looking into the hatch, 'dead men can't talk, and so, as you're bound to be alive, you'd better come up out of that, and smartly too—d'ye hear?—or you'll find this the worst attempt at skylarking that was ever made.'

"There was a short silence, and you'd see all hands straining their ears, for there was light enough for that, given out by a lantern one of the men held.

"'You couldn't catch me because you couldn't see me,' said the voice in a die-away tone, and this time it came from the direction of the main hatch, as though it had flitted aft.

"'Well,' says the captain, 'may I be jiggered!' and without another word he walked away on to the poop.

"I told the men to clap the hatches on again, and they did this in double-quick time, evidently afraid that the ghost might pop up out of the hold if they didn't mind their eye.

"All this made us very superstitious, from the captain down to the boys. We talked it over in the cabin, and the mate was incredulous, and disposed to ridicule me.

"'Anyway,' said he, 'it's strange that this voice is only heard in your watch. It's never favored me with any remarks. The creaking and groaning of an old wooden ship is often like spoken words, and what you've been hearing may be nothing but a deception of the ear.'

"'A deception in your eye,' cried the skipper. 'The timbers

of an old wooden ship may strain and creak in the Dutch language, but hang me if they ever talked good, sensible English. However, I'm not going to worry. For my part,' said he, with a nervous glance around him, 'I don't believe in ghosts; whatever it is that's talking in the hold may go on jawing, so long as he sticks to that, and don't frighten the men with an ugly mug, nor come upon us for a man's allowance.'

"'If it's anybody's ghost,' said I, 'it must be the Italian's, the chap that was starved in the forepeak.'

"'I doubt that,' said the skipper. 'I didn't detect anything foreign in what he said. To my ear it sounded more like Whitechapel than Italiano.'

"Well, for another week we heard little more of the ghost. It's true that one middle watch a chap I had sent aloft to loose the main-royal had hardly stepped out of the lower rigging, after lingering in the crosstrees to overhaul his clew-lines, when he comes rushing up to me and cries out, 'I've been hailed from aloft, sir! A voice has just sung out, "Tommy, jump aloft again that I may have a good look at you!"'

"'Who's up there?' I asked him, staring into the gloom where the mast and yards went towering.

"'There's no one up there, sir. I'll swear it. I was bound to see him had any one been there,' he answered, evidently very much frightened.

"It occurred to me that some one of the crew might be lying hid in the top, and that if I could catch him I might find out who the ghost was. So I jumped into the rigging and trotted aloft, keeping my eye on the lee rigging, to make sure that no one descended by it. I gained the top, but nobody was there. I mounted to the crosstrees, but the deuce a sign of anyone could I see. I came down, feeling both foolish and scared, for you see I had heard the voice myself in the hold. There was no question that there was a voice, belonging to nobody knew what, knocking about the ship, and consequently it was now impossible to help believing a man when he said he heard it.

"However, it was necessary to keep the men in heart, and this was not to be done by captain and mates appearing scared, so I reasoned a bit with the man, told him that there were no such things as ghosts, that a voice was bound to come from a live person, because a spectre couldn't possibly have lungs, those organs being of a perishable nature, and then sent him forward, but no easier in his mind, I suspect, than I was. Anyhow, I was glad when eight bells struck and it was my turn to go below. But, as I have said, nothing much came of this—at least, nothing that reached my ears. But not many nights following the ship lay becalmed—there wasn't a breath of air, and the sea lay smooth as polished jet. This time I had the middle watch again. I was walking quietly up and down the poop, on the lookout for a deeper shadow upon the sea to indicate the approach of wind, when a man came up the ladder and said, 'There's some one a-talking to the ship under the bows.'

"'Are you awake?' said I.

"'Heaven help me, as I stand here, sir,' exclaimed the fellow, solemnly, 'if that there woice which talked in the hold t'other day ain't now over the side.'

"I ran forward, and found most of the watch huddled together near the starboard cathead. I peered over, and there was a dead silence.

"'What are you looking over that side for? I'm here!' said a thin, faint voice, that seemed more in the air than in the sea.

"'There!' exclaimed one of the seamen, in a hoarse whisper, 'that's the third time. Whichever side we look, he's on the other.'

"'But there must be some one in the water,' said another man. 'Anybody see his houtline? cuss me if I couldn't swear I see a chap swimmin' just now.'

"'No, no,' answered some one, gruffly, 'nothing but phosphorus, Joe, and the right sort o' stuff, too, for if this ain't old

Nick—'

"'You're a liar, Sam!' came the voice clear, and, as one could swear, plain from over the side.

"There was a general recoil, and a sort of groan ran among the men.

"At the same moment I collared a figure standing near me, and slued him round to bring his face fair to the starlight, clear of the staysail. 'Come you along with me, Master Dick,' said I, and I marched him off the forecastle, along the main deck, and up on to the poop. 'So you're the ghost, eh?' said I. 'Why, to have kept your secret you should have given my elbow a wider berth. No wonder the voice only makes observations in my watch. You're too lazy, I suppose, to leave your hammock to try your wonderful power on the mate, eh? Now see here,' said I, finding him silent, and noticing how white his face glimmered to the stars, 'I know you're the man, so you'd better confess. Own the truth and I'll keep your secret, providing you belay all further tricks of the same kind; deny that you're the ghost and I'll speak to the captain and set the men upon you.'

"This fairly frightened him. 'Well, sir, it's true, I'm the voice, sir, but for God's sake keep the secret, sir. The men 'ud have my life if they found out that it was me as scared them.'

"This confession was what I needed, for though when standing pretty close to him on the forecastle I could have sworn that it was he who uttered the words which perplexed and awed the sailors, yet so perfect was the deception, so fine, in short, was his skill as a ventriloquist that, had he stoutly denied and gone on denying that he was the 'voice,' I should have believed him and continued sharing in the wonder and superstition of the crew. I kept his secret as I promised, but, somehow or other, it leaked out in time that he could deceive the ear by apparently pitching his voice among the rigging, or under the deck, or over the side, though the discovery was not made until the 'ghost' had for a long time ceased to trouble the ship's company, and until the men's superstitious awe had faded somewhat, and they had recovered their old cheerfulness. We then sent for Dick to the cabin, where he gave us a real entertainment as a ventriloquist, imitating all sorts of animals, and producing sounds as of women in distress and men singing out for help, in the berths. Indeed, such was the skill that I'd often see the skipper and mate turning startled to look in the direction whence the voices proceeded.

"He made his peace with the men by amusing them in the same way, so that, instead of getting the rope's ending aft and the pummeling forward which he deserved, he ended as a real and general favorite, and one of the most amusing fellows that a man ever was shipmate with. I used to tell him that if he chose to perform ashore, he was sure to make plenty of money, since such ventriloquial powers as his was the rarest thing in the world, and I'd sometimes fancy he meant to take my advice. But whether he died or kept on going to sea I don't know, for after he left the ship I never saw nor heard of him again."

THE TERROR OF THE WATER TANK

by William Hope Hodgson

CROWNING THE HEIGHTS on the outskirts of a certain town on the east coast is a large, iron water tank from which an isolated row of small villas obtains its supply. The top of this tank has been cemented, and round it have been placed railings, thus making of it a splendid "look-out" for any of the townspeople who may choose to promenade upon it. And very popular it was until the strange and terrible happenings of which I have set out to tell.

Late one evening, a party of three ladies and two gentlemen had climbed the path leading to the tank. They had dined, and it had been suggested that a promenade upon the tank in the cool of the evening would be pleasant. Reaching the level, cemented surface, they were proceeding across it, when one of the ladies stumbled and almost fell over some object lying near the railings on the town-side.

A match having been struck by one of the men, they discovered that it was the body of a portly old gentleman lying in a contorted attitude and apparently quite dead. Horrified, the two men drew off their fair companions to the nearest of the aforementioned houses. Then, in company with a passing policeman, they returned with all haste to the spot.

By the aid of the officer's lantern, they ascertained the grewsome fact that the old gentleman had been strangled. In addition, he was without watch or purse. The policeman was able to identify him as an old, retired mill-owner, living some little distance away at a place named Revenge End.

At this point the little party was joined by a stranger, who introduced himself as Dr. Tointon, adding the information that he lived in one of the villas close at hand, and had run across as soon as he had heard there was something wrong.

Silently, the two men and the policeman gathered round, as with deft, skillful hands the doctor made his short examination.

"He's not been dead more than about half an hour," he said at its completion.

He turned towards the two men.

"Tell me how it happened—all you know?"

They told him the little they knew.

"Extraordinary," said the doctor. "And you saw no one?"

"Not a soul, doctor!"

The medical man turned to the officer.

"We must get him home," he said. "Have you sent for the ambulance?"

"Yes, sir," said the policeman. "I whistled to my mate on the lower beat, and 'e went straight off."

The doctor chatted with the two men, and reminded them that they would have to appear at the inquest.

"It's murder?" asked the younger of them in a low voice.

"Well," said the doctor. "It certainly looks like it."

And then came the ambulance.

A T THIS POINT, I come into actual contact with the story; for old Mr. Marchmount, the retired mill owner, was the father of my *fiancee*, and I was at the house when the ambulance arrived with its sad burden. Dr. Tointon had accompanied it along with the policeman, and under his directions the body was taken upstairs, while I broke the news to my sweetheart.

Before he left, the doctor gave me a rough outline of the story as he knew it. I asked him if he had any theory as to how and why the crime had been committed.

"Well," he said, "the watch and chain are missing, and the purse. And then he has undoubtedly been strangled; though with what, I have been unable to decide."

And that was all he could tell me. The following day there was a long account in the *Northern Daily Telephone* about the "shocking murder." The column ended, I remember, by re-marking that people would do well to beware, as there were evidently some very desperate characters about, and added that it was believed the police had a clew.

During the afternoon, I myself went up to the tank. There was a large crowd of people standing in the road that runs past at some little distance; but the tank itself was in the hands of the police officer being stationed at the top of the steps leading up to it. On learning my connection with the deceased, he al-lowed me up to have a look round.

I thanked him, and gave the whole of the tank a pretty thorough scrutiny, even to the extent of pushing my cane down through lock-holes in the iron manhole lids, to ascertain whether the tank were full or not, and whether there was room for someone to hide.

On pulling out my stick, I found that the water reached to within a few inches of the lid, and that the lids were securely locked. I at once dismissed a vague theory that had formed in my mind that there might be some possibility of hiding with-in the tank itself and springing out upon the unwary. It was evidently a common, brutal murder, done for the sake of my prospective father-in-law's purse and gold watch.

One other thing I noticed before I quitted the tank top. It came to me as I was staring over the rail at the surrounding piece of waste land. Yet at the time, I thought little of it, and attached to it no importance whatever. It was that the encircling piece of ground was soft and muddy and quite smooth. Possibly there was a leakage from the tank that accounted for it. Anyhow, that is how it seemed to be.

"There ain't nothin' much to be seen, sir," volunteered the policeman, as I prepared to descend the steps on my way back to the road.

"No," I said. "There seems nothing of which to take hold."

And so I left him, and went on to the doctor's house. Fortunately, he was in, and I at once told him the result of my investigations. Then I asked him whether he thought that the police were really on the track of the criminal.

He shook his head.

"No," he answered. "I was up there this morning having a look round, and since then, I've been thinking. There are one or two points that completely stump me—points that I believe the police have never even stumbled upon."

Yet, though I pressed him, he would say nothing definite.

"Wait!" was all he could tell me.

Yet I had not long to wait before something further happened, some thing that gave an added note of mystery and terror to the affair.

O N THE TWO DAYS following my visit to the doctor, I was kept busy arranging for the funeral of my *fiancee's* father, and then on the very morning of the funeral came the news of the death of the policeman who had been doing duty on the tank.

From my place in the funeral procession, I caught sight of large local posters announcing the fact in great letters, while the newsboys constantly cried:

"Terror of the Tank—Policeman Strangled."

Yet, until the funeral was over, I could not buy a paper to gather any of the details. When at last I was able, I found that the doctor who had attended him was none other than Tointon, and straightway I went up to his place for such further particulars as he could give.

"You've read the newspaper account?" he asked when I met him.

"Yes," I replied.

"Well, you see," he said, "I was right in saying that the police were off the track. I've been up there this morning, and a lot of trouble I had to be allowed to make a few notes on my own account. Even then it was only through the influence of Inspector Slago with whom I have once or twice done a little investigating. They've two men and a sergeant now on duty to keep people away."

"You've done a bit of detective work, then?"

"At odd times," he replied. "And have you come to any conclusion?"

"Not yet."

"Tell me what you know of the actual happening," I said. "The newspaper was not very definite. I'm rather mixed up as to how long it was before they found that the policeman had been killed. Who found him?"

"Well, so far as I have been able to gather from Inspector Slago, it was like this. They had detailed one of their men for duty on the tank until two A.M., when he was to be relieved by the next man. At about a minute or so to two, the relief arrived simultaneously with the inspector, who was going his rounds. They met in the road below the tank, and were proceeding up the little side lane towards the passage, when, from the top of the tank, they heard someone cry out suddenly. The cry ended in a sort of gurgle, and they distinctly heard something fall with a heavy thud.

"Instantly, the two of them rushed up the passage, which as you know is fenced in with tall, sharp, iron railings. Even as they ran, they could hear the beat of struggling heels on the cemented top of the tank, and just as the inspector reached the bottom of the steps there came a last groan. The following moment they were at the top. The policeman threw the light of his lantern around. It struck on a huddled heap near by the right-hand railings—something limp and inert. They ran to it, and found that it was the dead body of the officer who had been on duty. A hurried examination showed that he had been strangled.

"The inspector blew his whistle, and soon another of the force arrived on the scene. This man they at once dispatched for me, and in the mean time they conducted a rapid but thorough search, which, however, brought to light nothing. This was the more extraordinary in that the murderer must have been on the tank even as they went up the steps."

"Jove!" I muttered. "He must have been quick."

The doctor nodded.

"Wait a minute," he went on, "I've not finished yet. When I arrived I found that I could do nothing. The poor fellow's neck had been literally crushed. The power used must have been enormous.

"'Have you found anything?' I asked the inspector.

"'No,' he said, and proceeded to tell me as much as he knew, ending by saying that the murderer, whoever it was, had got clean away.

"'But,' I exclaimed, 'he would have to pass you, or else jump the railings. There's no other way.'

"'That's what he's done,' replied Slago rather testily. 'It's no height.'

"'Then in that case, inspector,' I answered, 'he's left something by which we may be able to trace him.'"

"You mean the mud round the tank, doctor?" I interrupted.

"Yes," said Doctor Tointon. "So you noticed that, did you? Well, we took the policeman's lamp, and made a thorough search all round the tank—but the whole of the flat surface of mud-covered ground stretched away smooth and unbroken by even a single footprint!"

The doctor stopped dramatically.

"Good God!" I exclaimed, excitedly. "Then how did the fellow get away?"

Doctor Tointon shook his head.

"That is a point, my dear sir, on which I am not yet prepared to speak. And yet I believe I hold a clew."

"What?" I almost shouted.

"Yes," he replied, nodding his head thoughtfully. "Tomorrow I may be able to tell you something."

He rose from his chair.

"Why not now?" I asked, madly curious.

"No," he said, "the thing isn't definite enough yet."

He pulled out his watch.

"You must excuse me now. I have a patient waiting."

I reached for my hat, and he went and opened the door.

"Tomorrow," he said, and nodded reassuringly as he shook hands. "You'll not forget."

"Is it likely," I replied, and he closed the door after me.

T HE FOLLOWING MORNING I received a note from him asking me to defer my visit until night, as he would be away from home during the greater portion of the day. He mentioned 9:30 as a possible time at which I might call—any time between then and ten P.M. But I was not to be later than that.

Naturally, feeling as curious as I did, I was annoyed at having to wait the whole day. I had intended calling as early as decency would allow. Still, after that note, there was nothing but to wait.

During the morning, I paid a visit to the tank, but was refused permission by the sergeant in charge. There was a large crowd of people in the road below the tank, and in the little side lane that led up to the railed-in passage. These, like myself, had come up with the intention of seeing the exact spot where the tragedies had occurred, but they were not allowed to pass the men in blue.

Feeling somewhat cross at their persistent refusal to allow me upon the tank, I turned up the lane, which presently turns off to the right. Here, finding a gap in the wall, I clambered over, and disregarding a board threatening terrors to trespassers, I walked across the piece of waste land until I came to the wide belt of mud that surrounded the tank. Then, skirting the edge of the marshy ground, I made my way round until I was on the town-side of the tank. Below me was a large wall which hid me from those in the road below. Between me and the tank stretched some forty feet of smooth, mud-covered earth. This I proceeded now to examine carefully.

As the doctor had said, there was no sign of any footprint in any part of it. My previous puzzlement grew greater. I think I had been entertaining an idea somewhere at the back of my head that the doctor and the police had made a mistake—perhaps missed seeing the obvious, as is more possible than many think. I turned to go back, and at the same moment, a little stream of water began to flow from a pipe just below the edge of the tank top. It was evidently the "overflow." Undoubtedly the tank was brim full.

How, I asked myself, had the murderer got away without leaving a trace?

I made my way back to the gap, and so into the lane. And then, even as I sprang to the ground, an idea came to me—a possible solution of the mystery.

I hurried off to see Dufirst, the tank-keeper, who I knew lived in a little cottage a few hundred feet distant. I reached the cottage, and knocked. The man himself answered me, and nodded affably.

"What an ugly little beast!" I thought. Aloud, I said: "Look here, Dufirst, I want a few particulars about the tank. I know you can tell me what I want to know better than anyone else."

The affability went out of the man's face. "Wot do yer want to know?" he asked surlily.

"Well," I replied. "I want to know if there is any place about the tank where a man could hide."

The fellow looked at me darkly. "No," he said shortly.

"Sure?" I asked.

"Course I am," was his sullen reply.

"There's another thing I want to know about," I went on. "What's the tank built upon?"

"Bed er cerment," he answered.

"And the sides, how thick are they?"

"About 'arf-inch iron."

"One thing more," I said, pulling half-a-crown from my pocket (where at I saw his face light up). "What are the inside measurements of the tank?" I passed him over the coin.

He hesitated a moment, then slipped it into his waistcoat pocket. "Come erlong a minnit. I 'ave ther plan of ther thing upstairs, if yer'll sit 'ere an' wait."

"Right," I replied, and sat down, while he disappeared through a door, and presently I heard him rummaging about overhead.

"What a sulky beast," I thought to myself. Then, as the idea passed through my mind, I caught sight of an old bronze luster jug on the opposite side of the room. It stood on a shelf high up, but in a minute I was across the room and reaching up to it, for I have a craze for such things.

"What a beauty," I muttered, as I seized hold of the handle. "I'll offer him five dollars for it."

I had the thing in my hands now. It was heavy. "The old fool!" thought I. "He's been using it to stow odds and ends in." And with that, I took it across to the window. There, in the light, I glanced inside—and nearly dropped it, for within a few inches of my eyes, reposed the old gold watch and chain that had belonged to my murdered friend. For a moment, I felt dazed. Then I knew.

"The little fiend!" I said. "The vile little murderer!"

I put the jug down on the table, and ran to the door. I opened it and glanced out. There, not thirty paces distant was Inspector Slago in company with a constable. They had just gone past the house, and were evidently going up on to the tank.

I did not shout; to do so would have been to warn the man in the room above. I ran after the inspector and caught him by the sleeve.

"Come here, inspector," I gasped. "I've got the murderer."

He twirled round on his heel. "What?" he almost shouted.

"He's in there," I said. "It's the tank-keeper. He's still got the watch and chain. I found it in a jug."

At that the inspector began to run towards the cottage, followed by myself and the policeman. We ran in through the open door, and I pointed to the jug. The inspector picked it up, and glanced inside.

He turned to me. "Can you identify this?" he asked, speaking in a quick, excited voice.

"Certainly I can," I replied. "Mr. Marchmount was to have been my father-in-law. I can swear to the watch being his."

At that instant there came a sound of footsteps on the stairs and a few seconds later the black bearded little tank-keeper came in through an inner door. In his hand he held a roll of paper–evidently the plan of which he had spoken. Then, as his eyes fell on the inspector holding the watch of the murdered man, I saw the fellow's face suddenly pale.

He gave a sort of little gasp, and his eyes flickered round the room to where the jug had stood. Then he glanced at the three of us, took a step backwards and jumped for the door through which he had entered. But we were too quick for him, and in a minute had him securely handcuffed. The inspector warned him that whatever he said would be used as evidence, but there was no need, for he spoke not a word.

"How did you come to tumble across this?" asked the inspector, holding up the watch and guard. "What put you on to it?"

I explained and he nodded.

"It's wonderful," he said. "And I'd no more idea than a mouse that it was him," nodding towards the prisoner.

Then they marched him off.

THAT NIGHT, I kept my appointment at the doctor's. He had said that he would be able to say something, but I rather fancied that the boot was going to prove on the other leg. It was I who would be able to tell him a great deal more than "something." I had solved the whole mystery in a single morning's work. I rubbed my hands, and wondered what the doctor would have to say in answer to my news. Yet, though I waited until 10:30, he never turned up, so that I had at last to leave without seeing him.

The next morning, I went over to his house. There his housekeeper met me with a telegram that she had just received from a friend of his away down somewhere on the South coast. It was to say that the doctor had been taken seriously ill, and was at present confined to his bed, and was unconscious.

I returned the telegram and left the house. I was sorry for the doctor, but almost more so that I was not able personally to tell him the news of my success as an amateur detective.

It was many weeks before Dr. Tointon returned, and in the meantime the tank-keeper had stood his trial and been condemned for the murder of Mr. Marchmount. In court he had made an improbable statement that he had found the old gentleman dead, and that he had only removed the watch and purse from the body under a momentary impulse. This, of course, did him no good, and when I met the doctor on the day of his return, it wanted only three days to the hanging.

"By the way, doctor," I said, after a few minutes' conversation, "I suppose you know that I spotted the chap who murdered old Mr. Marchmount and the policeman?"

For answer the doctor turned and stared.

"Yes," I said, nodding, "it was the little brute of a tank-keeper. He's to be hanged in three days' time."

"What," said the doctor, in a startled voice. "Little black Dufirst?"

"Yes," I said, yet vaguely damped by his tone.

"Hanged!" returned the doctor. "Why the man's as innocent as you are!"

I stared at him.

"What do you mean?" I asked. "The watch and chain were found in his possession. They proved him guilty in court."

"Good heavens!" said the doctor. "What awful blindness!"

He turned on me. "Why didn't you write and tell me?"

"You were ill. Afterwards I thought you'd be sure to have read about it in one of the papers."

"Haven't seen one since I've been ill," he replied sharply. "By George! You've made a pretty muddle of it. Tell me how it happened."

This I did, and he listened intently.

"And in three days he's to be hanged?" he questioned when I had made an end.

I nodded.

He took off his hat and mopped his face and brow.

"It's going to be a job to save him," he said slowly. "Only three days. My God!"

He looked at me, and then abruptly asked a foolish question.

"Have there been any more murders up there while I've been ill?" He jerked his hand toward the tank.

"No," I replied. "Of course not. How could there be when they've got the chap who did them!"

He shook his head.

"Besides," I went on, "noone ever goes up there now, at least, not at night, and that's when the murders were done."

"Quite so, quite so," he agreed, as if what I had said fell in with something that he had in his mind.

He turned to me. "Look here," he said, "come up to my place tonight about ten o'clock, and I think I shall be able to prove to you that the thing which killed Marchmount and the policeman was not, well, it wasn't little black Dufirst."

I stared at him.

"Fact," he said.

He turned and started to leave me.

"I'll come," I called out to him.

A T THE TIME MENTIONED, I called at Dr. Tointon's. He opened the door himself and let me in, taking me into his study. Here, to my astonishment, I met Inspector Slago. The inspector wore rather a worried look, and once when Tointon had left the room for a minute, he bent over towards me.

"He seems to think," he said in a hoarse whisper, and nodding towards the doorway through which the doctor had gone, "that we've made a silly blunder and hooked the wrong man."

"He'll find he's mistaken," I answered.

The inspector looked doubtful, and seemed on the point of saying some thing further, when the doctor returned.

"Now then," Dr. Tointon remarked, "we'll get ready. Here," he tossed me a pair of rubbers, "shove those on.

"You've got rubber heels, inspector?"

"Yes, sir," replied Slago. "Always wear 'em at night."

The doctor went over to a corner, and returned with a double-barreled shotgun which he proceeded to load. This accomplished, he turned to the inspector.

"Got your man outside?"

"Yes, sir," replied Slago.

"Come along, then, the two of you."

We rose and followed him into the dark hall and then out through the front doorway into the silent road. Here we found a plain-clothes policeman waiting, leaning up against a wall. At a low whistle from the inspector, he came swiftly across and saluted. Then the doctor turned and led the way towards the tank.

Though the night was distinctly warm, I shuddered. There was a sense of danger in the air that got on one's nerves. I was quite in the dark as to what was going to happen. We reached the lower end of the railed passage. Here the doctor halted us, and began to give directions.

"You have your lantern, inspector?"

"Yes, sir."

"And your man, has he?"

"Yes, sir," replied the man for himself.

"Well, I want you to give yours to my friend for the present."

The man in plain-clothes passed me his lantern, and waited further commands.

"Now," said Dr. Tointon, facing me, "I want you and the inspector to take your stand in the left-hand corner of the tank top, and have your lanterns ready, and mind, there must not be a sound, or everything will be spoiled."

He tapped the plain-clothes man on the shoulder. "Come along," he said. Reaching the tank top, we took up positions as he had directed, while he went over with the inspector's man to the far right-hand comer. After a moment, he left the officer, and I could just make out the figure of the latter leaning negligently against the railings.

The doctor came over to us, and sat down between us.

"You've put him just about where our man was when we found him," said the inspector in a whisper.

"Yes," replied Dr. Tointon. "Now, listen, and then there mustn't be another sound. It's a matter of life and death."

His manner and voice were impressive. "When I call out 'ready,' throw the light from your lanterns on the officer as smartly as you can. Understand?"

"Yes," we replied together, and after that noone spoke.

The doctor lay down between us on his stomach, the muzzle of his gun directed a little to the right of where the other man stood. Thus we waited. Half an hour passed, an hour, and a sound of distant bells chimed up to us from the valley, then the silence resumed sway. Twice more the far-off bells told of the passing hours, and I was getting dreadfully cramped with staying in one position.

Then, abruptly, from somewhere across the tank there came a slight, very slight, slurring, crawling sort of noise. A cold shiver took me, and I peered vainly into the darkness till my eyes ached with the effort. Yet I could see nothing. Indistinctly, I could see the lounging figure of the constable. He seemed never to have stirred from his original position.

The strange rubbing, slurring sound continued. Then came a faint clink of iron, as if someone had kicked against the padlock that fastened down the iron trap over the manhole. Yet it could not be the policeman, for he was not near enough. I saw Dr. Tointon raise his head and peer keenly. Then he brought the butt of his gun up to his shoulder.

I got my lantern ready. I was all tingling with fear and expectation. What was going to happen? There came another slight clink, and then, suddenly, the rustling sound ceased.

I listened breathlessly. Across the tank, the hitherto silent policeman stirred almost, it seemed to me, as if someone or something had touched him. The same instant, I saw the muzzle of the doctor's gun go up some six inches. I grasped my lantern firmly, and drew in a deep breath.

"Ready!" shouted the doctor.

I flashed the light from my lantern across the tank simultaneously with the inspector. I have a confused notion of a twining brown thing about the rail a yard to the right of the constable. Then the doctor's gun spoke once, twice, and it dropped out of sight over the edge of the tank. In the same instant the constable slid down off the rail on to the tank top.

"My God!" shouted the inspector, "has it done for him?"

The doctor was already beside the fallen man, busy loosening his clothing.

"He's all right," he replied. "He's only fainted. The strain was too much. He was a plucky devil to stay. That thing was near him for over a minute."

From somewhere below us in the dark there came a thrashing, rustling sound. I went to the side and threw the light from my lantern downwards. It showed me a writhing yellow something, like an eel or a snake, only the thing was flat like a ribbon. It was twining itself into knots. It had no head. That portion of it seemed to have been blown clean away.

"He'll do now," I heard Dr. Tointon say, and the next instant he was standing beside me. He pointed downwards at the horrid thing. "There's the murderer," he said.

IT WAS A FEW EVENINGS LATER, and the inspector and I were sitting in the doctor's study.

"Even now, doctor," I said. "I don't see how on earth you got at it."

The inspector nodded a silent agreement.

"Well," replied Dr. Tointon, "after all it was not so very difficult. Had I not been so unfortunately taken ill while away, I should have cleared the matter up a couple of months ago. You see, I had exceptional opportunities for observing things, and in both cases I was very soon on the spot. But all the same, it was not until the second death occurred that I knew that the deed was not due to a human hand. The fact that there were no footprints in the mud proved that conclusively, and having disposed of that hypothesis, my eyes were open to take in details that had hitherto seemed of no moment. For one thing, both men were found dead almost in the same spot, and that spot is just over the overflow pipe."

"It came out of the tank?" I questioned.

"Yes," replied Dr. Tointon. "Then on the railings near where the thing had happened, I found traces of slime, and another matter that noone but myself seems to have been aware of, the collar of the policeman's coat was wet, and so was Mr. Marchmount's. Lastly, the shape of the marks upon the necks, and the tremendous force applied, indicated to me the kind of thing for which I must look. The rest was all a matter of deduction.

"Naturally, all the same, my ideas were somewhat hazy, yet before I saw the brute, I could have told you that it was some form of snake or eel, and I could have made a very good guess at its size. In the course of reasoning the matter out, I had occasion to apply to little black Dufirst. From him, I learned that the tank was supposed to be cleaned out annually, but that in reality it had not been seen to for some years."

"What about Dufirst?" I asked. "Well," said Dr. Tointon dryly, "I understand he is to be granted a free pardon. Of course the little beast stole those things, but I fancy he's had a fair punishment for his sins."

"And the snake, doctor?" I asked. "What was it?"

He shook his head. "I cannot say," he explained. "I have never seen any thing just like it. It is one of those abnormalities that occasionally astonish the scientific world. It is a creature that has developed under abnormal conditions, and, unfortunately, it was so shattered by the heavy charges of shot, that the remains tell me but little. Its head, as you saw, was entirely shot away."

I nodded. "It's queer, and frightening," I replied. "Makes a chap think a bit."

"Yes," agreed the doctor. "It certainly ought to prove a lesson in cleanliness."

THE STRIDING PLACE

by Gertrude Atherton

WEIGALL, CONTINENTAL AND DETACHED, tired early of grouse-shooting. To stand propped against a sod fence while his host's workmen routed up the birds with long poles and drove them towards the waiting guns, made him feel himself a parody on the ancestors who had roamed the moors and forests of this West Riding of Yorkshire in hot pursuit of game worth the killing. But when in England in August he always accepted whatever proffered for the season, and invited his host to shoot pheasants on his estates in the South. The amusements of life, he argued, should be accepted with the same philosophy as its ills.

It had been a bad day. A heavy rain had made the moor so spongy that it fairly sprang beneath the feet. Whether or not the grouse had haunts of their own, wherein they were immune from rheumatism, the bag had been small. The women, too, were an unusually dull lot, with the exception of a new-minded débutante who bothered Weigall at dinner by demanding the verbal restoration of the vague paintings on the vaulted roof above them.

But it was no one of these things that sat on Weigall's mind as, when the other men went up to bed, he let himself out of the castle and sauntered down to the river. His intimate friend, the companion of his boyhood, the chum of his college days, his fellow-traveller in many lands, the man for whom he possessed stronger affection than for all men, had mysteriously disappeared two days ago, and his track might have sprung to the upper air for all trace he had left behind him. He had been a guest on the adjoining estate during the past week, shooting with the fervor of the true sportsman, making love in the intervals to Adeline Cavan, and apparently in the best of spirits. As far as was known there was nothing to lower his mental mercury, for his rent-roll was a large one, Miss Cavan blushed whenever he looked at her, and, being one of the best shots in England, he was never happier than in August. The suicide theory was preposterous, all agreed, and there was as little reason to believe him murdered. Nevertheless, he had walked out of March Abbey two nights ago without hat or overcoat, and had not been seen since.

The country was being patrolled night and day. A hundred keepers and workmen were beating the woods and poking the bogs on the moors, but as yet not so much as a handkerchief had been found.

Weigall did not believe for a moment that Wyatt Gifford was dead, and although it was impossible not to be affected by the general uneasiness, he was disposed to be more angry than frightened. At Cambridge Gifford had been an incorrigible practical joker, and by no means had outgrown the habit; it would be like him to cut across the country in his evening clothes, board a cattle-train, and amuse himself touching up the picture of the sensation in West Riding.

However, Weigall's affection for his friend was too deep to companion with tranquillity in the present state of doubt, and, instead of going to bed early with the other men, he determined to walk until ready for sleep. He went down to the river and followed the path through the woods. There was no moon, but the stars sprinkled their cold light upon the pretty belt of water flowing placidly past wood and ruin, between green masses of overhanging rocks or sloping banks tangled with tree and shrub, leaping occasionally over stones with the harsh notes of an angry scold, to recover its equanimity the moment the way was clear again.

It was very dark in the depths where Weigall trod. He smiled as he recalled a remark of Gifford's: "An English wood is like a good many other things in life—very promising at a distance, but a hollow mockery when you get within. You see daylight on both sides, and the sun freckles the very bracken. Our woods need the night to make them seem what they ought to be—what they once were, before our ancestors' descendants demanded so much more money, in these so much more various days."

Weigall strolled along, smoking, and thinking of his friend, his pranks—many of which had done more credit to his imagination than this—and recalling conversations that had lasted the night through. Just before the end of the London season they had walked the streets one hot night after a party, discussing the various theories of the soul's destiny. That afternoon they had met at the coffin of a college friend whose mind had been a blank for the past three years. Some months previously they had called at the asylum to see him. His expression had been senile, his face imprinted with the record of debauchery. In death the face was placid, intelligent, without ignoble lineation—the face of the man they had known at college. Weigall and Gifford had had no time to comment there, and the afternoon and evening were full, but, coming forth from the house of festivity together, they had reverted almost at once to the topic.

"I cherish the theory," Gifford had said, "that the soul

sometimes lingers in the body after death. During madness, of course, it is an impotent prisoner, albeit a conscious one. Fancy its agony, and its horror! What more natural than that, when the life-spark goes out, the tortured soul should take possession of the vacant skull and triumph once more for a few hours while old friends look their last? It has had time to repent while compelled to crouch and behold the result of its work, and it has shrived itself into a state of comparative purity. If I had my way, I should stay inside my bones until the coffin had gone into its niche, that I might obviate for my poor old comrade the tragic impersonality of death. And I should like to see justice done to it, as it were—to see it lowered among its ancestors with the ceremony and solemnity that are its due. I am afraid that if I dissevered myself too quickly, I should yield to curiosity and hasten to investigate the mysteries of space."

"You believe in the soul as an independent entity, then—that it and the vital principle are not one and the same?"

"Absolutely. The body and soul are twins, life comrades—sometimes friends, sometimes enemies, but always loyal in the last instance. Some day, when I am tired of the world, I shall go to India and become a mahatma, solely for the pleasure of receiving proof during life of this independent relationship."

"Suppose you were not sealed up properly, and returned after one of your astral flights to find your earthly part unfit for habitation? It is an experiment I don't think I should care to try, unless even juggling with soul and flesh had palled."

"That would not be an uninteresting predicament. I should rather enjoy experimenting with broken machinery."

The high wild roar of water smote suddenly upon Weigall's ear and checked his memories. He left the wood and walked out on the huge slippery stones which nearly close the River Wharfe at this point, and watched the waters boil down into the narrow pass with their furious untiring energy. The black quiet of the woods rose high on either side. The stars seemed colder and whiter just above. On either hand the perspective of the river might have run into a rayless cavern. There was no lonelier spot in England, nor one which had the right to claim so many ghosts, if ghosts there were.

Weigall was not a coward, but he recalled uncomfortably the tales of those that had been done to death in the Strid[1]. Wordsworth's Boy of Egremond had been disposed of by the practical Whitaker, but countless others, more venturesome than wise, had gone down into that narrow boiling course, never to appear in the still pool a few yards beyond. Below the great rocks which form the walls of the Strid was believed to be a natural vault, on to whose shelves the dead were drawn. The spot had an ugly fascination. Weigall stood, visioning skeletons, uncoffined and green, the home of the eyeless things which had devoured all that had covered and filled that rattling symbol of man's mortality, then fell to wondering if any one had attempted to leap the Strid of late. It was covered with slime; he had never seen it look so treacherous.

He shuddered and turned away, impelled, despite his manhood, to flee the spot. As he did so, something tossing in the foam below the fall—something as white, yet independent of it—caught his eye and arrested his step. Then he saw that it was describing a contrary motion to the rushing water—an upward backward motion. Weigall stood rigid, breathless. He fancied he heard the crackling of his hair. Was that a hand? It thrust itself still higher above the boiling foam, turned sidewise, and four frantic fingers were distinctly visible against the black rock beyond.

Weigall's superstitious terror left him. A man was there, struggling to free himself from the suction beneath the Strid,

---

1   "This striding place is called the 'Strid,'
         A name which it took of yore;
         A thousand years hath it borne the name,
         And it shall a thousand more."

swept down, doubtless, but a moment before his arrival, perhaps as he stood with his back to the current.

He stepped as close to the edge as he dared. The hand doubled as if in imprecation, shaking savagely in the face of that force which leaves its creatures to immutable law, then spread wide again, clutching, expanding, crying for help as audibly as the human voice.

Weigall dashed to the nearest tree, dragged and twisted off a branch with his strong arms, and returned as swiftly to the Strid. The hand was in the same place, still gesticulating as wildly; the body was undoubtedly caught in the rocks below, perhaps already half-way along one of those hideous shelves. Weigall let himself down upon a lower rock, braced his shoulder against the mass beside him, then, leaning out over the water, thrust the branch into the hand. The fingers clutched it convulsively. Weigall tugged powerfully, his own feet dragged perilously near the edge. For a moment he produced no impression, then an arm shot above the waters.

The blood sprang to Weigall's head. He was choked with the impression that the Strid had him in her roaring hold, and he saw nothing. Then the mist cleared. The hand and arm were nearer, although the rest of the body was still concealed by the foam. Weigall peered out with distended eyes. The meagre light revealed in the cuffs links of a peculiar device. The fingers clutching the branch were as familiar.

Weigall forgot the slippery stones, the terrible death if he stepped too far. He pulled with passionate will and muscle. Memories flung themselves into the hot light of his brain, trooping rapidly upon each other's heels, as in the thought of the drowning. Most of the pleasures of his life, good and bad, were identified in some way with this friend. Scenes of college days, of travel, where they had deliberately sought adventure and stood between one another and death upon more occasions than one, of hours of delightful companionship among the treasures of art, and others in the pursuit of pleasure, flashed like the changing particles of a kaleidoscope. Weigall had loved several women, but he would have flouted in these moments the thought that he had ever loved any woman as he loved Wyatt Gifford. There were so many charming women in the world, and in the thirty-two years of his life he had never known another man to whom he had cared to give his intimate friendship.

He threw himself on his face. His wrists were cracking, the skin was torn from his hands. The fingers still gripped the stick. There was life in them yet.

Suddenly something gave way. The hand swung about, tearing the branch from Weigall's grasp. The body had been liberated and flung outward, though still submerged by the foam and spray.

Weigall scrambled to his feet and sprang along the rocks, knowing that the danger from suction was over and that Gifford must be carried straight to the quiet pool. Gifford was a fish in the water and could live under it longer than most men. If he survived this, it would not be the first time that his pluck and science had saved him from drowning.

Weigall reached the pool. A man in his evening clothes floated on it, his face turned towards a projecting rock over which his arm had fallen, upholding the body. The hand that had held the branch hung limply over the rock, its white reflection visible in the black water. Weigall plunged into the shallow pool, lifted Gifford in his arms and returned to the bank. He laid the body down and threw off his coat that he might be the freer to practise the methods of resuscitation. He was glad of the moment's respite. The valiant life in the man might have been exhausted in that last struggle. He had not dared to look at his face, to put his ear to the heart. The hesitation lasted but a moment. There was no time to lose.

He turned to his prostrate friend. As he did so, something

strange and disagreeable smote his senses. For a half-moment he did not appreciate its nature. Then his teeth clacked together, his feet, his outstretched arms pointed towards the woods. But he sprang to the side of the man and bent down and peered into his face. There was no face.

A FISHERMAN AND HIS SOUL

by Oscar Wilde

EVERY EVENING the young Fisherman went out upon the sea, and threw his nets into the water.

When the wind blew from the land he caught nothing, or but little at best, for it was a bitter and black-winged wind, and rough waves rose up to meet it. But when the wind blew to the shore, the fish came in from the deep, and swam into the meshes of his nets, and he took them to the marketplace and sold them.

Every evening he went out upon the sea, and one evening the net was so heavy that hardly could he draw it into the boat. And he laughed, and said to himself, "Surely I have caught all the fish that swim, or snared some dull monster that will be a marvel to men, or some thing of horror that the great Queen will desire," and putting forth all his strength, he tugged at the coarse ropes till, like lines of blue enamel round a vase of bronze, the long veins rose up on his arms. He tugged at the thin ropes, and nearer and nearer came the circle of flat corks, and the net rose at last to the top of the water.

But no fish at all was in it, nor any monster or thing of horror, but only a little Mermaid lying fast asleep.

Her hair was as a wet fleece of gold, and each separate hair as a thread of fine gold in a cup of glass. Her body was as white ivory, and her tail was of silver and pearl. Silver and pearl was her tail, and the green weeds of the sea coiled round it, and like sea-shells were her ears, and her lips were like sea-coral. The cold waves dashed over her cold breasts, and the salt glistened upon her eyelids.

So beautiful was she that when the young Fisherman saw her he was filled with wonder, and he put out his hand and drew the net close to him, and leaning over the side he clasped her in his arms. And when he touched her, she gave a cry like a startled sea-gull, and woke, and looked at him in terror with her mauve-amethyst eyes, and struggled that she might escape. But he held her tightly to him, and would not suffer her to depart.

And when she saw that she could in no way escape from him, she began to weep, and said, "I pray thee let me go, for I am the only daughter of a King, and my father is aged and alone."

But the young Fisherman answered, "I will not let thee go save thou makest me a promise that whenever I call thee, thou wilt come and sing to me, for the fish delight to listen to the song of the Sea-folk, and so shall my nets be full."

"Wilt thou in very truth let me go, if I promise thee this?" cried the Mermaid.

"In very truth I will let thee go," said the young Fisherman.

So she made him the promise he desired, and sware it by the oath of the Sea-folk. And he loosened his arms from about her, and she sank down into the water, trembling with a strange fear.

Every evening the young Fisherman went out upon the sea, and called to the Mermaid, and she rose out of the water and sang to him. Round and round her swam the dolphins, and the wild gulls wheeled above her head.

And she sang a marvellous song. For she sang of the Sea-folk who drive their flocks from cave to cave, and carry the little calves on their shoulders, of the Tritons who have long green beards, and hairy breasts, and blow through twisted conchs when the King passes by, of the palace of the King which is all of amber, with a roof of clear emerald, and a pavement of bright pearl, and of the gardens of the sea where the great filigrane fans of coral wave all day long, and the fish dart about like silver birds, and the anemones cling to the rocks, and the pinks bourgeon in the ribbed yellow sand. She sang of the big whales that come down from the north seas and have sharp icicles hanging to their fins, of the Sirens who tell of such wonderful things that the merchants have to stop their ears with wax lest they should hear them, and leap into the water and be drowned, of the sunken galleys with their tall masts, and the frozen sailors clinging to the rigging, and the mackerel swimming in and out of the open portholes, of the little barnacles who are great travellers, and cling to the keels of the ships and go round and round the world, and of the cuttlefish who live in the sides of the cliffs and stretch out their long black arms, and can make night come when they will it. She sang of the nautilus who has a boat of her own that is carved out of an opal and steered with a silken sail, of the happy Mermen who play upon harps and can charm the great Kraken to sleep, of the little children who catch hold of the slippery porpoises and ride laughing upon their backs, of the Mermaids who lie in the white foam and hold out their arms to the mariners, and of the sea-lions with their curved tusks, and the sea-horses with their floating manes.

And as she sang, all the tunny-fish came in from the deep to listen to her, and the young Fisherman threw his nets round them and caught them, and others he took with a spear. And when his boat was well-laden, the Mermaid would sink down into the sea, smiling at him.

Yet would she never come near him that he might touch her. Oftentimes he called to her and prayed of her, but she would not, and when he sought to seize her she dived into the water as a seal might dive, nor did he see her again that day. And each day the sound of her voice became sweeter to his ears. So sweet was her voice that he forgot his nets and his cunning, and had no care of his craft. Vermilion-finned and with eyes of bossy gold, the tunnies went by in shoals, but he heeded them not. His spear lay by his side unused, and his baskets of plaited osier were empty. With lips parted, and eyes dim with wonder, he sat idle in his boat and listened, listening till the sea-mists crept round him, and the wandering moon stained his brown limbs with silver.

And one evening he called to her, and said: "Little Mermaid, little Mermaid, I love thee. Take me for thy bridegroom, for I love thee."

But the Mermaid shook her head. "Thou hast a human soul," she answered. "If only thou wouldst send away thy soul, then could I love thee."

And the young Fisherman said to himself, "Of what use is my soul to me? I cannot see it. I may not touch it. I do not know it. Surely I will send it away from me, and much gladness shall be mine." And a cry of joy broke from his lips, and standing up in the painted boat, he held out his arms to the Mermaid. "I will send my soul away," he cried, "and you shall be my bride, and I will be thy bridegroom, and in the depth of the sea we will dwell together, and all that thou hast sung of thou shalt show me, and all that thou desirest I will do, nor shall our lives be divided."

And the little Mermaid laughed for pleasure and hid her face in her hands.

"But how shall I send my soul from me?" cried the young Fisherman. "Tell me how I may do it, and lo! it shall be done."

"Alas! I know not," said the little Mermaid, "the Sea-folk have no souls." And she sank down into the deep, looking wistfully at him.

Now early on the next morning, before the sun was the span of a man's hand above the hill, the young Fisherman went to the house of the Priest and knocked three times at the door.

The novice looked out through the wicket, and when he saw who it was, he drew back the latch and said to him, "Enter."

And the young Fisherman passed in, and knelt down on the sweet-smelling rushes of the floor, and cried to the Priest who was reading out of the Holy Book and said to him, "Father, I am in love with one of the Sea-folk, and my soul hindereth me from having my desire. Tell me how I can send my soul away from me, for in truth I have no need of it. Of what value is my soul to me? I cannot see it. I may not touch it. I do not know it."

And the Priest beat his breast, and answered, "Alack, alack, thou art mad, or hast eaten of some poisonous herb, for the soul is the noblest part of man, and was given to us by God that we should nobly use it. There is no thing more precious than a human soul, nor any earthly thing that can be weighed with it. It is worth all the gold that is in the world, and is more precious than the rubies of the kings. Therefore, my son, think not any more of this matter, for it is a sin that may not be forgiven. And as for the Sea-folk, they are lost, and they who would traffic with them are lost also. They are as the beasts of the field that know not good from evil, and for them the Lord has not died."

The young Fisherman's eyes filled with tears when he heard the bitter words of the Priest, and he rose up from his knees and said to him, "Father, the Fauns live in the forest and are glad, and on the rocks sit the Mermen with their harps of red gold. Let me be as they are, I beseech thee, for their days are as the days of flowers. And as for my soul, what doth my soul profit me, if it stand between me and the thing that I love?"

"The love of the body is vile," cried the Priest, knitting his brows, "and vile and evil are the pagan things God suffers to wander through His world. Accursed be the Fauns of the woodland, and accursed be the singers of the sea! I have heard them at night-time, and they have sought to lure me from my beads. They tap at the window, and laugh. They whisper into my ears the tale of their perilous joys. They tempt me with temptations, and when I would pray they make mouths at me. They are lost, I tell thee, they are lost. For them there is no heaven nor hell, and in neither shall they praise God's name."

"Father," cried the young Fisherman, "thou knowest not what thou sayest. Once in my net I snared the daughter of a King. She is fairer than the morning star, and whiter than the moon. For her body I would give my soul, and for her love I would surrender heaven. Tell me what I ask of thee, and let me go in peace."

"Away! Away!" cried the Priest. "Thy leman is lost, and thou shalt be lost with her."

And he gave him no blessing, but drove him from his door.

And the young Fisherman went down into the marketplace, and he walked slowly, and with bowed head, as one who is in sorrow.

And when the merchants saw him coming, they began to whisper to each other, and one of them came forth to meet him, and called him by name, and said to him, "What hast thou to sell?"

"I will sell thee my soul," he answered. "I pray thee buy it of me, for I am weary of it. Of what use is my soul to me? I cannot see it. I may not touch it. I do not know it."

But the merchants mocked at him, and said, "Of what use is a man's soul to us? It is not worth a clipped piece of silver. Sell us thy body for a slave, and we will clothe thee in sea-purple, and put a ring upon thy finger, and make thee the minion of the great Queen. But talk not of the soul, for to us it is nought, nor has it any value for our service."

And the young Fisherman said to himself: "How strange a thing this is! The Priest telleth me that the soul is worth all the gold in the world, and the merchants say that it is not worth a clipped piece of silver." And he passed out of the marketplace, and went down to the shore of the sea, and began to ponder on what he should do.

And at noon he remembered how one of his companions, who was a gatherer of samphire, had told him of a certain young Witch who dwelt in a cave at the head of the bay and was very cunning in her witcheries. And he set to and ran, so eager was he to get rid of his soul, and a cloud of dust followed him as he sped round the sand of the shore. By the itching of her palm the young Witch knew his coming, and she laughed and let down her red hair. With her red hair falling around her, she stood at the opening of the cave, and in her hand she had a spray of wild hemlock that was blossoming.

"What d'ye lack? What d'ye lack?" she cried, as he came panting up the steep, and bent down before her. "Fish for thy net, when the wind is foul? I have a little reed-pipe, and when I blow on it the mullet come sailing into the bay. But it has a price, pretty boy, it has a price. What d'ye lack? What d'ye lack? A storm to wreck the ships, and wash the chests of rich treasure ashore? I have more storms than the wind has, for I serve one who is stronger than the wind, and with a sieve and a pail of water I can send the great galleys to the bottom of the sea. But I have a price, pretty boy, I have a price. What d'ye lack? What d'ye lack? I know a flower that grows in the valley, none knows it but I. It has purple leaves, and a star in its heart, and its juice is as white as milk. Shouldst thou touch with this flower the hard lips of the Queen, she would follow thee all over the world. Out of the bed of the King she would rise, and over the whole world she would follow thee. And it has a price, pretty boy, it has a price. What d'ye lack? What d'ye lack? I can pound a toad in a mortar, and make broth of it, and stir the broth with a dead man's hand. Sprinkle it on thine enemy while he sleeps, and he will turn into a black viper, and his own mother will slay him. With a wheel I can draw the Moon from heaven, and in a crystal I can show thee Death. What d'ye lack? What d'ye lack? Tell me thy desire, and I will give it thee, and thou shalt pay me a price, pretty boy, thou shalt pay me a price."

"My desire is but for a little thing," said the young Fisherman, "yet hath the Priest been wroth with me, and driven me forth. It is but for a little thing, and the merchants have mocked at me, and denied me. Therefore am I come to thee, though men call thee evil, and whatever be thy price I shall pay it."

"What wouldst thou?" asked the Witch, coming near to him.

"I would send my soul away from me," answered the young Fisherman.

The Witch grew pale, and shuddered, and hid her face in her blue mantle. "Pretty boy, pretty boy," she muttered, "that is a terrible thing to do."

He tossed his brown curls and laughed. "My soul is nought to me," he answered. "I cannot see it. I may not touch it. I do not know it."

"What wilt thou give me if I tell thee?" asked the Witch, looking down at him with her beautiful eyes.

"Five pieces of gold," he said, "and my nets, and the wattled house where I live, and the painted boat in which I sail. Only tell me how to get rid of my soul, and I will give thee all that I possess."

She laughed mockingly at him, and struck him with the spray of hemlock. "I can turn the autumn leaves into gold," she answered, "and I can weave the pale moonbeams into silver if I will it. He whom I serve is richer than all the kings of this world, and has their dominions."

"What then shall I give thee," he cried, "if thy price be neither gold nor silver?"

The Witch stroked his hair with her thin white hand. "Thou must dance with me, pretty boy," she murmured, and she smiled at him as she spoke.

"Nought but that?" cried the young Fisherman in wonder and he rose to his feet.

"Nought but that," she answered, and she smiled at him again.

"Then at sunset in some secret place we shall dance together," he said, "and after that we have danced thou shalt tell me the thing which I desire to know."

She shook her head. "When the moon is full, when the moon is full," she muttered. Then she peered all round, and listened. A blue bird rose screaming from its nest and circled over the dunes, and three spotted birds rustled through the coarse grey grass and whistled to each other. There was no other sound save the sound of a wave fretting the smooth pebbles below. So she reached out her hand, and drew him near to her and put her dry lips close to his ear.

"Tonight thou must come to the top of the mountain," she whispered. "It is a Sabbath, and He will be there."

The young Fisherman started and looked at her, and she showed her white teeth and laughed. "Who is He of whom thou speakest?" he asked.

"It matters not," she answered. "Go thou tonight, and stand under the branches of the hornbeam, and wait for my coming. If a black dog run towards thee, strike it with a rod of willow, and it will go away. If an owl speak to thee, make it no answer. When the moon is full I shall be with thee, and we will dance together on the grass."

"But wilt thou swear to me to tell me how I may send my

soul from me?" he made question.

She moved out into the sunlight, and through her red hair rippled the wind. "By the hoofs of the goat I swear it," she made answer.

"Thou art the best of the witches," cried the young Fisherman, "and I will surely dance with thee tonight on the top of the mountain. I would indeed that thou hadst asked of me either gold or silver. But such as thy price is thou shalt have it, for it is but a little thing." And he doffed his cap to her, and bent his head low, and ran back to the town filled with a great joy.

And the Witch watched him as he went, and when he had passed from her sight she entered her cave, and having taken a mirror from a box of carved cedarwood, she set it up on a frame, and burned vervain on lighted charcoal before it, and peered through the coils of the smoke. And after a time she clenched her hands in anger. "He should have been mine," she muttered, "I am as fair as she is."

And that evening, when the moon had risen, the young Fisherman climbed up to the top of the mountain, and stood under the branches of the hornbeam. Like a targe of polished metal the round sea lay at his feet, and the shadows of the fishing boats moved in the little bay. A great owl, with yellow sulphurous eyes, called to him by his name, but he made it no answer. A black dog ran towards him and snarled. He struck it with a rod of willow, and it went away whining.

At midnight the witches came flying through the air like bats. "Phew!" they cried, as they lit upon the ground, "there is some one here we know not!" and they sniffed about, and chattered to each other, and made signs. Last of all came the young Witch, with her red hair streaming in the wind. She wore a dress of gold tissue embroidered with peacocks' eyes, and a little cap of green velvet was on her head.

"Where is he, where is he?" shrieked the witches when they saw her, but she only laughed, and ran to the hornbeam, and taking the Fisherman by the hand she led him out into the moonlight and began to dance.

Round and round they whirled, and the young Witch jumped so high that he could see the scarlet heels of her shoes. Then right across the dancers came the sound of the galloping of a horse, but no horse was to be seen, and he felt afraid.

"Faster," cried the Witch, and she threw her arms about his neck, and her breath was hot upon his face. "Faster, faster!" she cried, and the earth seemed to spin beneath his feet, and his brain grew troubled, and a great terror fell on him, as of some evil thing that was watching him, and at last he became aware that under the shadow of a rock there was a figure that had not been there before.

It was a man dressed in a suit of black velvet, cut in the Spanish fashion. His face was strangely pale, but his lips were like a proud red flower. He seemed weary, and was leaning back toying in a listless manner with the pommel of his dagger. On the grass beside him lay a plumed hat, and a pair of riding-gloves gauntleted with gilt lace, and sewn with seed-pearls wrought into a curious device. A short cloak lined with sables hang from his shoulder, and his delicate white hands were gemmed with rings. Heavy eyelids drooped over his eyes.

The young Fisherman watched him, as one snared in a spell. At last their eyes met, and wherever he danced it seemed to him that the eyes of the man were upon him. He heard the Witch laugh, and caught her by the waist, and whirled her madly round and round.

Suddenly a dog bayed in the wood, and the dancers stopped, and going up two by two, knelt down, and kissed the man's hands. As they did so, a little smile touched his proud lips, as a bird's wing touches the water and makes it laugh. But there was disdain in it. He kept looking at the young Fisherman.

"Come! let us worship," whispered the Witch, and she led him up, and a great desire to do as she besought him seized on him, and he followed her. But when he came close, and without knowing why he did it, he made on his breast the sign of the Cross, and called upon the holy name.

No sooner had he done so than the witches screamed like hawks and flew away, and the pallid face that had been watching him twitched with a spasm of pain. The man went over to a little wood, and whistled. A jennet with silver trappings came running to meet him. As he leapt upon the saddle he turned round, and looked at the young Fisherman sadly.

And the Witch with the red hair tried to fly away also, but the Fisherman caught her by her wrists, and held her fast.

"Loose me," she cried, "and let me go. For thou hast named what should not be named, and shown the sign that may not be looked at."

"Nay," he answered, "but I will not let thee go till thou hast told me the secret."

"What secret?" said the Witch, wrestling with him like a wild cat, and biting her foam-flecked lips.

"Thou knowest," he made answer.

Her grass-green eyes grew dim with tears, and she said to the Fisherman, "Ask me anything but that!"

He laughed, and held her all the more tightly.

And when she saw that she could not free herself, she whispered to him, "Surely I am as fair as the daughters of the sea, and as comely as those that dwell in the blue waters," and she fawned on him and put her face close to his.

But he thrust her back frowning, and said to her, "If thou keepest not the promise that thou madest to me I will slay thee for a false witch."

She grew grey as a blossom of the Judas tree, and shuddered. "Be it so," she muttered. "It is thy soul and not mine. Do with it as thou wilt." And she took from her girdle a little knife that had a handle of green viper's skin, and gave it to him.

"What shall this serve me?" he asked of her, wondering.

She was silent for a few moments, and a look of terror came over her face. Then she brushed her hair back from her forehead, and smiling strangely she said to him, "What men call the shadow of the body is not the shadow of the body, but is the body of the soul. Stand on the sea-shore with thy back to the moon, and cut away from around thy feet thy shadow, which is thy soul's body, and bid thy soul leave thee, and it will do so."

The young Fisherman trembled. "Is this true?" he murmured.

"It is true, and I would that I had not told thee of it," she cried, and she clung to his knees weeping.

He put her from him and left her in the rank grass, and going to the edge of the mountain he placed the knife in his belt and began to climb down.

And his Soul that was within him called out to him and said, "Lo! I have dwelt with thee for all these years, and have been thy servant. Send me not away from thee now, for what evil have I done thee?"

And the young Fisherman laughed. "Thou hast done me no evil, but I have no need of thee," he answered. "The world is wide, and there is Heaven also, and Hell, and that dim twilight house that lies between. Go wherever thou wilt, but trouble me not, for my love is calling to me."

And his Soul besought him piteously, but he heeded it not, but leapt from crag to crag, being sure-footed as a wild goat, and at last he reached the level ground and the yellow shore of the sea.

Bronze-limbed and well-knit, like a statue wrought by a Grecian, he stood on the sand with his back to the moon, and out of the foam came white arms that beckoned to him, and out of the waves rose dim forms that did him homage. Before him lay his shadow, which was the body of his soul, and behind him hung the moon in the honey-coloured air.

And his Soul said to him, "If indeed thou must drive me from thee, send me not forth without a heart. The world is cruel, give me thy heart to take with me."

He tossed his head and smiled. "With what should I love my love if I gave thee my heart?" he cried.

"Nay, but be merciful," said his Soul, "give me thy heart, for the world is very cruel, and I am afraid."

"My heart is my love's," he answered, "therefore tarry not, but get thee gone."

"Should I not love also?" asked his Soul.

"Get thee gone, for I have no need of thee," cried the young Fisherman, and he took the little knife with its handle of green viper's skin, and cut away his shadow from around his feet, and it rose up and stood before him, and looked at him, and it was even as himself.

He crept back, and thrust the knife into his belt, and a feeling of awe came over him. "Get thee gone," he murmured, "and let me see thy face no more."

"Nay, but we must meet again," said the Soul. Its voice was low and flute-like, and its lips hardly moved while it spake.

"How shall we meet?" cried the young Fisherman. "Thou wilt not follow me into the depths of the sea?"

"Once every year I will come to this place, and call to thee," said the Soul. "It may be that thou wilt have need of me."

"What need should I have of thee?" cried the young Fisherman, "but be it as thou wilt," and he plunged into the waters and the Tritons blew their horns and the little Mermaid rose up to meet him, and put her arms around his neck and kissed him on the mouth.

And the Soul stood on the lonely beach and watched them. And when they had sunk down into the sea, it went weeping away over the marshes.

And after a year was over the Soul came down to the shore of the sea and called to the young Fisherman, and he rose out of the deep, and said, "Why dost thou call to me?"

And the Soul answered, "Come nearer, that I may speak with thee, for I have seen marvellous things."

So he came nearer, and couched in the shallow water, and leaned his head upon his hand and listened.

And the Soul said to him, "When I left thee I turned my face to the East and journeyed. From the East cometh everything that is wise. Six days I journeyed, and on the morning of the seventh day I came to a hill that is in the country of the Tartars. I sat down under the shade of a tamarisk tree to shelter myself from the sun. The land was dry and burnt up with the heat. The people went to and fro over the plain like flies crawling upon a disk of polished copper.

"When it was noon a cloud of red dust rose up from the flat rim of the land. When the Tartars saw it, they strung their painted bows, and having leapt upon their little horses they galloped to meet it. The women fled screaming to the waggons, and hid themselves behind the felt curtains.

"At twilight the Tartars returned, but five of them were missing, and of those that came back not a few had been wounded. They harnessed their horses to the waggons and drove hastily away. Three jackals came out of a cave and peered after them. Then they sniffed up the air with their nostrils, and trotted off in the opposite direction.

"When the moon rose I saw a camp-fire burning on the plain, and went towards it. A company of merchants were seated round it on carpets. Their camels were picketed behind them, and the negroes who were their servants were pitching tents of tanned skin upon the sand, and making a high wall of the prickly pear.

"As I came near them, the chief of the merchants rose up

and drew his sword, and asked me my business.

"I answered that I was a Prince in my own land, and that I had escaped from the Tartars, who had sought to make me their slave. The chief smiled, and showed me five heads fixed upon long reeds of bamboo.

"Then he asked me who was the prophet of God, and I answered him Mohammed.

"When he heard the name of the false prophet, he bowed and took me by the hand, and placed me by his side. A negro brought me some mare's milk in a wooden dish, and a piece of lamb's flesh roasted.

"At daybreak we started on our journey. I rode on a red-haired camel by the side of the chief, and a runner ran before us carrying a spear. The men of war were on either hand, and the mules followed with the merchandise. There were forty camels in the caravan, and the mules were twice forty in number.

"We went from the country of the Tartars into the country of those who curse the Moon. We saw the Gryphons guarding their gold on the white rocks, and the scaled Dragons sleeping in their caves. As we passed over the mountains we held our breath lest the snows might fall on us, and each man tied a veil of gauze before his eyes. As we passed through the valleys the Pygmies shot arrows at us from the hollows of the trees, and at night-time we heard the wild men beating on their drums. When we came to the Tower of Apes we set fruits before them, and they did not harm us. When we came to the Tower of Serpents we gave them warm milk in howls of brass, and they let us go by. Three times in our journey we came to the banks of the Oxus. We crossed it on rafts of wood with great bladders of blown hide. The river-horses raged against us and sought to slay us. When the camels saw them they trembled.

"The kings of each city levied tolls on us, but would not suffer us to enter their gates. They threw us bread over the walls, little maize-cakes baked in honey and cakes of fine flour filled with dates. For every hundred baskets we gave them a bead of amber.

"When the dwellers in the villages saw us coming, they poisoned the wells and fled to the hill-summits. We fought with the Magadae who are born old, and grow younger and younger every year, and die when they are little children, and with the Laktroi who say that they are the sons of tigers, and paint themselves yellow and black, and with the Aurantes who bury their dead on the tops of trees, and themselves live in dark caverns lest the Sun, who is their god, should slay them, and with the Krimnians who worship a crocodile, and give it earrings of green glass, and feed it with butter and fresh fowls, and with the Agazonbae, who are dog-faced, and with the Sibans, who have horses' feet, and run more swiftly than horses. A third of our company died in battle, and a third died of want. The rest murmured against me, and said that I had brought them an evil fortune. I took a horned adder from beneath a stone and let it sting me. When they saw that I did not sicken they grew afraid.

"In the fourth month we reached the city of Illel. It was night-time when we came to the grove that is outside the walls, and the air was sultry, for the Moon was travelling in Scorpion. We took the ripe pomegranates from the trees, and brake them, and drank their sweet juices. Then we lay down on our carpets, and waited for the dawn.

"And at dawn we rose and knocked at the gate of the city. It was wrought out of red bronze, and carved with sea-dragons and dragons that have wings. The guards looked down from the battlements and asked us our business. The interpreter of the caravan answered that we had come from the island of Syria with much merchandise. They took hostages, and told us that they would open the gate to us at noon, and bade us tarry till then.

"When it was noon they opened the gate, and as we entered in the people came crowding out of the houses to look at us, and a crier went round the city crying through a shell. We stood in the marketplace, and the negroes uncorded the bales of figured cloths and opened the carved chests of sycamore. And when they had ended their task, the merchants set forth their strange wares, the waxed linen from Egypt and the painted linen from the country of the Ethiops, the purple sponges from Tyre and the blue hangings from Sidon, the cups of cold amber and the fine vessels of glass and the curious vessels of burnt clay. From the roof of a house a company of women watched us. One of them wore a mask of gilded leather.

"And on the first day the priests came and bartered with us, and on the second day came the nobles, and on the third day came the craftsmen and the slaves. And this is their custom with all merchants as long as they tarry in the city.

"And we tarried for a moon, and when the moon was waning, I wearied and wandered away through the streets of the city and came to the garden of its god. The priests in their yellow robes moved silently through the green trees, and on a pavement of black marble stood the rose-red house in which the god had his dwelling. Its doors were of powdered lacquer, and bulls and peacocks were wrought on them in raised and polished gold. The tilted roof was of sea-green porcelain, and the jutting eaves were festooned with little bells. When the white doves flew past, they struck the bells with their wings and made them tinkle.

"In front of the temple was a pool of clear water paved with veined onyx. I lay down beside it, and with my pale fingers I touched the broad leaves. One of the priests came towards me and stood behind me. He had sandals on his feet, one of soft serpent-skin and the other of birds' plumage. On his head was a mitre of black felt decorated with silver crescents. Seven yellows were woven into his robe, and his frizzed hair was stained with antimony.

"After a little while he spake to me, and asked me my desire.

"I told him that my desire was to see the god.

"'The god is hunting,' said the priest, looking strangely at me with his small slanting eyes.

"'Tell me in what forest, and I will ride with him,' I answered.

"He combed out the soft fringes of his tunic with his long pointed nails. 'The god is asleep,' he murmured.

"'Tell me on what couch, and I will watch by him,' I answered.

"'The god is at the feast,' he cried.

"'If the wine be sweet I will drink it with him, and if it be bitter I will drink it with him also,' was my answer.

"He bowed his head in wonder, and, taking me by the hand, he raised me up, and led me into the temple.

"And in the first chamber I saw an idol seated on a throne of jasper bordered with great orient pearls. It was carved out of ebony, and in stature was of the stature of a man. On its forehead was a ruby, and thick oil dripped from its hair on to its thighs. Its feet were red with the blood of a newly-slain kid, and its loins girt with a copper belt that was studded with seven beryls.

"And I said to the priest, 'Is this the god?' And he answered me, 'This is the god.'

"'Show me the god,' I cried, 'or I will surely slay thee.' And I touched his hand, and it became withered.

"And the priest besought me, saying, 'Let my lord heal his servant, and I will show him the god.'

"So I breathed with my breath upon his hand, and it became whole again, and he trembled and led me into the second chamber, and I saw an idol standing on a lotus of jade hung with great emeralds. It was carved out of ivory, and in stature was twice the stature of a man. On its forehead was a chrysolite, and its breasts were smeared with myrrh and cinnamon. In one hand it held a crooked sceptre of jade, and in the other a round crystal. It ware buskins of brass, and its thick neck was circled with a circle of selenites.

"And I said to the priest, 'Is this the god?'

"And he answered me, 'This is the god.'

"'Show me the god,' I cried, 'or I will surely slay thee.' And I touched his eyes, and they became blind.

"And the priest besought me, saying, 'Let my lord heal his servant, and I will show him the god.'

"So I breathed with my breath upon his eyes, and the sight came back to them, and he trembled again, and led me into the third chamber, and lo! there was no idol in it, nor image of any kind, but only a mirror of round metal set on an altar of stone.

"And I said to the priest, 'Where is the god?'

"And he answered me: 'There is no god but this mirror that thou seest, for this is the Mirror of Wisdom. And it reflecteth all things that are in heaven and on earth, save only the face of him who looketh into it. This it reflecteth not, so that he who looketh into it may be wise. Many other mirrors are there, but they are mirrors of Opinion. This only is the Mirror of Wisdom. And they who possess this mirror know everything, nor is there anything hidden from them. And they who possess it not have not Wisdom. Therefore is it the god, and we worship it.' And I looked into the mirror, and it was even as he had said to me.

"And I did a strange thing, but what I did matters not, for in a valley that is but a day's journey from this place have I hidden the Mirror of Wisdom. Do but suffer me to enter into thee again and be thy servant, and thou shalt be wiser than all the wise men, and Wisdom shall be thine. Suffer me to enter into thee, and none will be as wise as thou."

But the young Fisherman laughed. "Love is better than Wisdom," he cried, "and the little Mermaid loves me."

"Nay, but there is nothing better than Wisdom," said the Soul.

"Love is better," answered the young Fisherman, and he

plunged into the deep, and the Soul went weeping away over the marshes.

And after the second year was over, the Soul came down to the shore of the sea, and called to the young Fisherman, and he rose out of the deep and said, "Why dost thou call to me?"

And the Soul answered, "Come nearer, that I may speak with thee, for I have seen marvellous things."

So he came nearer, and couched in the shallow water, and leaned his head upon his hand and listened.

And the Soul said to him, "When I left thee, I turned my face to the South and journeyed. From the South cometh everything that is precious. Six days I journeyed along the highways that lead to the city of Ashter, along the dusty red-dyed highways by which the pilgrims are wont to go did I journey, and on the morning of the seventh day I lifted up my eyes, and lo! the city lay at my feet, for it is in a valley.

"There are nine gates to this city, and in front of each gate stands a bronze horse that neighs when the Bedouins come down from the mountains. The walls are cased with copper, and the watch-towers on the walls are roofed with brass. In every tower stands an archer with a bow in his hand. At sunrise he strikes with an arrow on a gong, and at sunset he blows through a horn of horn.

"When I sought to enter, the guards stopped me and asked of me who I was. I made answer that I was a Dervish and on my way to the city of Mecca, where there was a green veil on which the Koran was embroidered in silver letters by the hands of the angels. They were filled with wonder, and entreated me to pass in.

"Inside it is even as a bazaar. Surely thou shouldst have been with me. Across the narrow streets the gay lanterns of paper flutter like large butterflies. When the wind blows over the roofs they rise and fall as painted bubbles do. In front of their booths sit the merchants on silken carpets. They have straight black beards, and their turbans are covered with golden sequins, and long strings of amber and carved peach-stones glide through their cool fingers. Some of them sell galbanum and nard, and curious perfumes from the islands of the Indian Sea, and the thick oil of red roses, and myrrh and little nail-shaped cloves. When one stops to speak to them, they throw pinches of frankincense upon a charcoal brazier and make the air sweet. I saw a Syrian who held in his hands a thin rod like a reed. Grey threads of smoke came from it, and its odour as it burned was as the odour of the pink almond in spring. Others sell silver bracelets embossed all over with creamy blue turquoise stones, and anklets of brass wire fringed with little pearls, and tigers' claws set in gold, and the claws of that gilt cat, the leopard, set in gold also, and earrings of pierced emerald, and finger-rings of hollowed jade. From the tea-houses comes the sound of the guitar, and the opium-smokers with their white smiling faces look out at the passers-by.

"Of a truth thou shouldst have been with me. The wine-sellers elbow their way through the crowd with great black skins on their shoulders. Most of them sell the wine of Schiraz, which is as sweet as honey. They serve it in little metal cups and strew rose leaves upon it. In the marketplace stand the fruitsellers, who sell all kinds of fruit: ripe figs, with their bruised purple flesh, melons, smelling of musk and yellow as topazes, citrons and rose-apples and clusters of white grapes, round red-gold oranges, and oval lemons of green gold. Once I saw an elephant go by. Its trunk was painted with vermilion and turmeric, and over its ears it had a net of crimson silk cord. It stopped opposite one of the booths and began eating the oranges, and the man only laughed. Thou canst not think how strange a people they are. When they are glad they go to the bird-sellers and buy of them a caged bird, and set it free that their joy may be greater, and when they are sad they scourge themselves with thorns that their sorrow may not grow less.

"One evening I met some negroes carrying a heavy palanquin through the bazaar. It was made of gilded bamboo, and the poles were of vermilion lacquer studded with brass peacocks. Across the windows hung thin curtains of muslin embroidered with beetles' wings and with tiny seed-pearls, and as it passed by a pale-faced Circassian looked out and smiled at me. I followed behind, and the negroes hurried their steps and scowled. But I did not care. I felt a great curiosity come over me.

"At last they stopped at a square white house. There were no windows to it, only a little door like the door of a tomb. They set down the palanquin and knocked three times with a copper hammer. An Armenian in a caftan of green leather peered through the wicket, and when he saw them he opened, and spread a carpet on the ground, and the woman stepped out. As she went in, she turned round and smiled at me again. I had never seen any one so pale.

"When the moon rose I returned to the same place and sought for the house, but it was no longer there. When I saw that, I knew who the woman was, and wherefore she had smiled at me.

"Certainly thou shouldst have been with me. On the feast of the New Moon the young Emperor came forth from his palace and went into the mosque to pray. His hair and beard were dyed with rose-leaves, and his cheeks were powdered with a fine gold dust. The palms of his feet and hands were yellow with saffron.

"At sunrise he went forth from his palace in a robe of silver, and at sunset he returned to it again in a robe of gold. The people flung themselves on the ground and hid their faces, but I would not do so. I stood by the stall of a seller of dates and waited. When the Emperor saw me, he raised his painted eyebrows and stopped. I stood quite still, and made him no obeisance. The people marvelled at my boldness, and counselled me to flee from the city. I paid no heed to them, but went and sat with the sellers of strange gods, who by reason of their craft are abominated. When I told them what I had done, each of them gave me a god and prayed me to leave them.

"That night, as I lay on a cushion in the tea-house that is in the Street of Pomegranates, the guards of the Emperor entered and led me to the palace. As I went in they closed each door behind me, and put a chain across it. Inside was a great court with an arcade running all round. The walls were of white alabaster, set here and there with blue and green tiles. The pillars were of green marble, and the pavement of a kind of peach-blossom marble. I had never seen anything like it before.

"As I passed across the court two veiled women looked down from a balcony and cursed me. The guards hastened on, and the butts of the lances rang upon the polished floor. They opened a gate of wrought ivory, and I found myself in a watered garden of seven terraces. It was planted with tulip-cups and moonflowers, and silver-studded aloes. Like a slim reed of crystal a fountain hung in the dusky air. The cypress-trees were like burnt-out torches. From one of them a nightingale was singing.

"At the end of the garden stood a little pavilion. As we approached it two eunuchs came out to meet us. Their fat bodies swayed as they walked, and they glanced curiously at me with their yellow-lidded eyes. One of them drew aside the captain of the guard, and in a low voice whispered to him. The other kept munching scented pastilles, which he took with an affected gesture out of an oval box of lilac enamel.

"After a few moments the captain of the guard dismissed the soldiers. They went back to the palace, the eunuchs following slowly behind and plucking the sweet mulberries from the trees as they passed. Once the elder of the two turned round, and smiled at me with an evil smile.

"Then the captain of the guard motioned me towards the

entrance of the pavilion. I walked on without trembling, and drawing the heavy curtain aside I entered in.

"The young Emperor was stretched on a couch of dyed lion skins, and a gerfalcon perched upon his wrist. Behind him stood a brass-turbaned Nubian, naked down to the waist, and with heavy earrings in his split ears. On a table by the side of the couch lay a mighty scimitar of steel.

"When the Emperor saw me he frowned, and said to me, 'What is thy name? Knowest thou not that I am Emperor of this city?' But I made him no answer.

"He pointed with his finger at the scimitar, and the Nubian seized it, and rushing forward struck at me with great violence. The blade whizzed through me, and did me no hurt. The man fell sprawling on the floor, and when he rose up his teeth chattered with terror and he hid himself behind the couch.

"The Emperor leapt to his feet, and taking a lance from a stand of arms, he threw it at me. I caught it in its flight, and brake the shaft into two pieces. He shot at me with an arrow, but I held up my hands and it stopped in mid-air. Then he drew a dagger from a belt of white leather, and stabbed the Nubian in the throat lest the slave should tell of his dishonour. The man writhed like a trampled snake, and a red foam bubbled from his lips.

"As soon as he was dead the Emperor turned to me, and when he had wiped away the bright sweat from his brow with a little napkin of purfled and purple silk, he said to me, 'Art thou a prophet, that I may not harm thee, or the son of a prophet, that I can do thee no hurt? I pray thee leave my city tonight, for while thou art in it I am no longer its lord.'

"And I answered him, 'I will go for half of thy treasure. Give me half of thy treasure, and I will go away.'

"He took me by the hand, and led me out into the garden. When the captain of the guard saw me, he wondered. When the eunuchs saw me, their knees shook and they fell upon the ground in fear.

"There is a chamber in the palace that has eight walls of red porphyry, and a brass-sealed ceiling hung with lamps. The Emperor touched one of the walls and it opened, and we passed down a corridor that was lit with many torches. In niches upon each side stood great wine-jars filled to the brim with silver pieces. When we reached the centre of the corridor the Emperor spake the word that may not be spoken, and a granite door swung back on a secret spring, and he put his hands before his face lest his eyes should be dazzled.

"Thou couldst not believe how marvellous a place it was. There were huge tortoise-shells full of pearls, and hollowed moonstones of great size piled up with red rubies. The gold was stored in coffers of elephant-hide, and the gold-dust in leather bottles. There were opals and sapphires, the former in cups of crystal, and the latter in cups of jade. Round green emeralds were ranged in order upon thin plates of ivory, and in one corner were silk bags filled, some with turquoise-stones, and others with beryls. The ivory horns were heaped with purple amethysts, and the horns of brass with chalcedonies and sards. The pillars, which were of cedar, were hung with strings of yellow lynx-stones. In the flat oval shields there were carbuncles, both wine-coloured and coloured like grass. And yet I have told thee but a tithe of what was there.

"And when the Emperor had taken away his hands from before his face he said to me: 'This is my house of treasure, and half that is in it is thine, even as I promised to thee. And I will give thee camels and camel drivers, and they shall do thy bidding and take thy share of the treasure to whatever part of the world thou desirest to go. And the thing shall be done tonight, for I would not that the Sun, who is my father, should see that there is in my city a man whom I cannot slay.'

"But I answered him, 'The gold that is here is thine, and the silver also is thine, and thine are the precious jewels and the things of price. As for me, I have no need of these. Nor shall I take aught from thee but that little ring that thou wearest on the finger of thy hand.'

"And the Emperor frowned. 'It is but a ring of lead,' he cried, 'nor has it any value. Therefore take thy half of the treasure and go from my city.'

"'Nay,' I answered, 'but I will take nought but that leaden ring, for I know what is written within it, and for what purpose.'

"And the Emperor trembled, and besought me and said, 'Take all the treasure and go from my city. The half that is mine shall be thine also.'

"And I did a strange thing, but what I did matters not, for in a cave that is but a day's journey from this place have I hidden the Ring of Riches. It is but a day's journey from this place, and it waits for thy coming. He who has this Ring is richer than all the kings of the world. Come therefore and take it, and the world's riches shall be thine."

But the young Fisherman laughed. "Love is better than Riches," he cried, "and the little Mermaid loves me."

"Nay, but there is nothing better than Riches," said the Soul.

"Love is better," answered the young Fisherman, and he plunged into the deep, and the Soul went weeping away over the marshes.

And after the third year was over, the Soul came down to the shore of the sea, and called to the young Fisherman, and he rose out of the deep and said, "Why dost thou call to me?"

And the Soul answered, "Come nearer, that I may speak with thee, for I have seen marvellous things."

So he came nearer, and couched in the shallow water, and leaned his head upon his hand and listened.

And the Soul said to him, "In a city that I know of there is an inn that standeth by a river. I sat there with sailors who drank of two different-coloured wines, and ate bread made of barley, and little salt fish served in bay leaves with vinegar. And as we sat and made merry, there entered to us an old man bearing a leathern carpet and a lute that had two horns of amber. And when he had laid out the carpet on the floor, he struck with a quill on the wire strings of his lute, and a girl whose face was veiled ran in and began to dance before us. Her face was veiled with a veil of gauze, but her feet were naked. Naked were her feet, and they moved over the carpet like little white pigeons. Never have I seen anything so marvellous, and the city in which she dances is but a day's journey from this place."

Now when the young Fisherman heard the words of his Soul, he remembered that the little Mermaid had no feet and could not dance. And a great desire came over him, and he said to himself, "It is but a day's journey, and I can return to my love," and he laughed, and stood up in the shallow water, and strode towards the shore.

And when he had reached the dry shore he laughed again, and held out his arms to his Soul. And his Soul gave a great cry of joy and ran to meet him, and entered into him, and the young Fisherman saw stretched before him upon the sand that shadow of the body that is the body of the Soul.

And his Soul said to him, "Let us not tarry, but get hence at once, for the Sea-gods are jealous, and have monsters that do their bidding."

So they made haste, and all that night they journeyed beneath the moon, and all the next day they journeyed beneath the sun, and on the evening of the day they came to a city.

And the young Fisherman said to his Soul, "Is this the city in which she dances of whom thou didst speak to me?"

And his Soul answered him, "It is not this city, but another. Nevertheless let us enter in." So they entered in and passed through the streets, and as they passed through the Street of the Jewellers the young Fisherman saw a fair silver cup set forth in a booth. And his Soul said to him, "Take that silver cup and hide it."

So he took the cup and hid it in the fold of his tunic, and they went hurriedly out of the city.

And after that they had gone a league from the city, the young Fisherman frowned, and flung the cup away, and said to his Soul, "Why didst thou tell me to take this cup and hide it, for it was an evil thing to do?"

But his Soul answered him, "Be at peace, be at peace."

And on the evening of the second day they came to a city, and the young Fisherman said to his Soul, "Is this the city in which she dances of whom thou didst speak to me?"

And his Soul answered him, "It is not this city, but another. Nevertheless let us enter in." So they entered in and passed through the streets, and as they passed through the Street of the Sellers of Sandals, the young Fisherman saw a child standing by a jar of water. And his Soul said to him, "Smite that child." So he smote the child till it wept, and when he had done this they went hurriedly out of the city.

And after that they had gone a league from the city the young Fisherman grew wroth, and said to his Soul, "Why didst thou tell me to smite the child, for it was an evil thing to do?"

But his Soul answered him, "Be at peace, be at peace."

And on the evening of the third day they came to a city, and the young Fisherman said to his Soul, "Is this the city in which she dances of whom thou didst speak to me?"

And his Soul answered him, "It may be that it is in this city, therefore let us enter in."

So they entered in and passed through the streets, but nowhere could the young Fisherman find the river or the inn that stood by its side. And the people of the city looked curiously at him, and he grew afraid and said to his Soul, "Let us go hence, for she who dances with white feet is not here."

But his Soul answered, "Nay, but let us tarry, for the night is dark and there will be robbers on the way."

So he sat him down in the marketplace and rested, and after a time there went by a hooded merchant who had a cloak of cloth of Tartary, and bare a lantern of pierced horn at the end of a jointed reed. And the merchant said to him, "Why dost thou sit in the marketplace, seeing that the booths are closed and the bales corded?"

And the young Fisherman answered him, "I can find no inn in this city, nor have I any kinsman who might give me shelter."

"Are we not all kinsmen?" said the merchant. "And did not one God make us? Therefore come with me, for I have a guest-chamber."

So the young Fisherman rose up and followed the merchant to his house. And when he had passed through a garden of pomegranates and entered into the house, the merchant brought him rose-water in a copper dish that he might wash his hands, and ripe melons that he might quench his thirst, and set a bowl of rice and a piece of roasted kid before him.

And after that he had finished, the merchant led him to the guest-chamber, and bade him sleep and be at rest. And the young Fisherman gave him thanks, and kissed the ring that was on his hand, and flung himself down on the carpets of dyed goat's-hair. And when he had covered himself with a covering of black lamb's-wool he fell asleep.

And three hours before dawn, and while it was still night, his Soul waked him and said to him, "Rise up and go to the room of the merchant, even to the room in which he sleepeth, and slay him, and take from him his gold, for we have need of it."

And the young Fisherman rose up and crept towards the room of the merchant, and over the feet of the merchant there was lying a curved sword, and the tray by the side of the merchant held nine purses of gold. And he reached out his hand and touched the sword, and when he touched it the merchant started and awoke, and leaping up seized himself the sword and cried to the young Fisherman, "Dost thou return evil for good, and pay with the shedding of blood for the kindness that I have shown thee?"

And his Soul said to the young Fisherman, "Strike him," and he struck him so that he swooned and he seized then the nine purses of gold, and fled hastily through the garden of pomegranates, and set his face to the star that is the star of morning.

And when they had gone a league from the city, the young Fisherman beat his breast, and said to his Soul, "Why didst thou bid me slay the merchant and take his gold? Surely thou art evil."

But his Soul answered him, "Be at peace, be at peace."

"Nay," cried the young Fisherman, "I may not be at peace, for all that thou hast made me to do I hate. Thee also I hate, and I bid thee tell me wherefore thou hast wrought with me in this wise."

And his Soul answered him, "When thou didst send me forth into the world thou gavest me no heart, so I learned to do all these things and love them."

"What sayest thou?" murmured the young Fisherman.

"Thou knowest," answered his Soul, "thou knowest it well. Hast thou forgotten that thou gavest me no heart? I trow not. And so trouble not thyself nor me, but be at peace, for there is no pain that thou shalt not give away, nor any pleasure that thou shalt not receive."

And when the young Fisherman heard these words he trembled and said to his Soul, "Nay, but thou art evil, and hast made me forget my love, and hast tempted me with temptations, and hast set my feet in the ways of sin."

And his Soul answered him, "Thou hast not forgotten that when thou didst send me forth into the world thou gavest me no heart. Come, let us go to another city, and make merry, for we have nine purses of gold."

But the young Fisherman took the nine purses of gold, and flung them down, and trampled on them.

"Nay," he cried, "but I will have nought to do with thee, nor will I journey with thee anywhere, but even as I sent thee away before, so will I send thee away now, for thou hast wrought me no good." And he turned his back to the moon, and with the little knife that had the handle of green viper's skin he strove to cut from his feet that shadow of the body which is the body of the Soul.

Yet his Soul stirred not from him, nor paid heed to his command, but said to him, "The spell that the Witch told thee avails thee no more, for I may not leave thee, nor mayest thou drive me forth. Once in his life may a man send his Soul away, but he who receiveth back his Soul must keep it with him for ever, and this is his punishment and his reward."

And the young Fisherman grew pale and clenched his hands and cried, "She was a false Witch in that she told me not that."

"Nay," answered his Soul, "but she was true to Him she worships, and whose servant she will be ever."

And when the young Fisherman knew that he could no longer get rid of his Soul, and that it was an evil Soul and would abide with him always, he fell upon the ground weeping bitterly.

And when it was day the young Fisherman rose up and said to his Soul, "I will bind my hands that I may not do thy bidding, and close my lips that I may not speak thy words, and I will return to the place where she whom I love has her dwelling. Even to the sea will I return, and to the little bay where she is wont to sing, and I will call to her and tell her the evil I have done and the evil thou hast wrought on me."

And his Soul tempted him and said, "Who is thy love, that

thou shouldst return to her? The world has many fairer than she is. There are the dancing-girls of Samaris who dance in the manner of all kinds of birds and beasts. Their feet are painted with henna, and in their hands they have little copper bells. They laugh while they dance, and their laughter is as clear as the laughter of water. Come with me and I will show them to thee. For what is this trouble of thine about the things of sin? Is that which is pleasant to eat not made for the eater? Is there poison in that which is sweet to drink? Trouble not thyself, but come with me to another city. There is a little city hard by in which there is a garden of tulip-trees. And there dwell in this comely garden white peacocks and peacocks that have blue breasts. Their tails when they spread them to the sun are like disks of ivory and like gilt disks. And she who feeds them dances for their pleasure, and sometimes she dances on her hands and at other times she dances with her feet. Her eyes are coloured with stibium, and her nostrils are shaped like the wings of a swallow. From a hook in one of her nostrils hangs a flower that is carved out of a pearl. She laughs while she dances, and the silver rings that are about her ankles tinkle like bells of silver. And so trouble not thyself anymore, but come with me to this city."

But the young Fisherman answered not his Soul, but closed his lips with the seal of silence and with a tight cord bound his hands, and journeyed back to the place from which he had come, even to the little bay where his love had been wont to sing. And ever did his Soul tempt him by the way, but he made it no answer, nor would he do any of the wickedness that it sought to make him to do, so great was the power of the love that was within him.

And when he had reached the shore of the sea, he loosed the cord from his hands, and took the seal of silence from his lips, and called to the little Mermaid. But she came not to his call, though he called to her all day long and besought her.

And his Soul mocked him and said, "Surely thou hast but little joy out of thy love. Thou art as one who in time of death pours water into a broken vessel. Thou givest away what thou hast, and nought is given to thee in return. It were better for thee to come with me, for I know where the Valley of Pleasure lies, and what things are wrought there."

But the young Fisherman answered not his Soul, but in a cleft of the rock he built himself a house of wattles, and abode there for the space of a year. And every morning he called to the Mermaid, and every noon he called to her again, and at night-time he spake her name. Yet never did she rise out of the sea to meet him, nor in any place of the sea could he find her though he sought for her in the caves and in the green water, in the pools of the tide and in the wells that are at the bottom of the deep.

And ever did his Soul tempt him with evil, and whisper of terrible things. Yet did it not prevail against him, so great was the power of his love.

And after the year was over, the Soul thought within himself, "I have tempted my master with evil, and his love is stronger than I am. I will tempt him now with good, and it may be that he will come with me."

So he spake to the young Fisherman and said, "I have told thee of the joy of the world, and thou hast turned a deaf ear to me. Suffer me now to tell thee of the world's pain, and it may be that thou wilt hearken. For of a truth pain is the Lord of this world, nor is there anyone who escapes from its net. There be some who lack raiment, and others who lack bread. There be widows who sit in purple, and widows who sit in rags. To and fro over the fens go the lepers, and they are cruel to each other. The beggars go up and down on the highways, and their wallets are empty. Through the streets of the cities walks Famine, and the Plague sits at their gates. Come, let us go forth and mend these things, and make them not to be. Wherefore shouldst thou tarry here calling to thy love, seeing she comes not to thy call? And what is love, that thou shouldst set this high store upon it?"

But the young Fisherman answered it nought, so great was the power of his love. And every morning he called to the Mermaid, and every noon he called to her again, and at night-time he spake her name. Yet never did she rise out of the sea to meet him, nor in any place of the sea could he find her, though he sought for her in the rivers of the sea, and in the valleys that are under the waves, in the sea that the night makes purple, and in the sea that the dawn leaves grey.

And after the second year was over, the Soul said to the young Fisherman at night-time, and as he sat in the wattled house alone, "Lo! now I have tempted thee with evil, and I have tempted thee with good, and thy love is stronger than I am. Wherefore will I tempt thee no longer, but I pray thee to suffer me to enter thy heart, that I may be one with thee even as before."

"Surely thou mayest enter," said the young Fisherman, "for in the days when with no heart thou didst go through the world thou must have much suffered."

"Alas!" cried his Soul, "I can find no place of entrance, so compassed about with love is this heart of thine."

"Yet I would that I could help thee," said the young Fisherman.

And as he spake there came a great cry of mourning from the sea, even the cry that men hear when one of the Sea-folk is dead. And the young Fisherman leapt up, and left his wattled house, and ran down to the shore. And the black waves came hurrying to the shore, bearing with them a burden that was whiter than silver. White as the surf it was, and like a flower it tossed on the waves. And the surf took it from the waves, and the foam took it from the surf, and the shore received it, and lying at his feet the young Fisherman saw the body of the little

Mermaid. Dead at his feet it was lying.

Weeping as one smitten with pain he flung himself down beside it, and he kissed the cold red of the mouth, and toyed with the wet amber of the hair. He flung himself down beside it on the sand, weeping as one trembling with joy, and in his brown arms he held it to his breast. Cold were the lips, yet he kissed them. Salt was the honey of the hair, yet he tasted it with a bitter joy. He kissed the closed eyelids, and the wild spray that lay upon their cups was less salt than his tears.

And to the dead thing he made confession. Into the shells of its ears he poured the harsh wine of his tale. He put the little hands round his neck, and with his fingers he touched the thin reed of the throat. Bitter, bitter was his joy, and full of strange gladness was his pain.

The black sea came nearer, and the white foam moaned like a leper. With white claws of foam the sea grabbled at the shore. From the palace of the Sea-King came the cry of mourning again, and far out upon the sea the great Tritons blew hoarsely upon their horns.

"Flee away," said his Soul, "for ever doth the sea come nigher, and if thou tarriest it will slay thee. Flee away, for I am afraid, seeing that thy heart is closed against me by reason of the greatness of thy love. Flee away to a place of safety. Surely thou wilt not send me without a heart into another world?"

But the young Fisherman listened not to his Soul, but called on the little Mermaid and said, "Love is better than wisdom, and more precious than riches, and fairer than the feet of the daughters of men. The fires cannot destroy it, nor can the waters quench it. I called on thee at dawn, and thou didst not come to my call. The moon heard thy name, yet hadst thou no heed of me. For evilly had I left thee, and to my own hurt had I wandered away. Yet ever did thy love abide with me, and ever was it strong, nor did aught prevail against it, though I have looked upon evil and looked upon good. And now that thou art dead, surely I will die with thee also."

And his Soul besought him to depart, but he would not, so great was his love. And the sea came nearer, and sought to cover him with its waves, and when he knew that the end was at hand he kissed with mad lips the cold lips of the Mermaid, and the heart that was within him brake. And as through the fulness of his love his heart did break, the Soul found an entrance and entered in, and was one with him even as before. And the sea covered the young Fisherman with its waves.

And in the morning the Priest went forth to bless the sea, for it had been troubled. And with him went the monks and the musicians, and the candle-bearers, and the swingers of censers, and a great company.

And when the Priest reached the shore he saw the young Fisherman lying drowned in the surf, and clasped in his arms was the body of the little Mermaid. And he drew back frowning, and having made the sign of the cross, he cried aloud and said, "I will not bless the sea nor anything that is in it. Accursed be the Sea-folk, and accursed be all they who traffic with them. And as for him who for love's sake forsook God, and so lieth here with his leman slain by God's judgment, take up his body and the body of his leman, and bury them in the corner of the Field of the Fullers, and set no mark above them, nor sign of any kind, that none may know the place of their resting. For accursed were they in their lives, and accursed shall they be in their deaths also."

And the people did as he commanded them, and in the corner of the Field of the Fullers, where no sweet herbs grew, they dug a deep pit, and laid the dead things within it.

And when the third year was over, and on a day that was a holy day, the Priest went up to the chapel, that he might show to the people the wounds of the Lord, and speak to them about the wrath of God.

And when he had robed himself with his robes, and entered in and bowed himself before the altar, he saw that the altar was covered with strange flowers that never had been seen before. Strange were they to look at, and of curious beauty, and their beauty troubled him, and their odour was sweet in his nostrils. And he felt glad, and understood not why he was glad.

And after that he had opened the tabernacle, and incensed the monstrance that was in it, and shown the fair wafer to the people, and hid it again behind the veil of veils, he began to speak to the people, desiring to speak to them of the wrath of God. But the beauty of the white flowers troubled him, and their odour was sweet in his nostrils, and there came another word into his lips, and he spake not of the wrath of God, but of the God whose name is Love. And why he so spake, he knew not.

And when he had finished his word the people wept, and the Priest went back to the sacristy, and his eyes were full of tears. And the deacons came in and began to unrobe him, and took from him the alb and the girdle, the maniple and the stole. And he stood as one in a dream.

And after that they had unrobed him, he looked at them and said, "What are the flowers that stand on the altar, and whence do they come?"

And they answered him, "What flowers they are we cannot tell, but they come from the corner of the Fullers' Field." And the Priest trembled, and returned to his own house and prayed.

And in the morning, while it was still dawn, he went forth with the monks and the musicians, and the candle-bearers and the swingers of censers, and a great company, and came to the shore of the sea, and blessed the sea, and all the wild things that are in it. The Fauns also he blessed, and the little things that dance in the woodland, and the bright-eyed things that peer through the leaves. All the things in God's world he blessed, and the people were filled with joy and wonder. Yet never again in the corner of the Fullers' Field grew flowers of any kind, but the field remained barren even as before. Nor came the Sea-folk into the bay as they had been wont to do, for they went to another part of the sea.

THE GHOST SHIP

by Richard Middleton

Fairfield is a little village lying near the Portsmouth Road about half-way between London and the sea. Strangers who find it by accident now and then, call it a pretty, old-fashioned place; we who live in it and call it home don't find anything very pretty about it, but we should be sorry to live anywhere else. Our minds have taken the shape of the inn and the church and the green, I suppose. At all events we never feel comfortable out of Fairfield.

Of course the Cockneys, with their vasty houses and noise-ridden streets, can call us rustics if they choose, but for all that Fairfield is a better place to live in than London. Doctor says that when he goes to London his mind is bruised with the weight of the houses, and he was a Cockney born. He had to live there himself when he was a little chap, but he knows better now. You gentlemen may laugh—perhaps some of you come from London way—but it seems to me that a witness like that is worth a gallon of arguments.

Dull? Well, you might find it dull, but I assure you that I've listened to all the London yarns you have spun tonight, and they're absolutely nothing to the things that happen at Fairfield. It's because of our way of thinking and minding our own business. If one of your Londoners were set down on the green of a Saturday night when the ghosts of the lads who died in the war keep tryst with the lasses who lie in the church-yard, he couldn't help being curious and interfering, and then the ghosts would go somewhere where it was quieter. But we just let them come and go and don't make any fuss, and in consequence Fairfield is the ghostiest place in all England. Why, I've seen a headless man sitting on the edge of the well in broad daylight, and the children playing about his feet as if he were their father. Take my word for it, spirits know when they are well off as much as human beings.

Still, I must admit that the thing I'm going to tell you about was queer even for our part of the world, where three packs of ghost-hounds hunt regularly during the season, and blacksmith's great-grandfather is busy all night shoeing the dead gentlemen's horses. Now that's a thing that wouldn't happen in London, because of their interfering ways, but blacksmith he lies up aloft and sleeps as quiet as a lamb. Once when he had a bad head he shouted down to them not to make so much noise, and in the morning he found an old guinea left on the anvil as an apology. He wears it on his watch-chain now. But I must get on with my story; if I start telling you about the queer happenings at Fairfield I'll never stop.

It all came of the great storm in the spring of '97, the year that we had two great storms. This was the first one, and I remember it very well, because I found in the morning that it had lifted the thatch of my pigsty into the widow's garden as clean as a boy's kite. When I looked over the hedge, widow—Tom Lamport's widow that was—was prodding for her nasturtiums with a daisy-grubber. After I had watched her for a little I went down to the "Fox and Grapes" to tell landlord what she had said to me. Landlord he laughed, being a married man and at ease with the sex. "Come to that," he said, "the tempest has blowed something into my field. A kind of a ship I think it would be."

I was surprised at that until he explained that it was only a ghost ship and would do no hurt to the turnips. We argued that it had been blown up from the sea at Portsmouth, and then we talked of something else. There were two slates down at the parsonage and a big tree in Lumley's meadow. It was a rare storm.

I reckon the wind had blown our ghosts all over England. They were coming back for days afterwards with foundered horses and as footsore as possible, and they were so glad to get back to Fairfield that some of them walked up the street crying like little children. Squire said that his great-grandfather's great-grandfather hadn't looked so dead-beat since the battle of Naseby, and he's an educated man.

What with one thing and another, I should think it was a week before we got straight again, and then one afternoon I met the landlord on the green and he had a worried face.

"I wish you'd come and have a look at that ship in my field," he said to me. "It seems to me it's leaning real hard on the turnips. I can't bear thinking what the missus will say when she sees it."

I walked down the lane with him, and sure enough there was a ship in the middle of his field, but such a ship as no man had seen on the water for three hundred years, let alone in the middle of a turnip field. It was all painted black and covered with carvings, and there was a great bay window in the stern for all the world like the Squire's drawing room. There was a crowd of little black cannon on deck and looking out of her portholes, and she was anchored at each end to the hard ground. I have seen the wonders of the world on picture-postcards, but I have never seen anything to equal that.

"She seems very solid for a ghost ship," I said, seeing the

landlord was bothered.

"I should say it's a betwixt and between," he answered, puzzling it over, "but it's going to spoil a matter of fifty turnips, and missus she'll want it moved."

We went up to her and touched the side, and it was as hard as a real ship. "Now there's folks in England would call that very curious," he said.

Now I don't know much about ships, but I should think that that ghost ship weighed a solid two hundred tons, and it seemed to me that she had come to stay, so that I felt sorry for landlord, who was a married man. "All the horses in Fairfield won't move her out of my turnips," he said, frowning at her.

Just then we heard a noise on her deck, and we looked up and saw that a man had come out of her front cabin and was looking down at us very peaceably. He was dressed in a black uniform set out with rusty gold lace, and he had a great cutlass by his side in a brass sheath. "I'm Captain Bartholomew Roberts," he said, in a gentleman's voice, "put in for recruits. I seem to have brought her rather far up the harbour."

"Harbour!" cried landlord. "Why, you're fifty miles from the sea."

Captain Roberts didn't turn a hair. "So much as that, is it?" he said coolly. "Well, it's of no consequence."

Landlord was a bit upset at this. "I don't want to be unneighbourly," he said, "but I wish you hadn't brought your ship into my field. You see, my wife sets great store on these turnips."

The captain took a pinch of snuff out of a fine gold box that he pulled out of his pocket, and dusted his fingers with a silk handkerchief in a very genteel fashion.

"I'm only here for a few months," he said, "but if a testimony of my esteem would pacify your good lady I should be content," and with the words he loosed a great gold brooch from the neck of his coat and tossed it down to landlord.

Landlord blushed as red as a strawberry.

"I'm not denying she's fond of jewellery," he said, "but it's too much for half a sackful of turnips." And indeed it was a handsome brooch.

The captain laughed. "Tut, man," he said, "it's a forced sale, and you deserve a good price. Say no more about it."

And nodding good-day to us, he turned on his heel and went into the cabin. Landlord walked back up the lane like a man with a weight off his mind. "That tempest has blowed me a bit of luck," he said. "The missus will be much pleased with that brooch. It's better than blacksmith's guinea, any day."

Ninety-seven was Jubilee year, the year of the second Jubilee, you remember, and we had great doings at Fairfield, so that we hadn't much time to bother about the ghost ship, though anyhow, it isn't our way to meddle in things that don't concern us. Landlord, he saw his tenant once or twice when he was hoeing his turnips and passed the time of day, and landlord's wife wore her new brooch to church every Sunday. But we didn't mix much with the ghosts at any time, all except an idiot lad there was in the village, and he didn't know the difference between a man and a ghost, poor innocent! On Jubilee Day, however, somebody told Captain Roberts why the church bells were ringing, and he hoisted a flag and fired off his guns like a loyal Englishman. 'Tis true the guns were shotted, and one of the round shot knocked a hole in Farmer Johnstone's barn, but nobody thought much of that in such a season of rejoicing.

It wasn't till our celebrations were over that we noticed that anything was wrong in Fairfield. 'Twas shoemaker who told me first about it one morning at the "Fox and Grapes."

"You know my great great-uncle?" he said to me.

"You mean Joshua, the quiet lad," I answered, knowing him well.

"Quiet!" said shoemaker indignantly. "Quiet you call him, coming home at three o'clock every morning as drunk as a magistrate and waking up the whole house with his noise."

"Why, it can't be Joshua!" I said, for I knew him for one of the most respectable young ghosts in the village.

"Joshua it is," said shoemaker, "and one of these nights he'll find himself out in the street if he isn't careful."

This kind of talk shocked me, I can tell you, for I don't like to hear a man abusing his own family, and I could hardly believe that a steady youngster like Joshua had taken to drink. But just then in came butcher Aylwin in such a temper that he could hardly drink his beer.

"The young puppy! The young puppy!" he kept on saying, and it was some time before shoemaker and I found out that he was talking about his ancestor that fell at Senlac.

"Drink?" said shoemaker hopefully, for we all like company in our misfortunes, and butcher nodded grimly.

"The young noodle," he said, emptying his tankard.

Well, after that I kept my ears open, and it was the same story all over the village. There was hardly a young man among all the ghosts of Fairfield who didn't roll home in the small hours of the morning the worse for liquor. I used to wake up in the night and hear them stumble past my house, singing outrageous songs. The worst of it was that we couldn't keep the scandal to ourselves and the folk at Greenhill began to talk of "sodden Fairfield" and taught their children to sing a song about us:

"Sodden Fairfield, sodden Fairfield, has no use for bread-and-butter,

Rum for breakfast, rum for dinner, rum for tea, and rum for supper!"

We are easy-going in our village, but we didn't like that.

Of course we soon found out where the young fellows went to get the drink, and landlord was terribly cut up that his tenant should have turned out so badly, but his wife wouldn't hear of parting with the brooch, so that he couldn't give the Captain notice to quit. But as time went on, things grew from bad to worse, and at all hours of the day you would see those young reprobates sleeping it off on the village green. Nearly every afternoon a ghost wagon used to jolt down to the ship with a lading of rum, and though the older ghosts seemed inclined to give the Captain's hospitality the go-by, the youngsters were neither to hold nor to bind.

So one afternoon when I was taking my nap I heard a knock at the door, and there was parson looking very serious, like a man with a job before him that he didn't altogether relish. "I'm going down to talk to the Captain about all this drunkenness in the village, and I want you to come with me," he said straight out.

I can't say that I fancied the visit much, myself, and I tried to hint to parson that as, after all, they were only a lot of ghosts it didn't very much matter.

"Dead or alive, I'm responsible for the good conduct," he said, "and I'm going to do my duty and put a stop to this continued disorder. And you are coming with me John Simmons."

So I went, parson being apersuasive kind of man.

We went down to the ship, and as we approached her I could see the Captain tasting the air on deck. When he saw parson he took off his hat very politely and I can tell you that I was relieved to find that he had a proper respect for the cloth. Parson acknowledged his salute and spoke out stoutly enough. "Sir, I should be glad to have a word with you."

"Come on board, sir, come on board," said the Captain, and I could tell by his voice that he knew why we were there. Parson and I climbed up an uneasy kind of ladder, and the Captain took us into the great cabin at the back of the ship, where the bay-window was. It was the most wonderful place you ever saw in your life, all full of gold and silver plate, swords with jewelled scabbards, carved oak chairs, and great chests that look as though they were bursting with guineas. Even parson was surprised, and he did not shake his head very hard when the Captain took down some silver cups and poured us out a drink of rum. I tasted mine, and I don't mind saying that it changed my view of things entirely. There was nothing betwixt and between about that rum, and I felt that it was ridiculous to blame the lads for drinking too much of stuff like that. It seemed to fill my veins with honey and fire.

Parson put the case squarely to the Captain, but I didn't listen much to what he said; I was busy sipping my drink and looking through the window at the fishes swimming to and fro over landlord's turnips. Just then it seemed the most natural thing in the world that they should be there, though afterwards, of course, I could see that that proved it was a ghost ship.

But even then I thought it was queer when I saw a drowned sailor float by in the thin air with his hair and beard all full of bubbles. It was the first time I had seen anything quite like that at Fairfield.

All the time I was regarding the wonders of the deep parson was telling Captain Roberts how there was no peace or rest in the village owing to the curse of drunkenness, and what a bad example the youngsters were setting to the older ghosts. The Captain listened very attentively, and only put in a word now and then about boys being boys and young men sowing their wild oats. But when parson had finished his speech he filled up our silver cups and said to parson, with a flourish, "I should be sorry to cause trouble anywhere where I have been made welcome, and you will be glad to hear that I put to sea tomorrow night. And now you must drink me a prosperous voyage." So we all stood up and drank the toast with honour, and that noble rum was like hot oil in my veins.

After that Captain showed us some of the curiosities he had brought back from foreign parts, and we were greatly amazed, though afterwards I couldn't clearly remember what they were. And then I found myself walking across the turnips with parson, and I was telling him of the glories of the deep that I had seen through the window of the ship. He turned on me severely. "If I were you, John Simmons," he said, "I should go straight home to bed." He has a way of putting things that wouldn't occur to an ordinary man, has parson, and I did as he told me.

Well, next day it came on to blow, and it blew harder and harder, till about eight o'clock at night I heard a noise and looked out into the garden. I dare say you won't believe me, it seems a bit tall even to me, but the wind had lifted the thatch of my pigsty into the widow's garden a second time. I thought I wouldn't wait to hear what widow had to say about it, so I went across the green to the "Fox and Grapes", and the wind was so strong that I danced along on tiptoe like a girl at the fair. When I got to the inn landlord had to help me shut the door; it seemed as though a dozen goats were pushing against it to come in out of the storm.

"It's a powerful tempest," he said, drawing the beer. "I hear there's a chimney down at Dickory End."

"It's a funny thing how these sailors know about the weather," I answered. "When Captain said he was going tonight, I was thinking it would take a capful of wind to carry the ship back to sea, but now here's more than a capful."

"Ah, yes," said landlord, "it's tonight he goes true enough, and, mind you, though he treated me handsome over the rent, I'm not sure it's a loss to the village. I don't hold with gentrice who fetch their drink from London instead of helping local traders to get their living."

"But you haven't got any rum like his," I said, to draw him out.

His neck grew red above his collar, and I was afraid I'd gone too far, but after a while he got his breath with a grunt.

"John Simmons," he said, "if you've come down here this windy night to talk a lot of fool's talk, you've wasted a journey."

Well, of course, then I had to smooth him down with praising his rum, and Heaven forgive me for swearing it was better than Captain's. For the like of that rum no living lips have tasted save mine and parson's. But somehow or other I brought landlord round, and presently we must have a glass of his best to prove its quality.

"Beat that if you can!" he cried, and we both raised our glasses to our mouths, only to stop half-way and look at each other in amaze. For the wind that had been howling outside like an outrageous dog had all of a sudden turned as melodious as the carol-boys of a Christmas Eve.

"Surely that's not my Martha," whispered landlord, Martha being his great-aunt that lived in the loft overhead.

We went to the door, and the wind burst it open so that the handle was driven clean into the plaster of the wall. But we didn't think about that at the time, for over our heads, sailing very comfortably through the windy stars, was the ship that had passed the summer in landlord's field. Her portholes and her bay-window were blazing with lights, and there was a noise of singing and fiddling on her decks.

"He's gone," shouted landlord above the storm, "and he's taken half the village with him!" I could only nod in answer, not having lungs like bellows of leather.

In the morning we were able to measure the strength of the storm, and over and above my pigsty there was damage enough wrought in the village to keep us busy. True it is that the children had to break down no branches for the firing that autumn, since the wind had strewn the woods with more than they could carry away. Many of our ghosts were scattered abroad, but this time very few came back, all the young men having sailed with Captain—and not only ghosts, for a poor half-witted lad was missing, and we reckoned that he had stowed himself away or perhaps shipped as cabin-boy, not knowing any better.

What with the lamentations of the ghost girls and the grumbling of families who had lost an ancestor, the village was upset for a while, and the funny thing was that it was the folk who had complained most of the carryings-on of the youngsters, who made most noise now that they were gone. I hadn't any sympathy with shoemaker or butcher, who ran about saying how much they missed their lads, but it made me grieve to hear the poor bereaved girls calling their lovers by name on the village green at nightfall. It didn't seem fair to me that they should have lost their men a second time, after giving up life in order to join them, as like as not. Still, not even a spirit can be sorry forever, and after a few months we made up our mind that the folk who had sailed in the ship were never coming back, and we didn't talk about it any more.

And then one day, I dare say it would be a couple of years after, when the whole business was quite forgotten, who should come trapesing along the road from Portsmouth but the daft lad who had gone away with the ship, without waiting till he was dead to become a ghost. You never saw such a boy as that in all your life. He had a great rusty cutlass hanging to a string at his waist, and he was tattooed all over in fine colours, so that even his face looked like a girl's sampler. He had a handkerchief in his hand full of foreign shells and old-fashioned pieces of small money, very curious, and he walked up to the well outside his mother's house and drew himself a drink as if he had been nowhere in particular.

The worst of it was that he had come back as soft-headed as he went, and try as we might we couldn't get anything reasonable out of him. He talked a lot of gibberish about keel-hauling and walking the plank and crimson murders—things which a decent sailor should know nothing about, so that it seemed to me that for all his manners Captain had been more of a pirate than a gentleman mariner. But to draw sense out of that boy was as hard as picking cherries off a crab-tree. One silly tale he had that he kept on drifting back to, and to hear him you would have thought that it was the only thing that happened to him in his life. "We was at anchor," he would say, "off an island called the Basket of Flowers, and the sailors had caught a lot of parrots and we were teaching them to swear. Up and down the decks, up and down the decks, and the language they used was dreadful. Then we looked up and saw the masts of the Spanish ship outside the harbour. Outside the harbour they were, so we threw the parrots into the sea and sailed out to fight. And all the parrots were drownded in the sea and the language they used was dreadful."

That's the sort of boy he was, nothing but silly talk of parrots when we asked him about the fighting. And we never had a chance of teaching him better, for two days after he ran away again, and hasn't been seen since.

That's my story, and I assure you that things like that are happening at Fairfield all the time. The ship has never come back, but somehow as people grow older they seem to think that one of these windy nights she'll come sailing in over the hedges with all the lost ghosts on board. Well, when she comes, she'll be welcome. There's one ghost lass that has never grown tired of waiting for her lad to return. Every night you'll see her out on the green, straining her poor eyes with looking for the mast-lights among the stars. A faithful lass you'd call her, and I'm thinking you'd be right.

Landlord's field wasn't a penny the worse for the visit, but they do say that since then the turnips that have been grown in it have tasted of rum.

BY WATER

by Algernon Blackwood

THE NIGHT BEFORE young Larsen left to take up his new appointment in Egypt he went to the clairvoyante. He neither believed nor disbelieved. He felt no interest, for he already knew his past and did not wish to know his future. "Just to please me, Jim," the girl pleaded. "The woman is wonderful. Before I had been five minutes with her she told me your initials, so there must be something in it."

"She read your thought," he smiled indulgently. "Even I can do that!" But the girl was in earnest.

He yielded, and that night at his farewell dinner he came to give his report of the interview.

The result was meagre and unconvincing: money was coming to him, he was soon to make a voyage, and—he would never marry. "So you see how silly it all is," he laughed, for they were to be married when his first promotion came. He gave the details, however, making a little story of it in the way he knew she loved.

"But was that all, Jim?" The girl asked it, looking rather

hard into his face. "Aren't you hiding something from me?" He hesitated a moment, then burst out laughing at her clever discernment. "There was a little more," he confessed, "but you take it all so seriously. I—"

He had to tell it then, of course. The woman had told him a lot of gibberish about friendly and unfriendly elements. "She said water was unfriendly to me. I was to be careful of water, or else I should come to harm by it. Fresh water only," he hastened to add, seeing that the idea of shipwreck was in her mind.

"Drowning?" the girl asked quickly.

"Yes," he admitted with reluctance, but still laughing, "she did say drowning, though drowning in no ordinary way."

The girl's face showed uneasiness a moment. "What does that mean—drowning in no ordinary way?" she asked, a catch in her breath.

But that he could not tell her, because he did not know himself. He gave, therefore, the exact words: "You will drown, but will not know you drown."

It was unwise of him. He wished afterwards he had invented a happier report, or had kept this detail back. "I'm safe in Egypt, anyhow," he laughed. "I shall be a clever man if I can find enough water in the desert to do me harm!" And all the way from Trieste to Alexandria he remembered the promise she had extracted—that he would never once go on the Nile unless duty made it imperative for him to do so. He kept that promise like the literal, faithful soul he was. His love was equal to the somewhat quixotic sacrifice it occasionally involved. Fresh water in Egypt there was practically none other, and in any case the natrum works where his duty lay had their headquarters some distance out into the desert. The river, with its banks of welcome, refreshing verdure, was not even visible.

Months passed quickly, and the time for leave came within measurable distance. In the long interval luck had played the cards kindly for him, vacancies had occurred, early promotion seemed likely, and his letters were full of plans to bring her out to share a little house of their own. His health, however, had not improved; the dryness did not suit him. Even in this short period his blood had thinned, his nervous system deteriorated, and, contrary to the doctor's prophecy, the waterless air had told upon his sleep. A damp climate liked him best, and once the sun had touched him with its fiery finger.

His letters made no mention of this. He described the life to her, the work, the sport, the pleasant people, and his chances of increased pay and early marriage. And a week before he sailed he rode out upon a final act of duty to inspect the latest diggings his company were making. His course lay some twenty miles into the desert behind El-Chobak and towards the limestone hills of Guebel Haidi, and he went alone, carrying lunch and tea, for it was the weekly holiday of Friday, and the men were not at work.

The accident was ordinary enough. On his way back in the heat of early afternoon his pony stumbled against a boulder on the treacherous desert film, threw him heavily, broke the girth, bolted before he could seize the reins again, and left him stranded some ten or twelve miles from home. There was a pain in his knee that made walking difficult, a buzzing in his head that troubled sight and made the landscape swim, while, worse than either, his provisions, fastened to the saddle, had vanished with the frightened pony into those blazing leagues of sand. He was alone in the Desert, beneath the pitiless afternoon sun, twelve miles of utterly exhausting country between him and safety.

Under normal conditions he could have covered the distance in four hours, reaching home by dark, but his knee pained him so that a mile an hour proved the best he could possibly do. He reflected a few minutes. The wisest course was to sit down and wait till the pony told its obvious story to the stable, and help should come. And this was what he did, for the scorching heat and glare were dangerous. They were terrible. He was shaken and bewildered by his fall, hungry and weak into the bargain, and an hour's painful scrambling over the baked and burning little gorges must have speedily caused complete prostration. He sat down and rubbed his aching knee. It was quite a little adventure. Yet, though he knew the Desert might not be lightly trifled with, he felt at the moment nothing more than this—and the amusing description of it he would give in his letter, or—intoxicating thought—by word of mouth. In the heat of the sun he began to feel drowsy. A soft torpor crept over him. He dozed. He fell asleep.

It was a long, a dreamless sleep, for when he woke at length the sun had just gone down, the dusk lay awfully upon the enormous desert, and the air was chilly. The cold had waked him. Quickly, as though on purpose, the red glow faded from the sky; the first stars shone. It was dark. The heavens were deep violet. He looked round and realised that his sense of direction had gone entirely. Great hunger was in him. The cold already was bitter as the wind rose, but the pain in his knee having eased, he got up and walked a little—and in a moment lost sight of the spot where he had been lying. The shadowy desert swallowed it. "Ah," he realised, "this is not an English field or moor. I'm in the Desert!" The safe thing to do was to remain exactly where he was; only thus could the rescuers find him. Once he wandered he was done for. It was strange the search-party had not yet arrived. To keep warm, however, he was compelled to move, so he made a little pile of stones to mark the place, and walked round and round it in a circle of some dozen yards' diameter. He limped badly, and the hunger gnawed dreadfully, but, after all, the adventure was not so terrible. The amusing side of it kept uppermost still. Though fragile in body, his spirit was not unduly timid or imaginative. He could last out the night, or, if the worst came to the worst, the next day as well. But when he watched the little group of stones, he saw that there were dozens of them, scores, hundreds, thousands of these little groups of stones. The desert's face, of course, is thickly strewn with them. The original one was lost in the first five minutes. So he sat down again. But the biting cold, and the wind that licked his very skin beneath the light clothing, soon forced him up again. It was ominous, and the night huge and shelterless. The shaft of green zodiacal light that hung so strangely in the western sky for hours had faded away; the stars were out in their bright thousands. No guide was anywhere. The wind moaned and puffed among the sandy mounds. The vast sheet of desert stretched appallingly upon the world. He heard the jackals cry.

And with the jackals' cry came suddenly the unwelcome realisation that no play was in this adventure anymore, but that a bleak reality stared at him through the surrounding darkness. He faced it—at bay. He was genuinely lost. Thought blocked in him. "I must be calm and think," he said aloud. His voice woke no echo. It was small and dead; something gigantic ate it instantly. He got up and walked again. Why did no one come? Hours had passed. The pony had long ago found its stable, or—had it run madly in another direction altogether? He worked out possibilities, tightening his belt. The cold was searching. He never had been, never could be warm again; the hot sunshine of a few hours ago seemed the merest dream. Unfamiliar with hardship, he knew not what to do, but he took his coat and shirt off, vigorously rubbed his skin where the dried perspiration of the afternoon still caused clammy shivers, swung his arms furiously like a London cabman, and quickly dressed again. Though the wind upon his bare back was fearful, he felt warmer a little. He lay down exhausted, sheltered by an overhanging limestone crag, and took snatches of fitful dog's-sleep, while the wind drove overhead and the dry sand pricked his skin. One face continually was near him; one pair of tender eyes; two dear hands smoothed him; he smelt the perfume of light brown hair. It was all natural enough. His whole thought, in his misery, ran to her in England—England where there were soft fresh grass, big sheltering trees, hemlock and honeysuckle in the hedges—while the hard black Desert guarded him, and consciousness dipped away at little intervals under this dry and pitiless Egyptian sky.

It was perhaps five in the morning when a voice spoke and he started up with a horrid jerk—the voice of that clairvoyante woman. The sentence died away into the darkness, but one word remained: Water! At first he wondered, but at once explanation came. Cause and effect were obvious. The clue was physical. His body needed water, and so the thought came up into his mind. He was thirsty.

This was the moment when fear first really touched him. Hunger was manageable, more or less—for a day or two, certainly. But thirst! Thirst and the Desert were an evil pair that, by cumulative suggestion gathering since childhood days, brought terror in. Once in the mind it could not be dislodged. In spite of his best efforts, the ghastly thing grew passionately—because his thirst grew too. He had smoked much, had eaten spiced things at lunch, had breathed in alkali with the dry, scorched air. He searched for a cool flint pebble to put into his burning mouth, but found only angular scraps of dusty limestone. There were no pebbles here. The cold helped a little to counteract, but already he knew in himself subconsciously the dread of something that was coming. What was it? He tried to hide the thought and bury it out of sight. The utter futility of his tiny strength against the power of the universe appalled him. And then he knew. The merciless sun was on the way, already rising. Its return was like the presage of execution to him.

It came. With true horror he watched the marvellous swift dawn break over the sandy sea. The eastern sky glowed hurriedly as from crimson fires. Ridges, not noticeable in the starlight, turned black in endless series, like flat-topped billows of a frozen ocean. Wide streaks of blue and yellow followed, as the sky dropped sheets of faint light upon the wind-eaten cliffs and showed their under sides. They did not advance; they waited till the sun was up—and then they moved. They rose and sank. They shifted as the sunshine lifted them and the shadows crept away. But in an hour there would be no shadows any more. There would be no shade!

The little groups of stones began to dance. It was horrible. The unbroken, huge expanse lay round him, warming up, twelve hours of blazing hell to come. Already the monstrous Desert glared, each bit familiar, since each bit was a repetition of the bit before, behind, on either side. It laughed at guidance and direction. He rose and walked, for miles he walked, though how many, north, south, or west, he knew not. The frantic thing was in him now, the fury of the Desert. He took its pace, its endless, tireless stride, the stride of the burning, murderous Desert that is—waterless. He felt it alive—a blindly heaving desire in it to reduce him to its conditionless, awful dryness. He felt—yet knowing this was feverish and not to be believed—that his own small life lay on its mighty surface, a mere dot in space, a mere heap of little stones. His emotions, his fears, his hopes, his ambition, his love—mere bundled group of little unimportant stones that danced with apparent activity for a moment, then were merged in the undifferentiated surface underneath. He was included in a purpose greater than his own.

The will made a plucky effort then. "A night and a day," he laughed, while his lips cracked smartingly with the stretching of the skin, "what is it? Many a chap has lasted days and days!" Yes, only he was not of that rare company. He was ordinary, unaccustomed to privation, weak, untrained of spirit, unacquainted with stern resistance. He knew not how to spare himself. The Desert struck him where it pleased—all over. It played with him. His tongue was swollen; the parched throat could not swallow. He sank. An hour he lay there, just wit enough in him to choose the top of a mound where he could be most easily seen. He lay two hours, three, four hours... The heat blazed down upon him like a furnace... The sky, when he opened his eyes once, was empty... then a speck became visible in the blue expanse, and presently another speck. They came from nowhere. They hovered very high, almost out of sight. They appeared, they disappeared, they—reappeared. Nearer and nearer they swung down, in sweeping stealthy circles... little dancing groups of them, miles away but ever drawing closer—the vultures.

He had strained his ears so long for sounds of feet and voices that it seemed he could no longer hear at all. Hearing had ceased within him. Then came the water-dreams, with their agonising torture. He heard that... heard it running in silvery streams and rivulets across green English meadows. It rippled with silvery music. He heard it splash. He dipped hands and feet and head in it—in deep, clear pools of generous depth. He drank; with his skin he drank, not with mouth and throat alone. Ice clinked in effervescent, sparkling water against a glass. He swam and plunged. Water gushed freely over back and shoulders, gallons and gallons of it, bathfuls and to spare, a flood of gushing, crystal, cool, life-giving liquid. And then he stood in a beech wood and felt the streaming deluge of delicious summer rain upon his face; heard it drip luxuriantly upon a million thirsty leaves. The wet trunks shone, the damp moss spread its perfume, ferns waved heavily in the moist atmosphere. He was soaked to the skin in it. A mountain torrent, fresh from fields of snow, foamed boiling past, and the spray fell in a shower upon his cheeks and hair. He dived—head foremost... Ah, he was up to the neck... and she was with him. They were under water together. He saw her eyes gleaming into his own beneath the copious flood.

The voice, however, was not hers. "You will drown, yet you will not know you drown!" His swollen tongue called out a name. But no sound was audible. He closed his eyes. There came sweet unconsciousness.

A sound in that instant was audible, though. It was a voice—voices—and the thud of animal hoofs upon the sand. The specks had vanished from the sky as mysteriously as they came. And, as though in answer to the sound, he made a movement—an automatic, unconscious movement. He did not know he moved. And the body, uncontrolled, lost its precarious balance. He rolled, but he did not know he rolled. Slowly, over the edge of the sloping mound of sand, he turned sideways. Like a log of wood he slid gradually, turning over and over, nothing to stop him—to the bottom. A few feet only, and not even steep; just steep enough to keep rolling slowly. There was a—splash. But he did not know there was a splash.

They found him in a pool of water—one of these rare pools the Desert Bedouin mark preciously for their own. He had lain within three yards of it for hours. He was drowned, but he did not know he drowned.